NO DAMAGED GOODS

NICOLE SNOW

ICE LIPS PRESS

Content copyright © Nicole Snow. All rights reserved.
Published in the United States of America.
First published in February, 2020.

Disclaimer: The following book is a work of fiction. Any resemblance characters in this story may have to real people is only coincidental.

Please respect this author's hard work! No section of this book may be reproduced or copied without permission. Exception for brief quotations used in reviews or promotions. This book is licensed for your personal enjoyment only. Thanks!

Cover Design – CoverLuv. Photo by Michelle Lancaster.

Website: Nicolesnowbooks.com

ABOUT THE BOOK

Fearless firefighter. Silver tongue. Single dad.
My grouchy hero pushes all my freaking buttons...

The red hot stranger who just saved my bacon might be the end of me.

Blake Silverton could sweet talk an angel into sin.

Fierce small-town fire chief. Rough velvet voice. Drop dead gorgeous.

Don't even get me started on the tortured single dad thing.

Wintering in Heart's Edge wasn't a choice when my van went *kaboom!*

Neither is gawking at the human bulldozer who keeps charging to my rescue.

If only we could stop butting heads over...everything.

But I can tame a grumpasaurus in my sleep.

Oh, I'm hardly obsessed.

I'm not tuning into his radio love line *every single night.*

That charred lump of coal he calls a heart isn't *that* fascinating.

I can *handle* one itsy bitsy insta-wildfire kiss.

Those fires some deranged punk keeps setting around town, though...

Maybe I need a hero after all.

He insists on playing house to protect me.
Being under Blake's roof isn't scary.
But when the heart falls hard for damaged goods?
It's out of the frying pan and into the fire.

I: ALL FOR A LARK (PEACE)

*Y*ou know, I don't *normally* question my decision-making skills.

If I did, I wouldn't be me.

My dad used to call me a flower on the wind.

Maybe I'm small and soft and fragile and have a hippie name—

But that just makes me light enough to move with the breeze, soar high, drift into the sky, and let every gust take me to new horizons and beautiful things.

That's what sent me jetting out of Oahu.

What sent me flitting through New Orleans, St. Louis, Nashville, Chicago, and lately Denver.

What put me on the road to Vancouver, too, for my next big adventure.

…and what's currently left me stranded on the side of the road on a remote mountain looking out over a town called Heart's Edge.

Freezing my butt off, with no way to warm up except for my old clunker of a van.

Which is currently on fire, belching plumes of thick, dark smoke up into the sky.

Yep.

Sometimes when you're a flower on the wind, you find yourself adrift on a beautiful sea.

And sometimes you land face-first in a burning garbage fire, desperately flailing to alter course but sinking deeper anyway.

It's my own fault.

I'm the only one who decided I needed to go for a drive after dinner, packing up my van like I'm part of Scooby and the gang, gearing up in the Mystery Machine.

Honestly, my ride's probably even older than that technicolor beast in the cartoon, but it's served me well.

Until now.

I'd been puttering along just fine, listening to some local radio station and this really weird little show.

At first, I thought it was a variety show, but it turned out to be some kind of call-in advice line. The guy hosting it had a warm, kind voice, deep and sort of gritty with a weathered edge.

He sounded like he laughed a lot. And he'd sure as hell been laughing when someone called in looking for advice on what to do if a woman caught her husband stealing her underwear—*to wear them.*

He'd been gentle as he'd said, "Maybe get used to sharing, ma'am, or maybe get him his own." I'd been able to hear the grin in his voice as he'd said it. "We ain't quite made to fit in the front of them lacy things, and he's gonna stretch yours plumb out. Whatever floats his boat, though."

Most guys would've made fun of the guy and his wife. *Oh, poor gal,* that kind of thing.

This guy, though...

He'd just laughed like it was no big deal, live and let live. It made *me* feel better even though it wasn't even my call or my issue.

I'd been giggling too, feeling kind of warm inside, as I'd listened to him say "Next caller..."

But I missed out on what the call was about, because right then my van decided it was hotter for this guy's voice than I was.

And it just blew.

Spontaneously combusted.

Big old *boom* that split the night like a gunshot, sending smoke and plumes of flame spewing out from either side of the flower-painted hood.

Good thing I was going slow, I guess, being extra careful with the snowy roads and steep slopes.

Still, it must've been the scariest thirty seconds of my life while I wrestled the burning van over to the side of the road, grabbed my things, and scurried out.

The funny thing is, I can still hear the radio going, while whatever's under the hood crackles and burns.

"I don't know," Mr. Advice Guy's saying. "I mean, you ask me to pick between football and sex and UFO sightings..."

Someone else at the station guffaws. He sounds older, heartier. "Oh, c'mon. I know which one you'll pick, and so does everybody else. You're dang-near the last single man standing, Blake. Everybody wants a slice of that in this town. Bet you're getting a piece every night."

There's an odd pause. Weird, heavy.

And when Advice Guy speaks again, it's almost...melancholy, even if there's still a smile in his voice. "Guess so," he says. "You know me. Real heartbreaker."

Ouch.

I wonder what happened to make him sound like that.

There's real pain living in his voice. The kind of buried agony that has teeth.

Pain is something I know in my line of work.

And I know what it sounds like when someone's got a heart that's taken a direct hit from a sledgehammer.

Listen to me. Sitting here worrying about this guy, when I should be taking care of myself.

I'm a warm-weather girl. Even bundled up in a thick coat,

I'm about to shiver my *toes* off, and the clear night sky looks heavy.

I need to get off the side of the road before another storm comes down.

And, you know, before my van explodes into stabby confetti.

I fumble my phone from my pocket with half-numb fingers and dial 911. I'm hoping I did the call routing right.

It's always a little iffy with the way I travel. Never know whether 911 will route to the office closest to the nearest cell tower or will try to hit the 911 for my old Hawaii zip code. I've never needed to test it much, except one night when I got mugged in Chicago.

But I'm in luck because after a couple of rings, a drowsy, thick male voice slurs, "Langley."

I blink.

I'm used to *911, what's your emergency?*

But after a moment I say tentatively, "Um...is this the police? The Heart's Edge PD?"

"Sure is. Sheriff Langley at your service, Miss, and I'm guessin' you're one of the out-of-towners if you don't know that."

"Yeah." I smile wryly. "Listen, my van broke down and it's kind of on fire—"

"Fire? I ain't the one you need, then, but lemme get you right on over to the main man."

I don't even get to protest *Wait!* before there's a weird buzzing sound.

It's like...the line's not disconnected, but he's not there.

I wait a second, listening to the idle murmur of voices from the radio. There's a rattling, a clicking, and a different male voice comes on the line.

"Fire and rescue." Deep, crisp, business-like. "What do you need?"

Wait.

Why do I hear his voice twice?

The second time, it's coming from my van in this weird half-second delayed echo.

But I try, "Um, hi, my name is Peace and my van broke down and caught fire."

Now I'm hearing it again.

The echo, only this time...

Oh, crap.

That's *me*.

And it's coming from the radio inside the van.

I'm live on the air with the advice line guy, who's apparently also the emergency responder for the town's fire team.

"Um," I fumble again, then continue, "I called the sheriff's office and the second I said *fire*, he routed me to you."

"Where? How much fire we talkin'?" the man snaps off quietly—Blake. I think that's what the other guy on the radio said his name was.

His friendliness is gone, replaced by an authoritative calm. His tone eases a little knot of nerves I hadn't even realized I was holding on to until it started to relax.

"I'm not sure...a little flame, a lot of smoke." I don't like the echo of my voice coming from the radio, when I sound way more scared than I really want to be, but I'm kind of stuck here. Helpless. "I'm from out of town, and I was just driving around to check out the woods and mountainsides—"

"Can you see the town from where you are?" he asks.

I turn slowly, scanning. Just sky, forest, road, and a break in the trees, but no lights of the town. "Nope."

"What can you see?"

I step closer to the edge of the trees, pulling my thickly felted peacoat tighter, my breaths icy on my tongue and puffing out in front of me. I squint through the narrow trunks, the spindly leafless branches.

"Through the trees...there's a valley." I squint, looking down at dry slopes of red earth dotted with half-dead scrub and a dark chunk of rocky slope with what looks like the remnants of a pretty big building in front of it. "And what looks like some old, damaged abandoned place. Ruins?"

"Paradise Hotel. Gotcha. Direction?" he barks.

That I can answer a bit more confidently, looking up and scanning the sky. The North Star twinkles just bright past the building clouds that are gathering way too fast for my liking. But it's still there, brilliant and white against the deep blue.

"East," I say.

"Any other nearby landmarks?"

I rack my brain, trying to remember the things I'd passed by in the shadows. "Yeah, think I passed a hunting shack on the side of the road, about a mile and a half back?"

"I know where you are." I can hear rapid movement both on the radio and over the phone, and on the line he goes a little distant with a murmur. "Take over, Mario. I'm heading out."

Then his voice growls stronger again, aimed at me. "Stay put, lady. I'm coming. Keep your distance from the vehicle in case a gas line catches."

I nod as if he can see me.

Then curse myself for being an idiot.

I bite my lip, stuffing the hand not holding my cell into my pocket, curling it together for warmth. I hadn't brought gloves since I hadn't expected to be outside. "Blake? That's your name, right?"

There's a pause, then an oddly quiet, "...Yep. How'd you know?"

I smile faintly. "I was listening to you on the radio before my van went *boom*. I just...I think it's going to start snowing soon."

Another long silence passes before his crisp tone gentles. His voice is so expressive, and I get why anyone in town would tune in to listen to him. It's like he can lead you with his voice, this slow, rolling cadence of baritone roughness that wraps you up like velvet and carries you in and out of whatever feeling infuses those rich words.

I'm a music nerd; it's in my bones.

And his voice is like music, even when he says something as simple as, "What's your name?"

"Peace," I answer. "Peace Rabe."

He lets out a soft, husky laugh, and something tightens in my chest. "Rabe? Like a rabe of broccoli?"

"*Don't*," I groan around a laugh. "I had to deal with that in high school."

"Okay, Little Miss Broccoli. I won't."

"You just *did*."

"Maybe," he says, and my gut clutches up at the soft edge in that single word, almost like a sigh. "But you're not worrying about the snow anymore, are ya?" He stops, then adds gently, "You're gonna be okay, Peace. I'm on the way."

"Okay, Blake," I answer, and even though I'm so cold my toes feel like frozen nubs, I'm freaky warm all over, too. "I'll be waiting."

The line goes dead.

I pull the phone back and stare at the screen, running my tongue over my teeth, pulling my collar up around my mouth and nose to trap in the warmth of my breath.

My chest's all fluttery as I listen to the last murmur of Blake's voice on the radio. He says something unintelligible before he fades out. The other man's voice takes over, laughing.

I guess help's on the way.

And I shouldn't be hoping the man coming to rescue me is as intense as that rolling, lyrical, perfect lion voice.

* * *

Oh, God.

So he's not just intense.

He's...

No.

Nope.

Nada.

I totally shouldn't be staring at the tall man climbing out of the fire truck the way I am. Not when I'm so cold I feel like I must be blue from head to toe, and it's starting to make me feel sick to my stomach.

Maybe I'm just light-headed from impending hypothermia.

I think I could live with that excuse for this indecent freaking *gawking.*

It must be the real reason why I can't take my eyes off Blake as he and two other men swing down from the fire truck with lithe, easy movements, strength in every line of them, their fire-retardant coveralls sitting on their frames with rakish ease, outlining their every movement.

I don't know how I'm sure the man with the dark rusty-brown hair must be Blake.

One of them, handsome with a thick head of black Grecian curls, seems far too young to go with that voice. The other guy, sandy-haired and serious-looking and old enough to be my dad, just...doesn't fit.

But the tall man with the thick, gruff beard and the streaks of silver in his hair, with the blue eyes so dark they make the night look bright, with the brisk moves and the quiet confidence in every step...

That's got to be him.

That's *so* Blake.

He's out here with his coveralls rolled down around his waist and tied, his tight black t-shirt straining against his chest, his biceps bulging in hard knots. He roars something to his men.

They swing into action—hauling the heavy hose down from the side of the truck like it weighs nothing, turning the watery blast on the hood of my van. I guess it's a good thing it's a small fire. That heavy jet of hissing water has to come out of the truck's reserves instead of a hydrant, but honestly I'm *not* thinking about logistics right now.

I'm listening to Blake's voice—calm, commanding, rough—as

he directs his men to douse my poor rickety van until the fire simmers down into damp smoke, and sad, quiet metal.

It's almost like I'm not even here.

He's so focused on what he's doing. Exactly why I nearly jump out of my skin when he turns his head.

And those dark-blue eyes lock right on, capturing me in their hold like beaming spotlights.

The red and gold flashing emergency lights of the truck play over his profile, highlighting how weathered his tanned skin is.

Lines of age and maybe frowns, maybe laughter, trace wild history around his mouth, his eyes. He's got cheekbones for days, a mouth like a cruel kiss, and his pulse ticks in stark highlight against his strong, firm throat as the light glides over him.

Oh. My. God.

He's grimmer than I expected.

Harder.

An absolute *stone* of a man.

That softness I'd heard in his voice isn't there in his face. Almost like his body's a granite vault for holding the gentleness hidden away inside.

Why, Blake? I can't help wondering.

But I think I get a little hint of an answer as he turns, striding toward me.

He moves like a man who knows how powerful he is.

Slow and controlled, smooth ripples of chiseled musculature trailing down from broad shoulders, over the sweat-darkened pull of pecs against his clinging black shirt. The tight line of his abs and narrow hips switch in a rhythm that's as sensuous as a hunting panther's slink.

But he also moves like a man who knows what hell is.

Somehow, I don't think it's just firefighting that taught him.

He's favoring his left leg. Some kind of injury, the kind of walk that says he's learned how to hide it, but he can't always keep it down.

His strength fights against his own weight. He's built to

support that wall of a body, but every ounce of well-crafted muscle is also another ounce of pressure crushing down on the invisible wound, making him list just slightly to the left with every stride.

I probably wouldn't notice if I wasn't used to searching for pain.

That's what massage therapists do.

Learn people's pain, so they can tame it and chase it away.

But he's stoic, withdrawn, as he stops in front of me, scanning my body with a critical eye that makes me feel kind of like one of those dummies they teach you first aid on.

Eep. So much for all those flutters. My butterflies just iced over.

"You Peace?" he growls.

I smile faintly, pulling my frozen fingers from my pocket to wiggle them at him in a little wave. "Only person out here with a burning wreck. Blake, right?"

He only grunts, giving me another one of those looks. "You're not hurt?"

"No." I shake my head. "I jumped out and got away as soon as I had the van parked on the side of the road. I'm just *cold*."

"Lucky it's not quite cold enough tonight for hypothermia, but you'll still catch a chill."

He takes a step back then, retreating to the fire truck, and digs out one of those massive, thick fire jackets from a side compartment. It's deep grey with reflective yellow and orange bands on the sleeves and back.

Slowly, he returns to me and swings it around my shoulders.

For a moment, I'm almost wrapped up in his arms. He reaches around me to pull the jacket tight, draping it over my shoulders and then drawing it in to bundle me up.

Now, my butterflies are thawed.

And it's definitely not the jacket leaving my face so *hot* my ears burn against the cold, the contrast bordering on painful.

Oh, no.

Why did he have to be so...so...

That.

All of that, including the faint whiff of cologne and Goliath I get as he straightens, still looking at me with this fierce, unmovable gaze.

"Thanks," I say faintly, curling my fingers in the jacket, drawing it closer. "For coming out here."

"It's my job."

"Right." I'm really playing it smooth here.

So I bite my lip, searching for something to say, then glance past him at the other two men who have shut the hose off and lifted the hood of my van to see inside. "You doused it out fast. I'm a little amazed. It's not every day I see—"

"A dude with a leg as fucked as mine doin' this kind of work?" he cuts me off. "Heard it a thousand times, darlin'."

Oh, crap city!

Wrong tack.

Absolutely the wrong tack.

He can't possibly think I meant—

Ugh. He caught me staring like a deer in the headlights.

I realize it the instant his eyes go practically black, savage and dark, and his mouth tightens. There's no other hint I've hit the wrong button, but it's enough when the air around us drops a hundred degrees as he turns away, giving me his broad back.

The lines of his shoulders, his trapezius, are so tense.

Like he's carrying boulders around inside him.

"Blake, I'm sorry," I fumble out. "I didn't mean—"

"Forget it. Don't know what you're talking about," he says flatly, and that empty, detached voice sounds nothing like the gentle man who'd reassured me over the phone.

He stalks over to my van, reaches in the open driver's side window, and snaps off the radio that's been babbling in the background the entire time.

I trail after him.

I feel lost, unsure what to say. This is definitely in the top ten most surreal nights of my life.

"Hey, I'm sorry," I offer again to his back. "I wasn't trying to be rude or nosy. I'm just—you know, I'm a massage therapist and—"

"I heard about you!" One of the other men—the one with the mess of dark Grecian curls—looks up from under the hood with a grin. "You set up shop at the inn, right? Trying to get the snowbird crowd?"

I smile slightly. "Yep. Figured if I was going to put down roots for winter, settling in with the tourists wouldn't be a bad way to make a living."

He laughs, straightening and pulling one of his big bulky gloves off to offer me his hand. "Not just the tourists. We get more stress in this town than we have any right to. Hell, we've probably got collective PTSD by now after all that Galentron—"

"*Justin,*" Blake growls, snapping a look at him, dark with warning.

"Sorry, Chief." Justin winces, but he keeps grinning, his big hand still outstretched. "I'm being unprofessional."

"It's fine." I shake his hand, quickly and warmly. "I'm not real big on professional. Most hippie kids aren't."

"Figured you had some punk in you. Nice hair, by the way."

He's talking about the ombre purple tips dyed in my hair. Most people usually are. It gets me looks in small towns like this, but I'm used to it and don't mind when it's a good icebreaker.

I smile at Justin. "Thanks, dude."

Then his grin broadens.

"Hey, you mind if I snap a few photos? I like keeping albums, and uh...this is my first burning van in the middle of the night around these parts. It's not too far from the old Paradise Hotel ruins, might even be able to get them in the same shot off in the distance..."

Hotel ruins? Hmm.

I groan out a laugh but wave toward the van. "Knock yourself out. Just promise you'll send me the pics for insurance purposes. I'll even trade you a massage."

Justin laughs, already pulling his other glove off and fishing in his pocket for his phone.

While Justin lines up shots on his screen, the flash snapping in sharp bursts over the night, I glance at Blake.

He's ducked under the hood of the van, glaring, but he doesn't really look like he's seeing much of anything. I shuffle my feet together.

"So, if anybody on the fire crew wants to stop by, I'm happy to give a big discount for my daring rescuers."

Blake might as well not have even heard me.

Justin perks, saying, "Yeah? Sweet."

Meanwhile, the other guy, the sandy-haired one, lifts his head, his expression clearing to focus on me.

"What kind of discount do you give for vehicle repairs?"

I laugh. "Why? Think you can get me a lower rate?"

"I'm only a part-timer on the fire crew. Rest of the time I work at Mitch's Autobody." He grins. "Just ask for Rich."

"Will do."

For some reason, that seems to get under Blake's skin.

His shoulders ripple, and his hands go hard against the edge of the hood, knuckles ridged. He pushes himself up, flinging me a look. "Get anything you need out of your van. We'll give you a lift back to town and send a tow truck for the van in the morning."

I blink.

I don't know why I feel so oddly deflated.

Maybe because for a few seconds I'd built up a schoolgirl fantasy around that coaxing, growling voice, the feelies it gave me, wondering how it might feel to have that voice purring against my ear, sweet and dark and jagged.

Meh.

Gruff Jerk: 1.

Lonely Girl: 0.

You win this round, Blake.

My name may be Peace, but I don't go down without a fight.

If Mr. Snarly-saurus doesn't want to play, it's his loss.

* * *

I'M LESS THINKING about fighting and more about sleep by the time I dig my stuff out of my van.

I keep a lot of supplies in there since I often use my van to travel to clients, instead of them coming to me. Justin, Rich, and Blake help, though. It's a pretty weird look with my folding tables and gear and crates of massage oils stacked on the back of the fire truck by the ladders, but it works.

No obvious smoke damage to my stuff, thank gawd.

The whole time Rich and Justin gab at each other and me, warm and friendly and joking, and it's not hard to tell they're trying to make sure I stay calm.

Blake, on the other hand, is completely silent.

It feels almost like he's trying to disappear.

But I can't help watching him.

Except for the one time he catches my eye, I linger on the way his limp grows deeper while he hauls my stuff, and a pang of guilt builds inside me when it's my fault he's out here hauling my junk.

Another dark flash goes through his gaze again, as if I'd done something *wrong* by seeing his weakness, and I look away quickly.

It's not hard to see he's one of those men who builds walls out of pride.

It's only my own pride that keeps me awake, though, as the three men bundle me into the front cab of the fire truck. Good thing I'm small, or it'd be a snug fit with all of us.

Rich has me sandwiched up against the door, and it's hard for me not to fall asleep against his warmth while the cab's heater melts the icicles under my skin. He kind of reminds me of my dad, especially when he talks about getting home to read his kids a bedtime story, words traded in murmurs with Justin while they leave me to drowse.

It's like they're a sandwich of good company, caught between the silence of me against one door and Blake behind the wheel.

But it's kind of endearing.

Honestly, it's the first time I feel like I'm close to a group like family, ever since I cast myself into the wind.

I'm nice and toasty, almost asleep, by the time the fire truck pulls up outside the Charming Inn—this quaint touristy spot I really love—with its white-columned plantation house for the main hotel and a field full of cottages leading off to the gorgeous cliff-front views.

I perk up as the fire truck eases to a halt, the engine still running, all three men looking at me in silent question.

"That way," I say, pointing to a side lane that runs along the fence enclosing one side of the property. "I'm staying in one of the cottages back there. I don't want to wake anybody up at the main house. I think the owners have a kid."

"Warren and Haley," Blake grunts softly. "They'll have just put their kids down."

Oh.

Oh, no.

I don't know how I developed a crush this hard, this fast.

Maybe it's damsel in distress syndrome.

But there's that tick of warm, husky affection in his voice when he says *Warren and Haley*.

That hint tells me the owners of the inn are important to him. Friends. Maybe family.

Lucky them, when I just want to hear him say *Peace* in soothing baritone again, with that same gentle heat.

But he doesn't say anything else as he cruises the fire truck forward to take that little turn-off and head down the lane, the dirt and twigs cracking under the wheels.

The first flakes of a snowstorm, thick and fat and heavy, are just beginning to streak down from the clouds by the time I get out, adding to the small, half-melted dunes that cling here and there around the property. I'm sure the deeper, burying snows won't be far behind this dusting.

I'm lucky I didn't get stranded in a blizzard.

It's quiet as everyone helps me offload things from the fire truck. We carry them into the wooden slat cabin with its tall floor-to-ceiling windows and glass doors.

As the last crate rattles down on the coffee table, though, I turn to Blake, offering my hand. "Thanks again for—"

I'm looking at his back.

His back, and the tight clench of his left fist, pressed against his thigh. Clearly trying to knuckle out the pain and walk straighter, his spine stiff.

Yeah.

I know that habit.

There's a clear wound, maybe something he got as a firefighter, maybe something else. He's got that kind of dense corded muscle that says ex-military.

Maybe he's been in physical therapy, maybe he's recovered, but it's never going to fully heal.

And he looks like the kind of man who doesn't really listen when people try to talk to him about pain management.

"Hey," Justin says with an easy smile, just as the door slams shut behind Blake. "Don't mind him. He's just...not good with attention. Too many people staring at him already around town, so add one more pretty stranger and he's going to clam up."

I frown. "Why are people staring at him?"

Justin laughs and sucks in a deep breath.

Rich snorts, rolling his eyes. "Oh, don't get him started. It's his favorite story. The—"

"Heroes of Heart's Edge!" Justin finishes. His eyes are bright.

I lift a brow.

He can't be more than a few years older than me, maybe close to thirty, but there's definitely a case of fanboy hero worship in his boyish smile. "That's what they call 'em in the papers. They just keep making *all* the headlines. Making some folks believe in heroes again."

"Headlines about *what?*" I blink, leaning around Justin to peer past Blake's silhouette, slowly melting away into the falling snow and the shadows of night, barely visible through the glass.

"Um, let's see..." Justin ticks off his fingers, tilting his head, screwing his mouth up thoughtfully. "Got rid of a big-time drug runner, stopped an evil research company from killing the whole town, stopped them again from burning us down..."

I stare, my heart skipping just a little faster. "Okay, wow. The tourist guidebooks did *not* warn me about any of that. I thought this place was just a sleepy, peaceful little place?"

Justin grins, clapping me on the shoulder. "Aw, don't worry. We're back to being a sleepy small-town nothing again since autumn. Nothing's gonna happen to you here."

"Except a terminal case of boredom," Rich adds. "The only big shindig for the next few months is the winter carnival. Besides that, it's just socialites wanting to play at being rustic for a month or two, until they get sick of the crappy Wi-Fi connection."

I laugh. "I'm not really worried as long as Netflix works."

"Might cut out a little with everything else when the first big snow hits," Rich says. "For some reason, the underground internet cables get weird this time of year. But it's usually fine after a day or two." He nudges Justin's arm. "C'mon. Little lady's had a rough night. Let her get some rest."

He pitches his voice to me again. "I'll get your van in the morning and tow it into town. You can come by Mitch's when you're up. Warren or Hay will give you a lift into town, I'm sure. Ask for me."

I kind of wish I could ask Blake to give me a ride.

It's hard to resist a mystery.

That friendly warmth when he'd been on the radio, and then the soft, almost intimate way he'd spoken, coaxed, reassured me.

The way he'd said my *name* like it was a musical note rolling off his tongue.

Only to go cold and gruff and withdrawn the moment I'd noticed his pain.

He makes me think of a song, wrapped up in the shape of a man.

Melody in his movements.

Raw lyricism in his every breath.

I haven't had a good muse in a long while. Maybe *he* could be my spark.

So even as I wave Justin and Rich off with my thanks, my thoughts are hooked on Fire Chief Blake.

On the discord of pain in his music, and what I could do to tease them out until he's in harmony again.

I should pick up a rental car while they're working on my van at the garage, if it's even salvageable.

Pick up a rental, settle in, explore the town a bit more...

And hope maybe I run into my dark knight in fire-retardant armor one more time.

We'll just see if we can start over on the right foot.

II: OFF NOTE (BLAKE)

*G*oddamn, I'm an idiot.

Had a pretty gal right there, gunning to do something about this damn bum leg of mine.

And I just *had* to go baring my teeth at her like a rabid dog and run her off.

I mean, fuck.

It's her frigging job, and if she's any good at it, I'd have to be a card-carrying fool not to take her up on it.

Guess I'm dumb.

'Cause I ain't quite sure how I'm not gonna crash this fire truck trying to park it when my leg's so locked up it won't even unbend.

Shit.

At least I can manage the gas and brake with my right foot, but I'm exhausted. Not just tonight. The last couple years have been one round of serious business after the next. First old Warren and the drugs, then Doc and Galentron, then Tiger—I mean, Leo—and Galentron *again.*

It's enough to drive a man under the covers in the comfort of his own bed and make him stay there. Only, seeing how I'm the guy who keeps Heart's Edge from burning down, I don't have that luxury.

My thigh is chewing me up by the time I ease the truck in its bay and kill the engine.

I'll have to do the maintenance check tomorrow.

Right now, I need my bed, plus a Vicodin or twelve.

Mostly, I need home, and my daughter.

Not another starry-eyed single girl dumped on this town like it's some kind of fucking chick magnet and some naked little cherub just decided it was *my turn.*

That's how they got Warren *and* Doc.

Damsels in dead cars.

Weird shit around here sometimes, man.

Weird shit.

Gritting my teeth, I shove myself out of the cab of the truck —and nearly collapse.

My leg's been groaning at me for months, always has, but tonight? It's had *enough.*

Thank God there's nobody here to see me like this. I dropped off my guys after I shot myself in the face by turning down Peace's massage.

I catch myself with one hand, gripping hard at the door, my good leg holding me up. All while that fucking traitor thing attached to my hip dangles there uselessly, burning like I've shoved it into hot lava.

It ain't usually this bad. I've done a lot worse to it and never had it flare up like this.

But I've been feeling weird all day.

Groaning, I sink down on the footboard, leaning my back against the cold metal of the fire truck, and thump my fist against my thigh, pounding against the thick ridge of scar tissue I can feel through my coveralls.

Fucking shrapnel wound, well over a decade ago.

Lucky I survived it, I guess.

If you call this surviving.

Sometimes that burning lance of pain takes me right back to the fateful day under the hot Afghani sun. Blood spouting everywhere as people got ripped apart in a metal hail. Felt like I was standing in a cloud of bees, sharp edges tearing at me, zipping little lines of blood along my face, my arms, my chest.

The one that hit me was less like a bee and more like a bullet. An explosion of howling agony as a chunk of searing metal buried itself in my thigh.

It shouldn't feel so real. Not after all these years gone by.

But even if the wound's closed up, even if the smell of my own blood is just a visceral memory...

Sometimes it hurts like it never healed.

Sometimes I hurt like I never healed, either.

Shit.

It dawns on me slowly. I know what's wrong with me.

And I tilt my head back, staring up at the snow-dotted sky and breathing in its scent, letting it clear me and calm me down while I beat that knotted-up muscle till it starts to relax so I can limp home.

No forgetting what today is.

It's the day Abigail died.

It's been four goddamn years.

Four years, and I still don't know how to feel about losing the mother of our daughter and the woman who'd promised to make my life a perfect forever and instead made it a living hell.

How do you grieve when you've fallen out of love but you still had a kid?

When she might not have been *the one*, but she was sure as hell someone?

It's like that question is snarled up in all the hurt in my body, and every time I run up against it, my leg just knots worse. Telling me this is how I get to hurt.

Never figured out what to do with my heart, so all that pain gets roped up in my body.

I don't know how long I stay here at the fire station. Kinda lost track of time when that call came in, with that pretty redhead with her purple-tipped hair and those green eyes that make her look pure vixen.

Peace.

Peace fuckin' Broccoli—oh, sorry. *Rabe.*

Who the hell names their daughter Peace?

Probably the same kind of person who'd raise a chick who'd go mountain-trucking in a van that looks a whole lot older than she is, covered in hand-painted flowers in bright, bursting colors all over the finish.

That chick looks like she couldn't have been born any earlier than 1990, but she's got the look, all right.

Looks like she'd groove around naked covered in henna in a witch's communion circle or something, flowers in her hair and wreaths around her wrists and ankles...

...and I should *not* be thinking about a stranger naked.

Make that a damned curvy, cute, smart-mouthed stranger with a petite body and a pert, pretty, impish face.

No excuses.

Even if it's been a long-ass time.

I'm lucky when my phone yanks me out of my thoughts, buzzing in my pocket. I dig it out and swipe the new text —then wince.

GDI Dad u were here and u just left me?

Aw, hell.

I'd forgotten Andrea was at the Charming Inn with Haley, taking art lessons. I was supposed to pick her up.

I check the time.

Shit.

Like, twenty minutes ago.

Yeah, my leg's being nasty, but she doesn't need to know it. Nobody does, and that goes double for my little girl.

She's sixteen.

I don't need her worrying herself silly over me when I'm the parent here, and she's got enough on her plate.

My leg's not being too big a dick, at least, when I haul myself up. Hurts like a motherfucker, but at least it holds me up as I swagger off to my old military Jeep.

The top's all covered in snow. I sweep it off before hauling myself behind the wheel, flicking the headlights on and heading out into the night to pick up my daughter.

It's barely a mile's drive past the outskirts of town and back to the Charming Inn.

I tell myself I ain't looking as I drive past the field full of cabins.

I swear, I ain't paying attention to that light still on in one set of windows.

Not at all.

When I pull up around the front of the big house, Andrea's waiting outside with Haley and Ms. Wilma. She's bright, animated, talking to Haley with her sketchbook clutched to her chest, while Ms. Wilma watches with her wizened face set in an expression of kindly amusement.

Andrea swings herself around like a pinwheel, throwing up her hands between laughs.

I've seen so many little girls raised to make themselves small. To not take up too much space.

I love my daughter *because* she takes up space.

She isn't afraid to make her presence known, isn't afraid to be herself, from that punk mouth on her to the wild crop of half-shaved hair that's mostly pink at the tips, but still the vivid, wild purple underneath that makes her my Little Violet.

One brave flower, standing bright.

As she looks up and sees me pulling in, her brightness vanishes into a sullen scowl.

I sigh, dragging a hand over my face.

Look, I love my daughter, but she's a sixteen-year-old girl who thinks her dad is the biggest cringe embarrassment on the planet. I already know I'm in the shit from that mouth before she even gets in the car.

I ain't wrong.

She comes clomping down the steps in those big combat boots she wears—still don't know where she got 'em, huge and clunky things and she never fucking laces 'em and she's gonna kill herself like that—and slings herself into the car.

Then immediately tucks herself into the corner, glaring out the window.

Okay.

No mouth, then.

Silent treatment tonight.

I try to wait her out, lifting a hand in a friendly wave for Hay and Ms. Wilma, before jacking the Jeep into gear and reversing out of the drive to head back into town.

The silence is a knife over my skin.

I'd wonder what the hell I did wrong this time, but frankly I'm not sure I ever stop.

As we pull back into town with the light of the Brody's sign flickering like a second moon over the main street, I glance at her. She's got on thick black wool tights under her ripped, frayed denim skirt, but they're all busted out at the knees.

Another sigh spills out. "Andrea, you either gotta sew those up or let me buy you new ones. It's winter."

She scowls, just a hint of her face twisted up in profile. "I like them like this."

"You like freezing your kneecaps off?"

"I don't get *cold*, okay?" she snaps. "I'm fine. You're not Mom, so stop trying to mother me."

Ah. There it is. Didn't take long.

The *real* reason she's pissy, and tonight of all nights, I don't blame her.

For four years, my little girl's been mad at Abby for being the one to leave, and at me for being the one to stay.

I think she'd be the same way with Abigail, maybe, if I'd been the one Andrea found dead on the floor. Mad at me for going, and at her ma for staying. Who knows.

What she really wants is her whole family back in one piece, even if we'd been quietly broken way before Abby's accident.

"Hey," I try quietly. An olive branch or something. "You wanna stop by Brody's? They got the milkshake machine fixed so they can do the extra-thick ones again and—"

"I already ate with Haley," she snaps back. "And I don't have time. I have homework."

"It is kinda late," I concede. "Sorry I was slow picking you up. Had an emergency call."

"Yeah, I *heard*." She sniffs, almost offended. "It was on the radio."

I wince. She doesn't like my show, but goddammit I need something to do with myself. It was Warren's idea, way back, something to take my mind off things.

I didn't expect I'd start having fun with it.

Half the time people call in to prank me, 'cause that's how we roll here in Heart's Edge.

Everybody knows everybody, and we like to mess around.

Keeps people entertained.

Keeps me busy, answering questions about relationships or the latest Bigfoot sighting since the Legend of Nine ain't a thing anymore.

And every now and then, I get to really help people. Can't say I mind that one bit. Even if it embarrasses the hell out of my kid.

I wait several seconds for the simmer between us to die down a little, then try, "If you need help with your homework—"

"I'm *fine*." She doesn't even let me get it all out. "I've got straight As. It's all baby stuff. I don't need anything. And I don't need you to pull this stupid shit."

"Hey, watch your damn language."

"Oh, that's great. Curse at me while you tell me to stop cursing." She throws a sharp, hard look at me, crackling like wildfire. She's got her mother's light-brown eyes, and they're like sparks when she's this mad, amber-bright. "I know what you're trying to do. Okay? I know. It's the day. *That* day. And you're trying to make up for Mom being dead when you *can't*, and I hate it when you try. So just *stop*. Leave me alone, Dad. If I need somebody to cuddle me, I've got Mr. fucking Hissyfit."

I can't even get on her for that F-bomb.

Not when her words hit me like a ton of bricks, stinging more than the throb still in my thigh.

I'd close my eyes against the pain, if I didn't have to keep them on the road.

Goddamn, my daughter knows how to throw a punch.

I don't know what hurts more.

That she can see through me with so much contempt...or that she'd rather get squeezed half to death by her pet albino boa constrictor, rather than take a hug and a little comfort from her old man.

I don't know what to say.

So all I say is, "Okay, Andrea. Fine."

Sometimes, all you can do is let people burn themselves out. Especially when they're sixteen and their emotions run so hot.

I want to fix this for her. I want to fix *everything*.

But she's right about one thing—I can't.

So I'll respect her wanting to grieve in her way.

Meanwhile, I try to wrestle up some way to work through this crap on my own.

* * *

We don't say a word to each other for the rest of the drive home.

Whatever. I've got other things on my mind besides my firecracker daughter and my burning leg when I pull into the driveway. My headlights sweep over the car sitting off to one side.

It's nice. A Benz, looks like, brand new, glossy black.

I don't have a clue who it belongs to.

But I get my answer a second later when my headlights pick

out a familiar figure standing on the porch, cold smoke huffing out of his mouth with every breath.

Someone I haven't seen in years, lounging there like Lucifer himself come to pay back a grudge.

Holt.

Fuck my life.

I don't need this tonight.

Without even waiting for Andrea, I park the Jeep and throw the door open. I can't even feel the pain as I get out, standing and stalking toward the front steps.

"*No,*" I bite off before my brother can even say a single word. "Whatever it is you want, the answer's always no."

I've already got one snake inside the house.

Now I've got another one on my fucking porch.

Holt even moves like a serpent. The Biblical kind. We're about the same height, only a couple years apart, but that's where the resemblance ends.

Half-brothers, technically, and he takes after the good-for-nothing fuck who swept through town one night and left our single mama pregnant. His hair's dark as sin, contrasting with those sharp, feral features just made for the lazy, carnivorous, smug smile he turns on me now.

"You don't even know what I want," he says. He's almost slinky as he straightens and spreads his hands. "For all you know, I don't want a damned thing."

"You *always* want something," I growl, even as the door to the Jeep slams behind me and I hear Andrea moving up behind us. "I have yet to see you show up without your hand out."

"Uncle Holt?" Andrea says faintly. "Is...is that you?"

Holt's eyes flick past me. They're so pale brown they're almost yellow-gold, glinting in the porch light.

Like I said.

Fucking *snake man*.

"Hey, kiddo," he says with an almost rueful smile, holding his arms out. "Wow, you shot up. Come give your uncle a hug, hey?"

"*No*," I spit out again and shove myself between my daughter and my brother. Maybe I'm possessive, but he's got a bad habit of putting his hands on what doesn't belong to him and trying to keep it. "Stay away from her. You tell me what the hell you want, then you leave."

"Jesus, Dad," Andrea mutters at my back. "You're *mortifying*."

"Thanks for the ten-dollar word," I mutter back. "Holt, *talk*. You've got sixty seconds, and that's me being generous."

Holt sighs. "We can't do this inside?"

"You're not welcome in my house."

"Ah, c'mon. You'd think I'm fucking Dracula. Can't come in unless invited."

"Close enough," I bark back. "You drain everything you touch dry."

"Harsh," he says, arching one brow and dipping a hand into the pocket of his black leather racing jacket. "Especially since I came to give you this."

He offers a slim folded slip of paper.

Frowning, I take it and flip it open—and slowly realize what I'm staring at.

A check.

For five hundred thousand dollars, signed by the law firm that handled Ma's estate after...

Yeah.

Last year.

I ain't having a good few years with the people around me staying alive.

Maybe that's why I get so psycho protective with Andrea.

And maybe that's why I'm not interested in some pretty redhead with a splash of purple in her hair trying to get an angle on me. Don't need more problems.

Hell, as much as I call Holt a vampire, I'm like the kiss of death.

And this check feels an awful lot like blood money.

My jaw feels like it weighs a ton as I look up at Holt. "She left it all to you. Don't know why the fuck you're giving me this."

"Because it's the right thing to do, Blake," Holt points out quietly.

"Bull. You wouldn't know the right thing to do if it leaped up and bit you in the ass." I crumple the check in my fist—then think better of it. I unfurl it, then rip it to shreds, tearing it clean down the middle. "You're trying to buy forgiveness. I ain't that easily paid off."

"Dammit, man," Holt growls, slipping into his old small-town accent for a second and tilting his head back with a groan. "You're still mad at me about that?"

"She was my *wife*—"

"And it was already over. The ink just wasn't dry on the papers yet," he throws back. "Nothing even happened. And you don't understand the real situation—"

"Will you both *stop?*" Andrea flares, her voice thick, choked.

Holt and I both grow silent, turning our heads to look at her.

She stands on the steps with her face screwed up in a mask of gleaming teary-eyed fury, her fingers digging into the cover of her sketchbook, glaring at us.

"That's my *mom*," she sputters. "You're standing here arguing over my mom and she's *dead*. And *your* mom is dead too, Dad? I had...I had a grandmother I never knew about? And you never told me she died? And now you're gonna stand here and argue over flipping money like nothing else matters?" Her lips tremble. "Assholes! You're *both* assholes, and I hate that I'm related to you."

Before either of us can say anything, she shoves past Holt and goes racing across the porch. There's barely a frantic rattle of her house keys, and I catch a sniffle, a repressed hitch of breath that could be a sob.

Then she's gone, disappearing inside, running away from us.

Fuck me.

I think I'd run, too.

Holt turns his head, craning over his shoulder, before looking at me with a small, almost sad smile I've never seen on that snake before.

"Well, she's not wrong," he says softly. "Maybe I took the wrong tack with this. I should've waited before I—"

I take a deep breath, letting the scraps of the check flutter free from my fingers. "Gonna need you to go. Right now," I snap. Quieter, but I'm still pissed off. "This is not the day for this shit, man. This is so not the day. I can't deal with you and your fuckery, Holt. *Go.*"

I half expect him to argue. Say something oily, slick, persuasive.

Snarling, I hold up a fist, fully ready to throw it into his nose if he gives me any lip.

But all he does is nod, looking at me strangely. "Okay, Blake. Okay."

Sighing, he steps off the porch, brushing past me, shoulder to shoulder. Then, just a step past me, he stops and turns.

"I'm sorry," drifts back, so quiet and strangled I barely hear it. "I didn't mean to hurt you. Not tonight or...ever."

I don't know what to do with that.

I just don't.

So I don't say anything.

I just listen as his footsteps crunch across the gravel, before his fancy-schmancy car door slams and the engine cranks up.

And finally, I'm alone again, one flash of his headlights washing over me in a blinding rush before he drives away.

Guess Holt's not the only one failing at making big dramatic peace offerings tonight.

I just want to talk to Andrea. Without making my own daughter want to jab a knife through my guts.

I'm not too proud to admit I'm nervous.

Scared, even.

Fuck, if I can't reach my daughter now, this rift's only gonna widen.

Suddenly, it won't just be the anniversary of her ma's death when she's too angry to look at me.

It'll be every day.

And somehow we'll end up like me and my own ma, like me and Holt.

So far apart we're barely even blood, nothing but poison resentment between us.

I wasn't there when Ma died. I had my reasons. But I know one thing.

When Andrea's grown up and has kids of her own, I don't want history repeating itself.

Don't want them knowing me as nothing but a funeral announcement showing up by mail, and them not even knowing I existed till I was weeks cold in the ground.

Hell.

I feel sick. It doesn't stop me from knocking on Andrea's bedroom door with a quiet impact.

"Violet?" I call softly. "You awake?"

Usually that nickname's enough to get her yelling at me to fucking stop it, it's embarrassing, but this time there's nothing. Deafening silence.

Sighing, I rest my hand on the door and press my brow against the wood.

"C'mon, kiddo. I just want to talk. At least let me in to say goodnight. I ain't gonna fight with you no more. I just want a hug for your big dumb dad."

Nothing again.

Goddammit.

Okay. Whatever.

I ain't gonna push it here.

I know Andrea's temper full well.

Pushing her right now will just make it worse and hurt her even deeper.

So I'll give her time to spool down, and then maybe tomorrow, we can talk like normal people.

If I even know what the hell to say. It's a funny thing, me being Mr. Radio Man and all, making people's day and helping 'em tidy up their own lives. Meanwhile, I can't even put out the dumpster fire of my own.

When people call in every night to talk to me, I always find something to say.

But when it comes to my own kid, my own past, I'm empty.

There's nothing worse for a dude than running out of words when he needs them most.

III: WINTER SYMPHONY (PEACE)

I should be asleep.

It's almost midnight, and I'm exhausted.

I've been putting my stuff in the second bedroom that I use as a workroom, rearranging my supplies so they're not piled up in the living room. But if I'm being honest?

I'm feeling real shaky after tonight.

Sure, it was just a minor breakdown. Something that could've happened to anybody rattling around in a van older than Moses.

I'm just so used to being self-sufficient.

It's always been me, myself, and I, moving from pillar to post, port to port. I'm not used to asking for help.

But if I hadn't been able to get anyone on the horn tonight, if lazy old Sheriff Langley hadn't picked up the phone in this sleepy little town, I'd have probably had to try to hoof it back.

In the snow.

Alone.

In a place I don't know.

Anything could've happened to me then. Not something I like to think about. It brings up bad memories.

My mother tried to smother me when I was a kid. After Dad

went away on deployment and never came home, she had this horrible fear that if she let me out of her sight, I'd disappear, too. I think it's what made me so rebellious, like my dad's free spirit was trying to live again through me.

But sometimes I get these awful reminders that it really *would* be too easy for me to up and vanish. Totally.

Stop thinking about it, Peace, I tell myself. *Just finish organizing and go to bed.*

I distract myself with thoughts of a lovely baritone voice and the scent of cologne mingled with testosterone and gruff mountain man.

That's a more pleasant thought, and I focus on it intently as I finish organizing bottles of scented aromatherapy oils, then dust my hands off and head into the kitchen to brew a cup of chamomile tea.

But something catches my eye. I stop.

Through the windows over the kitchen sink, there's a fire flickering through the trees.

Maybe I'm a little extra sensitive to flames, considering my van just spontaneously combusted.

I'm pretty sure there shouldn't be anything burning out there at this time of night, though.

And even with the little hills of snow dotted everywhere, something feels *off.*

There's a lot of dry branches and dead leaves. A lot that could catch flame and spin wildly out of control.

"Crap," I mutter.

Setting my mug on the counter, I grab my coat, and then shove my feet into my battered old hiking boots before pulling a messy hand-crocheted cap over my hair and ducking out into the cold.

It only takes a minute to bustle across the field and hop the fence. The woods run along the other side of the dirt path. As I slip into the trees, I realize I'm not alone.

Voices.

Oh, crud.

I may be somewhere I don't belong, but...

Just to be safe, I'd better check things out and make sure no one's out here about to burn the forest down.

So I dial it down, slipping from a walk into a creep.

This isn't new. It's not like I haven't snuck around forests myself for years, from exploring for hidden caves to slipping out in the dead of night to get a certain flower for a special oil.

I'm silent as I make my way through the trees, making sure to keep tree trunks between me and the flicker of golden orange drifting through the branches. The biting, crisp scent of smoke hits my nose.

Edging over, I peer around a tree trunk, taking a good, long look.

The scene in front of me looks familiar.

Because I've done this a lot over the years, too.

Starting in high school and never really stopping, from sneaking out with my friends to not being so sneaky in college to meeting up with a random Roma caravan out in the Ozarks and staying for a drink and a song.

Five kids sit around a bonfire on fallen logs and rocks. Three girls and two boys.

The one who stands out the most is a tall, reedy-looking girl with a shock of pale purple hair, shaved in the back but long in the front and falling into her face, the tips dyed pink, much brighter than mine.

It's punky and cute, and it makes me smile at her ragged eighties throwback style.

And it's not hard to tell she's into the super tall, artsy-looking boy with a ragged pile of platinum hair sitting on the log next to hers.

Even as she swigs from a bottle of something clear and passes it to him, she won't look at him.

And he won't look at her.

I try not to giggle. It's funny how teenagers always think

they're going to fall in love by completely ignoring each other, but it's plenty adorable.

"I'm bored," one of the other girls says. "There's nothing fun around here anymore. Used to be you could at least go hunting for the monster in the woods."

"Some monster," the other boy says, a small dark-haired kid with a snub nose. "Turned out to be some burned dude. 'Mr. Regis' or whatever the fuck they're calling him now."

"Stop it," the purple-haired girl snaps. "He's a nice guy and he helped save the town. Leave him alone. He's got a lot of really cool stories. Like, he was in some freaky CIA thing."

"Hey," the blond boy says, standing with the bottle. "You're bored? Watch this."

He takes a swig, then sets it down, wedging it into the snow next to his log before leaning forward and plucking a twig from the burning bonfire.

Oh.

Oh no.

I know what he's about to do.

He holds the twig in front of his face, then blows hard, spraying fine particles of liquor.

They catch on the twig and ignite into a roaring blaze. It seriously looks like he's breathing fire in a plume that lights up the night in dancing orange.

The other kids gasp, letting out excited shouts, and the purple-haired girl looks up at him with total adoration, her eyes shining.

To a starry-eyed teenager, it's pretty cool.

But kids their age shouldn't be messing with stuff like that surrounded by trees.

I'm torn.

I've done my fair share of stupid stuff. It's part of growing up. Part of finding myself. I don't want to ruin it for someone else.

I also don't want to be the moron who looked the other way

while a bunch of kids started a wildfire that takes down half the town.

So I rock back on my heels, thinking how to approach them. Only for my boot to catch on a thick branch and snap it in half.

Even with the crackle of Senor Firespout over there, the noise zips through the night.

The kids tense, bolting upright, scattering like alley cats in police headlights.

Including the firestarter kid, gasping and choking as his plume sputters out...and the rapid whip of his head sends sparks flying freaking *everywhere.*

They drift up, catching on the last few tattered dry leaves clinging to the twigs overhead.

There's maybe half a second where I hope the sparks will smolder and die.

Only for a breeze to make them flare to light, and suddenly, the entire branch goes up in a sudden fiery burst.

Crap!

I'm moving before I even realize what I'm doing, my heart tripping over itself while I whip off my hat, exposing my face to the blistering cold, dashing across the clearing. I try to beat the flames out.

Next thing I know, there's someone right next to me and a quiet voice saying, "Not like that! You'll burn your hands, lady."

Before I can stop her, Purple Girl nudges me aside.

She's calmer than me, taking her coat off—one of those big clunky military surplus things punk girls her age love so much—and wrapping it around the branches, smothering the fire into nothing in half a second, before it even has a chance to singe her coat.

She holds it a minute longer, then pulls the coat free from the now-smoking but no longer burning branch, shaking the cloth free before sliding it on.

The look she gives me is wary, suspicious, like she's

wondering if I'm friend or foe, because let's face it, she did the right thing. She turned back to put out the fire.

Which means she basically just turned herself into an adult.

"You're new," she says carefully, then flicks her gaze to my hair. "Nice hair job."

"The red's natural," I answer. Easy icebreaker again. "But looks like we've both got a thing for purple."

"Yeah." She takes a step back, and I can tell she's ready to bolt, but I offer my hand.

"Hey," I say. "It's cold out here, and you've been drinking. Come on inside and sober up with me. I'll make you some tea, so you don't go home to your parents smelling like..." I glance at the bottle. "Whatever that cheap crap is."

She actually flinches.

I'm not sure what I said, but her expression crumples.

She looks away from me sharply, her lips working, her mouth trembling. She glares at the bottle. "Why would you do that?"

"Because I was the kind of kid who'd do the same dumb shit you just did. Only, I'd probably have set my hair on fire trying to put the tree out."

That gets a laugh from her. "...yeah, uh, yarn is really flammable. That was kind of silly."

"Guilty as charged." I grin, my hand still outstretched. "What's your name?"

For several seconds, she looks at my hand like she's trying to make up her mind, before stepping forward and slipping her fingers into mine. Even as cold as it is, without gloves, snow falling around us in soft little poofs, her fingers are warm.

Like she's just bursting with brightness and life.

"Andrea," she says, squeezing my hand. "Andrea Silverton. How 'bout you?"

"Peace," I say, and the weirdest look passes over her face.

Horror, amusement, dread, disgust, resignation.

Every spectrum of emotion I've seen before when I lay my name on strangers.

"Wait. Oh my God, that was *you* on the radio tonight!" she says.

I let out a groan, squeezing her hand back before letting go.

"My infamy precedes me," I say dryly. "Including my misfortune with fire." I toss my head. "C'mon. Let's go get warmed up."

* * *

I'M STARTING to think Andrea's a little repressed.

I make us both cups of blueberry hibiscus tea. It gives off a nice smell to cover up the liquor on her breath—moonshine, I think. I caught a whiff as we walked back. *Oof.*

With the hibiscus to calm her down, hopefully it'll help her sleep a little easier with less of a hangover in the morning.

Over her cup of tea, she watches me, settled on the couch nearby.

"How'd you know we were out there?" she asks.

"Smoke and fire show up easy at night. Especially with the snow reflecting everything." I smile and shrug, pressing my mouth against the rim of my mug, leaning against the arm of the couch. "You were pretty visible from the kitchen window."

"Fuck." She closes her eyes, cradling her mug but not drinking much. "I told my idiot friends we were too close."

"If you'd been any deeper, where the trees grow thicker, you could've caught a lot more than a few branches on fire."

"That was *Clark*," she spits out with the kind of annoyed vehemence that can only be a girl in love with a boy who's only dumb because he hasn't told her he's in love with her, too. "I just wanted to forget everything, I guess. Bad night. My dad's a dumbass, my mom's dead, my uncle's weird, and I have no clue why he's even here. Then Clark had to go and show off, and now everything's just...just..."

She's lost me.

I have no idea what's going on, really.

But I don't need to in order to listen.

Sometimes, we just need people to hear us. It sounds like Andrea's wanted someone to hear her for a long time.

And maybe I'm not the right one, the best one, the person who really needs to hear all of this.

Still, I can stand in, let her relieve some of the pressure until she's ready to talk to the folks she truly needs.

"Hey," I say softly. "Sometimes our friends are dumb when they're trying to distract us. And our parents do even dumber stuff when they're trying to figure out how to help us after..." I make a helpless gesture. "After all that."

Andrea gives me a miserable look. I think she's hiding behind her mug so I don't see how her lips tremble to match her voice.

"What do you know?" she whispers.

Her hostility doesn't bother me. She's young, drunk, miserable.

I've been there.

So I just smile, taking a bracing sip of tea. "My dad died when I was a few years younger than you," I say. "And my mom didn't know how to handle it. She kinda turned into an asshole."

Andrea's eyes widen, as if she can't believe an *adult* just cursed in front of her. She glances around quickly like she's waiting for someone to pop up and catch us, before lowering her eyes to her tea. The steam piping up makes her hair curl and frizz, but she doesn't seem to mind.

"Yeah," she says softly. "That's...yeah. Mom died like today. Not *today* today, but...this is the day. Four years ago." She swallows, her eyes glimmering. "And my dad's so stupid. He always says the wrong thing."

"Dads usually do." I hesitate, considering what to offer, and then try, "Even my dad sometimes, and he was amazing. I think that's what hurt the most, when he died and Mom changed. It's like she forgot everything she loved about him that was so free, so wild. She turned into the total opposite. It felt like she was trying to erase every part of me that was like him, so I wouldn't grow up to *be* him and then die and leave her, too."

"*Yes!*" It comes out of Andrea in an aching cry, one that nearly breaks my heart. "It's like, fine. I know Mom and Dad were gonna split up anyway, but I'd rather have her divorced and *alive*, but it's like...like he doesn't even want to *think* about her and doesn't want me to either. Maybe he didn't love her anymore, but I *did!*"

"Andrea..." I set my tea down on the coffee table and shift closer to her, carefully slipping my arm around her shoulders. "It's probably just that he doesn't know how to show his feelings in front of you. It's complicated for him, I'd bet."

Instead of pulling away from me like I half expect, she rests her mug on her knee so she can turn into me, hiding her face in my shoulder.

"It doesn't have to be that complicated," she mumbles against me. "If he'd just be honest."

"Yeah, well, men are kind of like that." I smile slightly, giving her a squeeze. "Hey. You ever been to Oahu?"

The distraction works.

She perks, lifting her head a little to peer at me curiously. "Isn't that in Hawaii? No way, I've never left *here*."

She says it with the scorn of any small-town girl who's longing for new skies. I can't help laughing.

"Yes, Hawaii. Home sweet home. You should ask your father to take you some day. I think you'd like it, even if it's *hot*."

"Awesome. I'm so sick of it always being rainy or snowy or just plain drab around here. It only gets really bright in the summer, and even then it's never *hot*." Andrea wrinkles her nose. "Plus, I doubt Dad would take me somewhere that cool."

I frown. "Who is your dad, anyway?"

She doesn't even get a chance to answer. There's a knock at my door, sharp enough to rattle the doorframe, but with a certain restraint.

Who in the heck, at this time of night...?

NICOLE SNOW

The last thing I expect when I peer over my shoulder and through the glass of the door is *him*.

Blake.

Mr. Grumpy Silver Tongue himself.

From the frozen look on Andrea's face...well, now I know who Daddy Dearest is.

And I also know Silver Tongue isn't too far off from *Silverton*.

"Hey," I promise her, giving her another squeeze before standing, keeping my voice low. "It'll be okay. I won't squeal about the liquor, but maybe take a few more sips of that tea."

Wide-eyed, she nods, lifting the mug to her lips while I cross to the door.

Blake looks particularly intimidating in the light falling through the glass. Big arms folded over his chest, thickly honed forearms bulging against the sleeves of his coat, his mouth set like a steel trap.

Yikes.

But I smile ever so sweetly anyway, pulling the door open.

"Hey!" I say. "I'm guessing the lost kitten here is yours?"

"Correct," he says grimly. I barely get to step aside before he's stalking inside, his big bulk taking up so much space in my little cottage living room. "Andrea?"

She winces but sets her mug down and shuffles over, her head down.

Only for Blake to throw his arms around her shoulders, dragging her in close, enveloping her in this massive, sheltering hug that actually takes me by surprise. His expression softens as he buries his face in her hair and cups the back of her head.

"Goddammit, girl," he whispers roughly. "I didn't even know you weren't home. Thought you were freezing me out. Then Haley called in the fire and I *knew*."

Andrea makes a soft, hurting sound, clinging to Blake, knotting her hands in his shirt. "M'sorry, Dad. Sorry. I know it was stupid, we could've...we could've set the whole woods on fire—"

"The Inn too," he growls, his eyes drilling into her. "You don't want to hurt Ms. Wilma or Warren and Hay that way, do you? This town's had enough fire damage the past year."

"No, no, of course not." Miserably, Andrea buries her face in his chest. "I just wanna go home, Dad."

"I know." He squeezes her tighter for a moment, then pulls back, gently nudging her. "Go wait in the Jeep. I'll be out in a second."

She holds on to him for a few more seconds, then pulls back and slogs away, the living portrait of tired dejection as she clomps out into the snow.

It's my guess she'll be out cold before they even get home.

Blake lingers, awkward in his thick flannel wool-lined coat, jeans, and boots. Apparently, changing out of his fire gear and into everyday stuff takes zero points away from the sexy department.

I try to quit gawking.

"How did you know you'd find her here?" I'm not even sure what to say, so I try a smile.

He gives me a flat look, then reaches into his back pocket and retrieves something.

My crocheted cap, several spots of it blackened and singed.

"You had this on earlier," he says. "And it's pretty distinctly ugly. But if you want it back..."

"Nah, I don't really think it's any good anymore." I wince, glancing away. "Sorry. I didn't know she was your little girl, or I'd have tried to call, or something. I saw them out in the woods, went to check out the fire, and they bolted. One kid was being reckless. A few twigs caught fire, but Andrea put it out. Now I know where she gets her fire safety tips from."

If I'm not mistaken, there's actually a touch of pride flickering in his eyes. Pride in his daughter. It warms me to see it.

And it does jack squat to dispel this ridiculous crush.

He rakes a hand through his thick hair, making it spike wildly around his sharply patrician features. "Yeah, well, thanks for looking out for her."

"Oh, it's no big!"

He starts turning away.

My lip digs against my teeth. Hey, I might as well shoot my shot while he's here, right?

Better than desperately trying to chase him down later.

"Hey," I say quickly, starting forward. "Listen, um...I was wondering about the stories Justin was talking about. The stuff about you and your friends and all the stuff that happened here? Heroes of Heart's Edge?"

It's the wrong thing to ask.

I *know* it's the wrong thing to ask, when I remember far too late that Justin said the whole thing makes Blake touchy.

I'm tired, I'm confused, I'm not thinking straight, and I'm regretting opening my mouth.

Sigh.

I expect him to slam down on me, to go gruff and cold and incisive the way he'd been earlier tonight.

I'm just a stranger, after all. A very *nosy* one.

But the man actually smiles.

It's so sad, though. And I can't help but wonder what made him that way as he says, "You're plenty welcome to ask other folks those stories. Warren. Doc. Even Leo. They're the heroes, and they do the talkin'. I don't need to be nobody's hero, Peace."

Then he's turning away again, and this time, I don't have the heart to stop him.

Especially when his voice floats over his shoulder, and the music in it comes out like a haunting dirge, making me ache to tease out what's at the heart of it.

"Not interested in heroing anyone these days but my little girl."

IV: BOUGHT FOR A SONG (BLAKE)

I survived the school week.

Barely.

I'm pretty sure the only reason Andrea hasn't murdered me in my sleep is because she's out of the house for twelve hours a day. Still, that little moment we had at Peace's cabin the other day went flat real fast when I told her she was grounded.

Look, she did good putting that fire out quick.

But like *hell* that tea or whatever Peace gave her was gonna mask the smell on her breath. Her breath stank like rocket fuel.

I know she was out there drinking, and probably with that firestarter kid Clark.

Little goddamn punk.

She's slowly relaxed, at least over awkward dinners where she spends half the time pretending to ignore me *with her sketchbook at the table* and the other half drawing furiously, applying the lessons Haley's shown her. That's the one thing I'll relent on —letting her spend two evenings a week at the Charming Inn.

I have to be her dad.

I'm not going to be her prison guard.

Can't stand seeing her grow up feeling crushed, stifled, run down.

Not the way I did.

By Saturday she's more animated, though—maybe because her grounding's lifted, and after dinner I finally give her permission to go out and find her friends.

She's been pretty pissed at them. Mad enough that making up between classes hasn't been possible, but she never stays angry at them for long. Small-town life gets even smaller when you're a teenager.

So she mostly saves her hellfire for me, I guess.

I'm shocked she actually kisses my cheek as she bounces toward the door. "I'll be home before midnight," she says, slinging her messenger bag over her shoulder.

"Ten thirty," I growl after her, and she lets out an exaggerated sigh.

Not really mad at me.

Just putting on a show. I hide my grin.

"Compromise," she says. "Eleven."

I stroke my beard, pretending to consider, then nod. "Eleven it is."

Rolling her eyes, tossing her head back, she groans, "God, you're *such* a dad," before bouncing out into the night.

Leaving me alone, in the quiet of my house.

I don't usually notice the emptiness when I have the rare evening to myself—no fires to put out, no cats to rescue from trees, no other crises, no call-in show, my growing daughter out having a life of her own. I'm usually too tired to think about anything but resting my feet and getting some shut-eye.

I've been trying to read the same book—*Gone Girl*—for nearly six damn months. Doc's idea. I get two pages in and then pass out, even if he's right about it being a fast-paced thriller.

But I'm not that tired now.

Maybe it's the ghost of my ma, riding in Holt's wake. Or maybe it's the lingering memory of Abby, her shadow haunting us all week, but hell.

I don't think I *want* to be alone right now.

It's not hard to know where I'll find the guys. Unless it's Warren's turn with a cranky kid or two—Doc also, now, damn all my friends are settled in with kids and wives, but one out of two ain't bad—they're always at Brody's.

It's a clear sky tonight. No fresh snow, though it smells like it's biting cold, the kind that makes the air feel thinner. With my leg not acting up, it's almost relaxing to make the drive under the bright full moon, everything gone silver under the snow.

I can get a beer in with enough time for it to wear off and leave me safe to drive home to see if Little Violet listens to my curfew.

The flashing sign at Brody's draws me in.

I park and head into the long, low weathered building, a classic roadhouse style pub that looks like it was put together from driftwood some thirty or forty years ago. Inside, it's still rowdy, even at just after nine. Mostly 'cause the college kids come in from a couple towns over.

They know the bartenders don't check IDs as often as they should and they love going up to the cliff to make out and throw flowers over the edge.

No flowers for me tonight.

Looks like the whole crew's here. I home in on Warren, Doc, and Leo, settled at their own table—and the moment Warren catches sight of me, my name echoes over the bar in a hearty boom.

"Blake!" he calls, waving. "Get over here!"

I catch a fast-moving waitress' eye and signal for a beer, then cross the room to sling myself into a chair in their booth. We're four big men, and it's a tighter fit than it used to be, especially with Leo being a new addition.

Or I should say a new *old* addition. We used to play together as kids, and my dumb ass called him Tiger, mixing up my Latin. Only for him to disappear, then show up again years later as the monster-turned-hero of Heart's Edge, formerly known as Nine.

I almost don't belong here with these brave damned men who keep risking it all for this town.

Peace's voice resonates in the back of my mind. That soft sweet girl, all vivid eyes and fire and charm, asking me to tell her those stories.

They ain't mine to tell.

I'm not here for grand showdowns and attention.

I'm just trying to raise my daughter in one piece and stay alive.

"Hey, man," Warren says, clapping me on the shoulder as I settle into the creaking wood. "Been a while."

I groan, folding my arms on the table. "Had to stay home with Andrea to make sure she *stays* grounded. Girl's better than old Mozart at sneaking out."

Warren chuckles. "That big ol' poofball does more sleeping than sneaking these days. The kids spoiled him rotten over Christmas with scraps of turkey and ham. He's got himself a buddy, too."

"Yeah, that big grey monster with the ears chewed off. You've got yourself a two-cat household to go with the two munchkins. What're you calling the new guy again?" I scratch my neck.

"Van Gogh. Hay's idea. I wanted to keep the crazy composer naming thing going, but..." He shrugs.

"No worries, man. Still got your two babes and two big cats beat with one angry teenager, love her to death." I flash him a grin.

Leo grimaces, the inked burn scars down his neck and jaw pulling tight. "Guess I'm up next with the terrible teens, huh? Shit."

I grin. "Zach is fuckin' *smart*, dude. Like, Andrea's honor roll, but Zach's like..."

"Don't say it," Leo grumbles. "I caught him trying to build a particle accelerator out of *kitchen tools*."

He's groaning, but there's clear pride.

Yeah. I get it.

I get it far too well.

"August will catch up to him soon," Doc says with a sniff, pushing his glasses up his nose, his sharp green eyes glinting. "She's quite the wit. Takes after her father, naturally."

I laugh. "Little Gus ain't even talking yet, let alone walking or building things. Give it ten years, man. Then maybe she'll join you and her mama at your vet clinic."

He growls. "Do not call my daughter *Gus*."

That just makes me grin wider. "Aw, why not? You call your wife Ember instead of September."

"I—"

Leo cuts us off with a patient sigh. "C'mon, boys. Don't start. I think we're all too tired for the comedy bit tonight."

"I feel that," I say, offering Doc a smile as an olive branch.

He sniffs again, looking away from me in that cool way he has, but it ain't hard to tell I'm forgiven.

If I wasn't, he'd have flipped me off.

"Hey," I add. "You need any help with her? The first kid's always the toughest, and you and Ember are plenty busy chasing animals at The Menagerie. Ain't she gonna be teething soon?"

In half a second, that icy demeanor vanishes and Doc winces, sagging and burying his fingers in his hair. "She already *is*. I feel like I haven't slept in *years*."

"Now, now, she can't have been fussing more than a few days, young as she is." I nudge him with my elbow. "Listen, I got a few tips to help her calm down. Andrea was a fussy teether, too."

Doc gives me a haggard look.

"Please," he says. "Teach me the wisdom of your ways. I had to let Ember deliver an entire litter of kittens on her own this week because I nearly fell asleep in the delivery room."

"Well then," I say. "Strap in, and let the advice man tell you what's up."

* * *

THERE'S something about helping people that takes me outside myself.

Think that's why I like it so much.

Feels like I've been stuck in a rut for so long, I'd damn rather deal with somebody else's. Most folks look at their lives as a line from beginning to end, stretching clean through space.

Me, though?

My life's kind of like that line came to a screeching halt.

The night Andrea's mother died, somebody just picked up the pen and made the line cut short, but that whole damn piece of paper's still there, sprawled out in front of me.

It's like I was supposed to die too when the ink line stopped, but since I didn't...

Now, I'm just waiting in blank white limbo, wondering what I'm even here for.

I mean, nah. I *know* who I'm here for.

Andrea's reason enough to wake up in the morning and haul my bones out of bed. She's everything.

But one fine day she's gonna be fully grown up and gone, and then what?

Who the fuck am I gonna be?

The funny man on the radio who alternates love advice with wild late-night conspiracy rumors, I guess. The dude who puts out fires.

Because I'd rather focus on other people's problems than that blank sheet of paper. And that's what has me laughing, completely absorbed in my buddies as we trade tips and horror stories back and forth about our kids.

It's a weeknight, though, and before I know it I gotta get home to make sure Andrea does, too.

My beer's worn off. I'm clearheaded as I clap my guys on the shoulder and stand.

That's when I catch sight of Justin, who sure as hell ain't clearheaded at all.

He's slumped over a barstool, head on the bar, damn near

drooling. His fingers are curled stubbornly in a half-filled beer mug's handle while the bartender tries uneasily to tug it away from a grip that just won't relax.

Goddammit, poor kid.

I have an inkling why he's gone all soggy tonight.

He always does around this time of year.

Something about the dead of winter brings out the loss in a whole mess of people in this little town, not just yours truly.

Sighing, I weave my way through the crowd of people wandering to the exit, make my way over to the bar, and hold up a hand to the bartender.

"Hey, man, I got it," I say. "Leave him to me."

The bartender, Bruce, gives me a wary look, then nods, his plump hand falling away. "I need him out of here in fifteen minutes," he says. "Coming up on last call. I already took his car keys. He one of your guys?"

"Yeah, he's on the crew. It's okay. I'm sober. I'll give him a lift."

Another suspicious look before the bartender slips away. I frown, leaning down to try to peer at Justin's face, but all I get is a mop of black curls and a hint of his brow. He's buried himself in his folded forearms.

"Yo, Justin," I say. "Hey, man. It's me. Let me get you home."

For a minute, I think he might actually be blackout drunk. Unconscious.

Shit.

I might just have to carry him at this rate.

But then he lets out a soft gurgle in the back of his throat. Not just the booze, it's ragged with grief. I think if he were a little more drunk, he'd be crying. If he were a little more sober, he'd be fighting it.

Where he is now is no man's land.

It's an awful, heartbreaking place where you hear wounded animal growls coming from a grown man's throat.

"Everybody dies here," he whispers, slurring his words, and

I'm wondering how many damn beers he's had. "Everybody. Maybe *she* didn't die here...but they brought her body back. They brought her body back to lay it home."

Fuck.

Yeah.

Yeah, I know what this is about.

Justin's young enough to be my kid, almost. Twenty-seven.

And he *was* a kid one time, with the big Paradise Hotel fire almost a decade ago.

These days, everybody can't shut up about the Heroes of Heart's Edge.

You wanna talk about a *real* hero long before we hooked up, though?

Talk about Constance Bast.

Justin's ma.

A lot of folks died the night that hotel burned, but she managed to get a hell of a lot of people out of there, people who would've been trapped if she hadn't stepped up.

She'd just been the receptionist.

She was never meant to be a martyr.

I still remember.

I wasn't too old back then either. Just a junior on the fire crew between tours serving Uncle Sam. And that woman in the debris, covered in soot, she'd shown bravery I didn't see again till Afghanistan.

She'd been okay, at first.

Until she'd collapsed, hacking up a bloody, black mess.

"Justin." I nudge his shoulder gently. "Thinkin' about your ma tonight, huh?"

"Chief?"

"Yeah, dude. It's me."

"F-forty-three days," he rasps, and my throat knots. It's so wretched, so awful. "She held on for forty-three days."

"Yeah, bud," I whisper. "I remember."

NO DAMAGED GOODS

Forty-three days while the doctors in Spokane tried to fix the brutal smoke damage to her lungs.

And failed.

She left Heart's Edge a hero.

She came home to a coffin.

Seems like that's the story of a lot of good people around here who die too young.

Warren's sister, Jenna, for one. Killed in a devious setup overseas.

Even more folks the past few years have had their own brush with the Reaper and lived to tell the tale.

Warren himself, and Haley, and Leo, and Clarissa, Doc, Ember...fuck.

I wonder sometimes if this place is cursed. Even if all those spooky legends about Nine aka Leo are just history now, there's something eerie and unnatural about life in Heart's Edge.

Add one more body from my side.

Abigail was no hero when she died. But nobody needed to die like her.

I close my eyes, taking a deep breath, pushing the thoughts away.

Instead, I keep my focus on Justin and slip my arm around his shoulders to coax him off the stool. "C'mon, bud. Let's get you home."

"Forty-three days, Chief," he repeats miserably, even as his body slides limply off the seat.

"I know, man. I know."

It's like moving a bag of dry cement, he's so heavy and boneless. But I manage to get his legs under him and prop him against my side, mostly supporting his weight on my right leg so I can steer with my bum left leg. This ain't the best way, but I just gotta get him to the Jeep.

"Let's go," I say, while Justin makes a hurting, horrid sound against my shoulder.

I wish I could give him more than useless words—but that's all I'm good for.

"Chief..."

"Hush. Talkin' takes a lot of energy right now. Let's get you put away for the night."

* * *

Dropping Justin at his apartment feels a little melancholy.

It's sparse, utilitarian, like he doesn't really *live* there.

Just sleeps and wakes up to go to work.

I frown. He hasn't bothered making it any kind of home, not even for a young guy. Nothing personal there except the rows of photo albums lined up on the wall shelves—well, at least he's got himself a hobby. He's good with a camera.

Turning away from them, I tuck him into bed and lock up, then push the spare key back up in the hidden holder over the door.

I should really make some kind of effort to break him out of his funk.

He's not my kid, nah, more my peer than anything, but I'm the chief of the volunteer fire crew and he's one of my boys.

He doesn't have much. No other family in town or anywhere else in the area I know of.

I can at least invite him to drink with us now and then.

Might help keep him from getting so shitfaced.

I'm still pondering that as I slip into my Jeep and head home, idly massaging my knuckles against my slightly sore thigh.

Thankfully, any pain I'm in vanishes behind weary irritation as I pull into my driveway, cut the engine, and crawl into bed.

For once, Andrea's home on time.

For once, my mind isn't overflowing with worries over fire damage or work or whose evil ass I have to run out of town next.

For once, I let my mind wander off to happier places, even if they're also kind of sad.

Little Miss Broccoli gives me plenty to think on as I drift off. Maybe it's just the booze or the wintry calm limbering me up, but I let myself linger on her memory.

Those strawberry lips. That hot red-purple mane a man could do outrageous fuckin' things with. Those hips that look like they could ride me to next Christmas.

And how it must be the worst irony ever that she got stuck with a name like a *Rabe* of damn broccoli when it doesn't fit her one bit.

She's a sweet, bright-eyed slice of cherry pie, a delicate morsel ready to be devoured by some lucky SOB. Even if he won't be me tonight or any night, a man's gotta have his dreams, his fantasies, his dirty little secrets.

I fall asleep feeling thankful for one newcomer in Heart's Edge who brings sweet dreams instead of more nightmares.

* * *

THE NEXT DAY, I put in my hours welding, hoping I'll get lucky to come home to some peace and quiet for the second day in a row.

Nope.

There's that damn Benz again, parked outside.

Holt.

I'd bet every penny Andrea's home and let him in, since the car's empty and dark. There's no one on the porch, and the lights are on in the living room.

Goddammit.

I'm not in the mood for this today. Or the other day. Or *any* day.

It's a hell of a thing when I don't even want to go into my own house, but I can't just stand out here in the fucking snow. I feel the cold down the back of my neck like a collar against the heat of annoyance flushing my skin.

Muttering, stomping snow off my boots on the front walk, I push the door open—the *unlocked* door, dammit, Andrea—and step inside the sweltering warmth.

My brother sprawls in my easy chair—my *favorite* chair—like he owns the place.

This time, I can't help noticing how immaculately he's dressed.

Like a real slick-dick big city boy.

Like he never tripped in ditches and came home covered in mud in this little mountain town just like I did once upon a time.

You wouldn't guess it. Not from his fine black suit, the wide lapels and cuffs of the white shirt under it, the perfect razor-sharp trim of his scruff, the blocky platinum ring on one finger.

Holt steeples his fingers, watching me over them with a hint of a smirk making his hazel eyes glitter. Once again, I feel like I'm facing down Lucifer.

The devil himself in my own living room, ready to offer me a bargain I want fuck all to do with.

"*What*." I snarl.

"Poor Blake." Holt lets out an exasperated sigh. "All these years and you still have *zero* manners."

"Like you do, asshat? You work construction. Why the fuck are you dressed like a lawyer and blabbin' like New York City?"

A smirk curls his lips. "I wasn't aware 'blabbing like New York City' was a thing."

He knows damn well what I mean. His smirk only widens as I bare my teeth at him in a silent growl.

"You're having a grand old time spending Ma's money, huh?"

"It's an *investment*," he retorts smoothly, crossing his ankle over his knee and slouching with casual ease.

"The hell you mean?" I hate how comfy he looks up in my space, while I'm vibrating, on fire, out of place.

"I'm investing in Heart's Edge. Investing in my hometown." His smile turns cunning, carnivorous, and fuck if I have any clue how we're related. "Maybe a few of the local single ladies wouldn't mind welcoming me home, since I hear you've rejected them all. They must be *starved*."

"I hate you," I bite off.

"Wish you didn't, brother."

"And I wish you'd stop talking in circles." I rip my jacket off just to give myself something to do. "What the hell are you talking about, investing in Heart's Edge?"

"I mean," he says slowly, "that I used my inheritance wisely to graduate from lowly landscaper to starting my own construction company." A pause, and I swear to God he's doing it for dramatic effect, the shit. "And it just so happens I've just landed the contract to rebuild several portions of the town damaged in the big museum fire last year."

Fuck me six ways from Sunday.

Blowing out sharply, I lean against the door, crossing my ankles and folding my arms, eyeing him warily. "So you're saying you're gonna be in town awhile? Great."

"Exactly." Holt looks at me strangely.

It's weird seeing him trying to be honest, but damn...I remember when we were kids. Sometimes, he'd look at me that way too, before he turned into this slick skirt-chasing snake.

I give him a look that makes it feel like July in January.

"Listen, we're going to be around each other a lot, Blake. I'd like it if we could bury the hatchet and start over."

"You don't fucking start over when your own brother tries to seduce your wife." My fists whiten my knuckles, so ready to meet his smart-ass face.

"You were already practically separated," he points out coolly. "And you don't know the entire situation."

"Bullshit. I *know* that separated or not, she was still Andrea's ma, and I didn't need my daughter trying to process her mother fucking her uncle."

He blinks and actually looks hurt for a moment before he turns his face away.

When he's not smirking, he actually looks more angel than

devil, almost pensive like he's bitten into a lemon so sour it gives him a soul.

But then, I'm sure Old Scratch had his pondering moments before he fell from grace, too.

Holt sighs and mutters quietly, "There is that. But it's also a moot point, isn't it?"

That? Right.

There's that creepy stillness between us. That silence. That reminder of death and bad blood.

I don't even know what to say.

It's like if I acknowledge it, I'm inviting more in.

After a little while, Holt says, "Andrea's growing up to be an amazing young woman, Blake. She showed me some of her art before she ran off to her room." His smile actually seems genuine—and I hate it more. "You're doing a good job with her."

Go fuck yourself, I want to say.

Because the best way to get under my skin is to say my girl's exactly as wonderful as she is.

I grumble, looking away, scrubbing a hand through my hair. "Yeah, well, I'm trying. Hope I'm not doing too bad on my lonesome."

"Hey," Holt says, an odd catch in his voice.

I glance at him warily. He's watching me intently, and for a split second...

Yeah.

There's my brother.

Just the two of us huddling in the same bunk, listening to the creak of our ma's footsteps, hoping if we didn't make too much noise, she'd walk past and not peer in and find us awake and make us suffer.

Ma had ways to torture kids that didn't mean laying a finger on us.

She never hit us. That'd be too easy.

But she *knew* how to make us scared.

And I remember the echo of that fear, having to clamp my

hand over Holt's mouth to silence his sniffles while her shadow passed under the door.

"Hey," he says again. "You're...you're not Mom."

"You're damn right I'm not," I spit back. "And I know I'm raising Andrea better than Ma or Abby ever could."

Holt cocks his head, studying me thoughtfully.

"I think...I envy you, Blake," he says. "You got out earlier. Left me alone with her. You broke free, while I got sucked in deeper."

I don't want the rush of guilt that hits, but there it is.

It's an anvil, crushing down on my chest, heading straight for the heart.

Fuck.

"Whatever." I duck my head, swallowing, feeling something gritty. "I'm sorry for that. The second I saw the chance to run..."

"Oh, I don't blame you. It's just how things turned out." There's a whisper of fine wool against the ratty plaid of my easy chair as he shrugs. "But maybe I want to start over, too. Find out what it's like to have a good family."

I inhale slowly, and exhale just the same.

I know what he's asking.

He wants me to *forget* that fucked up night I walked in on him with Abby in his arms, and he'll forget that I left him alone in our ma's clutches and abandoned him to deal with her shit, her demands, and then her care in old age till the bitter end.

Yeah.

Then it came, she died, and he was free too.

In the worst way possible.

Don't rightly know if I can forgive that. Or if he can forgive me.

But I'm thinking about Little Violet right now, how upset she was that she had a grandma she never knew.

She might never forgive me if I refuse to let her know her uncle, too.

"Okay," I say grudgingly. "Look, you can do dinner tomorrow. That's it. No more promises. But we don't talk about Ma,

59

understood? We don't talk about the past at all. You play nice, you keep it light, and you fucking behave yourself in front of your niece."

He grins then, and the devil's back as he claps his hands together. "Perfect. Have I ever not behaved?"

"*Holt.*"

He laughs—but it's not that oily laugh he turns on when he wants to seduce women with his wild purr and those too-sly whiskey eyes.

It's a real, hearty chuckle. This goofy kind of awkward small-town thing I recognize in my brother.

"Okay, okay," he says, standing, raising his hands in surrender. "I promise. I'll be good. You want me to bring wine, though?"

"This is a beer house," I growl. "And we don't do business formal."

He smooths the lapels of his shirt. "I'll make sure to adhere to the dress co—"

He's cut off by a sound I'd know anywhere and dread.

The shrill of a ringing line from across the room.

It's tinny, a weird, vibrating sound, because the phone's old as hell. Bright red, a little scratched and dinged up.

I found it in a thrift shop and bought it for the novelty, but when that landline rings, there's only one thing it ever means.

There's a fire somewhere in Heart's Edge.

V: MOVE TO THE BEAT (PEACE)

*H*eart's Edge is totally not what I expected.

Especially when I'm sitting on a bench across from a pretty candy store, talking to a man big enough to pull off the *I am the Brute Squad* quote with a straight face.

He's covered in burn scars, fused with tattoos in freaky artistic patterns that turn a sad disfigurement into a portrait of something strange and beautiful.

One look would tell anybody he *should* be a brute.

But he's got this gentle smile and warm eyes that look nearly black at first, until he brushes his hair back from his face. Then they catch the light, turning this unique amethyst-violet hue.

"Not gonna lie," he says a bit sheepishly. "I thought you were another reporter looking to crawl up my ass."

"Nah." I grin. "Just a goofy massage therapist who writes songs sometimes. I feel like there's a good country-rock ballad in Heart's Edge somewhere."

"Country-rock? Oh, hell." He lets out a bark of laughter. His voice has a slight burned, raspy edge.

"You know, like Garth Brooks style. Telling the story of a band of four desperadoes moving across the plains, rolling thunder, lightning strikes, that sort of thing."

That gets another laugh from him, incredulous. "Where you gonna find a horse big enough for me, then?"

"Ahhh, that's why we're lucky it's fiction." I hold a finger up. "Just a little pinch of truth. Just enough to make it feel real."

"So no names," he says, a touch warily.

I get the feeling he's heard his name said too many times, in all the wrong ways.

"Well, since I don't even know yours..." I tease.

"You know." He gives me a dry look. "Or you wouldn't be talking to me about your song. I'm probably the easiest person to ID in town."

I incline my head. "Fair. I hope you're not mad."

"Nah." He chuckles. "I don't mind. Just no more of that tabloid shit."

"Nothing of the kind." I cock my head, hugging my arms to myself.

It's bright out, the sun reflecting warmly off a thin new layer of snow that settled in overnight, but even with the sky bright and blue and soaring overhead, I'm numb through my coat.

At least I remembered gloves this time.

"So should I call you Nine or Mr. Regis?" I ask.

"Leo's fine." His smile is wry, self-deprecating. "Don't think I've ever been Mr. Regis except on national TV. And 'Nine' is full of some memories."

"Yeah? What kind?"

"Prison," he says. It's honest, but grim and a touch regretful. "I did the wrong thing for the right reasons, wound up in jail. My prisoner number started with nine. And when I escaped, living like a wild man around these hills...it just stuck."

I glance at the candy store across the street, visible past the hood of my little purple nugget of the compact rental car I've left on the sidewalk. The shop is called Sweeter Things, and a tall, beautiful woman with rich mahogany hair moves around inside busily, an adorable little chestnut-haired boy trailing in her wake.

"Anything to do with her?"

"My wife?" Leo chuckles. "Yeah. *Everything* to do with Rissa."

"Sounds like one hell of a love story."

"One for the ages." He studies me discerningly. "You gonna write a song about that, too?"

"Maybe." I bite my lip, and I know I'm not being subtle, but... "So where does Blake fit into this?"

He blinks, leaning back a little. "Blake Silverton?"

"Um, I guess." I grin nervously. "He does the radio show, right? I haven't heard him on the air lately..."

Something about the way Leo looks at me makes me feel like a kid with her hand caught in the cookie jar. "So you've been listening for him?"

Crap. Crap. Crap!

Wincing, I duck down into my shoulders. "*Mayyybe.* Can we keep that between us, though? Oh, *God.*" I drop my face into my lumpy purple hand-knitted gloves. "This is so high school."

"Don't worry, Peace. I won't tell the hunky fireman you got a crush."

"*Leo!*" I sputter.

But I'm laughing, and he's grinning, and it's just nice.

It's cool making a friend out here when I've avoided putting down roots for so long.

He lets out a hoarse laugh, then shakes his head. "He hasn't been at the radio station all week because Andrea's been grounded, I hear. Girl's slipperier than her pet snake. If he takes his eyes off her, she'll be gone like a cat in the night."

"Wowza." I wince. "I feel like I might've had something to do with that. I was there the night she almost set the inn on fire. Hid her out in my cabin until he came to get her."

"Yeah? No wonder Blake hasn't said a frigging word about you," he laughs.

Ouch. I deflate.

"...Not even a little?"

"Well, he usually doesn't talk about things that get under his skin," Leo says, stroking his stubble, and I almost want to kick myself for the way that makes my heart jump. "You looked after his kid? If you're really into him, that's a big favor. He ought to appreciate it."

I glance over my shoulder.

No fooling, this really does feel like high school, making sure my secret crush isn't eavesdropping.

"He's a good dad, isn't he?" I ask tentatively.

I can't help but remember that night. He'd pulled Andrea close and wrapped her in a hug that could've stopped time.

He'd been angry, sure, it wasn't hard to see.

But it was the kind of protective fury that comes from a man who's afraid someone he loves has done something reckless that could take her away forever.

And as he'd hugged her, the way his brows knit together and crumpled left an impression, all right.

I'm melting just thinking of it.

The warmth in his face was written so clearly, utterly real and unashamed, because he loves Andrea *that much*. That's not something you find in most places.

Maybe Leo's right and he doesn't talk much about his feelings, but when his guard comes down, they come pouring out like a rushing waterfall.

"Hey. Earth to Peace."

"Uh?" I blink, then shake myself, warmth chasing the chill from my cheeks. "Sorry. I drifted a little."

"Somebody's moonstruck."

"Am not!" I splutter. "I don't even know him. Not really."

"Then you'd best get on that—"

He breaks off, eyes widening, his entire body going stiff as he stares past me and then bites off, "Oh, *fuck*."

Too many things happen in the next ten seconds.

Leo bolts to his feet, digging his hand into his pocket and grabbing his phone. My stomach clutches nervously tight as I scramble to my feet after him, turning so fast I almost slip on the icy sidewalk, whirling to see what he's looking at.

Then I see the thick plume of smoke billowing up from behind the candy shop.

Oh, no.

Oh, *crap*.

It's like fire follows me everywhere, I swear.

But Leo's already barking something into the phone, while I stand there helplessly, watching him charge across the street, waving his arm over his head. Inside the shop, several customers and the mahogany-haired woman and boy look up quickly before rushing to the door.

Suddenly, the street's pure chaos.

People pour out of the candy store and every shop around, from the diner to whatever store is in the back. Looks like there's a narrow alley, and the smoke could be coming from either building. Alarms shrill, doors fling open, people's voices burst the quiet.

It's all happening so fast.

I feel like I'm the only bit of stillness in the entire space, helpless and frozen, not knowing what to do.

It's a relief, though, to see Leo ushering his wife and the boy outside, getting clear, even as the fat plume of greasy-looking, thick black smoke thickens.

Then the sound of sirens rips through the morning, drowning out the panicked voices. The crowd scatters like a flock of pigeons as a fire truck comes careening down main street, lights flashing.

And there they are—Blake, Justin, Rich, alongside two other men I don't recognize. They move like a well-coordinated unit as they slew the fire truck across the mouth of the alley, screeching it to a halt.

In seconds, they've leaped down, Blake directing everyone with the commanding authority that makes him seem like he can handle anything.

His smooth, rolling voice urgent, demanding obedience, but calming.

Still promising everything will be *okay*.

The morning light flashes off the smooth gleam of his hair and the stark line of his temple as he directs his men to connect the hose to the hydrant on the corner while others gear up, shrugging into thick fire jackets.

The flames billow higher.

I can see them now, rising up past the back of the shop, and there are screams from inside. Somewhere. I think the building behind it—*Jesus.*

Horror knifes through me, making the cold of the day that much heavier.

It sounds like people are still *trapped* inside.

I hate this.

Hate standing here, helpless, watching.

I feel like I've latched on to Blake as this avatar of hope, straining toward him like I can reach out to him and push him just a little harder, a little faster.

Like something my small, supporting hands could do would make him stronger, when I know the pain he's hiding under that firm, broad stance.

For the briefest second, it almost feels like he senses me.

As if there's this wavelength between us, this single struck chord vibrating to the same frequency.

He turns his head, looking over his shoulder.

One dark-blue eye locks on me.

It's like a piece of night cut out of the day. I feel that cool, soothing darkness folding me up, telling me everything's going to be all right.

Blake looks away, draws his helmet down, and leads the charge down the alley to the flames.

Three men wrestle a giant high-pressure hose as if handling an anaconda. It's like Hercules against the hydra, all strength and rippling muscle and grim purpose as they aim the bursting stream of water at the fire.

Wild spray arcs out in rainbow-rippling droplets in the sun. They step closer, closer to the wall of fire I can see spreading past the buildings, blocking my line of sight.

They're so determined.

So focused.

So sure of themselves.

And at their head is Blake, commanding them all with a militant confidence that captures and rivets me as much as the battle against the moving wall of flames.

The smoke billows thicker, but the leaping tongues of fire grow thinner by the second.

Though my heart skips, my throat clutches, just as Blake drops the head of the hose, barking at Justin to take it up.

Then he pulls the collar of his coat up and dives out of sight.

I can't stand it.

The next five seconds are too terrible, each one taking an eternity to grind out.

I know I shouldn't.

I know I'm risking myself.

I know Blake will yell at me later.

But I need to see him safe, like that odd wavelength between us has wrapped its chords around my heart and squeezed it too tight to beat when he's out of sight.

So I go darting down the other narrow alley flanking the opposite side of the building, pulling my shirt and coat up over my nose to filter out the acrid sting of smoke.

Peering around the brickwork at the corner, I don't see Blake —but I do see Justin and the others charging in while two more men aim the hose at the shop behind Sweeter Things.

The door is an employee entrance in the back, and it's not the only source of the flames.

There are more contrails billowing from the other side of the building, thick and dark.

The front entrance must be blocked.

Oh—oh, *God*.

Yet again that need to do something consumes me, but I know I'd only get in the way.

Too bad I can *hear* him. Voice like a beacon, calling from inside, roaring orders, searching, questioning. Other voices, too, but I'm only listening for his.

As long as I can hear *him*, I know it'll be all right.

It's still too long, watching frozen while the firemen point the hose at the flames pouring through the door, then guide it inside. I can only guess how the battle's going by the high-powered water blast, the steady hiss of flame.

Then the slowing plumes of smoke pouring from front and back.

But I can't breathe.

I can't breathe, not until it happens.

That door bangs open again.

And with his temples glistening and smeared with soot, his jacket pulled off and wrapped around a shaking, sobbing little boy, Blake steps out in all his glory.

Steam rises off his shoulders. He's drenched and scorched but whole. And just as courageously angry and focused as ever.

I'm so relieved to see him I almost don't catch the limp.

But as someone else comes tumbling out behind him, a crying woman in the uniform of the clothing shop currently sinking into a smoldering wet pit, the door bangs against him, and he stumbles forward.

His left leg starts going out under him.

He catches himself, just barely, clutching at the little boy, standing a little taller like nothing ever happened.

I start forward but stop myself.

Then let out a cry as he tries to straighten.

Too late.

His body goes crashing to the ground in a slow, strained, broken mess.

My pulse stops. I don't even realize I'm moving.

It's just sneakers on pavement and then I'm there, catching the shrieking little boy before Blake can't hold him up anymore and he hits the concrete. I'm just in time, gathering him up in my arms.

"Blake," I gasp, but he's on his knees now, gripping at both thighs with white-knuckled hands, teeth bared in a grimace of agony and shame. His eyes are pinched shut.

"Take him. *Go*," he snarls through his teeth, deep and raspy with pain, the timbre cadence richer, almost velvety. "Oxygen mask!"

"On it, Chief," Justin says. And suddenly he's there, relieving me of the little boy, juggling him against his hip as he clamps an oxygen tank under one arm and fits a mask over the boy's face with his free hand.

Leaving me free to focus on Blake, this feral beast-man laid low by an invisible arrow to his muscle.

I step closer, then back, then stop, hands outstretched.

"Here," I whisper. "Let me help. What happened?"

He actually *flinches* back.

"Just a cramp." He opens his eyes, glaring up at me, blue irises fierce and snapping, the faint hints of lingering embers floating in his gaze. "What the hell you *doing* here, Broccoli? It's not safe."

"I..." I falter, swallowing. "I was worried about you. I was talking to Leo when the fire started. I just wanted to help and—"

"Don't need no *help*, woman," he snarls. "It's just a cramp, you hear?"

It doesn't matter how many times he says it.

It doesn't make it true.

I know what deep pain looks like—the kind of brute agony that takes up root and never goes away, coiled like a serpent under the skin.

But he doesn't want my help.

And I feel redundant as Leo thrusts himself around the corner and races to Blake's side, approaching him with a certainty I could never feel.

Blake doesn't flinch back from *him*, at least.

Leo grunts and loops his arm under Blake's shoulders, hefting him up with his jaw clenched. "C'mon. Let's get you on a stretcher."

There's nothing I can do.

Nothing but watch, while Rich joins Leo on Blake's other side and together they guide him away, limping heavily.

"Go home, Peace," Blake grinds out, his voice exhausted, drifting over his shoulder. "Before you get hurt. There's nothing for you here."

Ouch.

Damn.

I don't need to read between the lines.

I'm not wanted. I know it.

But I can't stop thinking about easing his pain.

One thing's for sure: I don't believe him anymore when he says he's not a hero.

* * *

Okay, so I haven't left.

Hear me out.

It's not because of Blake, I swear.

I *swear*.

I just...can't walk away. Not without seeing that everyone got out safe.

This town isn't even my home.

Even so, I can't stand seeing innocent people suffer. It's a relief when the last of the flames are doused and a final inspection declares the building empty, check-ins ensuring everyone's accounted for and no one's still missing inside the charred, waterlogged brick building.

The back of the candy shop took some real damage, too, a strange-looking blast of black char that looks almost like it burst against the brick, but the worst of it is the clothing store by far.

Good news: there were no lives lost today, and that *matters*.

Bad news: a town that's apparently already had some big fires recently just had one more.

Oh, and I managed to make a royal freaking bonehead out of myself.

Maybe it's the hippie kid in me. Lack of attachment to material things. Flower on the wind.

But things can be replaced. So can wounded pride.

People, on the other hand, can't.

I've managed to find myself a corner farther down the alley, well out of the way of the work that's being done to investigate the debris and figure out how the fire started. Rich and a few others duck in and out of the building, conferring with their heads held close.

I'm still not supposed to be here.

I'm trying to be invisible.

And I'm ready to get chased off when Justin appears from the mouth of the alley and his gaze gravitates to me.

He's just as dirty and disheveled and scorched as Blake, but where it makes Blake look rugged and dark and so *God*-like I could just lick him clean...

It just makes Justin look young, tired, and out of his depth.

But he offers me a friendly smile, pushing his mop of curls out of his face as he steps closer. "Hey, Peace."

I hold both hands up.

"I'll go," I say. "You don't have to tell me twice."

"Nah." He tosses his head back in the direction he just came. "The chief wants a minute with ya."

I blink, doing a double take.

"With me?" I ask, squinting one eye up. "Are you sure?"

Justin grins wearily. "Nobody else here he calls Broccoli, is there?"

"Fair point." I snort.

I shouldn't be so nervous I'm barely even peeved over the stupid nickname.

Blake probably just wants to give me a lecture on fire safety, the hazards of diving into an active scene.

Honestly, I'd probably deserve it.

With my stomach leaping and fluttering like the flames they just put out, I square my shoulders and lift my chin.

Then I march off to face my fate, leaving Justin pacing the alley behind me, taking photos of the blast marks on the wall with his phone.

More for his album, I guess. Or maybe he's trying to document stuff for the investigation, what with those strange marks.

Fate, right?

It's waiting.

My fate, however, is currently sitting on a stretcher with one leg hanging off and his bad leg propped up in front of him. He looks as grumpy as a bear with a burr up his butt, and his leg is so stiff it looks like a lump.

That position isn't good for you, I want to tell him, but I don't think it's something he wants to hear right now.

Curling my hands in their gloves, I venture, "Listen, Blake, I'm sorry for being so reckless—"

He cuts me off with a snort, almost amused. "Broccoli, since I found you down the side of the mountain next to a burning van, can't say I'm surprised 'bout you being reckless," he says dryly—but not without some warmth.

God, I could bask in those lilting, deep rolling syllables like they're a glowing hearth, even with the crackling edge of pain in them. "Am I really so obvious?"

"Yeah, darlin', you sure as hell are. And you don't get to apologize when I'm trying to do the apologizing."

I blink, staring into flashing blue eyes shadowed by the sharpness of his brows.

Laugh lines, I decide, tracing the furrows in his brow around his eyes, his mouth.

Even if I've barely even seen him smile, I know that look.

Blake looks like he's got a face meant to laugh.

Only, he's not laughing now while I stare at him, dumbstruck. "Um. Why are you apologizing to me?"

"'cause you keep catching me at a bad time, and I damn near chewed your head off. *Again.*" He grinds his teeth, jaw working back and forth, and looks down, hands gripping his thigh tightly to either side. He kneads himself so lightly it's easy to see he's struggling not to flinch at the slightest pressure. "You're not the only one who's obvious. I ain't good at dealing with pain, lady. Especially not when I go ass over elbows in front of someone else. I shouldn't have taken it out on you like a pissed off wolverine. You seen the shit those things can do?"

I almost choke on a laugh. "Wolverines? I—"

"Never mind. Point is, it wasn't right of me. Not today or the night your ride went kaboom. I'm sorry for slinging so much crap your way." His gaze sharpens.

"Oh." I can't stop my smile. I probably look like a total dope since I can't seem to look away from him. "It's fine. I mean, I'm used to getting snarled at by big man-babies who can't handle a little pain."

He lifts a brow.

I raise my hands, flexing my purple-coated fingers. "I'm small, but I'm fierce. I've done a lot of massages. Over a thousand. I've even taken down bigger men than you with these hands."

He'd started to scowl when I said *man-babies*, but as he stares at my fingers, his lips twitch briefly—before he ducks his head with a sound suspiciously like a repressed laugh. "Okay, little fuckin' Broccoli Girl."

Bad move. My hands drop, bunching up at my sides.

"Don't call me that," I say, my voice flat.

"Don't call me a man-baby."

We trade scowls. Then he grins at me, and it's a good thing I've got my feet planted firm to the ground, or my knees might just give out under me.

Yep, I officially hate whatever insanity this weird, electric sparky thing between us is.

Oh, but when Blake Silverton grins, you'd better *believe* it transforms his face.

So much emotion, it might be the full spectrum.

Wolfish. Feral. Rakish. Bright and full of secret laughter dancing in those midnight-blue eyes.

And so dangerously compelling, this magnetism that just *pulls* like he could draw me against his body with just a glance.

"*Riiight,*" I mumble faintly. "No man-baby. No Broccoli Girl. Deal."

Wowza. I've got to get over this and stop acting like a kid.

His smile fades, but the warmth lingers in his features, softening their crags as he studies me. "So you really as good as you say with those paws?"

"I'm usually not short on clients. And I don't stay in the same places long," I answer, forcing myself back to some semblance of focus. I can't let him see how much he flusters me, though I don't think I can hide how hot my face is. "And I get a lot of repeat customers, so I must be doing something right."

"Well, if you think you can do something with this..." He balls up his fist and thumps his thigh—then hisses, baring his clenched teeth. "*Fuck.*"

"I can't do much if you do that again," I say, folding my arms. "Stop. You're not helping. You're just creating more bruised tissue around the trigger point, and believe it or not, bruises tear muscle fiber. They're called micro-tears, and if you keep creating tears that have to heal around the pain source, you're going to actually make the pain spread."

It all comes tumbling out of me, motor-mouth central, but hey.

I know my job.

Blake seems like the kind of man who doesn't take advice unless it makes sense to him, so I might as well head him off at the pass and explain.

He just blinks at me, tilting his head before arching a brow.

"Yes *ma'am*," he says sardonically, with a tired half-smirk. "Hell, I've been doing this for years, probably making it worse. Damn miracle it's still more than a piece of gristle. Where you been all my life?"

I bite back my answer.

It sounds like a pickup line, but I'm smart enough to know it's not.

A man hurting like him isn't thinking about me as anyone but somebody who might be able to ease his pain.

So I smile and deflect. "Oahu, mostly, though I'm guessing for a part of it I wasn't even born."

He narrows his eyes, but there's a spark there, curious and assessing. "I'm only forty-two."

"And I'm twenty-five," I say. "So. Guess that's your answer."

I smile brightly. He's looking at me like I just poleaxed him between the eyes.

"Go on home and get some rest, Gramps. I want you at my cabin bright and early. Don't worry," I tease, turning away, unable to help a little toss of my hair, just a *little* flirt. "I'll take good care of you."

VI: SWEET REFRAIN (BLAKE)

I barely get half a second to stare after the switch of that firecracker's hips before I've got a face full of Leo.

Not the view I want right now, dammit.

He's got my full attention as he leans in close, though, dropping his voice so it only carries between us.

"We have a problem," he growls, brushing his hand against mine like he's just offering a brotherly bit of comfort over my throbbing, fire-burning thigh.

Except a crumpled bit of paper falls against my knuckles. I instinctively turn my hand to catch it in my palm and hide it in the curl of my fingers.

I look over my shoulder real quick. Nobody looking our way.

Justin, Rich, and the guys are on cleanup duty. Leo's watching me urgently, violet eyes shadowed with the sun at his back. I look down at the crumpled note on a little scrap of blue paper, smoothing it out with my thumb.

*You and your **merry band of assholes aren't as smart as you think, you scarred freak.***

. . .

What the fuck?

The instant surge of anger hits my guts like bad whiskey, wondering how anyone would *dare* call my friend a *scarred freak*. It's eclipsed fast when I realize what it means.

Shit.

I thought this fire felt weird.

The scorch patterns say it broke out explosively, force thrusting flames out from inside till they seared the surrounding buildings.

Fires that start off as accidents, usually retail or industrial, kick off in cluttered corners. Frayed electrical cords, a candle, old machinery, something flammable close by.

One spark jumps, catches the right material, and then there's no stopping it.

Disaster.

Still, without some kind of incendiary, the blast wouldn't race outward with that kind of punch.

I sigh, murmuring under my breath. I don't want anyone to get freaked out; this is between me and Leo right now. "You think it was set? Arson?"

"Had to be," Leo snarls. "This is practically a confession. Found it on the ground. Just waiting to be picked up, right there in the line of sight."

"Dammit, yeah." I twist my lips, frowning. "But who? If this is about you...do you think *they're* back?"

"Galentron?" Leo shakes his head. "Don't think so. Not really their style. Fuchsia Delaney doesn't have a good reason to fuck with us anymore, seeing how she ran off after the last dustup and hasn't been seen since. Hell, the rest of the company's in ruins, caught up in legal battles. I don't think anyone's even left with enough incentive to take revenge, considering how many people wound up in jail. Even Durham, the CEO. Plus, with the Feds in and out of here all the time...who'd risk it?"

"That's a good point." And a bad prospect, meaning we've got no obvious motive. "But can we really rule 'em out just like that? Seems like those evil pricks *live* to fuck with this town."

"It's just not their M.O., Blake," Leo says ruefully. "They're more likely to send a strike team or some kind of cloak and dagger subterfuge. Not...*this*." He gestures at the note. "It's too personal."

"Okay." I twist my lips, scanning the sharp dashes of handwriting. "So, who the hell hates you enough to try to kill a bunch of people?"

He narrows his eyes. "...how much time do you have?"

"Real funny." I sigh, glancing toward the open door of the shop.

Rich comes out with several half-burnt piles of clothing, sniffing them, and I'd bet you anything he's smelling some kind of accelerant. I sigh my lungs out.

"So we've got ourselves a problem. Again." The words taste numb rolling off my tongue. I'm so sick of this shit, always some new fire to put out every so many months in Heart's Edge. Figurative and literal.

"Do we ever not?" Leo echoes.

"I wouldn't mind a few months off, Tiger." I give him a wink, hoping his old childhood nickname tames the huge beast of a man.

I hardly feel the pain in my thigh right now, at least. My mind's on too many other things.

Like how I need Peace Rabe more than ever, if we've got trouble blowing into town. Just to keep me in top fighting shape. I can't have my leg crapping out if we're gonna have another run at the same kind of drama we've dealt with before.

"No worries, man. We'll handle it," I say. "Like we always do."

Like we always *will*.

Maybe I've never been comfortable with the Heroes of Heart's Edge thing, but I damn sure feel the camaraderie with my friends. They're better brothers to me than Holt will ever be.

Slowly, Leo nods, and I mirror his movement.

We're up.

Before whoever's gunning for Leo gets a chance to try to handle *us*.

* * *

Gramps.

I can't believe that little hippie brat called me *Gramps*.

Forty-something ain't that much like having one foot in the grave.

Hell if I know.

Maybe it is to her?

And maybe I shouldn't be thinking about why it bothers me, thinking that sweet-faced girl with her wild shock of ruby-violet hair thinks I'm past my prime.

Thinks I'm *old*.

Maybe that's why I almost don't show come morning.

Or maybe it's 'cause I don't want Haley or Warren noticing me creeping up in my Jeep out here, asking questions and flinging shit bound to turn my face beet red.

Hell, maybe it's that my mind's already where they're gonna lead it, and I don't want it to be.

I. Can't. Do. This.

I got a daughter to think about, and Peace is far too—

Yeah. Okay. Fuck.

I'm old.

Funny thing is, she doesn't look at me like I'm ancient.

She stares at me like she wants to kiss away every hard knot of pain in my body. Just like she thinks I haven't been with a woman in so long I don't know what it means when she's watching real intently from under her long eyelashes with her skin all flushed and pale and pretty, and no, it's not the cold air.

And the way she'd said my *name* yesterday...

Christ.

No.

Nope.

I'm here for therapy. Trying to do something about this fucking bum leg of mine, and nothing else.

Leo had to practically carry me home last night. Andrea tried her best to help me get into a hot soaking bath to loosen my thigh up enough so I could get around without a crutch.

My rabid leg fought back every time I tried bending it. The pull from my hip to my knee sent searing pain ripping through me, just as bad as one hot, unlucky Afghan day too many years ago.

So I frog-marched myself around till I could toss a double dose of Vicodin and fall into bed.

The Vicodin at least held through morning. I'm worried about getting hooked on that shit the longer this goes on. Another reason I *need* Little Miss Broccoli to work on my meat —innuendo be damned.

Right now, my leg feels like dead weight as I let myself out of the parked Jeep and drag myself through the gate to Peace's cabin. I can already see her inside, through the glass, this whirlwind of vibrant color.

I'm starting to think the girl's color-blind. She always looks like she just stepped out of an explosion at a paint factory.

Today's no different.

She's got on big old bell-bottom jeans like the seventies never ended, only they're the modern throwback style, the denim covered in Magic Marker graffiti. Even loose, they're so far down her rocket hips they might fall off.

Oh, and of course she's got a navel piercing, nestled in the rounded, sweet-pale slope of her toned belly.

Just a wicked little glimmer of diamond, drawing my eye in and up over the dip of a waist that's almost too tiny for the swell of her hips, the arch of her rib cage. Smooth pale skin vanishes into the tie-dyed button-down shirt she's wearing completely unbuttoned and knotted between her tits. They spill down against the open *V* of cloth in the front and *fuck my life* am I really standing on this woman's porch, staring at her knockout melons and the tick of her pulse against her throat?

Blake, get your shit together, man.

I groan, dragging a hand over my face, then lift a hand and knock. I brace my other hand against the porch railing so I don't have to be obvious about taking my weight off my leg.

Guess she must've been preoccupied.

Don't know how she didn't see me coming when the cabins are more glass than wood—but she jumps, hands fumbling on the bottles of oil in her hands. She blinks at me, her green eyes so wide. With a flustered sound I see in the movements of her lips but don't hear, she grips the bottles tighter and bends to set them on the coffee table.

Then she scurries around the coffee table and the long padded...cot? massage table?

Whatever it is, it's in the middle of the living room. Her hips switch enticingly, the broad flares of her jeans moving in counterpoint rhythm, making me focus on just how tight those bell-bottoms fit against her curvalicious thighs.

Goddammit.

I yank my eyes up from her thighs to her face just as she opens the door with a sunny smile.

I'm so boned.

Worse, she's got the kind of mouth that's naturally red like a ripe strawberry, and when she's not smiling, it looks small and round. When she grins, it spreads nice and wide and lights up her whole face, putting *plenty* of dangerous ideas in my head of what to do with that mouth.

Her hair's been pinned back messy in chopsticks, the red parts sweeping at her face, the purple tips spraying out in a colorful fan behind her head.

I don't know how I never realized how short she was. Not till the moment she looks up at me and has to tilt her head back, her eyes glittering in the shadow I cast over her.

She hardly comes up to my shoulders.

But somehow, she's larger than life.

All that bright energy bursting out of her takes up a lot of real estate.

Not in an invasive way.

More like she's warm water, flowing in to fill the cold and empty corners around her till everything is soft and comfortable.

The fuck am I thinking?

I clear my throat, straightening, taking my hand off the railing.

"Hi."

Her smile brightens. "You *came!*"

Oh, hell. Here we go.

"What made you think I wouldn't?" I huff.

Her smile turns teasing, her body swaying back and forth a little. "I don't know, Papa Bear. Maybe all the snarling you do."

"*God.*" I rake a hand through my hair. "You gonna let me in or not? It's freezing out here. And I thought we had a truce? Stop with the old man nicknames."

She laughs.

I *feel* damn old—old and lecherous for almost craving the way she moves, the way she flits, the way she's the fluttering moth *and* the dancing flame hounding my dick to Hades and back as she slips inside and holds the door open.

My pride gets the better of me as I follow her inside.

I can't even fucking bring myself to limp. Even though every attempt at a natural step makes my whole leg lit with white-hot pain.

Fuck.

I don't want this gorgeous girl seeing how broken I am.

But I guess I can't hide anything from her.

I barely make it a step inside before she reaches out and catches my hand in both of hers, stopping me in my tracks.

Her fingers are soft and delicate against mine, so warm. My

mouth goes dry as I look down at her. Her mouth has gone full and sweet with worry, her eyes dark and liquid.

"Don't," she says softly. "Don't hurt yourself even more. You don't have to hide it. I'm here to work with your pain, Blake. Not judge it."

Everything in me wants to rebel with pride.

I fucking can't.

Not when she's looking at me like it'd break her heart if I refused her after I came out all this way.

So I just nod, shifting my weight to my right leg, lifting the pressure on my left.

Even that makes pain crunch up in an awful fiery knot. The muscle contracts with the movement, and I can't stop my hiss, the growl in the back of my throat.

A thunder roll that eases away as she squeezes my hand in hers.

No, it doesn't stop the pain.

But it makes a dude feel a little better, my chest warming. She turns to lead me toward her massage table, moving slow with her hand in mine and waiting without rushing for me to limp forward one step at a time.

It's a relief to hoist myself up on the table, wincing as I settle down on the edge.

I promptly choke on my next breath.

Peace smiles at me merrily, twirling her finger.

"Okay, then," she says. "Clothes off."

I splutter. There's a tightness in my gut that has nothing to do with pain or apprehension. "What? *Why?*"

Her laughter trills, and for a moment, wicked eyes dart over me before she turns her back. "You haven't ever had a massage before? I can't do it through your jeans for this kind of deep work. Don't worry. I won't look."

"You're gonna *have* to look to work," I growl.

"Towel." She points over her shoulder without turning back, before bending over the coffee table and giving me a sweet view of the curves of her ass and the dip of her silky spine. "You can cover yourself up pretty well."

Good thing I ain't naked right now.

My jeans are the only thing holding me in.

Fuck.

I tear my gaze away from her and look at the towels folded at the foot of the table.

Fine. Okay. Hell.

"Shirt too?" I ask, and she laughs again.

"Shirt too."

"...you ain't working on anything but my leg," I mutter, shooting her a look.

"Oh, you'd be surprised where we hold tension in the body, and how it affects pain in other areas far from the source," she says softly, her voice countered by the soft clink of glass vials moving together as she picks them up, reads their labels, and sets them down again. "So if I really want to work with your pain, I'll need to find your tension centers and trigger points. Trust me, Blake. I know what I'm doing. This is the only thing I actually stayed in school for."

"*Hnngh.*" I grunt but shrug out of my jacket and look around, before just tossing it toward the couch. It hits the arm, and I start unbuttoning the flannel shirt underneath. "I mean, can't be any worse than a doctor visit."

Her head turns like she'll glance over her shoulder at me—before she stops and looks firmly forward. "You don't trust doctors?"

"Never have." I toss the flannel next, then peel out of my undershirt and throw it on the pile before hooking my thumb in the fly of my jeans. It's less the pretty girl worrying me right now and more how I'm gonna wiggle out of these without a damn sigh of pain. "Doctors left me fucked up like this. Bad stitch-up job. Muscle never healed right. It was a combat situation, sure, and I get they did their damnedest, but..."

"And physical therapy never worked?"

Most of the time that question gets my hackles up like nothing else.

It's a judgmental question. Like the pain I'm in is my fault because I just didn't try some obvious thing or didn't do it hard enough.

Only, the way Broccoli Girl asks is different.

It's gentle. Honest. Kind.

It's part of this weird music in her voice and the soft *tink* of glass oil vials.

It doesn't feel like she's judging me.

Just seems like she wants to hear my story.

That's what I tell myself, anyway, as I mutter out slowly. "Tried therapy for a few years. Couldn't even walk when I came back from Afghanistan with shrapnel embedded so deep in my leg they told me at first they'd have to leave it in. They cut it out, eventually, but not without carving me up real bad first. And the way it healed, fuck. PT just made it worse, I guess." I shrug. "There's something knotted up in there real nasty. Every time they'd try the exercises, it'd always pull something else loose. The surgeons messed me up, though they were trying their best, too. I *guess.*"

Bitter much? Fuck yes, I am. A Purple Heart framed up in the corner of my basement can't take away years of total agony.

I hadn't meant to tell her all that. Too late.

And although Peace ain't supposed to be looking, for a minute she turns back, just gazing at me with those warm green eyes that make me feel like it's spring in the middle of this snowy, ice-scoured day.

"Sometimes people's best isn't good enough. It's okay to accept it," she says. "You're allowed to be angry at the surgeons for leaving you in this kind of pain, Blake. You don't have to excuse it."

"I..."

I'd never really thought of it like that.

That I was making excuses for the mess they made of my leg,

or if I just downplayed it, maybe it wouldn't be such a big deal and the pain would disappear.

I make a huffy noise in the back of my throat.

"You ain't supposed to be looking, remember?"

Yeah. No way in hell I'm misinterpreting the way her gaze dips over my naked chest, her lashes coming down in a soft sweep before a smile tugs at her lips as she turns away.

"Not looking," she says with this singsong lilt in her voice. Girl must sing a lot. "Pick a scent. Manly pine, sandalwood, or amber?"

I flick the button of my jeans open. "Pine's gonna sting my nose. Sandalwood's too strong. The fuck does amber smell like?"

She picks a bottle up and flicks the cap with her thumb, then sniffs. "Morocco."

"That ain't a scent."

"It's the best word I can come up with." She laughs.

"Fine, fine. Make me stink like Morocco."

Her only answer is another laugh. I let it hold me up, bracing myself for torture, and then lift myself up on one hand, tugging my jeans out from under me and since she said naked, dragging my boxer-briefs with.

There's a brief burst of agony, one that makes me groan in the back of my throat. Then I let myself down, using my hands to shimmy my clothes down my legs, kicking my boots and socks off in the process. I'm trying damned hard not to look at my hard-on, and grab a towel to cover it up quickly, cinching it clumsily around my hips.

"Uh," I mutter. "How you want me?"

"On your back," she answers, moving away from me, leaning over to light a single candle before circling the room.

There are candles everywhere, I realize. She touches each wick delicately with a spark of flame that flicks in little gold tongues.

"Don't worry, Fire Chief Silver Tongue, there's nothing flammable near the candles."

"*Silverton*," I snarl, correcting her.

Why the fuck are my ears burning?

Even with her back to me, I can hear the grin in her voice. "I don't know, I've heard your show. Silver Tongue sounds about right."

I make a sputtering noise. Is this girl openly flirting with me now?

I've gotta ignore it.

So I focus on shifting to my back instead. The massage table feels a little small for me, but it doesn't wobble as I ease myself back with my bum leg stretched out, smoothing my towel. Peace turns back toward me.

And immediately bursts out *laughing,* pressing her fingertips to her lips.

I scowl. "*What?*"

"You're stiff as a board, my dude," she says, stepping closer to the table. Her soft fingers brush my bare arm, my inner elbow, and rest there in little pinprick points of warmth. "It's like you're taking up planking as an Olympic sport."

"Planking? No clue what you just said."

"Of course not." With an amused sigh, she presses down on my inner elbow. "Just relax."

I start to say something.

Only for something about that pressure to *click*, and a sudden looseness flows through my entire body. Just like all my joints decided to pop and turn liquid.

I groan, sinking against the warm linen cover of the massage table, gasping out in something close to pleasure. "What the...what was *that?*"

"Chakra point," she answers simply. "Almost like a switch, isn't it? It's a quick release of tension. Some folks say it's all psychological, kinda like a placebo. Others think it's from some mystical, higher place. For me, it's a good place to start, whatever you want to believe."

She leans over me then, a few wisps of her hair falling down to tease against my cheeks as she looks at me searchingly.

"Are you feeling any better?' she asks. "Like it might be safe to get started?"

"Yeah. Okay." I nod shakily.

Shit.

I think this girl might be about to ruin me in more ways than one.

"Okay," she murmurs, pressing her slim hands flat to my stomach. "Close your eyes, then. And try to relax."

It's almost a relief to close my eyes—at first.

With my peepers shut I can't see her bent over me, the heavy curves of her tits on the verge of falling out of that damnable tied-up shirt, her body this pure graceful siren call and her face too pixie-like.

You know, everything that'd make the brutal pain in my dick a hundred times worse.

But it's actually *harder* with my eyes closed and nothing left to my senses but the imagination.

Underneath the scent of whatever she's pouring into her hands, this musky semi-sweetness that makes me think of sand and heat and spices, I can smell *her*.

She's almost got this creamy-thick scent, something I could sink my tongue into. It's as radiant and real as the warmth of her body leaning in close, the soft sound of her skin and her clothing against the edge of the table as she works.

And holy *damn*, her hands.

Her hands are hell on my skin as she strokes me from neck to shoulders to chest to hips. Just like she's waking me up, bringing my body back to life one square inch at a time.

I'm sizzling, prickling, electric charges in the shape of her palms left everywhere she touches. I don't think it's the oil warming slick against my skin, smoothed on in a soothing layer.

It's *her*.

And if she keeps it up, no frigging pain's gonna stop me from embarrassing myself under this flimsy towel when my cock spikes up a tent.

"Hey," I growl without opening my eyes. "That ain't my thigh."

Peace stops, lower, somewhere near my knees.

When her hands lift away from my body, she sounds almost wounded. "I'm trying to help you relax so the treatment will be more effective."

"Peace," I sigh. "Please. Humor me."

There's a pause before I hear her moving, her heat shifting, and then those soft hands rest just above my knee. "All right," she says. "If that's what you want...but it may end up hurting more."

"Don't see how that's possible."

I damn well find out a few seconds later.

I don't have to open my eyes to know the shape of the scar.

It's like a gnarled knot in a twisted tree trunk, blazed against my skin, starting a few inches above my knee and snaking in a strange contortion halfway up my thigh. The muscle somehow swirled into place around where that chunk of metal slashed my flesh.

Muscle ain't supposed to knot like that. It goes straight up and down, sometimes with a twist.

Too bad they put me back together wrong.

When her fingers press down on that knot, searching, looking for a single string to start unraveling, holy merciless fuck.

My leg *explodes*. Pure riptide pain shoots up my hip to my knee, then ricochets back to throb up to my groin.

I let out a low bearish sound, grappling at the edges of the table with my palms, digging my fingers in, spine arching. It hurts too much for me to even kick out, my teeth grinding like I'm trying to fucking crush them down to nubs.

"I'm sorry," Peace says softly, her touch gentling. "You're carrying so much tension here. It's like a land mine. Everything I do will hurt at this stage. I can try to work my way in from the outer edges to let you get used to it."

Part of me wants to say *fuck this*.

I don't know how hurting like this is supposed to help me at all.

My eyes open to slits, watching her as she stands next to my thigh, looking at me with such warmth, such concern, still asking me to *trust her*.

Kind of like I asked her to trust me that night on the side of the road, alone and frightened and waiting for me to come find her.

Whatever.

Taking several shaky breaths, I nod, digging my fingers in harder to the plush table cover till I feel the wood underneath. "Go ahead, woman. Do your worst."

She offers me a faint, almost sad smile.

The next time she touches me, it's farther from the center of the wound. The pain's more a soft burst versus the supernova blast it was before.

I close my eyes, swallowing hard, trying to endure it, counting out my breaths as her hands work and knead my flesh like it's putty. She goes in a radial path around the most concentrated bits of the scar.

It's this weird, rhythmic dance of pain.

Sometimes the pressure of her palms is enough to flatten it into nothingness, before it fights as soon as the pressure eases.

"Hey," she murmurs, her voice part of the rhythm, soft and low. "Talk to me. Anything to take your mind off it. It'll help."

It's hard to speak through gritted teeth. "Don't know what you want me to talk about."

"Tell me about Andrea?"

There's a warmth in her voice when she says my daughter's name that nearly undoes me.

I know she only met Andrea once.

That night I came to fetch my daughter, it'd been a hell of a something to see her through the windows, talking to Peace so easy. My Violet has a rare trust she's been hard pressed to give to many since her ma died.

"She's a good kid," I start. "No—that ain't even right. She's the *greatest*. Stubborn as hell, smart as hell, too. Determined to be this wild child artist and I'm gonna let her if that's what she needs to be, as long as she keeps out of serious trouble." I smile faintly. "She's nothing like her ma. I think I'm glad for that."

Peace doesn't answer for a long time.

"She mentioned her mother passed," she murmurs.

"Yep. Abigail." It's weird to say her name out loud. When Andrea and I are locking horns, it's always just *your ma*. "Four years ago last week. Freak medical condition. We were days away from signing the divorce papers anyway, but she was still Andrea's ma. I was ready to work with that. Just because things went to hell in a handbasket with my lady didn't mean it needed to spill over to my little girl. Didn't want it destroying her."

Too fucking honest? Maybe.

Hard to help it when I'm lying here under a pretty girl's gaze, practically buck naked, letting her wonder-fingers torture me back into something resembling a functional human being.

"She seems to still be taking it hard," Peace says.

"Sure. We manage most of the time, but that's one subject where we just butt heads. Can't seem to speak the same language."

Peace doesn't answer. I realize her hands are still working, and I'm actually starting to enjoy it, the pain more of a low mellow burn melting like hot wax through my flesh.

"You're afraid of something," she says. "It's making you lock up again. Relax, Blake. Tell me what's eating you."

If that ain't a sucker punch.

How the hell is this young woman—emphasis on the young—reading my body like it's tarot?

She's not wrong, though.

And I feel that fear tighten in my throat as I say, "I'm

worried she blames me for killing her ma." Then I move on quickly. "Not that there was ever anything violent! I ain't that kinda guy. Real coward piece of trash who'd ever put a hand on a woman. Abby would...I mean, she'd hit on me a little sometimes, but that was just the way she was. Never hurt none. I just took it, gave her a look, and asked her if she was *done*."

There's almost too much awed understanding in Peace's silence.

Fuck, this feels like some weird confessional, those hands kneading me in prayer.

"Andrea was mad about us toward the end, yeah," I try again. "Pissed that I was breaking our family up 'cause Abby and I just weren't seeing each other no more. I married a woman too much like my ma, and that was the biggest mistake I ever made. Then she went and had a freak fucking brain aneurysm, swift and sudden."

Peace gasps. Her eyebrows knit together in this sad puppy dog sympathy I don't fucking need.

"That's not the point. Think I'm just worried deep down she hates me because I pushed her ma away and drove her body to fail her."

"But you didn't!" Peace says it with the same gentle firmness she works in my flesh. "You didn't do that, Blake. You tried to make a decision that was best for Andrea, for your family, because things weren't happy...and then nature or chance or something else stepped in and did things that were totally not your fault." Her thumbs sweep inward, just barely touching the deepest ridge of my scar.

I hiss, digging my teeth into my lip so hard I taste a smidge of blood.

"And I don't think Andrea hates you for it. She's just young. Her feelings are in and out, confusing her all the time. Especially her feelings toward the man she values most. I'm sure she craves your approval as much as she needs to break your authority, so..." She giggles softly. "Andrea's going to be a little rage-bucket at you pretty often. I know that's how I was."

I let out a breathless laugh. I hurt, and not all of it's the pressure turning my flesh into warm putty.

My chest hurts, too.

Fuck.

I've never told anybody these deep dark secrets. It's like they cut me inside on the way out of my mouth.

"You're not old enough to have a teenage daughter," I tease, trying to deflect. "How do you know all this?"

"Because I used to be that girl who loved and hated her old man," she answers. The wistfulness in her voice hovers around her. "And then he was gone on deployment, and then just gone, and I was left with my mother. She buried herself in work. I just needed to feel like something stable would *stay*, just for once. My father didn't." She sighs. "So I got angry and ran away from missing him, and wound up not staying anywhere at all."

I'm struck by the sudden urge to hug her.

It's irrational as hell. Even if she's working on me and I don't want to interrupt this quiet stillness building between us with her hands.

"Sorry," I murmur. "You're allowed to be pissed at your folks for leaving you without any closure, even if they couldn't help it. Same thing you told me earlier. No crime in being human."

"You sound like you're speaking from experience."

"Well." Damn, she's just hitting all the pain points today, physical and psychic. "My ma died last year. She wasn't good to me, or to..." I almost mention Holt, but something about the thought of him pulls me up short. "...my family. But I left, and I never got to say a lotta things to her, y'know? Things I needed her to hear. And now that chance is gone, and my family's still a mess."

"Maybe not." Her grip shifts and the heel of her palm kneads the knot of my scar.

It actually *doesn't* hurt. There's a searing heat instead, like that stuff inside a stress ball moving under my skin, and it ain't half bad.

I sure as hell feel it creeping up, spreading higher and higher, toward my hips—tension everywhere else getting lighter. That's 'cause it's all flowing toward one specific place.

"Sometimes we just need to be heard," she whispers. "It doesn't matter by who. I'm not your mother, but I can listen to what you need to say."

Any other time, I might've actually taken her up on the offer.

It's kind, genuine in a way I'm not really used to when most people just fall back on pity and useless platitudes. Anything to get out of this kind of conversation ASAP.

I can't believe I've been telling her all this shit.

Just like that.

Shit I won't say to people I've known my whole life.

This strange little spitfire pulls it out of me.

I don't dare tell her that.

Not today when I've done enough spilling.

Not when I can't think about my ma and what those soft hands are doing to me on the same frigging wavelength.

I got a lotta fucked up shit going on in my head, but not *that* fucked up.

So I just give her an uneasy laugh, trying to take my mind off both things nagging at me. My mother, and the fact that Peace Rabe's hands are doing *terrible* things.

"Maybe some other time, Doc. I didn't exactly come with a prepared speech for a shrink."

She half-smiles. "I thought *Doc* was your friend. Don't get me mixed up with him."

"Pretty sure there's no way in hell I could. Doc doesn't look anything like you."

It's out before I can stop it.

Shit. Believe it or not, it could be worse.

I barely stopped myself from saying *Doc ain't got a body like that*. I mean, it doesn't mean a damn thing because Doc *doesn't* look like her, but hell.

We both know what I meant.

She stops, her hand resting lightly against my thigh, her eyes locked on mine, wide and questioning.

I never quite noticed the shade of green in her eyes before. I've always been looking at her in the dark or in firelight, never with clear sunlight reflecting in those glassy pools.

They're pale. Like the soft jade tokens I saw in the window of a shop when I visited Chinatown in Seattle once. It's a misty color, but mist was never this clear, this vibrant. Like I can see all the way to the bottom of her soul if I just look hard enough.

Glacial runoff, I think.

Glacial lakes, their green so pure, so vivid, and so pale.

But her eyes could never be as cold as ice, watching me with a warmth I have no fucking clue what to do with.

So I tear my eyes away before hers do a Medusa trick on me. Eyes that pretty could turn a man to stone, and it'd almost be *worth* it for the poor sucker who stares at her too long.

Clearing my throat, I turn my face to one side.

"Feels like you're done," I mutter. "Haven't we been at this an hour?"

I hear her breath catch, and then her hands drop away. "For now, yep. You'll need more than one session to see lasting results instead of just temporary relief. How do you feel?"

I shift my leg gingerly—and I'm surprised how easy it moves.

I'd been locking up, bracing for agony, but instead my leg flexes nice and smooth, bending and unbending, with only a little soreness that could be just as much from the kneading those nimble fingers gave me as from the injury.

"Huh. Not bad," I say.

Dumb, I know, but that's all I got.

I push myself up on one arm, staring down at the scar. It's still there, still the same angry red, but it doesn't feel like this vampire parasite, sucking my life out through its burning teeth right now.

"Well?" She taps a foot, giving me a smile.

"It ain't perfect, but I think I can stand without wanting to holler myself blue. Warren and Haley's little niece would never shut up about the damn *swear jar* if she ever heard me go off."

Peace giggles.

"We wouldn't want you going blue or bankrupting yourself," she says.

I let myself look at her again. But she's not looking at me.

She's turned away, her hands busy wiping the oil off on a towel.

I think it might be deliberate.

Feels like she's hiding from me, almost.

Did I just fuck up?

Maybe a little.

"Hey." I swing my legs over the side carefully, then drop down to my feet. My left leg's still a little shaky, but it holds me pretty well as I stand and reach over for my clothing. "You did good, darlin'. I'm sorry I ever doubted you. How much do I owe?"

She glances over her shoulder. Her smile comes faint, wistful, sad; those jade-green eyes are suddenly clouded, and I can't see to their bottoms.

"Freebie this time," she says, quiet and strange. "Call it thanks for saving me from turning into Frosty the other night."

"You, uh..." I scrub my hand against the back of my neck, then busy myself stepping into my boxer-briefs and jeans. Maybe if I'm more clothed, I'll feel less naked, but something about this has nothing to do with my damn body. "You want to schedule another appointment?"

She studies me. Her head tilts to one side.

Christ, she's so young, but sometimes when she looks at me it's with this wordless wisdom that makes me feel like she sees so much beyond her years.

Sees *me*.

And that shouldn't make me want to freak as much as it does.

"How about," she murmurs, "you find me when you need me?"

There's so much unsaid there.

So much I can't read, even if I want to.

So I pull my shirt on, throw my coat over my arm, and nod.

"Sure," I say numbly. "Thanks."

Then I turn and get the hell out of Dodge, leaving that cabin and heading into the morning so the cold winter air can slap some sense into my fool head.

If I'm lucky, it'll knock this girl clean out of my thoughts.

* * *

Call me paranoid, but there's a part of me that doesn't want Holt in my house.

Call it a holdover.

When you walk in on your brother with his arms around your wife, leaning in with his mouth half an inch from hers, and she's a blushing, flustered mess, *shit gets real.*

You get territorial.

Your fists go on autopilot.

Your throat can't roar loud enough, even when it's shaking the whole house.

And years later, you meet your brother for dinner at the local diner, instead of making him welcome at your kitchen table. Last minute change, I know, but he doesn't argue.

Doesn't matter what was going on between me and Abby.

He could've at least waited till we were done sorting our shit and officially separated before he made his move.

Too bad Holt's always liked having things he shouldn't.

That's where the rush is for him: the wrong woman, the wrong decision, the wrong three-day bender in Venice with a half-plastic Italian chick on his arm.

The fact that he's here looking for reconciliation with me and a relationship with my daughter is just sending up so many red flags it'd make the old Soviet commies blush.

Since Holt always wants things he shouldn't, it makes me wonder why he wants this.

At least he's keeping my mind off Peace, though.

Off the way the sunlight buried itself in her hair like loving fingers as she bent over me, caressing that vivid red to gold fire dipped in blazing purple.

Off our last weird little interaction. Where I knew I'd said too much, and she felt me holding back, and both of us maybe regretted being too open, too intense, too *real*.

We're perfect strangers. And even if I saved her from a pretty routine fire under the hood and she massaged away my pain, we don't *know* each other. We've got no good reason to.

Fuck. Right. *Not* thinking about Peace.

Not that the subtle glare Holt gives off is much better.

He's Mr. Congeniality, all smiles as he regales Andrea with tales of New York City. Hell, I hadn't even known he'd lived in NYC so long. Last I heard, he was still in Coeur d'Alene with Ma and then spending time in the Air Force, but I guess he's been living it up rich with the money she left behind.

But as he gears up into a story about a one-night stand with not one, but *six* supermodels, I grunt, leaning forward to pick up the soda I really wish was a beer right now.

"Hey," I bite off. "That's not appropriate in front of my kid."

Andrea's smile vanishes.

So much for putting out fires.

My fucking talent is killing my daughter's buzz.

"*God*, Dad," she groans. "I'm not a kid. I'm sixteen. There're worse things on Netflix."

Holt grins—that wide, charming devil's grin I despise. "She's right. I mean, when you were sixteen you were—"

"*Hey!*" I snarl, my ears going red-hot. "Listen, that's *definitely* not appropriate in front of my kid!"

NO DAMAGED GOODS

But Andrea's eyes light up, and she's all for it, leaning in with a wicked grin that makes the Silverton blood resemblance shine. "Oh, no. I think this is *definitely* appropriate. You've got embarrassing stories about Dad?"

She's not even paying attention to her food going cold on her plate, the ice cream in her root beer float melted away into a foamy white slurry on top of the soda.

There are no words for how much I hate this, even if it's making my daughter smile.

And even if I know it's technically Holt's job as her uncle.

I might not trust him, but at least he's doing his best to get along with her.

"Look, babe," Holt says, spreading his hands with the devil's own grin. "Your dad was an even bigger player than me in his day."

"I was not a damn player!" I protest.

Holt turns a sly look on me. "How many high school girlfriends did you have?"

My eyes widen. I recoil. "I, uh...can't remember. Long-ass time ago. Why's it matter?"

"You mean you lost *count*." He smirks. "I didn't. I was jealous. The answer is sixteen, by the way. The freshmen used to say you'd get a new girl every season."

Holy crap.

I'm dying.

And Andrea just laughs herself red in the face, a little hyena slumping back in her seat and covering her mouth with one hand, watching me over her fingers. "You're such a hypocrite, Dad."

But she's not saying it with any malice, just giving me a dig, and I accept it with a reluctant grunt.

"Eat your food, Andrea," I growl.

"'Kay. But you puff up like a porcupine if I even think about a guy, and you were like, sleeping with everyone in high school."

"Yo!" Oh fuck, people are gonna stare at us if I get any more flustered. Or loud. "No one ever said I slept with all of them, and I don't need that kind of talk coming out of your mouth. I'm your old man."

Andrea just sticks her tongue out merrily.

Damn.

She's got me by the tail and she knows it. She's enjoying being the one to embarrass her stupid dad for once.

Bah.

I still want to power-kick Holt under the table when he catches my eye and winks.

Whatever. So besides dying of mortification, it ain't going half bad for a family dinner.

Still doesn't mean I'm just gonna sweep the past under the rug.

Especially after another half hour or so of giving me shit and tag-teaming me while I bury myself in my burger. Time to say goodnight.

Andrea's got school tomorrow, and I should probably drop by the radio station tonight. Mario, my right-hand man, can only fill in for so long. He just doesn't have the same knack for it as me. And Rex Natchez, station owner, said listener numbers have been way down since I got so busy.

I really ain't sure why people tune in the way they do.

Still, it's nice to feel like I'm doing something useful, even if it's just giving folks a good old laugh at the end of a long day.

I'm not laughing, though, when we signal for the check and Holt takes the billfold from the waitress without even letting me look at it. Bastard's already pulling a pretty nice-looking leather wallet from his pocket, fishing out his metallic credit card.

"Hey," I growl. "Lemme see what our share is."

Holt waves before slipping his card into the billfold and passing it back to the waitress. "It's on me. It's the least I can do to thank you for humoring me."

I swear to God, the entire room flashes red.

From the table, to the dim overhead lights, to the sly gleam of my brother's eyes.

I'm going to fucking kill him.

Thrusting back from the table, and if it hadn't been a booth I'd probably have knocked both the seat and the table over, I stand.

"No," I snarl, even if I'm so pissed I can't even articulate what I'm saying no to just yet.

He stares at me. So does Andrea. Holt looks confused and stricken, while Andrea just looks horrified.

Dad's embarrassing her again, I guess.

But I can't hold it in.

I can't let him pull this.

"I told you," I bite off, "I don't want your money. Not one dime. No matter how you want to sneak it in. Fuck you, and fuck Ma's cash."

Holt's face actually crumples. "Blake, it wasn't about that—"

"I don't care!" I roar—then make myself drop my voice.

People are staring now.

I am being an asshole, shaming Andrea and myself like this.

I need to get out of here before I fully lose my spaghetti.

"Andrea, come on," I snap, pulling a couple crisp bills and throwing them on the table. "We're gone. Your uncle wants to pay, he can finish off his portion."

Andrea just gives me the most horrified look ever, then thrusts to her feet and sweeps toward the door, practically running, leaving me behind.

Leaving just me and Holt staring at each other, the air practically vibrating between us.

"So," he asks softly. "How long you gonna hate me?"

It's slipping. That slick-dick city accent he puts on. The country boy's coming out the longer he stays in Heart's Edge.

That just makes me want to punch him in his smug face even more.

"As long as I need to," I retort.

Then I turn and stomp out before he gets the last word.

Whatever his stories are, I don't want to hear them.

He says I was a player in high school, and maybe there's a shred of truth, but Holt's always been a different kind of player. I got past my teenage sins and *grew up*.

Holt, he'll say anything to get what he wants.

I just don't have to listen.

Andrea's already in the Jeep by the time I push the swinging door open and leave it slamming closed behind me in a jingle of the overhead bell.

She's tucked in the passenger seat, scrunching herself in the door like she's trying to seat herself as far away from the driver's seat as possible.

And when I crunch through the fresh-fallen snow, she goes stiff—only to turn her face away and glare out the window as I let myself inside and settle behind the wheel.

I sit there for several long, helpless moments, sighing and just staring through the windshield.

Doesn't help that I can still see Holt inside the diner, just sitting back against the seat with this hangdog look on his face.

I don't want to see it.

"Listen," I try. "I'm sorry. Me and Holt...we got bad blood. Bad history."

"Must be nice," she snaps, though it's a sort of sullen mumble, talking more to the window than to me. "Having someone to *have* history with. Thanks to you, I don't have anyone. No brothers. No sisters. No uncle. No grandma. No *mom*."

Shit.

That one stings like a screaming slap to the face.

Not nearly as much as when she finishes, "All I have is *you*."

I close my eyes, curling my hands tight against the wheel, wishing I could squeeze the pain out of me through my hands and soak it into the leather.

Part of me gets it.

She's sixteen.

She's mad.

She's smart as fuck and just as emotional, but she doesn't have the maturity to know the way she can cut people deep with words. She just knows she's hurting, and that makes her lash out to hurt someone else, like she can punish me for making everything so messy.

Maybe she should.

I sigh again, opening my eyes and starting the engine.

"Maybe I'm being a little hard on him," I admit.

She doesn't answer, won't even look at me.

"We'll try again some other time, Violet," I tell her.

"Don't call me that," she mumbles, but it's softer, less furious.

Fine. That's something.

"Sure, Andrea," I say as I pull out of the diner's parking lot and hit the road for home. "Sure."

We don't say anything else for the rest of the ride.

I just wonder how the hell it is I can give everyone else in this town advice, but I can't get my own shit together to save my life.

VII: GAMBLER'S SONG (PEACE)

Is it sad I've been listening to the radio every night?

I mean, the music's not bad. It's a mix of old eighties and nineties and aughts top hits, the kind of thing you find way out in the boonies where the local stations either have to rebroadcast bigger stations or go for the stuff with cheap licensing fees.

It gives Heart's Edge this kind of homey, lost-in-time feel.

I like it.

But what I'm really listening for is Blake freaking Silverton.

I've only heard him one time since the night he picked me up.

The night after I gave him his first massage. The inside of my chest was still hurting and feeling oddly hollow after listening to him talk about all those little cuts that built up under his skin the same way his scars did.

He'd been so quiet on the air that night. Subdued. Whispered.

No wisecracks about people calling in about kinky stuff or humoring the tinfoil dude who swore the evil Galentron people were beaming signals into his head.

In the time since I'd seen him, something happened to cut Blake open again and leave him bleeding from fresh wounds.

And I'd sat curled up in bed, hugging my arms to my chest, listening to the ache of compassion and pain in his voice as he comforted a girl named Felicity. Apparently, she owns a place in town called The Nest.

She'd called asking how she could sleep at night when every time she tries, she remembers the bad man who locked her up in a basement and tried to burn her alive along with her cousin and her aunt.

God, the things that *happen* to people here.

The trauma in that girl's voice, when she talked about her nightmares.

And the kindness in Blake's as he soothed her so gently. Told her that one fine day, she'd wake up and this would be nothing but a bad memory, and she'd be too far away from it to hurt anymore.

He said she was too close to it now, it could sink its claws in, but every day was another step forward. Another step she could put between herself and the pain. The pain was stuck in place, locked in that moment, but she wasn't.

He didn't offer useless platitudes.

Didn't tell her to try things that would only be a Band-Aid.

He just honored her pain. Talked to her like he knew it was real...and that it didn't have the power over her she thought it did.

Wow.

I wonder if anyone's ever told him the same thing.

I wonder if he needs to hear it.

I shouldn't be wondering if he wants to hear it from me.

But tonight, as the radio show comes on right on schedule around ten, when all the good little boys and girls are in bed and there's no one left but us late-night degenerates and night owls...

...I can already tell he's feeling better.

The intro jingle passes and he launches in with this soothing, musical voice, starting with a rumbling "Good evening, Heart's Edge."

The name of the town might be a metaphor for my heart whenever I hear him—pushed to the edge, teetering on the brink of falling.

When he talks like that, he takes my breath away.

And makes me remember him lying nearly naked under my hands, his body tanned and hard and thick with corded muscle, dusted with bristles of coarse, rusty brown hair.

That's Blake. Part Greek God, part black bear, and so *much* to explore.

He was striated with scars, old wounds that looked like they came from blades and other sharp edges, a few bullet nicks, though that knot on his thigh was the worst of it. His body had a sort of crude, sensuous artistry, like some kind of natural formation that time had worn into grace and beauty while still remaining feral.

Go ahead. Call me smitten.

He's as beautiful to look at as he is to listen to with those strong thighs and thick hands, with that broad chest and—*God*—the tick of his pulse against his throat when he swallows because he's struggling with his own vulnerability.

I know.

I *know* I have it bad.

I also know perfectly well I'm breaching every professional rule a massage therapist follows, swooning over her own freaking client when he's under her.

But Blake isn't exactly a traditional client. And I don't typically meet men who make me come undone when I lay my hands on them.

"First caller, you've got Blake on tap. How can I help?"

I'm listening with bated breath as Blake croons from the little alarm-slash-radio speaker on my nightstand.

The girl on the line sounds anxious, insecure, very young. "Um. There's...there's a guy at school that I like. But...he's a senior and I'm a sophomore."

"That's not such a big difference, honey. Just seems that way 'cause you're young and grades mean more than age does," Blake says gently. He's got a different tone when he's talking to kids, this sort of soft encouragement that doesn't talk down to them. More like he's taking their problems seriously. "Do you think he likes you, too?"

The girl lets out a nervous laugh. "I don't think he even knows I'm alive. I just hope he's not listening tonight."

"I won't ask your name, then, sweetheart," Blake says with a low laugh. "Have you ever tried talking to him?"

"Oh God, talk? *No way!*" the girl squeaks.

Man, do I know how she feels.

Every time I think about trading banter with Mr. Silver Tongue again, maybe seek some common ground, I just clam up inside.

I'm not ready to quit, but this little game isn't easy.

The more he winds me up, the scarier it gets to put myself out there.

It doesn't hurt when a stranger rejects you, not really.

It's a whole different thing when a man's been under your hands, laying himself bare.

"What if he hates me?" the poor girl goes on, her voice shaky.

"Well, young lady," Blake says, "he can't hate you if he doesn't know you. Anybody who'd hate you without knowing a darn thing about you ain't worth your time. So maybe give him a chance to know you first, yeah? Find out if you two have anything in common. Then it's all just talkin' about things you both like, and that ain't so hard at all."

She hesitates. "He...he really likes comic books, and so do I."

Blake lets out a soft, encouraging chuckle. "That's a good start. You know his favorite superhero?"

"Yeah!" she gasps. "He likes She-Hulk. That's one of my favorites, too!" Then she pauses, her voice dropping. "Ugh. I really hope he's not listening. I sound like a creepy stalker."

"C'mon now. It's not stalking to notice stuff about your crush."

No, it's really not, I think, grinning to myself.

I've noticed too many things about Blake.

How he dotes on Andrea.

How he takes on too much, like he's destined to carry the entire weight of his life on his shoulders without ever asking anyone to help, even just a little bit.

How he seems to be trying to atone for something, and I can't imagine what.

I have a feeling it has to do with his dead wife.

Andrea's mother.

Maybe he's apologizing to his daughter all the time for being the one she was left with.

It makes me wonder what kind of woman her mother was, considering things hadn't worked out between her and Blake.

But Blake must've loved her once, even if things went sour.

So what *kind* of woman did he love?

Enough love to have a daughter as feisty and smart as Andrea with?

I'm so caught up in it I almost miss him speaking again.

"Hey, I know the bookstore's restocking titles tomorrow, right?" he draws. "Bet he'll be there after school. Why don't you show up too?"

"Eep." The girl makes a mortified sound. "Won't that seem weird?"

"Nah," he says. "You're just there to pick up a new comic or two, right?"

"R-right," the girl says, then a bit more brightly. "Right! So I just...what? Talk to him?"

I cover my mouth, suppressing a giggle.

"That's all it takes, sweetheart," Blake says, his voice low thunder. "In the end, that's all relationships are. Two people who like talking to each other more than they like talking to anybody else. Then they get to that point where they don't need to talk at all, and it's good to just *be* together without saying a single darn word."

Okay. I can't help a soft sigh. Or *three*.

I'm as bad as that high school girl. But the man has a way with words.

I'd love to find out how they fit into his life.

Talking to Blake until all hours of the night, until we don't need words at all.

And maybe we could talk with lips, with hands, with skin...

My stomach tightens, my thighs tensing, this fierce pulse echoing in my blood. And I try to drag my mind from the gutter.

Not so easy. Not when his smooth as bourbon voice pours over me in shivers, like rough fingertips over my skin, submerging me in heat and friction from head to toe.

You ever get hot flashes before?

I know that makes no sense, but it's like your body gets so warm it makes you shiver, and it gets your nerves all crossed so they make you feel cold while you're still hot.

That's how it goes listening to Blake.

He's sweet, sending the girl off with a little more encouragement.

"Next caller," he says.

Only for another male voice to come over the radio, one that sounds almost like Blake's, but darker. *Slicker.*

This purr, dark and heady and a little too knowingly sexual for me.

It's sexy, kinda, but it doesn't have Blake's gentleness, his warmth, his honesty.

And without that, it's nothing.

"Hey, Blake. I've got a question," the man says. "What do you do when your brother's a stubborn donkey who won't listen when you try to make amends?"

Whatever I'm expecting, it's not the harsh, cold "Mother*fu*—" that comes next. Or how Blake clears his throat, probably to stop the station from getting slapped with a fine for live vulgarity.

Oh, crud.

Eyes widening, I shift to my knees, leaning toward the radio, listening closely.

Who is this guy?

And why does Blake sound so *angry*?

"This isn't funny," Blake bites off. "Why'd you call here?"

"Because you wouldn't pick up your phone, brother," the stranger says.

Okay. Wow. Crap.

So his life is more complicated than I realized.

Suddenly, I wonder if I'm just making things harder for him, wanting to self-insert in his world.

Sometimes, somebody wanting to comfort you can just be *too much* when you need time alone to clean up your own mess.

Blake lets out a soft snarl. "You're not broadcasting our business to the entire town. I don't have anything to say to you."

"Too bad," his brother says. "I have a lot to say to y—"

He's cut off, abruptly. There's a long pause before Blake sighs, soft and defeated. "Sorry about that, folks. Prank caller. Some people like to be knuckleheads." He pauses, then asks, "Do we have another caller up, Mario?"

That older male voice I heard the first night answers. "Not yet. You want to go to commercial or put on some tracks?"

No, no—don't!

Not yet, I think, and I scramble for my phone.

I'd saved the call-in number a few days ago, just in case I ever got brave.

And now I frantically tap the button before I can ask myself what I'm doing. *Why* I'm doing this, when just five seconds ago, I'd been questioning the wisdom of trying to get closer to Blake and possibly making things harder for him.

But I can't stand hearing the pain in his voice. The frustration. The sheer, quiet agony. The anger.

I've made it my life's work to soothe other's pain.

I can't not *try*.

So I listen with my heart in my throat as my phone rings against my ear, waiting for someone to pick up.

"Oh, wait," the older man says on the radio. "We've got a new caller!"

"Great," Blake says, though he sounds resigned for a moment before it picks up, a smooth warmth slipping into his voice again.

I hear a click, then an echo on both my phone and the radio.

"Hey, caller. What can I do for you?" Blake drawls.

"I—"

I wince, stopping as there's a weird feedback screech, jerking the phone away from my ear.

"Ow!"

Blake lets out a startled laugh. "Darlin', you gotta turn your radio off while we're talking."

Oops.

I reach over and turn the volume down to nothing on the clock radio, then murmur into the phone sheepishly. "Sorry. My bad."

"It's all right," he soothes. "First-time callers do it a lot. And if you're a first-timer...you ain't from around here, are you?"

My turn to *eep!*

Does he recognize my voice?

Does he realize it's me?

"Not from Montana, no," I say. "I guess I blew in on the autumn wind and decided to stay for winter."

"People do that around here a lot," he says. "Though some people come here to run away, too."

"I don't know if I'm running away," I admit. "If I'm running, then I've been running for a long time."

"How long?"

I pause, then say softly, "Probably for most of my life. Ever since my dad died, I just..."

He's silent, then prompts gently, "You just what, darlin'?"

"I think I'm scared to get attached to anything," I say, slowly and carefully because God I don't think I even realized it until I was saying it to him. "It's crazy. He was everything to me, and then he just went away and didn't come back. It still doesn't feel real. He was overseas when he died. Like, in the back of my mind, he's still alive, out there somewhere even though I saw his body at the funeral, flag-draped coffin and all. But that wasn't *him*. It was just this show, and maybe if I keep running...maybe I'll run away from losing someone ever again, and one day I'll figure out where he's hiding. Like he's waiting for me out there somewhere. Crazy, right?"

Blake lets out a sigh, but he doesn't sound so angry anymore.

He just sounds *warm*, that sigh a sweet breath of thoughtful contemplation. "How honest you want me to be with you?"

I let out a shaky laugh. *Oh, shit snacks.*

How did he pull all of that out of me with just a few probing questions?

How long have I been bottling it up without even realizing it?

"Hit me," I say. "Whatever you want to say, Blake."

"Your dad's never gonna be dead as long as he lives in you," Blake says, every word a rolling and hypnotic rhythm, this soothing heat like being wrapped up in his arms. "As long as you remember him. But I don't think he'd want you to live your life chasing his memory. He'd want you to live for yourself, not for him. So if you wanna stop running, darlin', you gotta decide what you want to run *to*, instead of what you want to run away from."

Woof, that's a lot to take in.

Even if I like easing others' pain, even if I thought it was something that mattered to me, and it *does*...it's not enough.

Not enough to live like who I am to other people, and never stop to think of who I want to be.

"I like singing. Music," I say, blurting it out before I can stop myself. "It was just never the kind of thing that, you know, anyone believed I could do. I was never going to be some big pop star, no Milah Holly or anything, but I like writing my own songs and singing them. And...and I think if I ever slowed down, it might be for that. If I could make my life about music, I'd have no reason to run."

"Good start, lady," Blake says.

And God, I hope he realizes it's me. Hope he recognizes my voice.

Because I'm living for the warm approval in every word.

The way he makes it sound like it's not so crazy at all, and maybe it's an attainable dream.

But, man, this is heavy.

Me, the flower child flitting around on the wind, never getting too deep, never clinging too hard.

I'm getting way too attached, and it's scaring me.

"Maybe," I deflect with a laugh, "I could sing a few end bumpers for your show? That jingle you're using now stopped being cool in the seventies."

That gets a deep chuckle, while the older man, Mario, lets out a grouchy, "Hey! We gotta go with royalty-free stuff here."

I grin against the phone, cradling it close to me. "How about just *free?* I won't charge you a bit. Just give me a chance."

"You really wanna come play songbird for us?" Blake asks. "Dunno if I can trust you around this much equipment. You might just set something on fire. Seems to follow you around, *Rabe.*"

Oh, *holy hell*. The way he says it makes my mind substitute the word *Broccoli.* And I'm not even mad.

He knows.

So I laugh, covering my face with one hand. "Hey, *neither* of those incidents were my fault."

"Says the woman driving a van that outlived its service miles twenty years ago. That thing's older than you are."

"Yeah, but...age isn't really that big of a thing, is it? Just like you told the comic book kid."

He doesn't answer for a minute, and I worry I've misstepped. Overstepped. Over-somethinged.

I don't know why I care so much what this man thinks.

But then he says slowly, "Nah. Age really ain't that big a deal, sometimes. Long as everybody's cool with each other."

"That's not a bad milestone," I say. "And you know the rest...as long as they like talking to each other."

Like I enjoy talking to you.

I've closed my eyes. I don't want anything to take me away from his voice. It's almost a flipping physical sensation.

Like curling up against the flank of a powerful lion who won't eat your face. A tame, righteous one who'll only lash out at pricks who deserve a nice lashing.

It's amazing how his voice envelopes me, but with that rich thickness of a lion's velvety fur.

Just listening to him makes me feel *safe*.

And a few other things.

Sometimes, there's a certain way his voice *catches*. A certain rough edge that just makes my breath hitch in my throat and turns my entire body a little too buttery.

"Can't say I'm minding certain conversations much," he says, husky and slow. I shiver, pressing my thighs together.

I don't think he even realizes he's seducing me with small talk.

"You want to talk a little longer?" I ask slowly, unable to keep the breathy edge from my voice. "Maybe off air."

"Hey," the older man interrupts.

Dammit.

I don't know his name, but I could kill him right now.

"This isn't a phone sex line," Mario says with a stressed laugh. "Tone it down, Blake. Every night we always get at least one hopeful. Mr. Silver Tongue, getting all the girls."

Oh, I could *die*.

But I guess that's the splash of cold water in the face I need.

I'm not unique.

I'm not anybody.

And Blake's probably just as nice to everyone who calls in, letting them feel like he cares for them while he's just being polite so people won't get their feelings crushed.

So *I* won't get my feelings hurt.

I muster a laugh from somewhere, even though my stomach's sinking with utter humiliation.

"Don't even," I say. "No one's trying to hook up. I just wanted to talk about recording a song for you. I don't think your listeners want to hear all the tedious details of that."

"Right," Blake says—but he sounds funny. "Don't worry, I'll find you, and we'll get the details ironed out."

"Sure," I say.

Then I hang up, before this stabbing at my chest can get worse.

Could I really have been more *obvious?*

I feel like that girl who called in about her crush, knowing the boy might be listening, might recognize her voice, might think she was desperate and sad and not worth his time. High school boys can be cruel.

Grown men aren't any better. Sometimes they're even worse.

Blake's not like that, I tell myself.

But I don't dare let myself believe he wants me, either.

Not even when part of me turns giddy.

I'm too freaking happy at the thought that I have a reason to see him again, without just waiting for that prideful beast to come to me.

* * *

I won't lie: I'm restless for the rest of the week.

Part of it's waiting for Blake to follow up about recording a little bumper tune for the show.

The rest? I can't stop thinking about his advice. Making a career out of my music.

It's not like I'm gunning to be some huge star.

I don't even want to have my own albums.

For me, the money's an afterthought. It's not about the stardom, the spotlight, the legions of adoring fans.

I'd just be pleased as punch piecing together songs for others.

Like, remember that girl in *Coyote Ugly?*

I'm not quite her. I don't crave the attention on stage.

I just want to hear my songs on the radio, even if I'm not the one performing them.

And I've been scribbling away for days, trying out different lyrics, strumming chords on the old guitar I inherited from my father, playing riffs on my portable Casio keyboard. Hardly anything studio-worthy, but at least it helps me get ideas down.

It's coming together.

A song about a damaged desperado type. He keeps himself moving by fighting for the people he loves but never lets himself get too close. For him it's always look, don't touch.

Too real?

Guess so because I don't know how to wrap the song up.

No matter which direction I go, it feels like an unfinished story, and I'm not sure it's even mine to tell.

God.

I need to get out of my head.

And that's how I find myself at the main house with Haley and Andrea, sitting in on Andrea's art lessons.

I may be a musician at heart, but there are some fine arts totally out of my reach.

Haley promised to keep it simple, but her idea of *simple* is whipping out a lifelike chalk pastel portrait in no time. It's the big orange tabby lurking around the inn, and she's got Mr. Mozart sketched in wild meowy detail in under an hour.

Andrea's drawn a cat too, but hers is more like something off a goth metal album cover. All saber teeth and fur dripping like black ink with crazy yellow eyes. Total Marilyn Manson meets H.R. Giger vibes, and while it's creepy as hell, it's also really *good.*

She's got serious talent, and she moves her brush pen with these fluid strokes that make looping, flowing lines everywhere.

Then there's me.

Um...if I was five, my mom *might* stick this rickety mess of pencil scratches on the fridge.

It doesn't even quite look like a cat.

It's more like a...snake with legs and whiskers?

Hey, it was fun. Honestly, I didn't come here to learn to draw anyway.

I just needed company, friendly humans, and both of these ladies have been happy to let me butt in.

Especially Andrea. She's putting the finishing touches on razory cat claws when she asks, "So did you ever surf back in Oahu?"

I laugh—and try not to be obvious about erasing the second tail I accidentally drew on my cat. Kind of a lost cause. The paper is the kind that crumbs up and thins when you erase it.

"Oh, all the time," I say. "Though I always stayed on the small waves. My mom worried too much and wouldn't let me tackle the big ones. I guess she was scared I'd drown."

Andrea wrinkles her nose. "Ugh. My mom was like that, too. She just always..." She shrugs stiffly, staring down at her sketchbook. "It's like if I stepped out of line even a little, something awful was going to happen."

I take her in quietly: her punky clothes, her dyed hair, and I get it a little more now.

This is her way of mourning her mom and celebrating her freedom.

Trying to figure out who she is in grief and escaping from her mother's shadow.

Sad. If I know anything about grief, and about little girls...

Andrea would rather have her mom back than all the rainbow hair dye in the world.

"Moms worry a lot," I say gently. "I think once you have a kid, that gene just kind of kicks on and suddenly you can't stop thinking about all the things that could happen to them, to take them away from you."

"But I'm not the one who went away, am I?" Andrea says. Soft, forlorn, almost more to her sketchbook than to us.

There's a dense silence.

Haley and I glance at each other before she offers a touch of humor. "Too right. I think I'm turning into that kind of Momzilla. I'm just lucky if Cody and baby Jenna are out of my sight, I know they're with their great-grandmother so I don't have to worry as much."

Andrea smiles faintly. "I doubt you could ever be a Momzilla, Hales."

Haley grins. "Well, if *you* say so. My niece, Tara, might beg to differ. She has a grand old time every time she visits, laughing at how much running around I do like a chicken who's just had a date with Robespierre."

"The French Revolution is so cool." The reference gets a bigger smile out of Andrea. "All those ideas and heads rolling all over the place. I mean, not that it was right to just—"

"It's *Hamilton* for me, all the freaking way, thank you very much. Best part of the eighteenth century," I say, which gets a knowing laugh from Haley. "God, do I love that musical. Got myself kicked off an organic farm in Cali once because I wouldn't stop singing it."

When I shift over, bumping my arm playfully on Andrea right next to me, she laughs and shoves me back with her shoulder. Some of that melancholy tension leaves her.

I wish I could make things better. At least I can be her friend.

"Y'all sound like you're having fun," a familiar voice drawls.

And I hate how I blush down to my toes before I even look up. Blake leans in the doorway, arms folded over his chest in a way that makes his jacket strain against his body.

Holy hell!

The thick fleece does *nothing* to hide his rigid shape and just how hard-packed the muscle on his body is.

Of course he's looking right at me.

Do "eeps" come in extra large?

If this keeps up, the next fire he'll have to put out is right in front of him.

I hold those night-dark eyes for a few moments, then drop my gaze to my sketch.

I can't look at him.

I can't look, or else I'll remember sitting in my bedroom, breathing shallowly while his voice washed over me like a steaming tide.

Thankfully, Andrea's got plenty to say to break the awkward silence.

"You're *early*," she gasps.

"I'm right on time," Blake says lazily. "You just don't want to go home."

"With you? You're right I don't."

Oof.

That's harsh.

But when I look up, Blake just takes it in stride, a sort of weary patience that says he's used to this routine. Words are no match for superdad.

And I'm barely kidding because sometimes a dad needs to be the punching bag for a daughter who's angry at everything and nothing at once. Who else can she trust to love her when she's done raging at the world but her father?

Maybe I'm projecting.

Maybe I'm seeing what I want to see in him, what I admire.

But I'm not imagining the gentleness in Blake's voice when he says, "Having your favorite tonight, Violet. Pierogies. Plus, you're supposed to be helping with carnival prep."

I don't think I've ever seen anyone perk *reluctantly*, but Andrea pulls it off.

She closes her sketchbook, wrinkling her nose.

"Well, I guess." Then she glances at me, biting her lip. "Can

Peace come, Dad? She was telling me about Hawaii. I want to hear more."

I blink several times, clearing my throat. "I don't want to impose..."

"You wouldn't be!" Andrea says enthusiastically, and I'm starting to wonder if she wants me as a buffer between her and her father. "Just hearing your stories gives me ideas. So many crazy things happen on the islands—did you guys hear about the Navy SEAL who married this rich chick with amnesia? They even fought this crazy pirate mobster-dude and she had an illegal cat. I guess some freaking *turtles* saved their skins."

Blake just stares. So do I.

Andrea shrugs. "It was all over the news! God, you guys..."

"Nice knowing the insanity isn't restricted to Heart's Edge, I guess." I smile faintly. "Maybe your dad can take you to Oahu someday. It's hard to make it sound exciting when you grew up a local like I did and everything's so commonplace."

She rolls her eyes, making an exasperated sound. "Please. He'd probably get drunk and end up with a tenth-degree sunburn."

"No such thing as a tenth-degree burn," Blake growls back. "Think I can manage to avoid a little sun. It's almost like I know a thing or two about burnin' up."

"Whatever," Andrea snaps.

Haley clears her throat, jumping in quickly. "Er...Blake? Peace? I didn't think you two had met?"

Oh. Now I don't think I'm going to stop blushing until I *die*.

"We've met," he says quietly, his gaze flicking to my eyes.

Just that.

No clue how to read it when he doesn't say anything else.

I just know he probably doesn't want Haley knowing *how* we met.

Except I guess we're more obvious than we both realize because Haley jumps in with a soft gasp. "Oh, that's right! I heard you on the radio the other night. You were talking about recording something for the radio station, weren't you, Peace?"

Dear God.

Blake's eyes widen.

So do mine.

We just *stare* at each other.

Is he blushing under those wily whiskers?

I know I sure as hell am.

Neither of us seem like we're going to look away first, even though I'm practically squirming.

Thank God for Andrea to the rescue again.

"You *sing?*" she gasps. "Could you get any cooler?"

I let out a nervous laugh. "I'm...not really, I just..." I tear my gaze from Blake to Andrea. "It's just a hobby. Maybe one I want to do professionally, though. A songwriter for recording studios or freelance or something."

Andrea tilts her head. "You don't want to sing your own songs?"

"Demo tracks, maybe." I gesture at myself. "Do I really look like star material?"

"Yeah," Blake says. "You do."

Three shockingly serious words. They stop my heart before jump-starting it again.

Holy crap.

He's looking at me again.

And I still can't read one bit of him and his steely-blue eyes.

But I feel like he's tearing me apart with a single steady gaze, his eyes shadowed and hot, raking over me with vivid intensity.

I swallow so loud it echoes.

I can't find any words, my voice drying up in my throat. And I realize Haley's staring at us, her eyes slightly narrowed, something knowing and amused in the quirk of her lips.

Save me, I almost plead. I don't even know if I actually want to be saved.

There's something delicious about melting under Blake's gaze.

It's a new kind of nice seeing him so relaxed.

From the patient, tired father to the gentle mentor to the stoic hero, but with a bit of goofy humor I've only seen come out every now and again.

And now this side.

This quiet, intense man I can't figure out, but who seems to have taken some kind of interest in me, even if I'm almost scared to know what's got him looking at me so sharply.

Nothing, maybe.

Or maybe everything I'm starting to want.

Every freaking time I'm in his presence and a lot of times when I'm not.

Haley stands abruptly, clapping her hands together. "Well. If you don't get moving, Andrea's going to be late—and I have a feeling she doesn't want to miss a certain meeting."

"*Haley!*" Andrea hisses, nearly squirming herself. "I don't want to talk about that!"

She bares her teeth, then abruptly changes the subject. "Peace, you want to come check out the carnival? We're just getting stuff set up for the fireworks show, and like, they're building an ice castle and everything."

Blake grunts, finally looking away, leaving me almost cold without his eyes. "I'm still not okay with this fireworks thing. Especially with that kid running it."

"Clark isn't a *kid*, Dad." Andrea snarls. "He's a junior."

Oh, now I get it.

That's why she's so eager to get going.

It's the same boy she was so mad at the other night.

I grin, relaxing a little. "What's so wrong with fireworks?"

"It's a major fire hazard," Blake says, scowling. "They won't just be shooting off rockets. They're planning a full pyrotechnics show, and they're expecting *me* to sign off on the safety check."

"And Clark's uncle trained him well," Andrea fires back. "It'll be *fine.*"

"*I'll* decide if it's fine, young la—"

"So!" I interrupt before this can thunder into a bigger argument. "If you wouldn't mind showing me around..."

Andrea and Blake pull back sharply from glaring at each other to blink at me.

Then Andrea grins.

Blake groans.

And I'm definitely getting mixed signals when they both say "Sure" at the same time.

It's adorable how father and daughter mirror each other.

Only, one's way more reluctant than the other.

* * *

YEP.

I officially feel like a third wheel right now.

We're making the ride over to the carnival grounds in Blake's Jeep after dinner. Andrea's in the back seat, and I'm awkwardly tucked in the front while no one says a word.

Blake's gone all broody beast-man again, turned inward, shutting down quietly, while Andrea stays in her *Don't talk to me, Dad* mode, busy texting in the back seat.

I don't know what to say.

Part of me wanted to talk about that night on the phone over pierogies, but between Hawaii stories and the little dance of family tension, the subject never came up.

A small relief, maybe. It feels so *intimate.*

Too private to discuss in front of Blake's teenage daughter.

And maybe he'd rather forget it, too.

So I just lean against the door and watch the town pass by, idyllic little buildings in their perfect little settings. Glittery snow clings to the corners of the roofs, reflecting the clear night sky back in soft shades of blue.

The "carnival grounds" are actually a ways past the high school football field, which looks mostly like pasture that someone framed in rickety wooden bleachers. I can't help but grin.

Small-town life.

Considering how late it is, I'm surprised to see so much activity bustling around, but there are adults and teenagers buzzing around everywhere.

They're putting up scaffolding, setting up booths, laying out electrical wiring and strings of lights. On the far end, there's a really impressive effort going on to fill a ton of square tubs with water, I'm guessing to create ice blocks for the huge ice-castle Andrea mentioned.

All in all, it looks like a pretty big deal.

Even as we park, I catch sight of the tall, gangly boy who'd been with Andrea that night in the woods. He's with a few other kids and has a weird metal contraption cuffed to his wrist.

When he flexes his hand, dipping two fingers inward like Spider-Man using his web shooters, flame arcs out in thin, lashing bursts.

Wow.

Andrea apparently thinks it's the greatest thing ever. The engine's not even quiet before she's scrambling out of the back seat and shooting off, waving and shouting, "Clark!"

I raise both brows. "That boy must be dense."

"Most boys are," Blake grunts, killing the Jeep but not opening the door yet. He folds his arms on the steering wheel, his remote, quiet gaze following his daughter. "You want to stay in here? It's warmer. I just need to do the rounds for safety checks. Pretty boring shit."

"I don't mind the cold," I say carefully, smiling and shrugging.

I don't want to say *I definitely don't mind it with you.*

I don't want to sound that desperate.

He glances at me, raising both brows. "Yeah? Hawaiian girl out here in Montana, and you don't mind the dead of winter?

Figured you'd be missing the warmer weather like your own skin."

"Well..." I look out the window. The frost has fogged it up, and my breaths don't help, misting it until the whole world runs in watercolors through the glass. "I don't miss much about Hawaii anymore."

"Since your old man?" he asks.

Even if he's gentle, it aches.

My eyes flutter shut a few seconds longer than they should.

"Yeah," I answer thickly. "Since my dad."

His silence isn't awkward or censuring.

It's soft.

It's kind.

Gives me a moment to compose myself with his warmth here to keep me company. I wait until I can breathe without feeling like my throat is caught in an ever-closing noose.

"Anyway," I say, trying to smile. "I've been around colder places than Montana. I once spent a summer gutting fish in Alaska and stayed a few months longer."

"Fuck." His startled laughter rolls over me. "*Why?*"

"I wanted to know what it was like," I answer. "That's why I do a lot of things. I've tried organic farming, micro-brewing, hand-carving beads in communes. If it seems fun, I try it. And I'm usually right."

"Gutting fish was *fun?* You serious, lady?"

"It actually was. Just really smelly. I learned a lot of awful sailor jokes, though."

Blake snorts. "So why'd you quit, then?"

He relaxes as he leans against the steering wheel, his powerful body slouched in a lazy sprawl of taut musculature.

"I didn't want to mess up my hands." I hold up my purple-gloved hands and spread my fingers. "While I wander around, I can at least make a living with massage. But gutting fish gives you carpal tunnel, and that's if you don't have an accident with a knife sooner or later."

With an amused sound, he gives me the side-eye. "Can't have that. There's magic in those fingers."

There's something almost suggestive in the way he says it, in the way his gaze lingers on my outstretched fingers, very unsexy in their purple yarn sheaths.

Then he clears his throat and looks away, pushing his door open.

"C'mon," he says. "If you really want the grand tour, let's go."

I pull my coat tighter, drag my cap down over my ears, and slip out after him—and nearly yelp as the biting air hits me right in the face.

Yep. It's that time of year. The average temperature can drop drastically in the space of an hour as the winds pick up after dark in mountain towns like this. I'm shivering like a wet puppy as I turn my collar up to better cover my neck and jaw.

Blake barely seems to feel it, turning to lead us through the rickety wooden gate closing off the field.

It's comfortable walking with him.

Not really needing to talk, though now and then he explains what he's doing as we follow the perimeter of the carnival grounds, then start moving between different installations.

He's mostly checking for fire hazards.

Too many extension cords plugged into an outlet, for example, or hot-burning lights too close to a cloth awning. Open fire next to dry, brittle grass becomes perfect tinder with winter leaving it crackling and dead.

I'd never really thought about the infinite ways a fire can start. But Blake seems to see it all with this weird sixth sense.

He's mostly interested in the stage, which they've assembled inside a massive tent—I guess to keep everyone warm. Though if you ask me, I'd love to see it open-air, naked under the stars.

That's one thing that's always helped me decide to stay, whenever I pick a place to hunker down for the winter.

Just how well I can see the stars stretched over the yawning heavens at night.

Some places, larger cities like Portland and Chicago, I can't even see a single star. It's just smog or blaring lights reflected back, the sky always a strange shade of peach-purple. You can't even see the moon sometimes save for a faint glow peeking past the light pollution.

I never stay in places like that long.

I go where I can see the same stars I saw at home in Oahu, and counted sometimes with my father to make wishes again and again, always hoping they'd come true.

I look up at the glittering expanse of the Milky Way, lingering before I follow Blake into the tent and climb up on stage with him.

There's a heaping mess of plugs and cables belonging to hot spotlights.

I can already tell this is going to be bad, holding my breath.

"Shit," he mutters, crouching low to examine a few tangled wires.

"You're going to shut this whole thing down, aren't you?" I ask, staring at the bunched nest of cables sprouting from a multi-outlet splitter that looks like it's had about thirty others plugged into it. "Because this is a Carrie reenactment waiting to happen."

"You're damn right," he says grimly. "Shitfire. I taught these people *better* than this."

I grin. "Did you actually teach them, or just lead by example?"

"Hey, now. I lead a good fire safety seminar." He grimaces. "But it's been a few years. Seems like folks need a refresher course, and this time they need to jot crap down." Blake frowns, stroking his beard, thick workman's gloves rasping against the bristly hairs. "Come to think of it...that might be a good gig for Justin. Maybe lead a carnival event on fire safety."

"Justin?" I tilt my head, watching the faraway, thoughtful look in Blake's eyes. "The younger fire dude, right?"

His gaze darts to me, narrowing like I've said something wrong. "He's not that young. Closer to your age, matter of fact."

Weird.

Closer to your age than me, he's not saying, and I arch a brow.

"He's not my type," I say, and Blake's brows rise in answer to mine, almost teasing.

"Nah? You seem to like wounded animals, and he's definitely the broken puppy type."

I laugh. "I'm not attracted to boys still trying to get their crap together. I have a very specific type, hardly a puppy dog."

More like a coyote, a panther, a bear.

Something rangy, put together, and wild, with teeth sharp enough to *bite*.

"I'm not gonna set myself up by asking what that type is," he says dryly, leaving me sputtering—ugh, does he *know* how infatuated I am?—while he looks away, scanning over the nest of cables again. "Teasing aside, Justin might benefit from a visit with you. Just for stress relief, relaxation. He's carrying a lot of pain around all the time, and I feel like I've been neglecting him."

I step closer, looking up at the solemn lines of his brow. "Neglecting him? How?"

"He's part of my crew." He shakes his head, turning his head, looking down at me with those dark, thoughtful eyes. "It's my responsibility to take care of them. But Justin...well, he's all smiles on the surface. Easy to forget he's in pain. And he isolates himself, y'know? He'll only let you see him when he's smiling. But I know why he's hurting, and I haven't done right. Haven't done enough to make him part of things so he doesn't feel like he has to be alone."

"What happened to him?"

"His ma died," Blake answers, and there's a hint of something dark, something hurting, that says he's feeling this on a deeper level. "Happened way back. He was just a kid, but there was this huge fire out at the Paradise Hotel in the valley. Same ruins you saw when your van caught fire. We didn't get it put out in time. There was a lot of freaky quasi-military shit up there, stuff they were keeping hidden we only found out about years later, but that ain't the point. His ma, Constance, she got a lot of folks to safety, but she died a month later from smoke inhalation. He's real serious about firefighting, 'cause of her. Even if what happened still leaves him messed up."

My heart stops.

I want so much to reach for him right now.

To just wrap Blake up and hold him.

Right now, he's talking to me the way he does when he's on the radio, instead of shutting down and going defensive when he has to deal with me in person.

The man who's talking to me now feels so much empathy. He owns their pain, hoping to ease it if he can't take it away.

Well, crap.

So infatuation might not be the worst of it.

I think I might be a little bit in love with that kind, stubborn, strange heart of his.

For just a moment, I can't help but step closer, reaching up to rest my hand on his arm. Even through his thick coat, his arm is solid muscle, and it tenses under my palm.

"You can't make Justin let go of his pain, Blake," I tell him softly. "But it's good that you want to make him feel like he's part of something. Maybe giving him control over a fire safety event would help him feel closer to the town, take his mind off what happened."

The way Blake looks at me makes me wonder if I said something wrong.

His jaw sets tight, his eyes creased at the corners, and my heart plummets.

Before he can pull away from me, I draw my own hand back. But he only makes this rough, bearish sound under his breath.

"Hope you're right, darlin'," he mutters, before he turns away, tilting his head back to look up at the lights suspended in the rigging. "Somebody's gonna die in here."

I don't know why I feel a chill when he says that.

Almost like a creepy premonition.

Hugging my arms around myself, I push down the feeling of disappointment in my chest.

"I don't know anything about fire safety, but this looks kind of dangerous even to me," I whisper.

"Heh. Maybe you need Justin's course, too." He glances at me, his eyes softening. "Hey. You serious about wanting to sing for the radio show or what?"

The sudden switch leaves me reeling, spinning, and I blink at him.

"Sing? Oh. Sure thing!" My eyes narrow. "So how long did it take for you to know it was me when I called?"

Blake smiles his wry, easygoing grin. "Thought so right away. Nobody's got a voice like yours. Or a name like Broccoli."

Shooting him a dirty look, I rub my hand against my too-warm neck.

Hey, if anything, Blake's going to keep me from freezing to death out here by blushing. "I'd really like to try, if you think it's all right. Maybe come up with a little custom jingle for you or something."

"We can try. Don't really have pro level recording equipment or a sound booth here, but we can probably rig something up at the station, if you want to come down this weekend."

"Really?" My breaths suck in quickly, and my sinking heart rockets back up. "Thank you!"

Sometimes I hate how impulsive I am.

Without even thinking, I throw myself at him, pressing against his back and wrapping my arms around him from behind.

I'm just elated. Buzzing and fizzing and whirling like sparklers.

I'm also instantly embarrassed. He goes stiff as a board against me.

Heck, I feel like I'm undoing all my own handiwork, though it's been nice to see him not limping today.

But I'm selfish.

I cling for a moment longer and breathe him in.

He smells like a Blake.

Fresh snow and woodsmoke and soft citrusy cologne. I take that scent in deep so I can remember it as long as I need to.

Then my sanity catches up.

"Sorry," I whisper, peeling away.

He doesn't acknowledge my apology. He doesn't even move.

Blake just tosses his head, moving toward the edge of the stage. "C'mon. Let's finish up here and pry Andrea away from whatever she's doing."

Biting my lip, I watch him vault down from the edge of the stage, then follow, climbing down more gingerly. For a moment, the heel of my foot slips as I drop down, and he starts forward, hands reaching for me—but I catch myself just in time.

He pulls back with another of those gruff, almost embarrassed sounds, looking away as I land in the chilly grass and dust myself off.

I'm going to smile, I tell myself.

I'm going to smile no matter what.

It's not my fault he's so guarded. So wounded. So *Blake*.

Papa bear's got himself a cub to protect, all on his own, I get it.

There's no use in taking his icy-hot reactions too personally.

So I just beam up at him, straightening my coat. "Lead the way, Chief."

That earns me an utterly filthy look. "Don't *you* start calling me that, too."

"Aye-aye, sir," I retort with a salute, and he rolls his eyes.

"Am I a captain now? C'mon, Sailor Broccoli." Turning away, he strides across the grass. "Try to keep up."

"Hey!" I have to scramble to catch up with those long legs of his and even longer strides. "Stop calling me Broccoli! And stop being so flipping *tall!*"

Blake says nothing.

He just grins.

But he shortens his steps, letting me fall into rhythm with him as we move across the field, some of the tension dissipating.

It's quiet as he focuses on work. I try not to be too obvious watching him.

He's so *intense* it practically breathes electricity in the air. Completely absorbed in checking every minuscule detail—whether he's making sure the outlets are grounded or...

Okay. Confession.

Half the time I don't even know what fire chief stuff he's doing.

I don't care.

I just like watching the way his lips part on plumes of breathy frost-smoke, breathing through his mouth to warm the frigid air.

As we make our way to the edge of the field on the far side from the parking area, though, I get a wicked idea. I can't unsee it once it hits me in the face.

There's a slope leading down toward the valley, totally covered in snow.

And someone's left several sleds lined up in lanes, with flags at the bottom of the hill.

They must be planning sled races.

Grinning from ear to ear, Blake's eyes meet mine and do a double take.

"What's up?"

"Fun," I say, turning to walk backward in front of him. "Race you to the bottom of the hill."

His eyes follow to the sleds I'm pointing at.

He stares at me, blinking. "What? Shit, you can't be—"

"C'mon." I toss my head toward the sleds again. "Scared of taking a tumble?"

Another blink.

Then a wide, disbelieving, almost boy-like grin spreads across his face.

"You're fucking kidding me, Peace. What are we, twelve? I'm supposed to be Mr. Authority here."

"Maybe," I tease. "Listen, I'm not good at ignoring my impulses. So, I'm gonna sled down this hill. You can come with, you can watch, or you can keep being a boring adult, but I'm going to have some fun."

Something in Blake's eyes snaps, soft blue turning fiery, his grin sharpening. "You think I'm boring?"

"I dunno." I shrug flippantly with an innocent little whistle. "It's all safety this, safety that, barking orders..."

"With good reason." He snorts. "And speaking of safety, we could break our damn necks on those things plowing into a tree."

"All the more reason to try it out! So you can check for safety before the carnival races." Spreading my hands, I take a few steps back, then turn and dart for one of the sleds. "See you at the bottom, slowpoke."

"Hey!" he hollers after me, but I'm already running, flinging myself facedown on one of the wooden sleds in a totally graceless belly flop and shoving off with my feet.

Laughing uncontrollably.

Snow sprays my face in a dusty white plume as I go rocketing forward, surging over the peak of the hill and down way faster than I expected.

I let out a breathless sound that's half scream, half laugh, clutching tight to the edges of the sled.

"Goddammit, Peace!" Blake snarls after me, but he's laughing, and his voice sounds way closer than it should.

No, I don't want to crash. There's no real danger of trees, thankfully. They've already got this little plastic fencing set up to stop serious crashes.

I can't resist looking back over my shoulder as the bottom of the hill comes hurtling toward me.

Oh, God.

Oh my *God*.

Blake's barreling down after me, but he's sitting upright on his sled.

Only, it's too small for him.

His long, muscular legs jut out in the air, and his hands clutch at the front of the sled between his thighs, his entire body leaning back like he's trying to slow the thing down, bucking its nose in the air from his weight.

Yes, he's hollering fit to kill.

But he's laughing, too, breathless and startled and a little bit panicked.

He's also careening straight toward me. *Uh-oh.*

Gravity isn't my friend today.

Blake weighs a lot more than I do, and he's hurtling toward me at breakneck speed, moving twice as fast and bearing down.

Our eyes lock for half a second. He comes screaming in, trailing white plumes in his wake.

Then the nose of his sled plows the side of mine, and we both go airborne in a tangled mess.

I let out an undignified screech, laughing helplessly as I grab at him.

We don't fly far.

We're almost to the bottom of the hill anyway, and Blake's *heavy*, weighing us both down.

But my stomach still nearly drops out and buries itself in the frozen snow clinging to me as we tumble and roll and tangle together.

Finally, we hit the bottom, smashing into a snow drift with a dramatic *whump!*

At least we're not moving anymore, right?

I don't think I could if I wanted to, anyway.

And right now, I don't want to go anywhere.

Not when Blake's weight presses down, all heat and hardened man. The snow feels frigid against my back. It's already starting to soak my jacket and freeze my skin, but Blake is a couple hundred pounds of masculine fire caged in human skin.

Right. On. Top. Of. Me.

We're both breathing hard, panting, and he's collapsed with his head buried against my shoulder and neck, his arms braced to either side, keeping me pinned down.

Good.

So deliriously good, that thick, weighty, granite-hard frame of his molded to mine, heating me up until I can't even feel the winter night.

It's just Blake's rasping, heavy breaths, hot against my throat, suggestive and loud, and the sight of the stars dancing overhead. I stare up past the thick bulk of his shoulder.

I didn't mean to grab him the way I did, my fingers curled against his biceps.

But now that he's there, I don't want to let him go.

My face hurts from grinning, but I'm not smiling now.

Not when I turn my head toward him, my entire body pulsing with the feel of him, and my cheek brushes his.

Blake goes oddly quiet, still, his heavy breaths silencing, slowing.

He pushes himself up on his arms.

God, I can't stand feeling even the slightest bit of that delicious weight lifting, but...

When he looks down at me, snow in his messy hair and dusted all over his coat, eyes razor-blue and hot, leverage bringing his hips tight against mine, I'm *so* done.

Utterly breathless.

I just feel sparks all over, thrumming in my blood, lighting up bright and burning over and over and over again in little rushes.

Licking my lips, my mouth aches for the taste of him, the feel of him, the *need* for him.

It wouldn't be hard.

I could spread my legs so easy, let his narrow hips sink down between my thighs, shudder with his molten friction. If he'd just let me.

If that animal look in his eyes, something smoldering-dark, is an *answer* to the call of desire rushing through me. Raw heat strums between my legs. Focused. Brutal.

No lie, I could writhe on him and get off in *under a minute* just by rubbing my body against his.

I *want* to.

This roughed up tree trunk of a man makes me shameless.

But before I can move, before I can *do* anything, he parts his lips to speak—

Only for both of us to go stiff. A deafening roar sounds from up the hill.

Over his shoulder, I catch a pillar of flame shooting toward the sky.

Mega-crud.

"Shit." Blake jerks up, looking over his shoulder sharply, staring at that orange and gold plume for half a second before he thrusts himself off me and surges up the hill on powerful strides that churn through the snow, leaving me behind.

I lie there for a dazed moment, staring at the sky.

All the stars are laughing at me tonight.

Damn it all.

So close.

So close, but so far.

I drag myself to my feet with a wince.

Now that Blake's not on top of me, I feel the bruises from bouncing and tumbling around, not to mention the chill crawling over my skin.

Shivering, I dust myself off, then climb the hill in his wake, trudging up after him in the path he so helpfully cleared through the snow.

It's not hard to figure out where he went, judging by the thick coiling smoke rising over the field.

Everyone out working stares in that direction.

I follow the painfully obvious clues until I catch up with his broad back.

He's standing head and shoulders above a group of teenagers

—including Andrea and the tall, gangly boy dressed in black that I think I recognize as Clark, Andrea's crush.

He's a shaggy thing, all throwback emo style and piercings. Just the kind of kid I'd have been crazy for at her age, and it's not hard to see she's protective of him.

Considering she's positioned herself between her father and Clark, glaring up at him while Blake's eyes drill right back.

"The hell do you think you're doing?" Blake growls.

Andrea starts, "It's just part of the—"

Clark shakes his head, brushing his hand against her arm.

"It's okay, Ana," he says, then looks at Blake with a frankness beyond his years. "I was testing out a new launcher, and one of the fireworks cartridges had loose gunpowder. Wasn't packed properly. No one got hurt. We made sure to test it in a clear space, all the grass pulled, snow piled up to put out any sparks." He sighs. "I know what I'm doing, Mr. Silverton. Accidents happen."

"*Accidents* have nearly burned this damn town down too many times," Blake growls back.

My heartbeat goes to ten.

He's firm, clearly angry, but Clark's calm ownership of what he did seems to have knocked some of the protective rage out of him, leaving pure cold authority.

It's another thing I like about Blake. Even when his temper snaps, he gets it under control fast without turning into a stomping dick. "Your uncle's the licensed fireworks tech. He should be doing controlled tests. Not you, Clark."

"Shit came up with Uncle Rog today. He gave me permission," Clark answers evenly, but there's an edge there, defensive. "And if he'd done the test, it *still* would've flared. It was a packing issue, not me. I'm trained in this. Everything's fine."

"Everything is *not* fine. What you're doing is technically illegal." Blake works his jaw. "Leave it. This is over, for your own good—before you get in any more trouble or I haul you up in front of Sheriff Langley. All of you, get home." His gaze darts to Andrea. "Including you. Come on."

Andrea stares at him in total horror. I'm pretty sure the pink spots on her cheeks are pure rage, not the cold air.

"Oh my God, Dad," she nearly whispers, so strained it's like she can barely get her voice out. Her gaze darts to me for a second, pleading, but I'm just a helpless bystander.

It's not my place to intervene. When I offer a confused grimace, she just turns her glare on her father again. "I'm not going anywhere with you. I'll find my own way home."

"Andrea—"

He reaches a hand out, but she's already turning and stalking off, putting another girl between herself and her father as the group starts to trail away. Clark stops, though, glancing back with a resentful look.

"For someone who says he knows what he's doing," he murmurs, "you sure fuck up with her a lot. She doesn't *want* to hate you, you know."

Before he, too, turns and walks away.

Blake just stands there, staring, his eyes angry black and blue seas. Then his hand falls limply to his side before he curses and drags it through his hair, shaking out a bit of half-melted snow. "Goddamn. Now I got kids telling me how to raise my kid?"

I step closer to him, trying to offer support. "He's her friend. She'd tell him things she might not tell you."

"Maybe so. Doesn't mean I like it."

He looks so defeated.

So exhausted.

Honestly, I'm worried how it's going to affect his leg. Stress can cause tons of flare-ups with chronic pain issues.

But he looks down at me after a moment, sighing. "We're done here. Need a ride home?"

"Sure," I say.

It's not what I really want to say. But I feel like what I want to get out won't be welcome.

NO DAMAGED GOODS

The ride back to Charming Inn is quiet, Blake locked up and brooding in his own head, and I don't want to interrupt his thoughts.

I'm also a little distracted myself.

Considering I'm still shivering half to death from melted snow soaked into my clothes, I'm focused on getting as close to the heater vents as possible to dry off.

As he pulls up along the lane near my cabin, engine idling, I bite my lip and take a risk, reaching over to rest my fingertips on his forearm. He's rock-hard under my touch, so tense.

"Blake," I say. "It'll be okay. She's young and emotional. Everything makes her mad right now. She'll come around."

Whatever I'm expecting, it's not the cold, forbidding word he spits out.

"Stop."

Just one word, but it's enough to punch the breath from my lungs.

He stares straight ahead, not looking at me, his face a fixed mask.

"I'm sorry?" I say faintly.

"Just fucking stop," he repeats—low, grim, the voice that seduces me so much now feeling like a granite wall between us. "I get it. You just want to help, Peace, and I'm grateful. But I don't need it. I don't need therapy. I just need to get the hell on with my life." His fingers tighten on the steering wheel so hard I can hear the leather groan. "So how about we stick to you doing your radio spot, and leave the rest alone?"

That shouldn't hurt so much.

But it stings deep, stings hard, like needles at the corners of my eyes.

They prick with more than just the sharp, cold air. I shove the passenger door open and take several deep breaths of night, trying to choke down the lump in my throat.

"Sorry," I say numbly, my voice sounding dead, empty,

remote even to me. "I didn't mean to intrude or...or to upset you. Thanks for the ride."

He doesn't say anything.

Doesn't even look at me.

So I just turn and walk away, all messed up inside, and remind myself that every risk has its price.

Sometimes it's pleasure.

Sometimes it's nothing but pain.

I took a gamble and lost.

VIII: RHYTHM AND TONE (BLAKE)

I know.

I'm such an asshole.

That's all I've been able to think ever since the other night.

That I'm pure defensive scum for the way I talked to Peace.

It's like some switch flipped inside me when we were sitting in my Jeep. Her by the moonlight and the stars reflecting off the snow. All I could remember was how small and fragile and sweet she felt under me. And all I could feel was a strong dose of *fear* warning me not to fuck her up.

She's too young.

Too kind.

Too gentle.

She wants to *give* too much of herself.

And me? I ain't good at accepting that kind of thing.

Hell, I can't even let my brother give me money that's rightfully mine from Ma's inheritance.

How am I supposed to accept this sweet as pie girl who keeps wanting to support me like she can carry all my weight on her shoulders?

I glare down at the steel struts I'm working, just a mess of dark bars and hazy sparks through my welding mask. Day job. That kind of shit.

There's always something needing to be rebuilt around Heart's Edge, especially with the fire damage from that blowout back around Halloween. I'm usually not short on work.

But thinking about that just leaves me more pissed off, a reminder of how Holt's moving in on the town construction biz, too.

I've had to see him a few too many times over the last few days.

From a distance, sure, while he's organizing the crew of locals he hired to start rebuilding the public structures that took shrapnel damage from the big kaboom.

At least he's not signing my checks.

I hired on with a crew from here in town for that.

I don't think I could stand taking money I earned from my brother.

Tell you what, though, right now is the wrong damn time for my phone to be ringing.

I shut off the blowtorch, grimacing as the bastard phone quivers against my back pocket, then set the torch down, lift my mask, and pull off my gloves.

When I see the name on the caller ID, I go cold inside—which is a feat when I'm standing in a hot-ass room over superheated metal.

It's Rich. And he'd only be calling me for one reason.

I stand, swiping the call and shoving my phone to my ear. "Update me."

"Nothing major," Rich says. "It's already over. Just a grease fire at the diner. Didn't need a full response, but I wanted to keep you in the loop, Chief."

There's something he's not saying.

It's in the unsteadiness in his voice, in the strangeness of the way he pronounces his words.

I frown, glancing over my shoulder at the construction

crew. I hadn't even noticed them going on their lunch break, sitting around the tarp-covered stacks of supplies and eating out of paper bags from the one or two lonely fast food joints in town.

Then I step away, ducking into the hall of the temporary warehouse that's been erected to protect the supplies from winter.

"Talk," I say. "What are you not telling me?"

Rich hesitates. "I...shit. I wasn't alone on the response."

"Justin?" I ask. There's not many other people it could be. With a volunteer crew, you tend to have tiers of people—your regulars, and then folks you only call in when things are too much for the main crew to handle.

Justin's one of the regulars.

I've got a sinking feeling in my gut before Rich says, "Well, Chief, he kind of bugged out."

"Describe 'bugged out.'"

"It wasn't a big fire. Like, it hadn't even jumped from one burner, but you know how grease fires are. Justin, he just stopped. Froze up, went blank, nothing there behind his eyes. And he was just staring at it instead of helping me with the extinguisher. I had to say his name like five or six times to get him to snap out of it."

I drag a hand over my face, rubbing my temples. "Aw, shit. I was afraid of something like this."

Rich sounds worried. "I don't follow."

I sigh. Damn, I feel bad talking about Justin's private crap like this, but there's no way around it now.

"You know he's carrying a lot of trauma from the Paradise fire," I say. "Seems like he's been going through a lot lately. I've been meaning to ask him about teaching a safety course at the carnival for the kids to take his mind off of it."

I just haven't gotten around to it.

Never got around to telling Rich and Justin about what Leo found, either, and that we might have an arsonist in town—one who's been laying low since the incident at the clothing shop, but I don't think they've given up yet.

Maybe that's why I've been so tense.

Or maybe it's that my daughter keeps crushing on a pyromaniac punk who's been the cause of a few too many fires of his own.

Everything's got me on edge lately.

I shouldn't have taken it out on Peace like that.

Goddammit.

I can't be thinking about her right now with Rich still silent on the line.

"Keep an eye on him. Report in if he has another incident, okay? Listen...was there anything else weird about the fire?"

"Nope. Looked like one of the younger kids in the kitchen wasn't doing the work with cleaning up the grease drippings, so they just caught." Rich sounds like he knows what I'm going to say already, though, when he asks, "Why? Something up?"

"Because." I hesitate. "That fire at Farley's Fashion. It looks like it might've been set."

I don't want to say anything about the note.

If this is Leo's past coming back to haunt us, even with everyone in town knowing about the Galentron company and their shenanigans now, I don't want it leaking and scaring people.

"Thought so," Rich says without even missing a beat. "Those blast patterns weren't right at the shop. Nothing goes up like that and creates those kinds of scorch patterns without a rapid combusting accelerant."

"Yep," I say. "Maybe it was a one-time thing. Some random asshole with a grudge or something. Leo's practically a national celebrity now. Maybe it makes some folks jealous. But let me know if you run across anything suspicious, yeah?"

"Will do, Chief." Rich pauses, then asks, "You told Langley about your suspicions?"

"Not yet. I don't want to get the sheriff worried and

bumbling around if it's nothing. I want to take another look at the scene first."

If I'm honest, I don't want to pull Langley into it at all.

This feels too personal.

The sheriff's a good man. He's just not cut out for the fuckery that's been going down here lately. Every time I see the man, I swear his hair has gone greyer.

"Listen," I add. "I gotta get back to work. But keep an eye out for me, would you?"

"Sure," Rich says. "I'll let you know if anything turns up. You want me to do a workup at the shop? Save you the trouble?"

"You're a lifesaver."

"It's what I'm here for. And besides, my three kids are less of a handful than your one. Get some sleep, Blake. You've been looking like hell lately."

"Thanks. Later," I mutter dryly, but I can't help but laugh before I hang up.

He's not wrong.

I've been feeling like hell, too.

Including my bum leg, ever since I chewed Broccoli's head off over nothing.

Worst part is, I don't even know where to start with apologizing.

Or if she'd even want to hear it.

* * *

BY THE TIME I get off work, I think I'd say anything to ease the agony ripping up my thigh.

It's like I took a hot-welded strut of steel rebar, still glowing at the tip from the blowtorch, and jammed it right into my flesh.

I barely get into the house after driving home in jerky fits and starts before my leg gives out under me, pitching me onto the sofa.

Sonofa...

I don't know how long I'm damn-near paralyzed there.

Just glad Andrea's not home right now.

As much as I love and trust my daughter, even when she's a handful, she doesn't need to see her old man stumbling around like this.

In a haze, I just keep massaging at my thigh till the dull, horrible throb of fire starts to fade.

I need a beer, not Vicodin.

I hate the fucking painkillers, hate how they haze me up, hate the potential for getting hooked. I'm so dull when that medicine kicks in.

Sure, beer gets me fuzzy, but I'm clearer and know it'll wear off in thirty minutes instead of six hours.

I *can't* be out of commission for six hours.

Not when someone might call with an emergency, and I can't let them down because I'm drugged out of my mind.

I roll over, thump myself off the couch, onto the floor, hitting my hands and knees before sheer pride shoves me to my feet.

Might feel like hell, but I ain't fucking crawling to the kitchen.

Zombie lurching isn't much better, but at least I'm standing on my two legs.

The first beer tastes like a sip of salvation. It goes down quick, cold pouring through me. The shock of drinking something that frigid so quickly actually distracts me from the anguish in my leg as chill spears shoot through my chest, leaving me gasping.

But it's exactly the liquid looseness I want when the booze gets in my bloodstream and makes my body go lax.

I'll sure as hell use that effect to my advantage till I can handle standing upright again.

Just long enough to get into a hot shower and let the heat do the work to get me loosened up enough to sleep.

Might even go down to the station tonight, I think, after I've had time to rest. I crack open a second beer, sip it more slowly, then prop my hip against the counter and pin most of my weight on my good leg.

Maybe some small part of me is hoping.

Hoping if I go in, if I put myself out there over the airwaves, Peace will call in tonight.

And maybe I can tell her over the radio what I can't say to her face.

The first thing being *I'm sorry*.

The second being *sorry as hell*.

The third being *don't know what the fuck's wrong with me when you're the prettiest thing I've ever laid eyes on*.

All tidied up for FCC regulations, of course.

That last one, I'm stuck on now, trying to get this girl off my mind. I force myself through the fog of pain and beer and into the shower. Temperature turned to scalding hot. It's awful for the first few minutes I step into the steaming, scouring spray.

After a while, though?

Pure bliss.

Water pours down my naked body, heat soaking into my thigh, the beer and the steam working through every muscle to leave me relaxed like nothing else does.

Except for Peace's touch.

Goddamn, here we go again.

The way her hands slid over me, teasing my skin, taming my hurt, it's like I can feel her in the water trickling over my flesh.

Every drip feels like a tongue licking over me, making me shiver as I close my eyes and tilt my head back into the spray.

She'd touched me like she already knows me.

Like she's just been waiting to find me.

And I can feel her little fingers on my skin, tracing my own fingertips down across my stomach, toward my throbbing, fast awakening cock.

I can't do it.

Can't let myself touch, feel, crave, *need* with this insistent hunger.

That means admitting I want her just as bad.

I want her fire, her softness, her wrapped around me and pressed up against my body and using those hands to do a hell of a lot more than therapy.

I can't get the thought out of my head.

I tell myself I'm doing it because the endorphins of jerking off will do more to ease my pain than the steaming shower.

That distracting shot of hormones, of bliss, makes me forget everything but raw, savage pleasure.

Too bad I know the real reason I'm doing it.

Because that girl's gotten under my skin. Her sassy little mouth, her dyed up hair, her hips that could blindside any fool.

I can't stop thinking about the ripeness of her lips and how they'd look, gleaming wet, as if she's here in the shower with me. I'd have her on her knees, my seething hands tangled in her hair, pushing her right the hell down on my full, throbbing, angry—

Fuck.

That does it.

My cock's up and hard and ready so quick I'm dizzy, blood draining down in a rush to make me stand up, the shaft rising with a jerk that bucks against my stomach.

One thing Holt and I have in common—the only thing—no Silverton boy ever left a chick wanting.

I groan, giving in, wrapping my hand around the base, squeezing like a vise. Makes me flushed that much faster, like I'm compressing this hunger down in my fist, squeezing it into my flesh, infusing me with this heady, groaning psycho lust.

My hand's not the one I want touching me, even if it does the job.

It's too rough, too callused.

I want softness. Delicate touches, sweetness, and fuck I bet she'd be so shy at first.

Then she'd dive in just like everything else, headfirst and reckless and completely unafraid.

But my hand's gonna have to do, stroking down over my

length. I feel the pounding of my pulse in the veins against my palms.

I shudder, thinking about what it'd be like to kiss Peace Rabe, up against the wall, thieving every moan out of her mouth like a starving beast.

Yeah, dammit.

That gets me going like nothing else, imagining the taste of her lips, wet and parted, the way they'd be all hot and soft and perfect. The little flick of her tongue.

It'd be pink—no, strawberry *red,* and she'd taste me nice and slow. Taking sips before melting against me with a singsong moan as she lets me have my way and steal inside her and kiss her deep.

I'd throw her arms around my neck, *fusing* her to me.

Her naked body against mine, those full, heavy tits slick and round and gleaming and so fucking *soft* against my ribs.

Her belly nudging against my cock between us.

And maybe if I slipped my hand down between those lush thighs, I'd find her pussy hot and slick all over my fingers as I slid two of them along her folds and felt her moan and arch.

My cock jerks against my palm, a painful little warning spurt surging from the tip.

Shit, I'd almost forgotten I was even *touching,* so caught up in this perfect frigging fantasy of Peace that it's like the sensations are real.

And it's not my hand making my cock swell, not my fingers making me gasp and catch growls in the back of my throat as pleasure rockets through me.

It's *her.*

The crush of her body, the softness of her skin, everything feminine and lush and perfect, turning my body into hellfire.

I'm lava. I'm lightning. I'm a human earthquake.

I stroke my dick faster, harder, throwing my head back and reveling in the water pounding down on my back, just another hot sensation biting my skin with desire and pleasure.

I just want to know her.

Just want to know what it's like to sink inside her with her hips wrapped around my thighs and her wet hot cunt sinking down to suck me in.

And that's when I've reached my limit.

My cock swells in my hand. I see white-hot stars.

That first long jet of warning pouring out of me is fuck-nothing compared to the money shot.

Like a storm ripping through me, surging out of me, making everything hurt in all the best ways as I come, cock jerking and spilling, overflowing in my shifting fist.

Like that one hot burst rips everything out of me and leaves me weak—my breath, my blood, my pain, my desire, all of it emptying out in searing, thick jets.

Growling, I sag against the shower wall, closing my eyes and just letting the rush bleed out of me, gasping for breath.

Fuck, that felt good.

And now I feel even guiltier.

After the way I snapped at her?

I got no damn right to have her in my thoughts if I don't make things right.

I wonder at all the things I don't know.

Do I have it in me to try for someone like her?

What do I have to offer her besides stress, an angry kid, and a whole lot of pain?

She keeps wanting to see me like Warren and Leo and Doc.

I ain't no hero.

I'm damaged goods, trying to be useful while I'm still here, while people can figure out what they can use me for.

That's why I push myself so hard on my leg.

I know I only got so long with it. One day, it might give out on me for good.

When that day comes, I won't be able to do much.

I'll end up like Ma.

In a wheelchair or something, with my poor kid looking after me.

You can't do that to Andrea, this furious voice in the back of my head whispers. *You can't turn bitter and ugly like Ma did to you, and the only thing you got left when you're stuck and lonely and helpless and hateful is fucking with people just to feel a little bit of power again.*

I used to go to physical therapy.

Years ago, I'd drive all the way to Missoula to see this quack who'd always tell me I was never gonna get better, but I could figure out how to *live*.

I didn't want to hear *never gonna get better*, so I didn't listen.

I just walked out and didn't look back, then tried to act like I wasn't hurt at all.

Maybe it's time for me to admit I need Peace's hands.

No, not to do the unspeakable shit I just imagined in the shower.

I'm starting to think I need her light, too.

I can't remember the last time I laughed the way I did when I went crashing down that dumb old hill on a sled five sizes too small for me.

I'd wound up right on top of her, pressed in close and gasping and wanting to just grind my entire body against that pixie girl trapped under me.

Ow.

I can't be thinking about her under me now. Not again.

My cock's still too sensitive, and dirty thoughts like to chase each other.

If I have another go with her dancing around naked in my head like that, might just give myself a stroke.

At least my thigh ain't feeling too bad anymore.

I reach to turn the water off—then freeze as the doorbell rings, echoing through the house.

What the hell?

Who's here this late?

Whoever it is, they get to deal with me stark fucking buff.

I'll put a towel on. Fine.

But I ain't hurting myself wrestling into jeans when I just got the pain to subside.

I grab a towel off the rack and drag it around my hips, knotting it on one side, then limp out of the shower. My leg still can't handle my full weight, but it holds up all right as I stagger to the door and yank it open, growling *"What?"* before I even see who it is.

Only to find myself looking into glacial green eyes, blinking up at me, a little too wide. Peace's cheeks are almost as red as her hair as she stares.

She's got her big folding table balanced under her arm.

And a bag slung over her shoulder, standing there like she means business.

I blink at her.

She blinks back at me.

"What're you doing here?" I blurt, wondering for a second if she's even real.

Not the first words I wanted coming out of my mouth when I spoke to her again.

Ain't I smooth?

Peace cocks her head, eyes flashing for a moment before her mouth sets. "You have an appointment."

"Huh?" I scratch the back of my head. "We didn't schedule nothing."

And I'm pretty sure last time we talked was a pretty clear "fuck off," not that I meant it but...well, damn.

And well *damn* again as she gives me an up-and-down look before marching right past me, her thick coat brushing against my naked, still too-sensitive skin, making my stomach jump *hard* as she struts her way into my house like she belongs here.

Girl's got stones. Lady stones. I'll give her that.

And she's flexing them at me right now. She nudges my coffee table aside with her calf and then snaps her folding table open, plunking it down with a decisive *thump*.

"Since you're already kind enough to be dressed down for the occasion," she says, stripping those ridiculous purple gloves off and lifting her chin, "you can just set yourself right down on the table. And don't even try to hide your limp. You're only standing on one leg right now."

She's got me.

And after I got my head all turned around and confused, I'm a little too flustered to deal with this hurricane standing here, staring at me like she'll fight if I argue.

You know what?

I think she just *might*.

And I'm not gonna risk getting knocked out by someone I could pick up with one hand and palm like a basketball in my bewildered state.

* * *

THAT'S how I find myself on her table five minutes later, lying on my back, adjusting my towel.

Trying real frigging hard not to think about the fact that I just got off to this woman.

At least it means I got maybe ten minutes or so before I have to worry about embarrassing myself under her hands.

She busies herself setting her bag down on the coffee table, then shrugs out of her coat and drapes it over the couch. She glances around the living room, taking my place in.

Whatever, I ain't worried about her judging my house. I keep it tidy to set an example for Andrea.

But there's still something about having this woman up in my life that makes me feel a little too naked, y'know?

I keep it to myself, though.

She drifts closer to the big glass aquarium against the wall. Inside, under the heat lamp that keeps him alive during winter, Mr. Hissyfit coils in miles and miles of pale ivory and yellow scales, lazy on the branches Andrea had meticulously arranged inside.

Peace makes an appreciative sound, whistling under her breath. "Whoa. That's one big snake."

"That's what she said," I say, before I can stop myself—and she laughs, her eyes brightening as she glances over her shoulder at me.

"Yeah? You got a lot of *shes* saying that to you?" Her smile is coy, teasing, and I'm amazed she's not holding a grudge for what a Hissyfit-sized dick I was the other night. "All those ladies calling in to see if they can tap into your heart line?"

I roll my eyes. "Listen, don't you start with that too. My fucking brother told my daughter about all the girls I dated in high school not too long ago, and now you're acting like I'm some kinda player?"

She turns to face me, sauntering playfully with a little skip of one step, lacing her hands together behind her back.

Tonight she's wearing a filmy, almost fluffy off-the-shoulder top in some kind of lilac fabric. The material floats around her with her every step.

Instead of hiding her body, it just teases.

The shirt wafts against the curve of her waist, the swell of her chest, their curves pushing up against that plunging neckline I could *bite.*

I grit my teeth, trying to ignore the way it lifts over a thin strip of her stomach, above jeans so low they're damn near obscene.

There's a certain thing that happens when a lady's got this mix of softness and tone, where her belly swells out with a little plumpness. All perfect and lush to the touch, but she's got muscle under it, too.

The creases where her belly blends into her thighs get real deep.

Real high, too, almost to her hips.

Peace has got it going on in droves.

Holy Hades, do I want to nibble my way along those little lines of flesh bared with her every movement.

"So," she asks sweetly, tilting her head, her hair falling against her bared shoulders in a wash of twilight and flame. "*Are* you a player, Blake Silver Tongue? Do you ever use that tongue for more than sweet-talking?"

"*Goddammit*, Broccoli!" I sputter, damned if I ain't blushing at the things this little monster's suggesting without an ounce of shame.

Especially when I still got the thought of her wrapped around me on my mind, and now I'm wondering what she tastes like.

Spent or not, my cock stirs again, painful and throbbing.

Peace just laughs, covering her mouth with one hand.

"You're so easy," she says, hounding me to kiss the insolence right out of her. "Now relax. If you're tensed up, this won't really do any good."

Relax.

Right.

When she just asked me if I use my tongue for something other than pretty words, and there's no missing what she means.

I want to use my tongue on you, I want to say.

I don't dare.

Still too many things left unsaid, unresolved.

Don't even know how to broach that apology now. Not when she's acting like my bad attitude never ever happened.

Okay.

Shit.

Relax.

I can do that.

Yeah.

I close my eyes, trying to chase out all the dirty thoughts with pitchforks.

Doesn't help when I hear a bottle cap pop and catch that musky scent of the oil she used on me last time.

My body's instantly alert, aware.

Remembering how it felt to have her touching me.

Relax.

"Hey," she says softly. "Are you hurting today? You're so stiff."

I'm in pain, all right.

But my thigh isn't the appendage giving me the most trouble right now.

"I'm fine," I say, gazing into those pretty green eyes looking down at me with clear worry, sweet and soft, while she warms the oil in her hands by rubbing them together. "Just spent a lot of time standing at work today."

She tilts her head. "You had a lot of fires to put out today?"

I can't help a small laugh. "I ain't a full-time fire chief. We don't have those salaries around here. I do welding work when I can, just to pick up the slack. I'm mostly set with my military pension and the skimpy pay from the town for fighting flames, but I can't *not* work."

"Sounds more like the type who can't stand to be idle."

She smirks and reaches for me—but I guess she remembers how I snarled at her the first time.

Instead of resting her hands on my chest like she'd started, she goes straight for my thigh.

I must be losing my mind, feeling sad to lose the feeling of those soft hands against my skin.

I did this to myself, being a defensive dick all the time.

Her brows knit as she smooths her hands over my thigh. I hiss as the muscle instantly jumps, locking as hard as a cramp, pain flaring.

"It's bad right now," she says softly, just resting her hands against the knot, trying to soak the pain into her warm, oil-smoothed palms, her gaze locked intently on my leg. "Worse than it was before. Blake...you've been stressing, haven't you?"

"You could say that," I grit out through my teeth.

Fuck, that hurts.

But I almost welcome the pain. It's keeping my cock under control.

No way that thin towel's gonna hide how I react to her.

Peace bites her lip, shaking her head. "You can't keep doing this. What will Heart's Edge do without its fire chief if you permanently disable yourself?"

I exhale, staring up at the ceiling. "It's gonna happen anyway. The physical therapists told me I can't stop it. Just delay the inevitable. Sooner or later, my leg's gonna snarl up for good. Might be able to get around with a brace, might not."

"I don't believe it." Slowly, she starts working again, using just the tips of her fingers now, prodding at the scar like she's trying to soften a hard-packed knot of dough.

Her voice drops to a soothing, intimate murmur, and yeah, I can hear the music in it, now.

I hear how she might sing, even though she's never let me listen yet.

"What makes you so sure?" I wonder.

"Injuries like this, they can be managed. You'll never be a hundred percent cured, but you can always get yourself back to a workable state as long as you start taking care of yourself and *don't stop.*" Her gaze flicks to me, and once again I'm struck by how she seems older than her years. "That's what most people don't get. They think it's a short-term thing, and one day they can quit, but they never can."

"Sounds like a prison sentence." I smile faintly. "But I guess I'd deserve one since I'm guilty of giving up."

"No. You don't seem like the type to give up for good," she says. "More like you just got tired and took a break."

I snort, wishing I could have her faith in me.

I'm clueless what to say, so I don't say anything.

Just let her do her thing.

I close my eyes while those soft hands take my pain and tease it out of me like she's a snake charmer and she's got every last bit of me coiled around her mystic fingertips.

Somewhere in the silence, it happens.

I slip away into memories.

Another time, another place, when I couldn't do a single damn thing to stop the worst from happening.

Couldn't stop the hurt that'd turn my little girl into the living fury she is now, the reason why all her pain is every bit as justified as my own.

* * *

Four Years Ago

I DON'T KNOW why we're planning a family vacation.

No, not true, I do know why.

Dammit, I know, and the reason is upstairs packing her bags in a whirlwind, excited about getting to camp out in Glacier National Park for the next two weeks.

We're trying for Andrea, not for us.

I'm not sure there's even an "us" left, when Abby and I haven't been seeing eye to eye for a good, long while.

It wasn't just Ma, always sticking her nose in everything early on and trying to tell me how bad Abigail was for me.

It wasn't just that my stubborn ass didn't want Ma to be right, when catching her getting up close and personal with my fuck-shit traitor of a brother not so long ago all but proves Ma *is* right.

Christ, we can't even afford this stupid trip. Abby spent every last bit of money I brought home, every last bit of her own check, all on this online shopping stuff. Pure impulse spending.

Next thing I know, Andrea's fully funded college account is half empty but there are two shiny cars in the garage, one sitting there waiting until she's old enough to drive it to a university she now can't afford to attend.

Maybe we could've found a way to work through that.

Through the fights, the way she'd dismiss how I felt about everything, telling me to man up and stop bothering her when she had shit to do.

But there was no working through the day I came home to Holt in our house, his arms around my wife, and Abby looking up at him with her lips parted and red, breathless, her lashes fluttering.

We hadn't even drawn up the fucking divorce papers yet.

Still looking at stuff like legal separation, maybe a trial thing.

And she couldn't even wait to move on.

With my own fucking *brother*.

That's all I see now, every time I look at her.

That lost, dazed, starry-eyed way she was looking at Holt.

Used to be how she looked at *me*.

But I don't quit.

If anything, we can stick it out a little while longer for our kid, and at least figure out how to do this separation without any collateral damage.

Even if everything went sour with me and Abby too quick...

One thing I know, whatever else she is, she loves Andrea just as much as I do.

So I'm loading up the car. I'm packing up all the camping supplies we shouldn't have spent money on because we're going to use them once and never again. It takes two to try, and we're way past trying, not even for the love of our daughter.

I'm trying not to break something with how hard I'm slinging things into the back of the trunk.

And I'm bolting upright, nearly banging my head on the frame of the car. That's when a high, tinny scream comes shrilling from inside the house.

Andrea.

I'd know the sound of my daughter in serious distress anywhere.

Before I can even blink, I'm rocketing into the house, slamming my way inside hard enough to make the front door bounce on its hinges. *"Andrea? Andrea!"*

She's there. Standing in the open-plan living room and kitchen, next to the kitchen island.

Just staring.

Stone-still, trembling, little hand shaking in front of her face, staring at something I can't see, her face white as a sheet.

Whatever it is, it's on the floor, and my stomach sinks with dread as she lets out a shaky whisper. "M-mom...?"

I feel like I'm walking through a nightmare, crossing the room numbly.

I don't want to see it.

What I fear is already there.

But it's too late. I can't avoid it.

I stare down at my wife's dead, empty face, her skin already rigid, her eyes milky and pale and completely devoid of everything that once made her the woman I loved and hated.

* * *

Present

I SNAP BACK into my own skin with a sharp gasp, sucking in a breath that makes my entire body heave.

Shit.

It's like waking up from a bad dream by being plunged into a frigid ocean, and I sit up sharply, ignoring the twinge in my leg.

Peace jerks back from me, stumbling, looking at me with wide eyes. "Blake?"

I stare at her.

It's...

Right.

I'm not there, not *then*.

My pounding, frantic heart doesn't quite seem to believe it, but I gotta remember.

That's in the past. This is the present.

Pressing a hand over my chest, I suck in several shuddering breaths, telling myself to calm the fuck down.

"Sorry," I manage. "Guess I fell half asleep or something. I just...*fuck*, I remembered some shit I didn't want to."

Her expression clears, soft with sympathy, understanding. "That's normal when you start relaxing under treatment," she soothes. "It can almost put you in a trance state. Releasing physical pain often opens up emotional scars. It helps a lot to just let it happen and work through it."

"Don't want to *work through it*," I bite off.

I can't take this.

This shitty feeling bottoming out my gut, this thing I never actually looked at before to recognize it for what it honestly is.

Guilt.

All these years I've been carrying a boulder of *guilt* for not saving my wife from a freak aneurysm I had no control over.

Like if I'd been a better man somehow, not only would our marriage not have fallen apart, but she wouldn't have died.

Wouldn't have left Andrea behind.

Crazy thoughts, I know.

No good reason it's my fault.

I just know that dark knot of hurt inside me swears it *is*. I can't take that shit right now when I'm still all tangled up with present-day guilt over being a mindless jerkwad animal to Peace, too.

Now, I'm doing it again.

Lashing out like a trapped beast who doesn't trust the person trying to clean the blood from its flesh, biting the hand that ought to soothe it.

I don't fucking know how to stop.

So the best thing is for her to get away from me, before I hurt her even more and have to see that crestfallen expression on her face again.

Same expression that's there right now, darkening her pretty eyes as she says, "Blake, you've got to stop fighting your fears."

"Don't need a therapist," I throw back, sliding off the table, dropping myself down on my good leg when I don't want to test the bad one right now.

As mad as I am, as fucked up in the head over this girl who tugs me every which way, it might just stress collapse on me.

"This session's over. No more appointments. I'm grateful, lady, but don't try this again. Just go home, Peace. There's nothing you can do to help me."

"No," she says softly, but with a firmness that says she knows she's right. "There's nothing I can do to help someone who doesn't *want* to be helped."

My jaw tightens.

I can't.

So I just listen to her packing up her things, turning my back on her—

And freezing as I see Andrea standing in the door, the cold swirl of night at her back, looking at me with the closest I've ever seen to contempt on my daughter's face.

"Wow," she says. "And I thought Mom dying fucked *me* up." Her voice bleeds with disappointment, with hurt, and shit if that doesn't cut me *deep*, knowing my baby girl looks at me and sees someone she can't believe in. "You can't even be nice to someone who's just trying to help you?"

"Andrea..."

"Don't *Andrea* me."

Don't know when my daughter grew up.

But she sounds more adult than I'm capable of being right now as she cuts me off with her quiet, withering words. She sweeps me over with a look that says I've let her down.

Then, shaking her head, she holds her hand out to Peace.

"Come on. I'll help you load your things in the car," she says, and even if I'm hurting, I'm so proud of the softness in Andrea's voice, the gentleness and sympathy she's showing Peace.

I don't even care that Andrea's taking Peace's side when she's *right*.

"Thanks," Peace says with a wistful smile, her head bowed.

And they leave me standing there in the middle of the living room, nearly naked in all but the heart I guard too well.

They walk out of the house and leave me alone to my bullshit.

* * *

THIS TIME, I can't skimp on the apology.

After Andrea and Peace left, I sat down in my bedroom for a long time, just thinking. Getting myself together, trying to work through these messy feelings that still make no sense.

The autopsy report said Abby's aneurysm was congenital.

She'd been born prone to high blood pressure and clotting, a lethal cocktail just asking for anything from varicose veins to deep vein thrombosis to clogged arteries to brain clots.

She hit the jackpot on the latter.

Wasn't anything but shit luck in life and maybe her folks gifting her a few genetic time bombs.

It probably would've happened sooner or later.

I stare at my clenched fists, listening to the sounds of Andrea coming home and shutting herself in her room with a slamming door.

Why am I doing this?

Why do I feel like I gotta save everyone, even people who can't be saved at all?

You ask a shrink, and they'd say I'm some kinda egomaniac. Savior complex. Gotta be everyone's hero but my own.

I don't think it's that, though.

I'm scared of losing more folks, so I feel like if I just try hard enough, then I won't anymore. Even though it doesn't work that way.

I still remember folks I fought with in Afghanistan. The people who died when that bomb went off and shredded my leg —people who were like my brothers and sisters.

Jenna Ford, too.

Warren's sister.

We grew up together, her always with War, inseparable twins. Everyone loved the shit out of Jenna like she was their sister, daughter, or the love of their life.

And I lost her because she saw the wrong things and a monster arranged an 'accident' to shut her up.

Lost my old man, too. Dead of a heart attack.

Lost Abby, slipping through my fingers when she was just feet away from me, going cold on the floor, me having no damn clue.

And then Ma.

Dying with Holt, and me not even there to see her go.

I get what Peace meant about not seeing her dad die so it's like his body wasn't real. He didn't really die.

That's how it is with Ma.

For all the weird conflicted feels I got with her, the love and hate and fear and frustration and resentment, there's still this weird void that can't think of her as dead.

I gotta let go.

But first I have to go apologize to Peace.

She was right. Brutally so.

And I gotta stop carrying around this poison, using it as a club to drive people away.

* * *

WHEN I HEAD on up to the Charming Inn, though, Peace's cabin is dark, and her little purple bug of a rental car is nowhere to be found.

Aw, hell.

Heart's Edge ain't exactly a jumping hot spot, so there can't be many places to find her.

Reluctantly, though, I go to the main house. I know there'll be questions. I know I'm gonna get grilled, when I feel like I'm the last eligible single man in Heart's Edge and everybody just *stares* whenever a girl comes anywhere near me.

Especially my friends.

Haley's a new transplant to Heart's Edge herself, ending up here after her car crapped out and she tumbled into Warren's lap.

She's become my friend, too, on top of being the wife of one of my lifelong buddies.

And she only has to take one good look at my face to know something ain't right.

I'm standing there in her living room, trying to figure out how to ask if she knows where that flower child has gotten off to, without being obvious.

Haley clucks her tongue in sympathy.

"That's one long face," she says, propping her laundry basket on her hip, a gurgling little boy inside it and reaching up to tug at her hair. "Funny thing is, I've been seeing a lot of that expression around here lately."

I wince.

If it's Peace she means, I know damn well it's my fault.

Taking a breath, I scrub my gloved palms against my jeans like that can soak the sweat into my gloves, and ask, "You uh...you seen her around?"

I don't even have to name *her.*

Hay just smiles sadly. "She left with Ember about an hour ago. I think they're at The Nest; she had a guitar with her."

A guitar?

Okay.

I feel a little creepy following her to Felicity's coffee shop, but I'll keep it simple.

Get in, say I'm sorry, and bug out.

Maybe it'll be easier in public, where she doesn't have to worry I'm gonna say something mean again and hurt her feelings when we're alone.

Goddamn, I really *am* an asshole.

I don't know when I got like this. Just know this isn't who I want to be.

It's not who I was when I was married to Abby.

It's not the example I want to set for Andrea.

And it's not how I want to treat Peace, when she deserves so much better.

I offer Haley a faint smile and flick her a quick salute.

"Thanks," I tell her. "Guess I'm suddenly in need of a little caffeine."

I turn away, but a soft "Hey," drifts toward my back.

I glance over my shoulder, raising a brow, but Haley just smiles.

"Good luck, Blake," she says.

I'm gonna need it.

I give her a lopsided grin and go.

* * *

IT'S ALREADY LATE, and The Nest is closing soon, but I've got time to catch Peace.

When I get to the café, though, I almost think it's shut down already. The lights inside are dim, just barely shining in a golden haze through the tall floor-to-ceiling windows.

But no, it's not closed, there are cars parked outside and people in there, seated in intimate little clusters.

So why is it so dark?

I get my answer when I step inside. The lights have been dimmed to shine a spotlight on the far end of the café.

Peace and Ember sit on stools. Peace with a weathered,

honey-toned guitar shining with the love of many hands, and Ember with her violin propped up on her shoulder.

And Peace starts singing so quietly, with all her heart in it, her voice winding in pure sweetness around the twanging notes from the instruments.

The entire room's silent, watching raptly.

Hell, so am I.

Completely spellbound.

I hardly see Ember, Doc's wife.

I've only got eyes for Peace, the way she sings like she's mourning and exulting, a whisper for the dead and a prayer for the living.

That's all I can hear, listening to her.

All that raw emotion overflowing till the words don't even matter.

She's singing her whole heart out, pain written on her expressive, lovely face in lines of sweetness.

And it's the most beautiful shit I've ever heard.

I shouldn't be here, eavesdropping on this.

Feels like I'm too dirty for something this sanctified, this beautiful, and maybe I'll ruin it if I stay.

I'm too broken for her.

Too much of a mess.

She can keep working at me with her hands all she wants, but she'll never shape me back into anything whole. That's not her responsibility.

It's not anybody's but my own, and I can't bring myself to ask her to wait for me to fucking try.

I gotta leave.

Only, I'm rooted to the spot, captivated by her, and I can't bring myself to walk away just yet.

I'm too conspicuous, though. Without ever taking my gaze off her, I drift over to the long coffee bar, letting the curve of it take me out of their direct line of sight.

But I can still see her, the spots shining down overhead, making her shimmer.

Why?

Why am I staying when it feels like she's plucking away inside me with every strum of the guitar strings, quivering me up with bittersweet pain?

No.

I've got to escape before she sees me and gets *that look* on her sweet face again.

I start turning away and get a serious déjà vu trip.

"Hey," another soft voice says.

Last time it was Haley.

This time, it's Felicity Randall, Ember's cousin and the owner of The Nest, slim and pretty and tired-looking in her apron. She wipes a rag down the counter, watching me with a sympathetic smile.

"You look like a desperate man," she murmurs, "who sees the thing he wants most, but it's just out of his reach."

I swallow, my throat tight. "Honestly, that ain't too far off base, Fliss."

"Makes me wonder why you're hiding over here. Almost like you don't want to be seen." Her smile turns wry. I only half hear her voice, still so lost in the mournfully gentle music; still so lost in Peace. "But I won't ask. You look dog-tired, Blake. How about a coffee for the drive home? On the house."

I finally tear my eyes from Peace, glancing at Felicity. "I look so rough *you're* handing out freebies?"

"You look that heartbroken," she answers with a laugh, something dark and haunted flickering in her eyes. "And I'm the coffee girl, so that's all I've got for comfort."

I try a smile, but I can't seem to get my mouth to move quite right. "Thanks, lady. I'd like that a lot."

She only lingers on me for a minute with that same sad smile, then slips away to snag a cup. A minute later, I've got a steaming cup of her best dark brew with a dab of sugar, just the way I like it.

It's bracing. Helps to clear my head, reminding me I need to make a choice.

And that choice is to leave and not thrust myself up in Peace's life when I'm just no good for her.

I'm no good for anyone.

Heading for the door, still trying not to be obtrusive about it, trying not to draw her eye, I push it open. Right into a group of kids who are just heading in as I'm leaving.

There's a brief, awkward tussle for the door, before I step out of the way to let them pass.

I'm almost worried Andrea's not with them when I recognize her friends, but she had a lot of homework tonight.

And I'm *glad* Andrea's not with them when I see that little bastard pyro, Clark Patten.

The boy catches my eye just as I catch his, lifting his pierced upper lip in a sneer.

Then he promptly flips me off with both middle fingers, before laughing and shoving away with his friends.

Little shit.

I don't like that kid.

No, I'm not so fucked up I'm gonna start a fight with a seventeen-year-old, when I know that's just how kids are and he's probably still mad at me for breaking things up at the carnival. I shoot him a dead-eyed glare instead. He smiles, then whips his head away, catching up with his friends.

That boy ain't right.

I've got to figure out how to keep Andrea the hell away from him.

Almost as much as I've gotta sort this shit with Broccoli Girl some night when I won't stomp all over her angel wings.

IX: PLAY IT AGAIN (PEACE)

I hadn't expected to draw such a crowd.

Good thing I don't get stage fright.

It's been a long time since I had a chance to sing in front of anyone else, or with anyone else at my side.

But it's been nice to lose myself—in the vibrations of guitar strings against my fingers, in the work it takes to find point and counterpoint and harmony with someone else. And in making a new friend, September, the cool lady who loves music and animals as much as I do. Haley introduced us.

I've needed the distraction.

I've needed to keep Blake off my mind.

With him, I just *can't* anymore.

Can't make him see what he doesn't want to see. Can't make him let go of his pain and try to find a new path forward when he doesn't want to.

All I can do is offer him my hand along the way.

And he made it pretty clear tonight he doesn't want it.

I'm not the type to cry over men.

Instead I sing, pouring all my feelings into the notes.

It's an old song Dad taught me, one I never knew the name for.

It's about birds in the sky and how they only come down when they're tired—so as long as you've got the heart, just fly, because the ground's only for people who've given up.

Just fly, I sing, while Ember follows me with her violin like she's known this song her whole life. It's amazing how fast she picks it up off a few strummed bars, trying them out in soft, keening notes of her own.

Just fly.

By the time the song ends, the whole café goes quiet.

Gentle, enthusiastic applause rises, breaking my trance. I lift my head, blinking.

Oh.

They're clapping for *us*, aren't they?

I smile sheepishly, glancing at Ember. "Well, I think we got everyone's attention."

"Oops," she says with a dazzling smile, blue eyes bright, a few wisps of her blonde hair slipping out of its bun to stick to her face, a faint mist of sweat on her skin.

I'm just as damp; playing is weirdly hard work.

It also leaves you *lit*.

Just buzzing with all this energy, even if it's secret and wordless.

Ember stands, lowering her violin and turning to pick up the case. Around us, the patrons of The Nest slowly start to slip back into their own hushed conversations.

"We should do that again," she says. "You're only in Heart's Edge for the winter, right? I'd hate to miss out on the chance to play with you some more."

"We'll figure something out," I answer, shouldering my guitar and slinging it to my back by its strap.

I don't really have a reason to stay past winter, do I?

That thought shouldn't make me as sad as it does.

Ember watches me as she puts her violin away with quiet reverence. "You know, I think you just missed Blake."

"Wh-what?" I jerk my head up sharply, staring at her.

How could she tell?

How could she tell so easily that I'm already missing Blake Silverton?

"He was just here," she says, and I suck in a breath. Oh. *Ohhh.*

That's what she'd meant.

"He was just kind of standing there, watching," she continues. "Then he got a coffee and left."

I frown. Why is she telling me this?

We barely know each other. Even I can't be *that* obvious.

I smile weakly. "I guess he was just...you know, late night or something."

"He could've made coffee at home. Speaking of which," she tosses her head with an impish smile. "C'mon. When you're related to the owner, you get free lattes."

I trail Ember over to the counter, trying to ignore the pinched feeling in my stomach.

Had Blake come in and left because of me?

Had he...oh God, had he heard me singing?

I keep my mouth shut as I slide onto a stool next to Ember. Her cousin—I recognize her as Felicity, the one who called into the radio show, talking about her nightmares—slides over with a grin.

"Y'all are welcome to do that any time," she says, her eyes merry as she tucks her brown hair back. "With how hard it is to keep business running, you could draw a crowd every night."

"I think Gray would lose his mind if I left him alone with the baby every night," Ember says with a laughing wink, tucking her loose hair back behind her ear. "He loves Auggie to death, but he gets so helpless dad sometimes. The man freaks out like she's made of crystal and he'll break her if he sneezes too hard."

"*Him?* Mr. Tall, Dark, and Icy?" Felicity laughs. "I'll believe it when I see the video."

Suddenly, though, her attention's on me—snapping to my eyes with an abruptness that makes me recoil.

She studies me. "You're quiet. Need a little caffeine to lift you up? Anything you want, on the house."

"Decaf," I say with a sheepish laugh. "Or else I'll never sleep tonight. Too wired. But maybe a decaf cappuccino?"

"Sure thing," she says. "Not planning to stay up to listen for the radio show tonight, then?"

Oh.

Oh, *damn it*.

The way she's watching me leaves no room for doubt.

She knows, doesn't she?

Everyone knows.

That's why Ember mentioned Blake being here.

That's why Felicity's watching me like a hawk with a knowing little smile.

Ugh. I guess in towns like this, everyone knows everyone's business. And they like that business a lot when it means *drama.*

It hits me then.

Of course they know. Everyone and their dog heard me being flirty with Blake on the radio.

I wince, rubbing the back of my neck. "I mean, I could..."

But I'm not calling in again.

No way.

Not even to hear Blake's voice go gentle the way I want so bad, when he's open and sweet and soft instead of this closed off, hyper-defensive beast. Fighting to protect himself as much as he's trying to protect Andrea from more sorrow.

"You know, I think I'll try a full-caf cappuccino after all," I venture, then quickly correct, "No. Half-caf. I have a nine a.m. tomorrow with rich folks who tip really well. I *have* to sleep at some point tonight."

"Half-caf it is," Felicity says, turning away with a sly look. "Blake got his coffee black with a pinch of sugar, you know. I have a feeling he'll be up pretty late himself."

Groan.

Oh my God.

I'm so obvious people are *trying* to play cupid.

But what good does it do if he doesn't want to be my match?

* * *

I shouldn't be awake.

Too bad.

It's after eleven, and I'm curled up in my pajamas—or at least what I call pajamas, an old ripped tie-dye t-shirt that's barely holding together by a thread and a pair of lace boyshort panties.

The heat in the cabin is so good I don't need anything else to stay warm besides a cup of calming tea. It tells my heart rate to normalize after the caffeine hit that was definitely a bad idea.

Sure.

The caffeine.

That's why I'm a jittery mess.

Not because I'm listening to classic rock tracks, waiting to see if Blake's coming on the air tonight.

Rod Stewart's fading off the air when I hear that faint click that says they've gone live.

My breath sticks in my lungs.

I'm such a mess, I swear.

And I wish so much the gentle thunder of Blake's voice was for me as he starts up. "You're tuned in to the heart of Heart's Edge, and our lines are open. Do we have any callers tonight?"

"We've got one," his sidekick, Mario, says. "She just says her name is E."

"Okay, E," Blake rumbles. It's so soothing listening to his rough velvet voice, so compelling, this hypnotic lyricism that just makes me close my eyes and *bask*. "I'm listening."

I nearly jump out of my skin when I hear the voice that comes over the line.

"Hey," Ember says, sounding just a little too innocent and cheerful. "I don't think you're going to get many callers tonight. Just a lot of listeners."

NO DAMAGED GOODS

Blake pauses and chuckles. "Oh? Why's that?"

"Because we're waiting," Ember says brightly. "And really hoping you don't screw this up."

"Screw *what* up, exactly?" Blake's voice sharpens.

"You know," Ember tells him softly. "We *all* know. I don't need advice, you know. I just called in to give *you* a little advice for a change."

"I ain't amused. Did Doc put you up to this? 'Cause if he did, I'll—" Blake snarls, and I giggle, hiding it behind my palm as if he can hear me.

This is absolutely mortifying.

And too adorable.

I can just *picture* him sitting there glaring daggers at the mic.

"Nope, this is my baby. But you should laugh more," Ember says.

"Laugh more? That the advice you've been keeping me waiting for?"

"No," Ember replies, her voice softening, the laughter fading to leave a sort of sweet fondness. "It's okay to be nice to people, Blake. It's okay to trust strangers sometimes...they're not all Galentron agents. Some people just want to take away your pain...and the rest of us just want to see you happy."

My breath catches, my chest aching.

God. I press my hand to my breastbone, trying to control my pulse again.

Blake's silent.

I almost think he's left in a huff until he says, "Well, thanks for that, lady. Sometimes, it helps when the boot's on the other foot and I'm the dude getting some wisdom."

"I know," Ember says. "But I'm going to go now and stop tying up the line. Good luck, Blake. You *know* what this is about."

There's another sandpapery sound from Blake, then the click as the line goes quiet, leaving just the sound of empty air with a hint of breathing.

"Well, uh..." Mario drawls out slowly. "Not sure what to make of that, boss."

"Maybe," Blake says slowly, thoughtfully. "If no one else is gonna call in, we wait for Broccoli? You out there, girl? I got some things to say."

My heart stops.

I just stare at the radio like it's Blake himself, not even breathing, my chest tight and my hands clenched into little fists until my nails bite into my palms.

Um, what is happening?

Right here?

On the open freaking air?

Not even pretending like he's talking to anyone but me.

And my heart remembers to beat again in velvety shivers as he croons in a husky tone, "C'mon. Don't keep a guy waiting. Everybody's listening."

I'm about to die.

And on my autopsy, cause of death will say *this man*.

I fumble for my phone. I can barely tap the numbers, but after an awkward minute, I manage.

"While we're waiting, let's talk Fuchsia Delaney, the best frenemy Heart's Edge ever had. Still can't figure out if she came to save this town or curse it." Blake says. "Nobody's seen that witchy woman since the night of the big museum fire. Nothing confirmed. But word on the street is, she's been seen skulking around everywhere from behind Brody's to way out in Spokane. What do *I* think? I ain't gonna trust her as far as I can throw her. But she *did* help dispatch the air support that helped my crew put out the big fire that crazy Halloween night. Don't know if this town's just looking for a new legend after Nine turned out to be our harmless buddy Leo, or what, but if she meant to come back and do any of us harm—"

"New caller, Blake. Line one," Mario says.

I clutch my phone in both hands, breathing in tiny rushes as the phone finally rings.

"Finally. You've got Blake." He picks up, voice all wildfire in my ear.

"Hi," I say, my voice tiny. "It's me."

Only for that screeching feedback loop to start again, howling out of the radio and my phone.

I yelp, jerking my phone away with a wince, and dive for the radio to turn it down.

Blake's already laughing.

Low and rolling and thunderously sweet, Blake's laughing just for me.

"You did it again," he says.

I smile, curling up against the headboard and hugging my knees against my chest.

"Sorry."

"It's all right. I'm glad you were listening and picked up that phone."

I'm vibrating inside, electric all over. I bite my lip. "Yeah? You...you said you wanted to say something?"

"I do," he murmurs.

God, even when he's murmuring it's like the roar of a mighty river.

I bite my lips, just *knowing* there must be a couple hundred people or more tuned in for this. But it feels like it's only us condensed down in our own little world.

Like *he's* here for me and nobody else.

I close my eyes to soak him in and let his voice roll over me.

"I'm listening," I whisper.

It's still several long seconds before he speaks again. Before he takes a slow, audible breath, shaky enough to tell me he's nervous.

Oh, God.

This tall, strong, powerful man is *nervous*...

...because of me.

And I realize why when he says, in no uncertain terms, "Listen, Peace, I'm sorry. And now I'm gonna be real straight..."

I suck in a breath. I don't know what to say—not at all.

And he's not done.

"You scare me, woman," he says. It's raw, quiet, sweet. "You make me freak because I've been hurtin' for so long I've forgot what it's like *not* to be in pain, and I got so used to it being that way I told myself it couldn't be different. But you...you just keep showing me that maybe it *can*. Maybe I'm wrong. And that scares me because it means accepting I've been the only idiot hurting myself all this time, and now I've got to make a choice: let go, or keep on sufferin'."

"Blake..." I whisper, but his voice keeps coming.

"Some guys, when they get freaked, they turn tail and run. But some men, when they get scared..." He sighs heavily. "They lash out first. And I ain't proud of being one of those dudes. Ain't proud of giving you cruel words while you tried to help with my pain, and I just held on like a stubborn ass and didn't want to let it go. Wasn't right. I'm sure as heck not gonna do it again. That's my little spiel about how it is with hurting for the good folks of Heart's Edge...and for you. And just for you, Peace, I want you to know again, I'm sorry."

If I could breathe, I might be crying.

I hadn't realized I needed this so much.

Blake, torn open and bared, heart in hand.

Blake, *caring* that he hurt me.

To care, and to actually apologize like a man, and mean it.

Right here tonight in front of the whole town.

I take a hitched breath, smiling fit to crack. "So you had to tell me that live on the air, huh?"

"Yeah, well. You know." He laughs faintly. "We were low on callers tonight. Figured it was either give folks some fireworks to keep 'em happy or else blabber away all night about more Fuchsia conspiracies."

I burst out a startled laugh. "Dick-butt. Uh, can I say that on air?"

"Yeah. And I kinda am." His voice softens. "But I really am sorry, lady."

"I know," I whisper. "And I know you were acting out of fear. It's okay. I'm not mad at you. I'm just glad you're ready to try to let go of old hurts. It won't be easy, but I know you can do it, Blake."

"You've got that much faith in me, huh?"

"I do." I'm hugging the phone like it's his hand, holding it so close to me, scrunched up with my eyes so tightly closed until it's just me and him in the darkness. "You heard me singing tonight, didn't you?"

"Sure did." It comes out of him raw, gritty with something I'd swear was appreciation, and I flush. "Your voice is something else, songbird. Prettiest thing I've heard in a good, long while."

"It's a song my dad taught me. I don't know the name, just the sound and the words." I swallow hard, my throat so tight. "It's this song about birds, and how they're made to fly. They're not made for the earth, just for the sky. The only time a bird comes down is when its wings can't hold it up anymore. So hey, maybe you and me, broken people like us...maybe we were meant to soar."

I'd slipped into the lyrics without meaning to.

It's such a sweet song, embedded forever in my heart.

And it feels like it could belong to his heart, too, if he'd just let it.

Maybe I could belong too, if he'd just let me.

"I didn't get to hear all of it," he admits. "But I'd love to hear it now. Will you sing it for me again?"

I make a soft sound in the back of my throat. "Right here? Live?"

"If it's okay." I can hear the smile in his voice. "Maybe you could sing this old town off to sweet dreams, Peace Rabe. Send them off real lovely. Send *me* off."

"O-oh."

Oh, wow.

I'm glad we're not face-to-face right now.

Because if he'd said those things to me with those dusk-blue eyes cutting through me, I'd never be able to make a single sound again. I'd be too lost in him.

"I'll try," I whisper, but I can't quite get a sound out just yet. My throat's too tight with emotion, too tight to draw the breath needed to actually produce a clear note.

But after a few calming breaths, I hold the phone closer, as if I'm kissing it, and let loose.

I sing.

No guitar this time. No Ember on her violin. No audience I can see.

Just me and Blake Silverton.

Two souls wrapped up in one sunny voice and the shadow of an ear.

My voice starts shaky, and yet I've got it, this song so much a part of me that I could sing it even if I'd lost my words forever.

I used to sing it in Dad's memory.

Now I sing it for Blake and Heart's Edge by proxy.

I'm asking if he'll soar with me.

He doesn't make a sound until it's over, and I'm trailing off with my breath and heart both going just a little too fast. The silence that follows makes me nearly hurt with the awareness of the wild riot of noise and feeling inside me.

He finally breaks the stillness with a low, appreciative *mm-hmmm.*

"Don't think I'm ever going to forget that," he says. "The way you sound when you're putting all your heart into notes like raindrops." He pauses, then adds, "Guess I'd better get on those Fuchsia stories and this caller who Mario says swears he played tag with Sasquatch...but maybe you'll sing for me again some time?"

"Maybe," I whisper. "Goodnight, Blake. Thanks for taking my call."

"Goodnight, darlin'," he rumbles against my ear.

The line goes dead, and I'm alone.

Except for the *millions* of butterflies taking flight in my belly.

* * *

I BARELY GET any sleep that night.

It's hard to pass out when I'm all twisted up, thinking about Blake.

About the way he teased me.

About the soft words of apology.

About the intimacy in his voice, the warmth, the gentleness, the tease.

All the little things that tell me this push and pull means something.

Something *more*.

And maybe I'm not just insane for losing myself in his magnetism.

I finally drift off, though, long after midnight.

In the morning I oversleep a little, but I wake up zinging—and I don't even need coffee to make my morning appointment with the rich folks who tip amazingly well, and then an older woman vacationing here at the inn. She says she used to be a silver medal skier, but time and age and repetitive stress injuries knocked her off her feet.

She's sweet. Teases that she likes places like Heart's Edge because they don't even tempt her to ski, with the trees walling off all the good slopes. And I'm full of laughter as I work around her joints and calves to loosen things up so she can walk and enjoy the cold beauty in peace.

I'm feeling good by the time I pack up.

I always feel good after a positive session, when I can leave people just a little happier, a little more free of their pain.

But who does that for you?

Oh—no, nope.

I'm not letting that thought in.

I know I had my little existential crisis a little while ago, but I'm not letting it come back today to chase my buzz away.

If I putter around the cabin, I'll either start brooding or thinking about Blake too much. As forward as I've been, I'm a little too embarrassed to give in to the urge to run and *find* him and hope that warmth he shows over the mic will be there in his face when he sees me.

God, what am I? A giddy teenager with a crush?

I need to get out.

So I bundle myself up, strap on a good pair of boots, and go.

I've got a little pocket brochure, courtesy of Haley and Ms. Wilma. They keep them for the tourists, showing all the best places for a scenic view. Haley mapped them herself with her hubby, looking for the best places to paint. I trust her judgment.

So I pick a spot on the map.

It's exhilarating to set out under a bright sun and yet still feel so *cold*, like all the wonderful things that energize me are bundled up in one: the crisp snow, the brightness of the day, and the beautiful blue sky.

Everything smells like frost, dry leaves, and something starker like ozone.

I love it.

And I love the little hidden trail in the woods I find by meticulously following little markers in the brochure—a broken signpost, a cairn of rocks, a poplar tree that looks like a praying woman.

It's like a scavenger hunt.

And it's a delight when I spot the smooth, flat rocks set into the earth, turning the trail into a set of steps leading up into the woods.

I park my rental car on the last bit of paved road before that hidden trail, get out, and slip up to mount the first step. It takes me up a winding path through tall, skinny trees with their leaves stripped off, giving me some footing on the ground in the snow.

Dead leaves crunch under my boots as I hike up and up and

up until my breath burns, and suddenly the trees open up on a peak that makes me feel like I'm on top of the world. I look out over stretches of mountains that seem to march off forever in the distance.

The brochure has a story in it, too. One variation of the lovers' cliff legend everybody seems to know around here.

It says that way back when the town was founded, the mayor's daughter and a farm boy fell in love.

But the mayor said the boy was too poor, so they couldn't be together. He forbade them to fall in love.

So they went to the half-heart-shaped cliff behind the Charming Inn, and jumped.

It's not as morbid as it sounds.

In the story, they turned into a shower of flower petals and blew away into the pretty mountains I'm looking at right now.

The legend says their love lives on, these strange creatures forever with the wind, and all their generations upon generations of children. Wood-waifs guarding every impossible love that blossoms in this town.

And that's why when people in the town fall in love, they go to the famous overlook and toss flowers over the edge.

They make a wish, with all their hearts, hoping their love will last forever.

I wonder if I can work that into the song I'm slowly piecing together. My tale of the wandering desperado, protector of a town he can never call home and yet always watches over.

Maybe there's a fire in him that can't burn out.

A fire in his heart, a love as lasting as wishes cast on petals in the wind.

I feel lyrics starting to take shape, so raw and real that I can almost *smell* the fire on the chilly midday breeze.

Wait.

It's not my imagination.

I smell smoke.

Again.

Lord, it's like fire follows me everywhere. I'm kind of getting sick of it—even if it summons the hottest man in town.

I'd rather have an excuse to see Blake that doesn't involve something smoldering.

I turn, scanning the horizon, then back to the forest.

There.

A plume of smoke rises against the trees, thick and black and oddly slender.

Probably a small, controlled fire. Burning brush or something.

I sigh.

If those kids are messing around again, though, or some idiot tourists...

Hold up. The last time I snuck up on kids playing with fire, I almost made it worse by startling them as soon as I stepped on that twig.

So this time I'm quieter, making my way through the trees, keeping the bigger ones in front of me as a shield, placing my steps slowly. I'm careful to avoid crunching down in the snow and leaves as I make my way down the slopes.

I stick to the path where I can, but as I get closer, I break off and crouch down behind some bushes as I sneak closer.

Movement. I freeze.

That's not the kids.

That's *definitely* not the kids.

I don't know who this man is, but considering he's dressed in black from head to toe and wearing a black ski mask that completely covers his face...

I think he might be trouble.

Especially since he's pouring water over a big pile of wood, making it flare with thick black smoke as the flames choke out.

He's tall. Imposingly high off the ground, but kind of wiry and lean.

There's something weird and *dangerous* about him.

I won't lie.

He scares me.

I feel like I'm seeing something out here I'm not supposed to see.

Time to get out of Dodge.

I take a wary step back, then freeze as my heel comes down on a twig.

And it *snaps*, the sharp sound as abrupt and harsh as the manic thud of my heart.

His head jerks up immediately.

Now, I'm cursing my love for bright colors. Even through the brush, he spots me instantly.

All I can see are his eyes, but they're oddly blank.

Strange.

Angry.

And they glaze in the coldest way as he cranes his head slowly to the side, staring dead at me.

Then he's charging forward, moving like a pouncing cat, from statue stillness to cheetah motion in less than half a second.

I scream and tumble back, scrambling onto my hands and knees with cold slushy snow flouncing up around me, soaking my clothes.

I think it's only the distance and my head start that saves me.

I barely risk glancing back—he's too *close*, this black blur rocketing at me—before I go flying down the slope.

It's a miracle I don't break an ankle on the stone steps, racing and tumbling and falling over myself, breathing harshly and painfully as I shove through the trees.

My car. I have to get to my car!

I clamber a few more steps, stealing another glance back.

But he's gone.

I fling myself onward, pelting down the path.

He might've just ducked out of sight, and I can't dilly-dally. I *have* to go now.

I can see the bright purple of my rental through the trees, and I dive off the path. Shortest path is best, right?

I'm snatching my keys from my pocket before I'm even at the door, and I nearly drop them as I trip off the edge of the slope, onto the road, and slam right into the side of the car.

Struggling to breathe, ears pricked to a new sound.

I stare blankly through the clouds of my own breath.

An engine comes growling from higher up the slope, around the bend in the road.

Don't look, I tell myself.

I look. I can't not.

A big, dark truck comes tearing around the curve, its engine roaring like a hell-beast.

Oh, *God*, it's him.

I can barely make him out through the windshield, the outline of his shadowy mask behind the wheel.

And those cold, glassy eyes locked right on me.

That truck is big enough to crush my little car.

Big enough to kill me, swatting me like a gnat.

And it's bearing down fast.

Ask me later, and I won't be able to tell you what takes over, what lets me escape.

Animal fight or flight instinct, maybe. Raw survival.

Suddenly, my fumbling fingers pop the door, and I'm behind the wheel.

Car started.

Foot on the gas.

And *gone*.

I tear off just as the truck comes up on my bumper, almost kissing my car's butt before I spin away with a little skid on the slick roads.

Oh, crap.

Slick roads!

I clutch the steering wheel hard enough to *hurt*, holding my breath, pushing the gas pedal harder and harder as I go ripping down that winding road, one eye on the rear-view mirror, one on the road.

Tight spirals of pavement coil every time I careen around, lose him for a second, then see him nosing around the curve seconds later in my mirror.

I've never been more thankful for tiny, shitty, cramped rental cars.

Because the truck's too big.

It tries to take the corners too fast, so I'm gaining ground. I feel an elated spark of hope as I see the break in the trees up ahead that spills out onto the main highway.

It's my only chance.

Because even if the truck's too big to take the corners, it's still faster, more powerful.

Gaining ground.

And coming up on me like he's about to steamroll me right off the road.

He almost *does*.

The second the last stretch of road to the highway opens up, I *floor* it—but so does he, and I feel like I'm being hunted by an angry bull charging down. Fear and adrenaline flare hot in the back of my throat.

I lean my whole weight into the steering wheel like I can make this crappy little snozzberry of a car go faster, faster, *faster* while he's racing *closer*—

And I swerve onto the highway, taking a sharp right, right as he comes slamming up on my bumper.

He clips my rear end, just enough to make me half fishtail.

But I screech and grab the wheel. He goes rocketing across the highway behind me, almost ending up in a field.

He grinds the truck to a halt at the last second, while I wrench myself straight on the road.

I stomp on the gas.

Town's not far. Charming Inn, even closer.

I just need to get somewhere safe, somewhere around other

people, and I'm trying not to *cry* as I beg the rental car to go a little faster, a little harder, just take me where I need to go, where I need to be, *please...*

That growl rises behind me again, just as I catch the peaked roof and columns of the inn up ahead.

I dart a desperate look in my mirror.

He's still there.

Hot on my tail, but...

Is he slowing down?

I can't.

I can't slow down on the off chance he might be easing off, so I just keep breaking the speed limit with every hair on my body standing up.

But no—that growl's slipping now.

He's falling behind.

When I check the mirror again, he's even more distant.

I don't know what he's doing, but I don't want to risk getting close enough to catch his license. It might be my last mistake.

I don't even know.

I need to be somewhere safe.

And I can't bring this nut to the Charming Inn with Ms. Wilma and Haley and Warren and their kids.

There's only one place where I'll *really* feel safe.

I don't even slow as I overshoot the inn and go rabbiting right into town.

* * *

EVEN IF I knew subconsciously where I was going, I'm still a little surprised as I pull up in front of Blake's house.

I don't think I've breathed the whole way here.

Not even when that truck slipped out of sight, and I was back in the middle of a sleepy small town, surrounded by people, buildings, normalcy.

I kill the engine and stare at Blake's sprawling house.

I'm okay.

But I won't feel okay until I'm not alone anymore.

It takes more effort than I can believe to peel my clenched fingers off the wheel, my knuckles aching and ligaments sore.

I manage, pushing out of the car. I scramble to the front door, darting nervous looks around, feeling far too exposed in the open.

And I'm grateful when he answers mere seconds after my frantic knock on the door.

Grateful, yet frightened as I look up into his confused frown and blurt out, "Blake, I think I just saw the man who set the clothing shop on fire."

X: DANCE TO YOUR TUNE (BLAKE)

Surprises just keep showing up at my door.

Last time Peace crashed on my doorstep, she showed up with her massage table and soft words threatening to split me open.

This time, she looks terrified, shivering, flushed.

And on the verge of tears.

I've been thinking about her ever since that call-in last night, and the soft, low way she sang her little heart out for me.

Aching to see her.

But not like this.

Not with the words, "Blake, I think I just saw the person who set the clothing shop on fire."

Everything in me bristles. I reach for her without thinking.

It's instinct, this feral urge to protect her from someone she's already escaped from.

Still, I slip my arm around her shoulders, stepping out on the porch. I put myself between her and the line of sight from the street, darting my gaze around suspiciously as I usher her in.

"Come on," I say. "Inside. Did they hurt you?"

She shakes her head, scrubbing her ridiculous purple knit gloves against her red nose and gulping audibly, her hair bouncing from under her rainbow knit cap in shimmers of purple and red.

"No, but he tried. Chased me through the forest and then tried to run me down in this big truck. I...I didn't get the color, like, maybe dark blue or grey or even green, I don't know."

"Hey. It's okay. You're with me now."

I nudge the door closed behind her, then sink down before her in the entryway, gripping both her hands. Even through the gloves, I can feel how cold they are, chilled to the bone, and I rub my hands over hers slowly for warmth, staring into her too-wide eyes.

"I want you to close your eyes," I say—and she does, instantly. "Count to ten, and the whole time, don't think about anything but the truck. Tell me what you see."

She takes a few shaky breaths, then I see her lips mouth *one*.

Then *two*, a hesitant pause, then *three, four, five*, all the way to ten.

The whole time her breath slows, the tension in her heaving shoulders relaxing.

She'd been gripping my hands for dear life, but now she eases up.

I count with her, silent, mirroring the shape of her lips.

She actually smiles, weak and shaky. "...you did that just to calm me down. You put on your radio voice."

I half-smile. "I got a radio voice?"

"Yeah. Whenever something's wrong, you talk this certain way." She shakes her head. "Like you really believe everything's going to be all right. No matter what. And it just soothes, wraps me up real warm like..."

Like you're holding me. It's on the edge of her voice.

Fuck.

I can't help a strangled sound.

Holding her right now doesn't sound half bad, but I have to focus. Some random asshole tried to kidnap her or hurt her or worse. Nothing's more important than that right now.

"Glad it helps," I say, squeezing her hands. "You feeling better?"

"Yeah," she says quietly, opening her eyes. "The truck was hematite, almost. Really dark grey, almost black, but shimmery, too."

I'm trying to think of anyone in town who has a truck like that, but that's the kind of flashy thing most people around here don't bother with.

Trucks out here get put to work, not lounge around looking pretty.

Something with a nice finish like that, it'd take too much effort to keep it perfectly polished and sparkling.

Means I'm drawing a blank, and I don't like it one bit.

Standing, keeping my grip on her hands, I step back slowly, guiding her to the couch. "C'mon. Sit down, I'll make you some cocoa, and you tell me what happened."

She nods, biting her lower lip, the red of it looking so swollen with the cold it's like an overripe cherry. When I let her hands go, she sinks down on the sofa, peeling slowly out of her winter gear.

"Sorry for the ambush," she says hesitantly. "My first instinct was to find you."

"Nah, glad you did," I say, stepping into the kitchen to rummage in the cupboards. I can still see her through the doorway, watching me with wide, curious eyes while I pull down mugs and a tin of cocoa powder. "But how'd you know someone set fire to the shop?"

She winces. "Well, your voice kind of stands out in a crowd. I overheard you."

"Goddamn. So much for keeping that under wraps."

"I haven't said anything!" she protests. "I'm smarter than that, jeez. If rumors got out, you wouldn't be able to find the arsonist. They'd be more secret."

"Pretty much," I grumble.

That's the way it should work, anyway. Shame something

about this shit feels different, like a puzzle with mismatched pieces.

I get some milk warming on the stove and fill the kettle with water. The best cocoa's a mix of both according to the Gospel of Ms. Wilma Ford's cooking.

"So why don't you start from the beginning and give me the rundown?"

While I let things heat, I move to the kitchen door and lean against the frame, folding my arms over my chest and watching her.

She looks up at me nervously, then ducks her head and tucks her hair behind her ear. After shedding her winter things, she's got on jeans, ski boots, a clinging sweater in thin white fabric that looks like it was hand-splattered with multicolored paint. All hugging her curves in just the right places.

Shit.

I try not to give my dick a dirty look. This is already *hard* enough.

Her tongue darts over her lips. "I was just out for a walk, taking in the scenery. There's a big pointed bluff, kind of like the one where Rafiki holds Simba up when he's first born? You know, The Lion King?"

I can't help cracking a smile. "I know the one you're talking about, darlin'."

"I was up there. Then I saw smoke back down the path and a bit to the..." She pauses, squinting. "Northwest, I think. You can probably find it; he was burning this pile of sticks, but he was already putting them out with a jug of water."

"Hmm." I stroke my chin, rubbing my fingers through my beard. "So he came to set a fire and then put it out, prepped with water? Fucking around with methods, maybe. What'd he look like?"

"I don't know." She shakes her head, looking at me mournfully like it's her fault when it damn well ain't. "He was wearing all black. Covered from head to toe, he even had a ski mask.

Couldn't see anything except his eyes, and I was panicking so much I didn't really catch the color. They were creepy and glazed. And he was really tall, almost this whipcord build?"

Damn.

Whipcord.

That rings a few bells.

My jaw tightens. *It better fucking not be.*

Not a gangly teenager who loves pyrotechnics, tall and playing with an attitude problem big enough to write checks his ass can't cash. And way too up close and personal with my little girl.

I scowl. "And he tried to hurt you?"

"I don't know if he meant to hurt me or just scare me, but...he wasn't fooling around with the car chase." She wraps her arms around herself tight, fingers making creases in the sweater's sleeves. "I stepped on a twig. He heard me, saw me..."

She looks up sheepishly.

"Not your fault. Go on, darlin'. Give me more."

With a flimsy smile, she tweaks the bright cap piled at her side. "Hard to hide with all my color. Then he just came charging after me, so I ran back to my car. I thought he took off, until I heard his truck starting. He chased me down the hill to the highway and clipped me a little, but he just trailed off when I started getting close to town." She winces, then. "Oh, hell. That's a rental. I don't think they're going to believe 'a masked man chased me down,' and my insurance won't cover it—"

"Don't worry about it," I say. "I know some folks. The fire department around here has pull with the cops, even if we're not the best paid. I'll smooth it over. Might even be able to get Rich to help buff out anything before it's an issue."

But I'm not really thinking about her huckleberry car.

I'm thinking about what the *hell's* going on here in Heart's Edge.

A fire set at the clothing store.

A nasty note for Leo.

Clark dicking around in the woods with fire. Then dicking around more at the carnival grounds without his uncle's supervision.

Holding a grudge because I made him stop.

Because I damn well don't want him anywhere near Andrea.

Fuck.

Was he playing with new ways to light shit up?

He knows fire almost like I do, inside and out. His uncle works in pyrotechnics, does big shows all over the country, and Clark's been his apprentice forever.

He wouldn't want to use professional gear, no.

Stuff that could be traced back to him.

So he'd have to experiment with new tools, whatever he could make look more reckless and accidental.

Damn, my mind's running away from me.

And Peace is just watching me with her pretty green eyes like I'm a human powder keg and she's just waiting for the blast.

I sigh, lifting my head, looking at her. "You don't feel safe at the inn, do you?"

She almost flinches, averting her eyes. "Well...not anymore. I know Warren's a big, tough guy just like you, but—"

"No buts. I wouldn't feel safe either, if I were you," I say—then make an impulsive decision. One I know I'm probably gonna regret before it's even out of my mouth. "You're staying here with me."

She'd started looking away, but now her gaze flicks back, full deer in headlights. "Wh-what?"

"You saw this firestarter prick. You didn't catch his face, but he doesn't know you can't identify him." I sigh, shaking my head, scrubbing a hand through my hair. "Look, I don't want to go to the cops with this just yet. There's been too many messes the last few months, all that Galentron crap and the big fire. Plus, our man, Langley, he's not the best at keeping secrets, much less solving 'em. So, just in case I'm off my nut, I don't want to cause a panic with folks on edge."

Sighing, I can't even quantify this feeling.

It's irrational, and I'm trying to rationalize it in words, trying to make it make sense for her in a way that doesn't just come out in this big flood coming out of my mouth. "This creep might also come looking for you, Peace. I'd rather have you where I can keep you safe."

Yep, she's still staring.

And I'm still standing here like a big dumbass.

Christ Almighty, I'm ruined around this girl.

Whatever happened between us on the radio the other night just made it worse.

Unplugged this whole frigging tangle of pent-up daggers in my guts. Now they're spilling out in this jumble of words that don't mean what they're supposed to mean.

Let me protect you.

Let me take care of you, Peace, because I can't stand it.

I can't let anything happen to you.

That's all I want to say. Instead, I'm just looking her up and down, wondering where that calm, put-together radio voice she loves so much ran off to.

She lowers her eyes, biting her lip, tucking her hair back in that sweet way she has. When she can go from brassy and bold to soft and uncertain in seconds, it's the little things that tell me when she's flustered, when she's confused.

"I mean, all of my things are at my place, though, and...I have appointments."

"I'm flexible. Unless something's burning down, that is. I've been doing welding jobs long enough to set my own schedule." I half-smile. "Don't think your clients are gonna want to get their massage in the same room as a giant boa constrictor, but if they're okay with in-home, then I'll drive you there and back if you're not feeling safe. And we'll bring your stuff here. Hopefully it'll be just crashing for a few days till we get this sorted out."

Her brows knit. "Why do you think anyone would set fires? Why here?"

"In this crazy town, I don't even know why anybody does anything no more." I snort, crossing the room to settle down next to her on the sofa, keeping a safe distance so I won't be tempted to *touch* her.

I just want to be close, to let her know she's not alone.

Her face tilts, giving me this brutal look that tells me she sees the hero I'm not.

"Listen. Whatever this asshole's deal is, it's not your problem. Promise you, anyone playing arsonist doesn't want you involved and doesn't even know who you are. It's just rotten luck that you saw him and he ran you off."

"Or maybe good luck," she whispers—and it's *her* touching me now, leaning over to bump me with her shoulder. "You've got a description to go on, if you're playing detective, Blake."

"Not really my strong suit, but, well, when you get thrown into it over and over again, you learn a thing or two." I grin, bumping her thigh with my knee. My cock wants *more,* but I'm thankful for the saving screech of the kettle, reining me in. "There's the cocoa."

I stand, wondering why I feel this tether tugging me back to her, something deep and hard.

Can't think about it too much, though, and I ignore it firmly as I head to the kitchen. "Let's get something warm in you. Then we'll go grab your stuff before dark and get you settled in at the Chat-two Silverton."

"Um." She quirks an eyebrow. "Isn't it pronounced *chat-teau?*"

I grin. "Languages never were my talent. Just ask Leo."

* * *

It's not much work getting Peace set up at my house.

No.

That's a lie.

It's a hell of a lot of work, but it's work that needs to be done.

The guest room is full of boxes and boxes of Abby's old things, sitting there gathering dust like it's some kind of mausoleum.

I don't know why I never got rid of 'em.

For Andrea's sake, maybe.

So someday when she's ready, she can see and touch things that belonged to her ma, bringing her back in little memories of Abigail wearing a certain dress or reading a book or laughing in the light from the window as she turned, her fingers glittering with delicate silver rings.

Things weren't always bad, once.

I fell in love with her when I was young and married her for a reason, even if those reasons wore thin real damn fast.

But it's time to put this stuff away until Andrea's ready.

Beyond time.

This heavy feeling knifes through me as I move, and I wonder if Andrea's the only reason I kept this stuff.

Why the hell do I feel this ache, swiping the dust off the stacked boxes and hefting one into my arms?

Is this what letting go feels like?

If so, I'm ready.

I turn with my arms loaded up and step out into the hall—only to bump right into Peace.

She looks up at me, bouncing back, then touches her fingers to the side of the box, tracing something.

My eyes lurch open. She's tracing my handwriting.

My jagged, angry Sharpie letters written so many years ago, blurred with rage. I'd been stabbing at the cardboard with the marker, trying not to be furious at Abby checking out on us the way she'd gone. Leaving no closure. And because it felt wrong to be pissed at the dead.

ABIGAIL – BOOKS

That's all it says. Just those two words.

I know deep down it says a hell of a lot more.

Peace smiles sadly, all the flighty sweetness that makes her who she is tied up in those soft pink lips.

My heart thumps so hard she must hear it.

"Need a little help?" she asks, and my throat constricts.

"Yeah," I say. "Think I'd like that a lot, darlin'."

She doesn't say anything else.

As much as she peels me open with those soft, understanding words, right now, it's her silence that gets me.

She rests her hand on my arm, squeezing gently, then slips into the bedroom behind me and grabs a box.

Together, we make our way to the attic with the first load of memories boxed up tight.

Memories which suddenly don't cut so bad at all.

* * *

With Peace's help, it doesn't take long to clear out the bedroom.

We don't talk until we're stripping old bedding and opening up the windows to let some light in, taking down curtains that have so much dusty fur on them I think they might damn well be alive.

"Sorry this place is such a mess," I growl. "Rest of the house is plenty clean. This room, we just shut up under lock and key."

"You kidding? This is nothing. That honey farm I lived on right outside Redding for a few months...I think I *slept* with the bees. They lived more in the wood of that rotted old house than inside their boxes."

Can't help but grin. "Been meaning to see about some beekeepin' myself one day. Doc swears up and down I'll get myself stung to death. I'm itching to prove him wrong."

We share a smile over easygoing banter for once. It's nice.

She's impressed I can get a fitted sheet on seamlessly.

Boot camp discipline and attention to detail as a grunt never leaves a man, I guess.

I'm impressed she nearly kills herself taking down a pair of lace curtains, flopping back into my arms when her balance craps out.

The two of us keep working for a few hours to turn this vault of dead memories into a living space for Peace. Before long, it's not too hard to breathe without choking on dust. The room comes alive, full of sunset light and the fresh smell of clean linens and brand new curtains.

There's a little glimmer of pride in us both.

On an unspoken agreement and a little toss of her head toward the door, we dust ourselves off and head out into the late evening to fetch her things.

We take my Jeep, leaving her car at my place for obvious reasons.

One, I don't want anyone to realize she's coming back to the inn, if they're watching for her—though if they're spying at her cabin, they'll see us getting out together. Whatever, I'm with her. I'm sure I can handle some gangly freak in a ski mask after taking down a whole group of lethal bandits months ago with nothing besides firecrackers, helping Doc's tight-lipped ass.

Two, if anyone followed her today, then I want them to see her car at my place.

Let them know she's *mine*.

Well.

Not mine-*mine*.

But damn it, she's with me, and I ain't letting a single thing happen to her.

We finish loading her stuff up pretty fast. There's plenty of room in the back of my Jeep, enough to hold all the cases and folding things and suitcases she'd had in that Mystery Machine van of hers, and then some.

There's more teasing, lightness, but what I like the most is that it doesn't feel like we have to make a thing out of it just now.

The air's easier between us, and she likes it, judging by how she keeps on beaming like the sun.

I like it, too.

It feels good to be out and about with her, the Jeep's top down briefly to let the winter breeze wash over us. She asked me how it works, so I showed her.

Then Peace lifts her hands up, letting out this soft *whoop* like she's riding a roller coaster, her cheeks flushed with the chill and her eyes so bright.

Yeah.

Shit.

This woman does things to my heart.

It's hard remembering she's too young for me. Not when she makes me feel like I'm the man I was before this bastard leg injury and the scars on my heart flayed me apart.

I sober up a little as we pull into the driveway back at my place.

Light's on in the upstairs window.

And there's angry heavy metal music thumping through the walls.

Andrea's home.

And my little violet and I need to have a *talk*.

I guess Peace picks up on the vibe. She goes sober as I park and cut the engine, scrubbing nervously at her cheeks.

"Hey," she asks softly. "Everything okay?"

"Yep." I flash her a smile. "Give me a sec, will you? I just need a few words with Andrea to let her know you'll be staying. Then we'll get everything unloaded and hauled up to your room."

The look on her face says she doesn't quite believe me—like that's all it is.

With a gentle smile, she lets it go, squeezing my arm again with those warm, nimble fingers—I *swear* I feel her heat even through those silly yarn gloves—before unlocking her passenger door and slipping out.

"I'll get a head start," she says. "Hopefully Andrea won't mind having another chick trying to sort her crap out up in her space."

I chuckle, but I'm not really feeling it.

It's go time, and I have no earthly clue how Andrea will react.

I pick up the heaviest suitcase, two birds with one stone, and heft it over my shoulder before I turn to follow her inside.

The music is deafening, so I guess it's a good thing we ain't got much to say to each other as we trek upstairs. I leave Peace with her bag and the case of oils she hauled in, tucking her away in her room before heading to Andrea's to knock on the door.

I don't think the girl even hears it over the racket.

"Andrea?" I call, pounding on the door harder. "Yo, Andrea!"

The music dies down for a second.

Then up again.

Damn her.

I haven't even done anything yet, and she's *already* mad at me.

I try the door, and...yep.

Locked.

I've got a key, sure. I mean, I respect my daughter's autonomy and privacy and I'm not gonna barge in on her unless it's critical, but I'm also a firefighter.

If something happens, I'm not gonna let a locked door keep me from saving my daughter in a crisis.

I'm just trying to figure out how much of an emergency this load of bull is.

I sigh, closing my eyes, thunking my head against the door hard enough to make it rattle.

"*Please,*" I say. "Open the hell up."

And the music cuts off.

I straighten up, blinking.

A few seconds later the door opens. Just a crack, enough for Andrea's wary, suspicious face to peek out, just a sliver of her nose and mouth plus one eye.

"What," she mutters. "You cleaned out Mom's stuff. *Why?*"

Oh.

That's why she's mad at me. I wasn't thinking.

Of course she saw the guest room when she came home.

"Didn't clean it out," I say. "It's packed up in the attic. It's still there, baby girl. That's your stuff now when you want it. I just needed the room. Thing is, somebody might be threatening Peace, so she's gonna stay with us for a while."

"What?!" Andrea's eyes widen.

She actually opens the door fully, peering down the hall at the square of light spilling out of the guest room.

"Peace is staying *here?*" she gasps, and that sullen edge is gone from her voice. "Really?"

Peace leans out from the guest room with a grin and waves.

"Really!" she says and tosses a wink at Andrea.

My daughter lights up.

"*Cool.*"

Peace disappears again with a laugh, while I let out a sigh of relief, offering a dry smile. "I didn't get a chance to tell you since you were out, and it was kind of sudden. It's only temporary—"

"It's fine, Dad!" Andrea says, her eyes gleaming.

I blink.

I think my daughter's got a case of heroine worship for the hippie girl down the hall.

Fine. Peace ain't a bad girl.

Not a bad girl at all.

Big heart, kind of flighty, but she's got common sense where it counts and she's smart as hell, plucky, brave.

I can think of worse people for my daughter to admire.

And with them having an understanding, it'll make it a lot easier to keep the peace in this house.

No pun intended.

I'm not *that* screwy.

Still, that's not the only reason I need to talk to Andrea.

"So, about where you were this morning?" I growl.

Her eyes narrow. She leans back, her grip on the door shifts, and I know I'm about to get it slammed in my face. "I was out with friends, Dad. It's Saturday. I don't have homework."

"Not worried about your schoolwork, Violet. You've never let me down that way." I sigh. "Just wondering who you were out with."

My fist trembles at my side.

If she tells me she was with Clark Patten...

I don't fucking know.

Maybe I'll know it wasn't him, the creep after Peace, even if I hate it.

But if it's not him, then who the hell is it?

Andrea eyes me suspiciously. "Why do you want to know?"

"I'm your father," I say. "Got a right to know who my daughter's spending her time with."

Wrong tack.

I know it before it's even out of my mouth, but it's too late.

Her mouth tightens, and she glowers at me. "Unless you've got a time machine, I don't think you can undo who I was with this morning," she bites off. "So, uh, why does it matter?'

It's not a question she wants an answer to.

It's not a question I get a *chance* to answer.

The door shuts in my face, hard enough to slam in its frame, making the entire wall around it vibrate.

I just stare.

Peace leans out the guest room door again, arching a brow at me. "That went well," she says lightly.

"Yeah," I grumble and sigh. "Welcome to the Silverton household."

* * *

I GUESS NOT EVEN Peace is enough to get Andrea to come down for dinner.

It's a quiet thing. I think Peace is feeling kinda awkward in the house with just the two of us around.

She doesn't even notice I made broccoli slathered in butter and garlic with dinner.

And I've got too much on my mind to tease her over it.

It's not that things are off between us.

Hell, there's not really an *us* to be *on*.

We're just on different planets right now. And she doesn't look like she wants to talk.

So after dinner's done, I clean up and stuff everything in the dishwasher. She offers to help, but I'm a stubborn SOB.

I got rules about houseguests, and houseguests don't work.

So with a faint smile and a murmur of thanks, she drifts upstairs to her room.

I head out back to the deck with a beer.

I know. I know I'm shutting her out. I know I shouldn't, but fuck. I don't know.

Andrea's my daughter.

I gotta handle this myself, and not put it on anyone else. Peace doesn't need to hear me worrying and getting all twisted up inside my own head.

She's got her own life, her own problems.

I don't need to pull her into mine.

I stare out over the snowy night as I crack my beer, and forget to even take a sip. I'm just fixated on the silhouettes of the trees against the sky, and I can't stop thinking about that truck Peace described. The guy.

I can name a ton of tall, lean guys in town. I wish she'd seen his eye color, might narrow things down. But that truck sticks in my head.

So does one perp.

Clark's uncle, Roger Patten, rents trucks for out of town work, sometimes.

He does these flashy things for rock concerts and like, EDM shows. He can't show up there in his grungy old beat-up camper with the big rust spots eaten out of the sides.

So he'll rent a big truck, something that looks professional.

Usually slaps a removable decal with his company's name on the side. Dolls it up like it's a company car.

Peel the decal off, though...

I glug my beer down in fast, angry swallows.

Without the sticker, Clark would have the perfect untraceable vehicle, whenever his uncle turns it back in to the rental place.

Fuck, I hate thinking like this.

Especially hate thinking that punk-ass kid might've tried to hurt Peace.

It's like thinking her name summons her.

There's a soft tread inside the kitchen a little while later, then the back door whizzes open.

"Hey." Her voice hits my back, warm as day.

I hadn't even realized I was freezing, my ungloved fingers numb and the tip of my nose frozen even with the fire pit crackling down to embers next to me. Not till that pixie's warm presence hits, beckoning as alluringly as ever.

"Do you ever sleep?" she teases gently. "Don't stay up on my account. Promise I'm not waiting to ambush you."

I can't help a smile.

She just brings it out of me.

I glance over my shoulder. She's in her pajamas, an oversized pair of pants with sailboats all over the off-white silk, plus a little clinging tank top just barely visible under her oversized coat. Her feet are tucked away, nice and warm in a giant pair of fuzzy pink bunny slippers with trailing floppy ears.

Nobody should be this damn cute, if I'm being honest.

Nobody should be this knockout sexy, especially wearing that, but my eyes can't stay off her hips.

It's like she's this collection of impulses she wears with pride.

My gut aches hot, my blood runs lava, wondering what it'd be like to just grab her and—

Yeah.

Pull her out of her moment, and into mine.

"So what does this count as?" I ask quietly, half-smirking. "'Cause it feels a little like an ambush to me. I got nowhere to go, now, unless I want to run off into the snow like a Yeti."

She laughs. "You're furry enough."

"*Hey*. I ain't that damn hairy past the beard. I've got a pretty average to slightly above average amount of hair for any normal dude."

"Oh, so you've quantified it? Interesting." Giggling, she steps out on the porch, letting the doors swing shut behind her, and pulls her thick coat tighter around her with a little shiver, exhaling a cloudy puff of breath. "Seriously, Blake, are you okay? I'm sorry if I brought more mess to your doorstep." She cocks her head, studying me.

"Not a mess. Just some welcome chaos." I stand up, offering her my chair. It's already warm, and I'm wearing a hell of a lot more layers and can stand the other chair. "Here. C'mon. By the fire pit. Those pants are too thin for you to be out here."

She settles down in the chair, tucking herself up in a comfy ball, leaning toward the fire.

I drag the other chair closer, add some wood to the flickering circle of orange light and warmth, and sit, leaning forward and resting my elbows on my knees.

My eyes catch on the flames, feeling like I dragged her into something, even if it's not my fault.

This mountain town is like an ocean.

Seems smooth and calm on the surface, but underneath, there are dark things aplenty.

Things with big teeth, waiting to drag you down and never let you come up for air again.

If you ain't careful, Heart's Edge will drown you.

And I'm scared I'm a weight pulling this girl under the surface and into that breathless dark, when she'd just wanted to spend a quiet winter here and then move on.

Someone like Peace ain't made to be held down.

She's the bird in that song she sang.

Meant to fly.

"Sorry," I say. It's out before I can stop it. "I regret getting you tangled up in this."

Peace makes a soft, quizzical sound. "I don't get what you're apologizing for? You didn't do anything."

"I did, though. I...fuck." I grind my teeth. "I think it's Clark. That kid Andrea likes. And I can't even fucking ask her about it because I'm a softie. Can't face down my own daughter, so I'm just dragging this out and if I don't do something, it could get even more dangerous. I wouldn't put it past that little shit to really hurt someone, whether he means to or not."

Someone like Peace.

No, dammit. I *have* to have that conversation with Andrea soon, like it or lump it.

She sucks in a breath. "Clark? The tall boy we saw at the carnival grounds?"

"Yeah," I grunt. "His uncle's a pyro expert. Does the holiday shows around here and big entertainment shit, too. Clark's been training with him. He knows fire, and he knows just how to piss me off because I don't want him around my daughter. I don't know how it got like this. How Andrea turned into such a scary little cactus. She used to be this sweet thing, and now...girl's a wild mess, hooking up with a reckless pyromaniac idiot."

"I don't think you're scared of her," Peace points out gently. "I think you're afraid of hurting her...and afraid of losing her. That's a different thing, Blake."

"Doesn't feel like it," I admit, my voice simmering to a growl.

I hate this shit.

Always turning so rough and worn around this woman.

And she just picks up all my pieces, smoothing them back together.

I swallow hard. "Feels like I lost her already anyway, honestly. She's so damn mad at me about everything."

I'm not expecting Peace to laugh.

It's a soft, soothing laugh, warm as the red-hot embers dancing in front of me.

Instead of feeling mocked, I'm just enveloped in her sweetness, lifted by that sound.

"She's *sixteen*," Peace says. "I didn't stop being angry at my dad for dying until I was twenty. And I was sad and missing him. You're right here, and you're an easy target. Of course she's mad at you. It's your *job* to make her mad at you, just by being dad. Because dad lays down the rules that keep her out of trouble. Later, she'll understand, especially when those rules mean you're the guy she can count on to be there when things go bad, too. But if your daughter's mad at you, then you're doing something right, Blake."

"Yeah?" I smile faintly. "I spent a lot of time real angry at my ma, but she didn't really do much right."

Peace doesn't say anything, at first.

I lift my head to find her watching me, her eyes glowing in the firelight, and my throat threatens to close.

She's so fucking beautiful it's blinding.

What I can't get? What in the world draws a chick like her to some gnarled wolf as screwed up as me.

But she reaches across the space between us, offering me her hand.

Right over the fire pit, like it's some kind of strange sweetheart ritual gesture.

"Want to talk about it?" she asks, with that same openness that makes her so disarming.

It's almost like I can't say no to her.

Fuck.

What can it hurt? I slip my hand in hers, and it's her who folds my fingers up and squeezes real tight, even though her hands are so small, so fragile in mine.

Doesn't matter.

She's a healer. Feels like she could hold the whole world in those hands.

I wonder if I'm losing it or is it just her superpower coming out as a massage therapist?

"I don't even know where to start," I say, swallowing to wet my dry mouth. "If you just look at one little thing at a time, it wasn't much. But when you add it all up over the years, it's a whole frigging mess. Ma, she'd pit me and my brother, Holt, against each other. Like, she didn't just play favorites. One of us would stop existing. Whoever was the golden child got everything, and the other would just get shit on. She wouldn't feed us; she'd forget us at school...I had to walk home in threadbare shoes in the late spring one day when I was nine. All because she picked Holt up and drove off like she didn't even see me."

Peace's expression crumples softly.

Almost like she sees that sad little boy I'd been.

"Blake," she whispers, squeezing my hand, stroking her thumb over my knuckles. "That's not how any mother should ever treat her sons."

"Don't I know it." It's hard to talk, but I can't stop, either. "She always had to be messing with us. Like we were her puppets, and she just had to have her fingers tangled up in our strings, mucking around in our heads. She'd lie to us, tell one boy one thing, one of us the other. We never knew what was true, what was real, but she'd gotten us so hooked on her approval. Instead of leaning on each other like brothers, we'd keep at each other's throats."

My free hand pinches into a fist. My chest hurts from harsh breathing, digging around inside me like claws, this sick feeling of razor-sharp memory. "Worst crime in her book was doing something she didn't approve of. Bitch did everything she could to stop me from marrying Abigail. I think that's half the reason I did it."

There it is.

There it is, fucking *out loud*.

Hell.

So maybe Abby wasn't the best mom, and a pretty lousy wife.

But maybe I was a shit husband, too.

Marrying her half for love and half to spite my Ma in the first place.

Growling, I hang my head, closing my eyes, starting to pull my hand back from hers. "Now you know. I'm goddamn trash. What kind of fucker marries a girl just to piss off Mama? Even if he was young and stupid."

"That's just it. Someone young," she soothes, never letting go of my hand.

Never letting go of *me*.

I pull her fingers in, tangle them around mine, and squeeze till she gasps real sweet for me.

God.

There are a thousand reasons I shouldn't be doing this, but a million more reasons why I can't stop.

"Someone who, I think, gets his daughter more than he lets on." Her other hand covers mine then, and I lift my head to find her watching me with so much compassion I almost can't stand it, being *seen* like this. "Did you ever hurt Abigail?"

"Nah, don't think so. Not the ways she backstabbed me." I'm searching deep here, going back in memory, pushing past the grief to try to really *see*. "Thought I loved her, Peace. I really did."

"We always *think* we're in love...until we realize we're not. That doesn't make us evil. It makes us human." She smiles, but her eyes are wet, glistening, like she's just stolen away my pain so she can cry it out because I'm too fucking proud to.

And she squeezes my death-gripping hand so tight. "And it's human to be afraid of hurting your kid, Blake. But it's also human to love Andrea so much you'd never hurt her the way your mother hurt you. You love Andrea that much, and more—and that's all that matters."

I want to believe her.

I want to believe her so much.

But I can't pin it all on her.

I've got this girl out here practically crying over me and my unresolved shit, when she should be inside keeping warm and getting rest after a madman scared her out of her wits.

Fuck this.

I need to handle my own mess.

Including figuring out how to keep Clark Patten away from Andrea before he gets her into trouble I can't get her out of.

I stand, gently tugging on my hand to free it from hers.

"Thanks, lady," I say. "I want to believe you. I do."

I shake my head.

Then on impulse, because she pulls me every which way, I draw one of those slender hands up and press my lips to the center of her soft, warm palm. Savoring the way her breath hitches and her chest rises, her eyes widening. I want to believe she's blushing for me and not the cold.

Her skin's so smooth. Plush against my lips, and I linger, rubbing my beard against her palm like I'm some wild beast marking her before reluctantly pulling away.

"Think I need something a little harder than beer," I tell her, taking a step back toward the house. "Shame I don't keep anything potent in the house with that little moonshine monster already sneaking crap with her friends. I grounded her hard last year when Leo brought her home drunk off her ass." I offer her a rueful, apologetic smile. "Go on inside before you freeze them little bunny ears right off your feet. Quit worrying over me and get some sleep."

And with her watching me, her eyes still so wide with confusion, longing, hurt, something *more*, we part ways.

I turn and walk, crunching away into the snow, rounding the side of the house.

I'm not running from this woman, I tell myself.

Or from the specter of two dead women who make me afraid to believe I could ever love again.

Tonight, I just need to *think*.

* * *

LUCKY for me that Brody's is crowded, but not *too crowded*.

I'm not in the mood for company tonight.

Warren, Leo, Doc, they all know me as the funny guy. The big goof.

I'm the dumbass who thought Leo's name meant Tiger back when we were kids. Not lion.

I'm always the one with an idiot joke, an easy grin, but the last one to get what's going on.

Hell, I'm the dude who lit up a bunch of those Galentron assholes with fireworks and yelled "Merry Christmas, chucklefucks!" right before my bum leg practically pitched me off the top of Gray's truck.

Yeah.

I'm the clown.

Because they only see me when it's just us, and everyone needs to wind down for a laugh. I always feel like I can't be the guy bringing the group down. Can't let 'em see when I'm screwed up or worrying about Andrea or remembering shit I don't want to with Ma, or Abby, or Holt.

So I laugh.

But I'm all out of laughs tonight, and I don't think I could pull one out even for my best friends.

I find an empty barstool and settle in to order a good hard shot of whiskey. I'd walked here on purpose, forgetting the vehicle. Partly because I needed to clear my head in the icy air, and partly because I know I'll be safer sobering up on a cool walk home than I would be driving.

I ain't gonna get too blasted, anyway.

I just need to be sober enough to think.

To figure out why it feels like this ain't adding up.

Clark's a kid.

A little asshole, sure.

But I'm having trouble believing a seventeen-year-old kid's got that much malice in him.

And that much forethought, to set a fire at the fabric store with prepared incendiaries for *what?*

Just to get my goat 'cause I don't like him?

And what about that vicious note for Leo?

Leo, formerly known as Nine, has turned into a local legend to the kids. Their favorite scarred-up superhero, especially since Leo gets all self-conscious and still goes hunting sometimes all cloaked and masked like something right out of a comic book.

He ain't nobody personal to Clark, as far as I know.

So why would Clark Patten be leaving him hate notes?

Trouble is, nobody besides Clark's uncle—who ain't no one to anyone, he's never in town long enough for anybody to love him or hate him—would have the expertise to do something like that, and the tools on hand.

Still no motive.

Still no lead except Clark.

I know I'm the big bad grizzly bear when it comes to protecting my little girl, but hell.

I ain't been *that* bad to the little punk.

I stare down at my whiskey, then take a deep, burning sip, letting it clear my head.

I'll figure it out.

If I have to, I'll bring in the boys. Maybe we can figure it out before I have to involve Sheriff Bumble.

Between us, we've got a decent head on our shoulders.

I sigh—then tense as someone slides into the empty seat next to me.

Great. All the stools free all along the bar, and someone's just gotta park down next to me like they want to be friendly.

But I breathe out a sigh of relief when I look up and see Justin, sinking down next to me with his movements heavy and tired, his face haggard. There are dark circles under his eyes, and he's a bit of a stubbly mess.

"Hey, Chief," he says wearily, folding his arms on the bar. "Mind if I join you? Can't sleep."

I give him a friendly smile. Here's one problem I might be able to make some progress with tonight.

"Sure," I say, lifting my glass in salute. "Been meanin' to talk to you anyway."

"Yeah?" He looks at me quizzically, even as he lifts one hand to the bartender. "What's up?"

"Nothing to worry about," I say. "But, say, how do you feel about dinner at my place sometime real soon?"

* * *

Okay.

Maybe I drank a little more than I meant to last night. The wicked hangover settling in tells me plenty in loud shouts of pain.

Still, I'm feeling pretty good about my decision to invite Justin over to dinner.

Whatever weight was bearing him down last night, it seemed to lift a bit when I made the offer. He'd relaxed as we'd sat and drank in near silence.

Lost in our own thoughts, each of us.

Sometimes it ain't bad to have a drinking buddy.

And I'd walked him back to his apartment, just to clear my head and make sure he got home safe. Something about his place still bugs me. It's too damn barren.

It seems so lonely, just him and those photos all lined up along the walls.

Kid like that needs company.

Maybe I ain't his family, no, but I can at least remind him he's part of something. Being with the fire team is no small feat.

You have to trust a man in the middle of hell with your life.

Once I saw him home, I wandered back to my dark house and collapsed into bed.

Tried hard not to think about Peace, sleeping just a little ways away, only a thin wall between us.

Fat chance.

I can't *not* think about her. Morning brings the smell of frying bacon and the sound of clanging pans drifting up the stairs.

I don't know if the smell makes me want to throw up or makes me hungry. That hangover messed with my senses something fierce.

One thing I know: that *noise* is gonna kill me.

Snarling, I crack one eye open.

Someone's been in my room.

There's a water bottle on the nightstand and the bottle of Tylenol that belongs in the medicine cabinet. Andrea didn't leave that.

Shit.

She's probably still holed up in her room, hoping I'll oversleep long enough for her to sneak out with her friends before I can say boo about the next week.

No can do.

I'm due out on a welding job at the Potter farm. Just a quick private gig, but not many others have the qualifications. They've got some framing that needs to be done up proper and safety-checked for a new well tank.

Welp.

Dragging myself out of bed, I grunt as my body protests with creaking bones and a throbbing in my thigh that matches the pounding in my skull.

Goddamn, what kind of rotgut did I drink last night?

The sound of Peace's soft singing echoes below, prying my mind off the pain.

I pause mid-reach for the water bottle to have a listen.

She's singing something sunny, something sweet, lyrics about California waves and tans.

Even with my skull splitting fit to blind me, I can't help but grin.

And with a bit more energy, I wolf down several pain pills,

chug the water, throw some clothes on, brush my teeth, and go clattering downstairs.

It's a good morning. An *easy* morning, like Peace just fits into the house in some odd little way. With nothing more than a good morning smile, she reveals another talent.

Knowing the perfect cure for a hangover: a big greasy breakfast, bacon and sausage and cheese and mushrooms and onions all slammed together into the largest, gooiest omelet I've ever seen.

Girl knows the way to a man's heart, all right.

"You're a lifesaver, darlin'." I toss her a wink as I settle at the dining room table and tuck in to the food.

Andrea even comes down, still in her pj's—girl's sixteen and *still* sleeps in a big purple fuzzy onesie, and somehow I'm just not surprised that Peace loves it.

That's another thing Broccoli's good at. Making Andrea light up as they chatter over breakfast.

I might as well not even be here, listening to Peace yammer on about the massive sapphire-blue waves people surf off the shores of Oahu and Maui with a glimmer in her eye.

As much as she swears she belongs to the continental US of A now, there's a part of her that'll always call that far off paradise home. And who can blame her? My ears prick up as she talks about the palm trees and big sea turtles and some wild story about this former SEAL dude taking down a modern-day high seas cartel for a very forgetful lady.

Same story she read up on after Andrea mentioned it, I guess.

I grin. She's a natural storyteller, her words just suck me in.

Not because I'm thinking about going to Hawaii.

I'm *not*.

Maybe for a vacation one day, with the way Andrea's eyes are shining.

Next winter, maybe.

Nice break from all the snow.

I don't mind being invisible, listening to Peace's stories as we cast little glances back and forth over the table.

"What?" she whispers emphatically. "I swear to God, that Valerie chick *did* have a wild cat when she washed up on shore with Mr. SEAL. A serval—er, half serval. I read all about it. I'm so not making this up."

"Careful, darlin'. You keep on bringing these Hawaiian romance thrillers here, and soon little old Heart's Edge won't be so freaky, and I won't have much to blab about on the radio."

"Perish the thought." Andrea chomps off a big bite of eggs and points her fork at me. "I can't figure out what's worse."

I quirk an eyebrow, waiting.

"You playing Mr. Conspiracy or Dr. Love. God, Dad, the things you tell some people."

"Hey, now, *some* people at this table have gotten pretty good advice," Peace says, flashing me a sun-shiny look that ignites my blood.

Andrea's face goes red. "I mean, well...it's not all bad. Like that chick who asked you about her crush, Tony the Comic Book Boy. Ugh. They're freaking inseparable now. Everyone just wishes they'd get a *room*."

We all burst out laughing.

For once, I ain't even fed up with her bullcrap. It's a rarity to have my little girl giving me a backhanded compliment, and today, I'll take it.

I can't even feel my headache now, absorbing the way Peace Rabe brightens up the whole house.

Maybe I get a little too comfortable. We're all moving around and murmuring over cleaning up the dishes and putting things away when it happens.

Without thinking, my arm brushes Peace, then it snags her around the waist and pulls her close.

Like we're one big happy family and I'm just kissing my girl goodbye on the way out the door.

I freeze as her body presses up to mine.

Shit, what am I doing?

I catch myself just inches away from bending down to steal her mouth.

She goes stock-still against me, not even breathing, staring up with those soft green eyes. They're still glacial forests, but they're also burning hot.

That's the kind of paradox she is.

All wild whims, and she pulls me all *her* witch ways when her body feels just like I imagined against mine.

Soft.

Lush.

Hot.

Like she's this plush marshmallow thing just melting against me in a whimper.

Her pert breasts against my stomach, my chest.

Her breath curled against my lips like the precursor to a kiss that shouldn't happen.

She's frozen with her hands held out from her sides, but slowly she lifts them against my chest, her gaze searching mine. "Blake?"

I can hardly hear her over my heartbeat.

Over my imagination going fuck-wild, thinking she's saying my name the way I'd dreamed it in the shower, *Blake, Blake, Blake, oh God, Blake*, her thighs gripping my hips and her body pumping down on mine and—

My whole body tingles, burning from the inside out.

Not nearly as much as the fire in my cock, the pounding blood roaring through my veins.

Fuck.

I swear under my breath, stepping back quickly, letting her go so sharply she stumbles. I reach out to grasp her arm and steady her.

"Sorry," I mutter. "Thought you tripped for a second there."

I'm a horrific liar.

She doesn't say anything. I have no idea what I'll say if she says *I don't believe that*.

So I just clear my throat.

I turn around, face the door, then do some more turning. Make sure Andrea isn't looking, but she's gone up to her room.

Screw it, here goes.

Her eyes go up in a fireball as I bring my mouth to hers, claiming this pixie who can't stop stirring me up without even trying.

Oh, but fuck do I *try* something right now, taking her tongue and her heat, leaving her delirious.

Believe me, it's mutual.

That first kiss is a freight collision, not just our mouths, but our bodies. Peace *moans* against my mouth as I take her, grasping her neck, lacing my fingers through her hair, and pulling gently so she dips real sweet for me.

It's everything I feared.

Fiery, divine, and so sexy I feel like I need a cold shower.

Her little mouth ripples again, pulsing another moan that sounds an awful lot like *Blake!* before I pull back for half a breath and take her again. This time she's ready. Her tongue dives at mine, starting a thirty-second battle of dueling tongues and teeth and breathless pleasure.

Fuck.

I'm grateful Andrea's still in the house.

It's the *only* shred of sanity that saves me from spinning her around, throwing her on the couch, and having my way right here and now.

I barely tear myself away, relishing her heat on my lips, watching her still leaning against the wall, wide-eyed and panting. "Blake...what...what was—?"

"That?" I finish. "That was my thanks for this morning, beautiful. I like having you around. See you for supper. Don't forget to keep the doors locked and call if you need anything. I'll have

Warren or Leo drive by a couple times to make sure everything's cool here."

I have to *go*.

Right the hell now before this turns into a conversation I don't have the time or clarity for.

So I charge out before she catches her breath, heading off to work.

* * *

IT'S A PRETTY long drive to the Potter place.

Heart's Edge is the kind of town where the population gets deceptive. You just don't know how many people are really living wild out in the hills on their homesteads and ranches and little logging cabins.

The Potters have a ranch way out on the other side of the valley, off the main road and down a long, desolate dirt road snaking across the valley floor. It's past the ruins of the Paradise Hotel and the boarded-up entrance to the silver mine that once was a secret Galentron facility.

Well, technically it's just one Potter now.

Liberty, Mark's daughter. He was a real smart scientist back in the day who called this place home forever before he passed away last year.

She's light on extra hands to help out and it seems like money, too. Old Mark wasn't a rich man, even if he was drawing a NASA pension, and I think he just inherited this place way back from his old man.

I give her a friendly smile, say hello to her horses, trade a few words about her dad—light stuff so I don't rub her grief raw—and get to work.

So, considering how deep in the wilds of rural Montana I am, working my blowtorch, helping Libby haul shit and set up scaffolding, I don't expect visitors.

Imagine my surprise when I step out of the barn and see a

familiar truck parked next to my Jeep on the dirt-packed front drive.

Warren.

He's just climbing out of his truck as I pull my gloves and welding mask off, frowning.

Dude looks grim.

Shit.

Something must've happened.

My mind flicks instantly to Peace, the house, and my gut sucks in. Had he been by?

Goddamn, I never should've left her alone today.

Gathering my courage, I step forward casually and say, "Hey, man. What drags you out here?"

"Take a look." He beckons to me, and then gestures fiercely into the back of his truck, so angry that his movements are jerky, pulling his jacket tight against his big straining arms. "This fuckery—I just—Leo told me about that fucking note. If someone's trying to endanger my *kids...*"

I don't understand. Not till I look in the back of the truck.

Then I start swearing up a blue streak.

Because there's no doubt what I'm looking at.

A crumpled, half-empty gas can and a bunch of bundled twigs and branches. They're tied up in a very specific way to make sure they'll catch fast, catch hard, and burn long.

Dry shit. The sort of material that'll suck up a flame and burst into a fireball in a hot second.

Goddammit.

I spit out a few more curses, then drag my hand over my face. "What happened?"

"Somebody tried to start a fire by your girl's cabin," he snarls.

I almost want to spit back *She's not my girl*, but I've got more important things to worry about.

Like the fact that I was right to keep her with me.

"Peace caught somebody setting fires up in the hills yesterday," I say. "She didn't get a good ID on him, but he must've been worried she did."

"Yeah, well, this bastard got unlucky. He propped it up in a snow dune and the melt put the fire out," Warren growls, his eyes flashing. "And he almost got a face full of Grandma's cookware. Wilma caught a prowler trying to light up the dry azaleas in the back garden and chased him off with a fork and a pot."

I can't help a laugh, imagining Wilma Ford up in arms, though it's brief, bitter, tired.

Angry.

Someone tried to *hurt* Peace.

Tried to hurt my friends and Charming Inn.

This is way beyond a stupid kid's prank.

I don't even know the half of it.

"That's not the end." Jaw tight, Warren fishes in his back pocket, then pulls out a crumpled bit of blue paper with singed edges, thrusting it at me. "I also found *this* at Jenna's grave."

Another note.

Christ.

My stomach sinks, deep and hard.

Sighing, I smooth it out with my thumb, reading the jerky handwriting. It's the same as the other letter—almost like there's hate etched into every letter.

JENNA WAS THE REAL HERO, **Warren.**
And you can't even protect her memory.

THE FEELING INSIDE ME RETURNS, black and thunderous.

What kind of sick, callous fuck would say something so cruel to War about his dead sis?

My dead friend.

Who died when Clark Patten was just a toddler.

What? This doesn't make *any* fucking sense.

Who could've done this who'd remember Jenna?

The answer screaming into my mind like a blood-red police siren is one I can't even stand, no matter how I feel about my brother.

Holt.

He'd been so damned in love with Jenna Ford back when we were kids.

All the way through high school.

Sometimes, I think it was the thrill of the challenge. She was the only girl who ever turned him down, even when we were teens.

Reject him, and he gets obsessed.

But...but...*nah.*

I can't.

It's too much.

Holt can't be this twisted perp.

I shake my head. "Fuck, man. I gotta think. I'd thought I knew who set the fires, but now I'm not so sure."

"Why the hell would they leave that on Jenna's grave?" Warren spits. "Covered in ash, no less. Like some kind of weird sacrificial offering."

"I don't know, War," I say gravely. "Let me start asking around. 'Cause we've got trouble, but I tell you one thing: I *won't* let it get any further."

XI: A LITTLE LOUDER (PEACE)

Not one day in Blake's house and I'm already breaking the rules.

By "rules" I mean waiting for the man who just kissed my soul out to ferry me around like my chaperone.

I know he means well.

I know he wants to protect me.

But nothing's going to happen in broad daylight, especially locked away safe in my customers' homes and hotel rooms.

Mr. Creepazoid Arsonist doesn't have access to my planner and has no idea where I'm going to be today.

It'll be *fine*.

And I'm right. It's absolutely fine.

I have a busy day seeing to housewives with tennis elbow and older bed-bound patients who can't get up to stretch their muscles, so they need someone else to help them limber up.

It's another good day for money.

A day where all I need is a soft touch and soft words and a little understanding to make someone's *life* better.

It's not playing God, but it's good.

And I'm feeling good by the time I get back to Blake's house. It's not a bad place to be.

I'm staying with the man who turns me inside out, makes me breathless, leaves me struggling to sort up from down.

And this morning, when he'd pulled me in for that knee-bending, breathtaking, *oh my God hot* kiss? I wish he hadn't stopped.

But Andrea was there, and he'd caught me off guard, and...

So many *ands*.

So many missed chances.

If his kiss was like the rain finally breaking over a parched desert, it's left me wanting *more*.

That kiss clings to my mind as I let myself into the empty house.

No sign of Andrea or Blake.

He must still be at work. I'm guessing Andrea's out enjoying her Sunday with friends before school drags her back to dreary Monday.

I don't mind having the place to myself.

It lets me settle in on the overstuffed sofa with my guitar, strumming soft chords, trying to get my mind to focus on something besides Mr. Silver Tongue. Oh, and now that I've had a taste, the name fits him too perfectly for other reasons.

Lyrics. Focus. Right.

Making this melody come together into something real, raw, true, and lovely.

That's my focus now.

Even if it *might* be an ode to how I feel about Blake.

Wouldn't that be funny?

Some pop starlet like Milah Holly picking up one of my songs and blasting it across the international air waves. Never knowing the wild man she's singing about, the desperado with the dust of his past on his shoulders is a living, breathing small-town tornado of a man.

The thought makes me smile.

Mr. Hissyfit seems to like it, too. He's happily twisting in his tank, moving like he's winding himself in rhythm to the music.

I'm so caught up in my strumming, in the turns of phrase and rhyme that fit the chords, I don't realize I'm not alone until a soft voice interrupts.

"Damn, you're good, lady!" Andrea chirps.

My fingers slip on the strings, and I glance up, blinking.

There she is, punky as ever in ripped jeans and a battered oversized military jacket over a crop top that leaves her belly exposed even in winter, henna designs inked around her navel along with a belly button piercing that I think would give Blake a heart attack...except I can tell it's fake. Costume jewelry.

And standing next to her, thumbs hooked into the loops of his torn black skinny jeans, is a sight that makes me tense.

"Hey," he says.

Clark.

Eep.

He's as sullen as ever, tall and lanky in this awkward teen boy way that makes him slouch naturally because it's just hard to deal with that much height and gravity at the same time.

He's dressed in all black, from his chain-spangled jean jacket to the black hoop in his lower lip. Total throwback to the eighties' glam goth crowd.

He doesn't look like an arsonist.

It's just hard to see it.

Sure, he's got some pent-up anger. What kid their age doesn't?

He's lashing out against the world.

But the way he looks at Andrea, there's something soft in it.

Something sweet and almost innocent.

Something that tells me there's just a confused, quiet boy under all that dark armor. He wouldn't ever hurt anyone close to Andrea, not even to get back at her overprotective daddy.

So, maybe I'm projecting, too up in my own clouds about love.

But I have a sixth sense.

"Cool shit," he says, echoing Andrea. "You play professional?"

I don't want to give away my thoughts, so I plaster on a smile and shrug, setting my guitar aside. "Just something I do in my spare time. What've you been up to?"

Andrea shrugs. "Just helping Clark get ready for the carnival. There's going to be a fireworks show over the ice castle at the end of the night, so we've got a *lot* to do for safety stuff if Dad's ever going to sign off on it." She rolls her eyes, and Clark snorts.

"He's such a pill," he mutters. "I know what I'm doing. So does Uncle Rog. Dude helped with Burning Man shows four years in a row."

I chuckle. "It's Blake's job as fire chief, that's all. If anything goes wrong, the first person they're going to come down on is him for not doing it right. He's just trying to keep everyone safe." I hesitate, watching Andrea, then venture, "...your dad's actually been needing a few words with you."

I don't know how else to hint.

How else to help, when I really shouldn't be sticking my nose in.

And I think I've made a mistake. Andrea instantly scowls, hissing under her breath.

"I bet he *has*," she spits. "And I know what it's about. Clark didn't do *anything*. God, Dad doesn't need to watch me all the time like I'm ten! I'm fine—*fine*, and he can stop being such a shitty jerk about everything! I'm not a baby anymore."

"You're not," I agree softly. "But maybe you need to tell him that, not me."

"I'll tell him something," Clark snaps. "I didn't set anything on fire that wasn't supposed to be on fire."

Woof.

I hope to God he doesn't say anything like that in front of Blake. It could be easily misconstrued as a subtle admission of guilt.

But I still don't see him as a criminal, much less the gangly, scary freak who chased me down the road.

Sure, he's tall and lean, just like the guy I saw.

NO DAMAGED GOODS

Still, he doesn't look quite right. The other guy was bulkier—whipcord lean, but older. With enough muscle to make it easier to hold his height up.

Stupid town full of stupid tall men.

Everyone here's got a lumberjack gene here or something.

Before I can say anything else, though, there's a slamming car door outside.

Everyone freezes, eyes widening.

Then Andrea hisses, turning to shove at Clark, pushing him toward the stairs. "Hurry up—hide! In my room before he sees y—"

"Too late," Blake growls from the doorway.

A frigid blast of air courses in from outside.

Uh-oh.

I feel like we're some kind of hivemind, all three of us turning slowly toward the door, my face feeling like as much of a frozen mask as theirs looks.

Crap.

Blake stands there, all protective Papa Bear with his shoulders squared, his feet planted, his huge arms folded over his chest, imposing and terrible and his face set in stone.

I didn't even do anything, and even *I* feel like I'm in trouble.

He's not focused on me, though.

His hawkish eyes are on Clark Patten.

If looks could kill, that boy would be on the floor with his feet up right now.

I try to catch Blake's eye, but it's no use.

Clark glares right back, fearlessly, straightening to his full height, and I cringe.

No, dude, no! Being tall right now is not *a good idea.*

Please don't put ideas in Blake's head, agh.

I have to do something.

Without thinking, I launch myself off the sofa, ducking around the coffee table to Blake's side.

My excuse is that I'm closing the door before all the warm air escapes.

This cold could hurt a warm-weather snake like Mr. Hissyfit, after all.

But really, I just want to lean in close to Blake, as I nudge him enough to get the door shut past his bulk, stretch up on my toes, and whisper, "It's not him. Trust me."

His gaze snaps to me, eyes widening sharply.

He leans down to let that rumbling velvet voice move against my ear. "You better be fucking sure, darlin'."

"I am." I turn my head.

Our cheeks brush, and if not for the kids, this might be way too intimate.

As it is, it's making my entire stomach knot up. "He's too skinny, Blake. The guy I saw was bulkier. Probably older," I whisper desperately.

Now I know how Moses felt trying to stop a fiery wrath.

Blake grunts, but straightens, and I hold my breath, waiting for the inevitable yelling or fists to fly.

But there's a gleam in his eye as he sees Clark—a sort of sharp-eyed assessment.

At least he doesn't look like he's about to commit a homicide anymore.

...maybe.

I bite my lip as he takes a step deeper into the room.

"You and me, Clark," he bites off. "We need to talk. Alone."

Clark narrows his eyes, lifting his chin. Kid's got pride; have to hand him that. "I don't have shit to say to you, Mr. Silverton."

"You better say something if you want to keep hanging around my daughter," Blake snarls.

"*Dad!*" Andrea's face flames red. "I hate you!"

His face whips back toward her. "Hate me all you want, Violet, but I don't want to hear your mouth right now. This is between me and him."

Holy Toledo.

This is a different Blake.

A calm, severe, deadly-serious Blake.

The kind of Blake you don't *ever* mess with.

And Andrea apparently realizes it. She goes pale, silent, her anger draining. It leaves her looking nervous as she stares helplessly between her father and a tense, motionless Clark.

He moves then, farther down the hall, and Blake follows, giving them a faint shield of privacy.

I almost feel like I shouldn't be here to witness this.

But I also feel like I might need to be here to break things up if they get nuts.

Peacemaker Peace.

Don't laugh.

I sit on the arm of the sofa, watching tensely as Blake gives Clark a slow once-over, looking him up and down from head to toe.

"I said we're gonna talk," he says quietly. "And I mean talk. Man to man, not man to boy." His jaw tightens. "Because if you're the one who's been setting fires around town, if you're pulling some kind of stunt, that's how they're gonna see you when you're standing in front of a judge. A man, not a boy. So I'm talking to you, Clark, and asking if you understand the seriousness of the situation."

The kid stays silent for several heavy seconds, his eyes narrow and dark, before he draws up a bit of bravery I can't help but admire. "You want to talk to me as a man, you're going to have to take my word as a man that I didn't do *anything*. I wouldn't. You're an asshole. Not enough of an asshole for me to risk jail over you, or risk hurting somebody. I've *seen* what burns do to people. You think I want to hurt anybody like that? What if I did something stupid, and *Andrea* gets caught up in it?"

Andrea's blush is back—but it's different now, softer, her eyes wide as they trail after Clark. She works her lips with a soft, nervous sound. Then she looks away and ducks her head, completely flustered, tucking her hair back with raking fingers.

Blake and Clark never look away from each other.

It's like a Wild West standoff.

I can't help seeing Blake as the desperado again, defending his town.

Finally, he inclines his head, grudging but accepting.

"Guess we've got one thing in common, Clark," he says. "We'd never do anything to hurt Andrea. So if we're on the same page there...you willing to answer some questions in front of Sheriff Langley just to get this on record?"

Andrea makes a mortified noise. "Dad, he just *said* he didn't do anything—"

I grab her arm gently, urging her voice down to a harsh whisper, then silence.

"That's right," Clark interrupts sharply, squaring his bony, angular shoulders. "I didn't do anything. So whatever, I'm not scared to say so in front of the sheriff, if that's what'll get you to calm the fuck down and get out of my face."

Blake *smirks*.

Actually smirks, instead of bristling in response to what's clearly a teenager lashing out and testing his authority. "You kiss your mama with that mouth, kiddo?"

I could kiss *him* right now.

For knowing when to be the big mean dad, and knowing when it's not fair to flex his muscle on a kid. He lets Clark have that hit to save his pride.

"My mom cusses worse than I do," Clark shoots back. "So are we done here?"

Blake shrugs. "Don't know, are you?"

Andrea sighs and speaks up. "Look, we're supposed to be working on our school project, Dad. Can...can we go *do* that, or do you want to embarrass me some more?"

Blake grumbles softly, then sighs. "Go on."

I've never seen two teenagers bolt away faster, their shoes scraping the floor.

I've also never seen a boy turn as red as Clark does, when Andrea grasps on tight to his hand and drags him upstairs.

"Keep your door open," Blake growls after them.

The only answer is the resounding *slam* of the door instead, and he hangs his head with a snarl, scrubbing his hands over his face.

"Well," I venture, holding back my grin. "That was eventful."

"Sorry you had to see that." Blake jerks, lifting his head and looking at me a bit sheepishly.

"It's fine. I'd rather be here if I helped even a little bit."

"You did, darlin'. Thanks for helping calm her down." With a firm glance, he settles down on the couch, his heavy weight sinking in—and I can't help but notice that he's favoring one leg again.

"Are you okay?" I ask softly.

"Never have kids, Peace. They'll kill you, if you don't kill them first. But I'm glad you were here, or I might have lit that little shit on fire myself. You're *sure* it wasn't him?"

"Not a hundred percent," I admit. "But ninety-nine-point-nine. He's just too skinny, and he doesn't carry himself the same way. I don't feel like Clark's that kind of kid. He's going through an angsty rebel phase, yeah, but not a crazy pyro phase."

Blake smiles tiredly. "In all your wisdom raising kids, huh?"

"Hey, I'm not completely lost." I laugh. "I know people, no matter their age."

"Yeah, you do." But Blake shakes his head. "I know you're right, anyway. That beat-up old Pinto he's driving ain't the right car. Plus, there's been another fire and a new note."

"Again? Was anyone hurt?" My heart sinks; my eyes widen.

"Could've been," he says grimly, lifting haunted eyes to me. "They tried to set the fire at your cabin, but the tinder tipped over into the snow and put itself out."

That hits me like a blow to the gut.

I...oh, no.

Now there's no more doubt.

The guy, the creeper, he wanted to hurt me.

He recognized me, knew who I was, and he wanted to *hurt* me, and I was off gallivanting around town today like nothing could ever happen. Totally oblivious.

I wrap my arms around myself. "But the note? What else happened?"

"Ms. Wilma chased somebody off her property but didn't get a good look at him. Here." He digs in his jacket pocket and retrieves a bit of blue paper, then passes it over. "Look for yourself."

Frowning, I take it and smooth it out.

Jenna was the real hero, **Warren.**
And you can't even protect her memory.

Yikes.

It's so ominous, so terrible, and I can't even explain why.

I shake my head. "Who's Jenna?"

Blake exhales slowly, propping his elbow on his thigh and leaning forward, pressing his knuckles to his temple. "Warren's sister. *Dead.* Almost a decade ago. She was murdered by one of our closest friends overseas while they were enlisted. All because she found out he had a terrible secret, some illegal shit he was smuggling in and out of Heart's Edge. He made it look like an accident in the line of fire when they were deployed, but Warren...he wouldn't quit till he found out the truth. Took him years to figure it out and win her some justice."

"That's horrible. So it sounds like whoever set the fire blames Warren for something?" I bite my lip and pass the note back to Blake. "What did the other note say?"

He gives me a skeptical look. "You didn't eavesdrop on that, too?"

"Um." I wince, half-smiling. "Sorry."

Blake looks so heavy, so burdened, and I wish there was more I could do. "It called Leo a scarred freak. Said he and his merry band of assholes aren't as smart as they think."

"Wow, that's cruel. So the arsonist is after the Heroes of Heart's Edge," I murmur as it clicks. "To him, you're not that heroic."

Blake's head comes up sharply. "All of us? Me and Doc, Warren and Leo? Shit." He stares at me, then swears, looking away and dragging his hand through his beard. "Yeah, guess that jives. And it helps me narrow my suspect list down to one, though I don't want to fucking think about it."

I can't help myself.

I can't stand seeing *anyone* in pain, least of all Blake.

So I slide off the arm of the sofa to settle down next to him, our hips just barely touching.

"Hey," I say, resting my hand on his arm. "Who do you think it is? Why would they want to hurt you?"

He doesn't look at me.

His arm might as well be solid steel under my touch, so tense, and I worry all this tension can't be good for his leg.

After a minute, he turns a long look on me, searching, before his hand falls to cover mine, warm and enveloping in its roughness.

He's not pulling away from me.

But he's not giving me any answers, either.

He just squeezes my fingers and says, "Don't worry about it, darlin'. Old family business. You've gotten muddied up in enough of my dirt around here. It's not your problem."

Then he leans in, stamping a kiss to my forehead.

It's chaste, not like the burn-me-down passion this morning.

I'm just as in love with it, anyway.

He kisses me like I'm a small, precious thing he wants to cherish, the rasp of his rusty-brown scruff against my temples, catching in my hair.

And even if it's so small, so simple, so sweet...

It takes my breath away, leaving me silent as he pulls back, the sadness in his smile whispering at an old, deep ache.

"You just let me look after you," he says, though he's already standing, drawing away, and putting that wall up between us again. "I'll get this wrapped up nice and quick."

* * *

No matter how long I stand at the window and watch him, I don't think Blake's going to look up and notice me.

And if I open the window and call out *Romeo, oh Romeo, wherefore art thou Romeo?*

I doubt he's going to climb the trellis to get me.

He's been sitting outside by the snowy fire pit for hours, well past sunset and into the dark of evening, moving only to crack open another beer from his six-pack or to top off the flames with a few fresh logs to keep it burning hot and bright.

I can't stand seeing him down there. Brooding. Hurting. Alone.

Sure, I'm supposed to be heading out to put on another show with Ember at The Nest while he's here, locked up inside his own head.

But I don't think I could sing with my real heart if I knew Blake was beating himself up over things that aren't his fault.

I don't want to cancel on Ember, either, though.

So I guess I've only got one option.

I finish pinning my hair up in a little twist with lacquered sticks that give it just the perfect *oomph* of messy I like while keeping it out of my face. Then I pull on a sweater over my little strappy tank top with my favorite pair of jeans—this lucky thrift shop find, bell-bottoms that are tight in all the right places, loose enough to earn their name, and embroidered with flower appliques all over them.

Yes, they're hokey, utterly kitschy, and totally me.

I pull on my winter boots, slide on my coat, sling my guitar over my shoulder, and head downstairs with hope bright in the back of my throat, like a quiet note waiting to burst into song.

Blake's so lost in his trance he doesn't even look up when I open the kitchen door and peek out back.

He's brooding in the firelight, golden light flickering off the edges of his stark, handsome profile. It catches in glints on his hair to make it gleam like polished dark wood and streaks of snow.

This man.

Achingly gorgeous, even when he's unaware he has an audience.

I never really think about how old he is. He just radiates this ageless vitality, even when he's in pain.

But I can see the lines in his eyes tonight.

The strain.

The pain reflected in icy-blue depths. They capture and give back the light from the fire pit in sapphire fragments.

He's living with the old ghosts tonight, I think. I can't leave him to their mercy.

"Hey," I say, smiling as I drift closer to his chair. Reaching down, I tap the empty beer can next to him. "Looks like you're all tapped out for the night."

He jerks slightly, waking up, even though his eyes are fully open. He looks up at me like he doesn't recognize me, too wrapped up in the thoughts of the Blake he was before he ever met me. Then his gaze clears and he smiles faintly.

"Whole fridge shelf waiting for me inside if I want it."

"I've got a better idea." I fold my arms against the back of his chair, leaning over his shoulders to watch him with a smile. "I think you need a nice hot cup of coffee instead."

"Eh." He shrugs. "Too lazy to brew up a pot."

"Good thing they make it for you at The Nest," I say with a grin, tugging at the collar of his jacket. "C'mon. You're coming out with me."

Blake makes an odd noise but doesn't budge. "I am? You want my buzzed ass around that bad, darlin'?"

"Yep. I'm playing with Ember at The Nest again, and I want you to come."

I sound firm, confident.

Honestly? I'm shaking in my boots.

This is halfway asking him out on a date.

It's openly admitting I want him there when I'm pouring my heart out in song.

And he's looking at me like he knows, his expression strange, brows knit together. He tilts his head and studies me in that gentle bear way he has.

Everything goes numb and warm inside.

He's got this way of looking at people that says he really *sees* them, open and frank and honest.

It's a little scary.

Like I've been waiting my whole life for someone to really see me, and now I'm in this man's spotlight.

After a moment, his eyes soften, his boyish smile returning—still small, barely there, but warmer. "You gonna sing that song about the birds made for the sky again?"

I flush, the heat in my cheeks chasing back the cold.

"If that's a request," I whisper. "So...you're coming? It's a lot warmer at the café than it is out here."

"Well...wouldn't wanna get frostbite, would I?" he asks flatly, leaving me in suspense.

There's something else to it, too.

That rolling, husky sweetness to his voice. Rich emotion that infuses every word to give them meaning, weight, life.

And all the words in my mouth dry up, leaving me silent as he chuckles and levers himself to his feet, bending over to pick up a pail of sand.

"Let me just put the fire pit out and sober up for a few," he says. "Then we'll drive on over."

* * *

I SHOULDN'T BE SO jittery.

I've played in front of customers at The Nest before, plus other little nameless cafes a hundred times over the years, but now?

It's different.

This time people *know* Ember and I are here to play for them, instead of it just turning into a random jam session. Word of mouth spread—and there's nearly twice as many people here tonight, settled in cozy little clusters, chatting, sipping their lattes and cappuccinos and dark roasts, watching with gentle curiosity while we set up.

Then there's Blake.

Last time I hadn't realized he was here until he was already gone, when Ember and Felicity told me he'd watched us play.

Now, he's settled at a small table near the window—just him, the tall cup of black coffee he'd ordered, and a small, curious smile on his lips, his chin propped up in one hand.

Yet, that sadness is still with him, too.

I'd felt it the entire time we were driving through the snow, silent save for the oldies jingling from the Jeep's radio.

He's carrying something so heavy, and still finding it in him to smile just for me.

So I flash him a smile back, telling the butterflies in my stomach to calm down as I climb up onto my stool next to Ember. She's checking her violin's bow. She glances over with a sweet smile, her eyes as sunny as her personality.

"You look a little shaky," she says. "It's easier singing to him on the radio, huh?"

I let out a flustered sound so awkward and so loud several heads jerk toward us.

My face *burns*, and I clear my throat, tossing out a quick smile for the waiting crowd before leaning close to Ember and hissing, "Can you *stop*? I feel like the entire town is watching and waiting for me to fall on my face. I'm Icarus flying too close to the sun."

"I don't think so," Ember says softly, watching me with gentle warmth. "The sun's out of reach, girl. I don't think what you want is."

My throat tightens. I look down, running my fingers lightly over my guitar strings, checking the sound, listening to the faint ripple of notes to make sure I'm in tune.

"How do you know what I want?"

"Everybody knows what you want, Peace. It's not hard to see there's something pulling you two together like the red thread of fate in those Chinese stories." She shakes her head with a soft laugh. "I think the only one who hasn't really figured it out is *him*."

"I've been pretty obvious," I say.

"Obvious to you probably isn't obvious to him." With a light-hearted little shrug, Ember lays the bow against her lap, next to the gleaming, well-loved violin resting on her thighs. "Look, I haven't been here that long. I don't know him as well as other folks do, but...I know he's got a lot going on inside his head. And he doesn't always see what's right in front of his face. With the guys he's kind of the last one to get it all the time, but it's not because he's dumb. It's just that he's worrying about so much *all the time*. So it's hard for him to pull away and see what's right in front of him."

I let my gaze drift back to Blake.

"Yeah," I murmur. "I can see that. He's got his hands full with Andrea and everything else."

Which makes me worry.

Do I really want to be another thing taxing Blake's thoughts, making him worry?

Do I even have the right to *want* to be something like that?

Everything in the sadness hovering around him says *no*.

But everything that aches inside me for the haunted need in those dark-blue eyes begs *yes*.

I already know what's happening.

Tonight, I'll sing for him like never before.

"You ready?" I settle my guitar across my thighs, glancing at Ember.

"Ready." She smiles. "How about you lead with whatever you want, and I'll harmonize? I'm pretty good at picking up a chord as long as you go steady. We'll improv."

I laugh breathlessly. "You know what that means, don't you?"

"Sure do. We're about to create genius that we'll never be able to repeat, and no one's even going to record it." She laughs, shrugging. "That's how it goes."

Right.

Just like those moments that are the most amazing in your life because you're too busy feeling to document them.

Those moments come in music, too.

When you just play with all your heart, and let it come out of you full of beauty and wildness.

I can feel something in my fingertips, something vibrating and needing to come to life. I only hesitate a second before touching my fingers to the strings, making them quiver, vibrate, and sigh.

I hardly notice the room going quiet, full attention drawn in on us.

Time to let go and follow my heart.

It's here. That song I've been working on, coming alive in my fingertips, this thing of burnt sparks across a dry landscape and the scent of cigarette smoke drifting from cynical lips, the weary creak of leather and boots, the movement of broad shoulders, the scent of blood in the desert and embers sparking in dry wood.

It's the story of a hero who can't let himself *be* a hero.

A man who can't see that the heart inside him isn't gunmetal, but gold.

And where I couldn't find the words before...

Now they pour out of me like I'm exhaling that smoke and

loveliness on my breath, taking in the pain on his lips, forming it into lyrics. And even with the haunting notes of Ember's violin squealing around me, I'm singing those lightning notes into existence.

It hurts.

It hurts in all the best ways like only the most beautiful songs do, reaching down and pulling out my emotions until I'm such a wreck, but it's all right.

It's okay to be a wreck because I can't look away from Blake Silverton.

He doesn't look away from me, either. There's something in his eyes, even if he's not smiling anymore.

One look that says he's walked every desert road I sing about.

He feels those heavy footsteps in his bones.

He's stood beneath desolate skies as blue as his eyes and looked up and counted all the stars shining against a moonless night.

And he's wished for something more.

Something that would ease his gunmetal heart, let it beat warm and alive and needy again.

Let it be me, I think, and that spills out in the chorus.

One line that I come back to, over and over.

"When you find somewhere to lay your head," I sing, my voice nearly breaking but still holding steady and true. "Please, baby, let it be me."

Let it be me, let it be me.

I sing it until my eyes are stinging and wet and there's not a sound in the entire café but me and Ember and hearts turning into crystal drops of shattering music.

Sweet Jesus.

Does he know what I'm asking?

Does he know I'm begging him to let it be me?

XII: HEART NOTES (BLAKE)

I don't think I've ever heard anyone sing like Peace.

There's something about her voice.

About the way she pours herself into it, and it feels like those strings she's plucking are twisted up in all the messy pieces of me. Every time she strums, it's not the guitar that twitches.

It's *me*.

It's me, shaking up all wild with these messy feelings, completely pulled into her glistening green eyes and the ache of want making her voice hitch and turn husky.

No, maybe she ain't studio-perfect, but she doesn't have to be.

She's perfect just like this.

I'd rather listen to her sing with all that rawness inside her bursting free like the sun coming up on a dead winter morning than hear the most flawless damn studio recording.

Shit. I hadn't meant to get swept away. I hadn't meant—

This.

When she'd asked me to come, I was just gonna stay for a song or two. Give her a little support, maybe get out of my own head, before leaving since she'd probably want to stay after and catch a ride home with Ember, anyway.

Now, I can't move.

Can't break free from the spell she's weaving with her voice.

And I'm hardly the only one.

She's got the entire café wrapped around her little finger. There are more than a few damp eyes in the house, plenty of breathless hitches in people's throats to go around.

I don't blame 'em.

That first song was the one that hit me like a sledgehammer.

This song about a lonely, desperate man, some gunslingin' cowboy who can't see himself as anything but broken and worn down and living only because he's got a duty to others.

Till somebody else sees him as something more.

Rusted gunmetal, with a heart of gold.

And the way she looks at me?

My blood runs nuclear. White-hot. I want to ask her.

I want to ask so damn bad.

Is that how you see me, darlin'?

But I'm completely lost for words. Clubbed over the head by her beauty, her sweetness, her sexy, shining eyes.

I can't go full caveman. I don't want to break this.

This magic that she makes, with every note she sings and strums. She pulls Ember into it until they're a haunting harmony that I could listen to for hours.

Fuck, I think a whole hour or more has passed with her singing her heart out, one song after another, and I realize I'm waiting.

I'm ready for that one song about how birds are meant to fly, so won't you fly with me?

Her voice is almost raw from singing. She's not even hiding the tears in her eyes.

That's when it comes.

That sweet, sad song her old man taught her, and it feels like it's a piece of her heart wrapped up in simple, quiet lyrics that still mean so much.

It's starting to feel like a piece of me, too.

Hell, I don't think I breathe the whole time she sings, with those liquid-gleaming green eyes locked on mine and a smile on her lips that's like heartbreak and sunlight had a baby.

Aw, shit.

I think I might be in love with this gorgeous girl's breathtaking, musical heart.

I've been trying so hard not to be *that dude*. Not let myself give in to the way she gets under my skin with that curvy body and delicate lips and her pillowy touch.

Except, somehow when I was trying to ignore my body, she got inside my head, inside my heart.

I'm not even gonna pretend my eyes ain't stinging.

By the time she trails off, gasping for breath, chest heaving, I'm grinning like a fool.

A silence falls that makes the café feel like a cathedral.

All of these people gathered here to worship the beauty those two girls made together.

Then Peace ducks her head, running a hand through her wildfire hair, letting out a shy, raspy laugh.

"Sorry," she says. "I think my voice has had enough for tonight. But I hope y'all enjoyed the show."

There's a soft chuckle from people who are clearly just as overcome with emotion right before the clapping starts.

Well deserved.

And Peace's eyes widen, blushing as the noise spreads. Everybody applauds, calling out soft praise, laughing. Just like there'd been this thunderhead of emotion that built up and now it's looking for an outlet just so we can all *breathe*.

I still can't stop smiling, and fuck if I don't hope she can tell how I feel.

She glances at me, then away, then back, smiling the whole time, tucking her hair back as she stands, holding the neck of her guitar.

I start to get up—I just want to be near her, even if I don't know what to say—but stop when a familiar figure steps in front of her, blocking my line of sight.

Holt.

I'd been so caught up in Peace I hadn't even realized that bastard snake was here.

The warmth and softness inside me instantly transforms into rage, hard-edged and dark and deadly. I watch him bend over her with that charming smile he turns on everyone, the fucking serpent crashing the party in Eden—but he's the apple too, and he always offers himself as temptation.

He's got his rogue look tonight, nice-looking button-down half-open at the throat and cuffed to the elbows, tucked into black slacks.

No suit coat, no tie, like he's some hot-shot executive slumming it in half-casual clothing.

Always gets the ladies going. Makes them wonder what other rules he breaks.

Like the rule that says you don't fucking put your hands on someone else's woman, and especially not someone else's *wife*.

Maybe Peace isn't *mine*.

Maybe I've been pushing her away more than I've been pulling her close.

But I see murder-red as I watch Holt offer Peace his hand, smiling down at her with his gaze dipping over her in a hungry way, those whiskey eyes of his gleaming.

And Peace smiles up at him, laughing as she takes his hand, shakes it, blushes at whatever he murmurs to her.

Don't do it, Blake. Don't fucking do it.

She ain't yours to claim, yours to defend.

I try too fucking hard to believe that.

When he bends down to whisper something in her ear and her eyes widen, her lips parting on a breath, I snap.

I'm out of my chair before I can even blink, shouldering through the people milling around with a snarl caught in the back of my throat.

I feel like a charging bull, just as big and clumsy and about to make a disaster, but it's like I'm disembodied and watching myself do all the dumbest shit in the world as I stalk up.

"*Holt,*" I bite off.

He stiffens, then turns, blinking at me before he offers an almost shocked smile. "Hey, Blake. What's up? Wasn't expecting to see you here."

"I can tell."

And suddenly I remember that note.

I remember Holt looking at Jenna in the same slimy, entitled way he's looking at Peace just now. A snake-man through and through, even when he was just a kid.

Raw doubt explodes inside me, wondering just who my brother really is.

How much like our ma he might be.

And if he's gonna be a big heaping problem.

If he's gonna be *dangerous*.

Rather than answer him, I turn my gaze on Peace, glaring down at her.

"I see you've met my brother," I snarl, then correct. "*Half-*brother."

Peace gives me an odd look—wounded, and I want to kick myself for being such a raging dick. She has no idea what's going on.

"He was just telling me he's your brother, yeah," she says, hugging her guitar a little closer like a shield. "We hadn't gotten a chance to meet yet. I never realized you had a brother in town."

"I'm working on the big rebuilding contracts," Holt says, smirking. "Might stick around a bit longer, though. Maybe put down roots. You planning to hang around here awhile, Peace?"

She opens her mouth to answer, but I don't let her.

"We should go." I flick a narrow-eyed look at my brother. "I'm her ride home."

Holt's brows rise slowly. He just gives me a long look, his

smile changing, turning sly, dark, as if to say two words that make me want to smash his face in.

Challenge accepted.

"Are you?" he asks softly, nearly purring, mocking and low.

I growl in the back of my throat, my tongue feeling thick.

But now it's Peace who cuts me off, her eyes flashing as she glares up at me with her mouth firming.

"Actually," she says, "I'll be staying a bit to talk chords with Ember. I think I need some more coffee to clear my head anyway." She flashes us both a tight, hard-edged smile. "So I'll say goodnight, gents. Blake, you can find your own way home."

Before she turns away, her shoulders stiffen. Then she tosses her hair and weaves her way through the crowd toward where Ember's relocated herself at the coffee bar, talking to Felicity.

Leaving me standing there like the jolly green jackass I am.

What the fuck was I thinking, barging in like this? Getting so jealous?

Acting like I have any right to be possessive?

Fuck, even if she *was* mine, I just made a huge swinging dick of myself.

My fists clench. Closing my eyes, I sigh.

"Way to go, Blake," Holt mocks. "I see you still have a sweet way with the ladies."

"Don't." I open my eyes, fixing him with a hard look. "Not in the mood for your bullshit."

I need to get the hell out of here.

"Watch yourself," I warn him. "Because I'm watching you."

Then I turn and walk away, shoving the door to the café open hard enough to make the bell jingle wildly.

The cold air is a slap in the face, punishment for *everything.*

Mostly, how I took a beautiful moment and turned it ugly.

All because I don't trust my brother, and I can't keep that old buried resentment under control.

I know it ain't really him I'm mad at. Not even after everything he did with Abby. Not even my present suspicions about him and the fires, either.

It's Ma.

But Holt's here.

Ma ain't.

And I can't quite let go of the way we grew up.

* * *

Many Years Ago

I DON'T THINK I've slept in a week.

Been too busy studying. Getting my shit together.

I'm gonna graduate at the top of my class.

Well, not quite. I'm not even going to be second in class.

I ain't dumb, but I ain't Albert Einstein either, and sometimes I don't wanna do homework.

But I'm gonna at least pull off straight As for this semester, 'cause that looks real good on transcripts when I'm applying to college.

And if I get those straight As, maybe Ma will...

I don't know.

Cut the fucking umbilical?

Damn, did I ace my finals. I know I did. I'm just waiting for the scores to come through while I get ready for graduation—checking in homeroom every day, looking for that report card. Being a goody two-shoes.

Hell, I even turned down taking Sally Jenkins to the dance because even though I like that girl so much, this whole idea's got its hooks in me.

Maybe I'm losing it.

I just know when my homeroom teacher sends me home on

the very last day of school for seniors, with my report card in my hand, I'm nearly beaming at the line of straight As.

And I go bursting into the house, calling "Ma? Ma! I got my report card!"

I don't realize Holt's already there, perched with a girl he's so proud of because she could've belonged to me.

Not till I see him sitting on the sofa with Sally Jenkins, his arm around her waist, and she's got her cute little shirt undone one extra button in the front even though Ma's there, too.

Right there, fawning on Holt, stroking his hair while she looks at his report card. "You did so good, baby. Look at this, when you had all Cs—you even managed to get this one up to a B, son!"

A frigging B.

Holt's almost flunked an entire semester, but she's petting him like a smug cat over a single fuckin' B.

And not even looking at me.

I step forward, offering her my report card.

"Ma," I say breathlessly. "Look."

It takes a few seconds for her to even see me.

And I know by now when she does that, it's on purpose.

So it'll cut deeper, harder.

So it'll hurt more, and I'll know she wants to make me feel invisible.

I feel Sally staring at me. Like I'm some pathetic weirdo, desperate for attention, and she's just now seeing me and realizing she picked the right brother. Not this loser gawking at his ma, eyes wide and breathing hard.

Ma slowly lifts her head, looking at me with a sigh like I'm bothering her, the smile on her lips turning into a tired grimace.

She takes my report card, flicks it open, scans down.

Stops.

She looks at me over the top of the paper, her mouth pursing, brows raised.

"What's this A minus in Calculus?" Her jaw tightens. "I expected better from you, Blake."

I just stare.

Fuck. I came home with my goddamn best, and it's still not good enough.

Holt's smirking.

Dead at me, all that ugliness under his pretty boy face, and as I dart my gaze between her and Holt, just trying to figure out what to do, what to feel, he says it.

"Mama's boy," he mouths, mocking and exaggerated.

I explode, launching myself at him with almost eighteen years of pent-up bullshit exploding out of me, while Sally thrusts herself away with a little scream.

And just like that, we're at it again.

Sometimes he's the one who throws the first punch.

Sometimes it's me.

But somehow, even as Sally scatters, Ma never stops us.

She just folds her arms over her chest, my report card fluttering from her fingers to the floor, and a glint of evil pleasure shining in her eyes.

She watches her boys tear each other apart.

* * *

Present

I DON'T KNOW how I wound up at the cemetery.

Thinking and driving too much, maybe. Remembering.

God, I'd been on such a hair-trigger back then.

That's what Ma trained us to do. Just hold things in, repress and repress and repress till it explodes like a cannon, and that's who I turn into again around Holt.

I hate it.

Hate who I am around him.

Hate who I am when I think of him.

And I can't go home as that guy.

So somehow I end up outside the cemetery gates, letting myself out to step beneath the iron arch into this world of snowy tombstones and tired statues draped with dead vines and leaves.

My boots crunch in the old leaves under the snow, making my way through the markers on a familiar path.

Until I find that one gravestone.

ABIGAIL SILVERTON.

And those dates.

Goddamn, she hadn't even been forty when she died.

Nobody should check out that young.

There are fresh flowers on her grave, though.

Purple, wrapped up with a black ribbon.

I don't even have to guess to know it was Andrea.

And I wonder how often she's been sneaking out here, without me ever knowing.

Considering the dead scattered petals and dirty, faded, tattered bits of ribbon buried in the snow around the tombstone...

A lot.

I sink down in a crouch, pushing a hand through my hair.

"Fuck, Abby," I whisper. "I have no idea what I'm doing. I didn't know what I was doing with you. I don't know what to do without you. I don't know what to do with Andrea, and I hate that I can't help her with how much she misses you..." I swallow back sandpaper.

"And I hate that I *don't* miss you at all. Feels like I'm doing something damn wrong with that, too. I still get sad. So fucking sad when I think about you. I wish you were alive, even if I don't wish you were with me. But I don't miss you. Just mourn you. I think...I think I'm finally starting to figure out the goddamn difference, you know? And it took this bright-eyed girl to show me, but I don't know what I'm doing with *her* either, and I just—*fuck*."

I stop, breathing hard, halting the bleed of words.

I don't even know what I'm saying, what I'm doing, why I'm really here.

For the second time tonight, my eyes are a mess. I'm struggling for every icy breath that cuts into my lungs and then comes out of me in a puffing cloud.

There's no answer from the silent headstone.

But there's a crackle of noise behind me that says I'm not alone.

I stiffen, rising sharply to my feet.

Footsteps. They're moving through the tombstones.

Then a dark silhouette.

Nobody should be here at this time, yours truly exempted.

Shit. Is the arsonist back?

Coming to defile Jenna Ford's grave some more?

I don't hesitate.

This time I let that headstrong bullishness send me running through the headstones, ducking low so I don't draw attention, but not trying to hide myself, either.

That shape is tall, lean, rangy, moving with a sort of gangliness that makes me think of how Peace described the asshole who chased her.

I tense, growling, ready to tackle him—

Until I realize I'm staring at my idiot brother.

Holt's wrapped himself up in a proper suit coat and a leather jacket, snow dotting his jet-black hair.

He's not even trying to be secretive about his movements as he winds through the headstones with a bouquet of fresh flowers in his hands, winter azaleas he probably plucked off someone's bushes and wrapped up in tissue paper.

And there's a sad, haunted look on his face as he stops in front of Jenna's grave marker, looking down at the snow-strewn stone still dotted with little heaps of ash here and there.

I stop.

Freeze in my tracks, watching him.

Holy damn *hell.*

I can't even process what I'm seeing.

Knowing how he once felt, and that he'd do anything to get ahead...

Setting fires in town like a rat, maybe.

Can't have a booming construction business in a town this small unless you've got shit to rebuild.

It'd be real easy to hire Holt's company to do the reconstruction work on the fabric shop, or anywhere else that "accidentally" burned down.

And fuck if he wouldn't have a reason to hold a grudge against the four of us.

He was never really one of us.

First he was the tagalong, the younger brat, always mouthing off for attention 'cause he was used to getting it from Ma. He didn't like that we didn't mess with that kind of shit.

Then he struck off on his own to be the playboy, but he always had a sneer for me and Warren and the others.

It's all coming together real ugly.

How Ma would play us off against each other, the monster she turned him into with that greedy need to always have everything his way without actually working for it.

Plus, the endless competition between us.

My heart can't take much more, and I don't want to admit it aches like hell, thinking my own brother could do this.

I wanted us to be real brothers, once, something better than this.

And I guess right now I'm just too raw to totally lose that hope.

"So," Holt says without looking up. "How long are you going to stand there and stare at me, Blake?"

I wince, looking away. "Didn't realize you knew I was here."

"You're not a little guy. Couldn't exactly miss you freight-training your way through the cemetery." With a sardonic sound, he bends and drops the bouquet on Jenna's grave. "You're disturbing the dead."

"Don't think they mind all that much." I fold my arms over my chest, growling under my breath. "Sure as hell not like the living being disturbed by all the shit that's been happening since you rolled into town."

Straightening, Holt rolls his head toward me with a weary sigh. "Are you really that angry? I made a move on your girl and now you think I'm setting fires here?"

"You'd do worse to get the upper hand." I force pure frustration through my teeth.

"Maybe." He shrugs, turning, regarding me with a sort of honesty I'm not used to from him, his tawny eyes unguarded and weary. Holt slips his hands in his pockets.

I cock my head, studying him.

"Sooner or later, you'll realize you're the only one playing games. Everyone else is too busy living," he tells me.

"I have no idea what the fuck you're on about." I shake my head.

Holt smiles faintly. "I guess you wouldn't, would you?" He turns his head then, looking at Jenna's headstone, eyes lidding. "You ever wonder what she'd think of us now? She was always everyone's conscience."

"Not that you ever listened."

Holt snorts out a bitter laugh. "Nope, I didn't. Listened too much to myself." He shakes his head, that laugh trailing into a humorless smile. "Tonight, I couldn't help thinking I never blamed her for turning me down. And I don't think she'd like what I've become."

"So you thought Peace would be a better option?" I bark at him.

Holt doesn't answer for several seconds.

Not till he turns his gaze back to me, his smile softening,

something almost *warm* in his eyes, something confusing I can't quite process.

"I thought," he says softly, "she should know my brother's so head over heels for her that her music moved him to tears."

I stop like I've been whacked across the face.

Just staring.

Staring at my idiot goddamn brother who sees how I feel about Peace when I can't even face that shit head-on.

"The fuck did you say to her?" I snap, and he laughs.

"Nothing. I didn't get a chance, since you came charging in the way you did. Smooth, by the way." And that smirk returns, and along with it the smart-ass prick I know too well. "Let me know if you need some pointers, brother. You never were good with sweet talk, even if you had your share of women."

I can't deal with this tonight.

The confusion, the questions, the doubts, wondering if he's playing me the way he's playing everyone else with that sociopath mask of vulnerability.

Wondering if I'm gonna be turning my own brother over to the cops.

Wondering if I can bring myself to do it, never mind the shitty history between us.

Nope.

Nah.

Can't answer that right now.

So I turn around and walk away, leaving Holt—and Jenna—alone, abandoning myself to the night.

* * *

There's no sign of Peace when I get home.

Just a dim light under Andrea's door, letting me know my girl's being good and obeying curfew, and I'm not alone.

But Peace's door is open, her room empty.

Shit.

Normally, I wouldn't blame her if she only came back to get her things.

Trouble is, how the hell can I protect her if she's gone because I can't even control myself?

* * *

SHE'S BACK BY MORNING, thank God.

Sound asleep in her bed, tucked up in a cozy little ball and so frigging guileless she just left her door *open.*

Like she doesn't even realize she's staying with a grown-ass man who's dying at the sight of her long, sleek legs poking out from the blankets, or the way she clutches the duvet against her chest in a way that makes her tits nearly burst out of her tank top, one slip of fabric away from pulling a Janet Jackson.

Maybe she realizes and just doesn't care.

Or maybe she knows it and trusts me not to go *insane.*

If that's it, the woman's too kind.

I'm quiet as I gently pull her door shut, then move through the house to usher Andrea out the door to school with some breakfast before I head to work.

Fire crew stuff, today.

My days are honestly erratic; I do what needs doing. It doesn't matter if it's welding or construction or safety inspections.

Just as long as I'm keeping busy and helping somebody out.

This time, it's the Clarendons, barely a few blocks over from my own house. They've got a faulty furnace, and I don't want them risking a nasty carbon monoxide leak. Good thing they replaced the batteries in their detectors last month, or we could've been looking at a tragedy.

They evacuated as soon as the alarm went off and called me in. Luckily, they've got family in town to stay with.

It doesn't take me, Justin, and Rich long to trace the source of the carbon monoxide back to the furnace, though we do a full-house inspection on the ducts to make sure it's not being funneled anywhere else.

It's quiet, near-solitary work. We move through the house with our detectors in hand, measuring levels and breathing through oxygen masks.

Then my path crosses Justin's in the hall.

He's looking better. A bit brighter, like maybe he's drinking less and sleeping more.

Good man.

And he actually looks worried about *me*, as he stops and gives me a long look, brows pinching together above his clear plastic mask.

"Hey, Chief." His voice filters oddly through the mask, more hollow. "You okay? You've been real tense lately."

"I have? Sorry, just got a lot on my mind." I pause, pulling my thoughts out of my notes, stopping my pen mid-scratch against my notepad.

"Like Peace?" he teases. "I think everyone tunes into the station just to see if she'll call in on your nights, now. It's the town's favorite show."

I scowl, my neck heating. "Nope. Not Peace."

She's probably still pissed at me anyway.

But Justin's been on point lately. I'm still trying to make sure he feels included in things, so there's no harm in telling him when Rich already knows. Another pair of eyes and ears might keep things safer.

I drop my voice, though, stepping closer to him. "Listen, keep this to yourself, but that fire at the fabric shop was set deliberately. And there've been a few hints around town of someone trying to start fires and failing. Some asshole leaving nasty notes, too."

Justin's eyebrows shoot up. He looks at me in stunned silence.

More than anything, hearing what I just said out loud confirms it for me.

It's not Clark Patten.

Because Clark *does* know what he's doing most of the time.

He wouldn't fail.

More signs are pointing to Holt.

I sigh. "I can't pull Langley in on this. Not yet. He's a wreck with the cases from last year. So I'm just trying to lock it down, keep things safe, and hope I can stop it from happening again."

Justin whistles softly, his eyes widening. "Chief, that's fucked. You got any idea who?"

I shake my head.

I have one good guess, and I can't make myself say it out loud.

So I just shrug. "Local firebug, most likely, but it's not adding up. So I'm just working the details through. I'll let you know when I come up with more."

"Sure thing. I'll keep an eye out myself and give you a shout if I notice anything funny." He pauses, then, tapping his pen against his mask. "Hey—we still on for tonight?"

Tonight?

Oh.

Right.

I'd invited him over for dinner.

My own phone saves me from that awkward memory lapse, buzzing in my pocket, and I nod as I fish it out, already turning away.

"We usually sit down around seven," I say over my shoulder. "Come casual, nothing special. Just hanging out." Then I swipe my phone, lifting it to my ear and talking awkwardly with it bumping against my mask. "Silverton."

"Hey, Blake," Sheriff Langley says. "I just got done talking to that kid. Clark? Whatever happened the other day...he was working at his uncle's. Got several people to back him up. Why'd you send me after him, anyway?"

"Oh, just making sure he's safe at the carnival grounds, Sheriff. You know how kids are. I told you about that little dustup.

He's got a smart mouth; I'm just making sure his head's in the right place with the big event coming up." I pinch my teeth together, grinding down everything I can't say.

"Pretty typical boy with a chip on his shoulder and a thing or two to learn. And if I were in your shoes, Blake, respectfully...I'd do the same damn thing with a boy going after my own daughter."

I swear softly but play dumb and mutter my thanks again before hanging up. The town gossip mill has no chill and no limit.

That's the final nail then.

Clark's too young, too good at what he does, too...everything that's not a reckless arsonist.

Which leaves me with the same suspect, my own flesh and blood.

And, right now, my number one enemy.

* * *

I wonder what it says that I won't let my own brother into my house for dinner, but I'll let Justin drop in like he belongs here.

Let's be real. Justin hasn't tried to sleep with my wife, doesn't piss me off at every turn, and isn't a suspect in a goddamn secret arson investigation.

He's just somebody who looks up to me, I guess.

It's a funny feeling, considering my own daughter sees me like the lamest dude to ever walk the earth.

Andrea's bright as hell tonight, though.

I don't know if it's because we've got company who's young enough to be cool but grown-up enough that she wants to impress.

Or is it because of Peace?

She's acting like last night never happened. Maybe she's forgiven me, once tempers calmed—or maybe she's putting on good airs for Justin's benefit since they're both guests here.

But she lights up the entire room, this whirlwind of warmth, helping Andrea set the table. I work over a rack of sauce-slathered ribs and a big ass vat of creamy mashed potatoes with plenty of garlic and bacon crumble.

It's nice.

She really lives up to her name. And no, I don't mean *Broccoli*.

Peace brings this glow with her wherever she goes, whether she's pissed at me or not. Don't know how I'm ever gonna let her go when it's time.

No, I don't own her.

Even if I kissed her ever-loving face off like I do.

I'm just trying to figure out how the hell to *ask* her if she wants to make a choice.

And maybe give this desperado another chance to find that gold under cold, hard gunmetal.

I don't feel all that cold or hard now, though, helping them haul the last of the stuff to the table and settle in to serve everyone—though it turns into a free-for-all. The way a family dinner should be.

It's nice to see Justin laughing as he reaches for the mashed potatoes and his hand smacks Andrea's. They both burst out laughing.

Yeah, this was a good idea.

Especially when I pass over the potatoes later for his second helping and ask, "So, how would you feel about helping out at the winter carnival?"

Justin blinks, almost dropping the serving dish before clutching it harder. "Me? What do you want me to do?"

"Well, we've got some numbsacks around here who like to play with fire too much—" That actually gets a snicker out of my daughter, not a glare, but she's in a bright mood tonight. "So, I'm thinking a fire safety course wouldn't be out of the question. You're young, and the kids like you, so why don't you lead it? Make it interactive or whatever they're saying now."

Justin's eyes widen, and he grins. "Really? Yeah, I can do that. I mean, is anyone even going to show up?"

"I will," Andrea says immediately, and I bite back a groan.

I already know what that's about.

She's head over heels for Clark. She'll memorize a whole course on fire control if it means getting closer to his passion.

She just doesn't want to learn it from *me* because I'm her stuffy, aggravating dad.

Fine.

Whatever makes her safer.

Justin turns his grin on her, bright-eyed and enthusiastic. He reminds me of a big kid himself sometimes, and I often forget he's older than Peace.

"That'd be cool, Chief," he says, then turns to Andrea. "And your friend Clark might be able to help out, right? You want to help, too?"

Andrea sucks in a gasp, her grin broadening. "Oh, yeah, totally! I'll ask him!"

I feel like I'm watching ping-pong with words.

Justin's just earned himself a friend for life, giving Andrea a good excuse to bring Clark into this.

While the two of them keep chattering away, Peace catches my eye.

And she smiles, something fond and approving in her eyes.

The sly smile I beam back at her sunny face tells me everything.

I haven't fucked this up just yet.

* * *

I AM ABOUT to kill Justin if he makes me take another damn photo with him, though.

Yeah, yeah, I know it's his thing.

Guess it's how he holds on to stuff, after the way he lost his ma—being able to capture and save the good moments so he'll have them even when people are gone.

I don't like smiling for photos.

Feels like I'm grimacing as he herds us into a tight cluster for a few selfies.

Though it doesn't hurt one bit to have Peace pressed against my side.

He finally lets us go and takes just a few more selfies with Andrea before we all break apart to start the kitchen cleanup. I tell Justin he doesn't have to help since he's a guest, but he's already gathering up dishes.

Whatever.

Like I said, I want him feeling like he's part of something, even if it's not quite family.

As he's helping me rinse dishes and load up the dishwasher, he glances over at me several times. It's this uncertain look that tells me he's probably got something emotional to say, but you know how younger guys are.

All ego and pride and being emotionally constipated. Like it's weird or some shit to just have a feeling in front of another man. Or anyone at all.

Can't say I have room to talk with the way I seize up around Peace till she splits me open with her sweetness.

"Hey, Chief...thanks," he manages finally.

It's gruff, quiet, but there, and he clears his throat, avoiding my eyes.

I don't push it, just nod, smiling to myself as I scrape the last of the half-burnt sauce out of the ribs pan and into the trash.

"Just dinner," I say, giving him an easy out so he won't be too embarrassed. "You're welcome over any time."

"Yeah?"

For just a second he's young again—eyes lit up, eager, head lifting to look at me with something almost like wonder. Then it's like he catches himself, and remembers we're supposed to be big tough manly men. He clears his throat again and takes the pan from me to angle it into the lower rack of the dishwasher.

"That'd be cool, maybe," he says.

Maybe.

Again, I keep my grin to myself, and we just settle back to work.

I think that's the end of it till we're almost done and I'm draining the sink.

Then he speaks so quietly I barely hear him, looking down at his hands as he dries them off.

"Thank you again. I mean...with my mother gone and who knows where my dad ran off to...it's cool. So I hope this isn't weird or out of line but...I've kind of always looked at you like a stand-in dad, Chief. And it's nice just to..." He makes an embarrassed sound, then finishes, "...to have something like a family."

Yeah.

Yeah, now I know one hundred percent I've done something right.

Ma never gave me a good example of what a family should look like, but I've been trying to work that out for myself come hell or high water.

One thing I've learned over the years is family doesn't always mean blood.

It means you can rely on each other. And I hope I can let Justin rely on me.

With a snort and a smile, I clap a hand on his shoulder.

"Just don't start calling me Dad," I tease and squeeze gently so he knows it's okay.

It's damned well okay by me.

Then I toss my head at the kitchen door. "C'mon, man. Let's go see what the girls are doing."

* * *

THE REST of the evening is pretty uneventful.

We chill and chat for a bit. Andrea gets tired of pulling Justin between grown-up conversations and curious questions and heads upstairs to sulk in her room.

Justin looks almost guilty, looking after her, but he's distracted soon enough. We talk about the safety course and listen to Peace tell stories about the weird places she's been all over the States where they do similar big shows with fire.

I'm tired by the time he heads out and go out back with one last beer for the night by the fire pit.

It's becoming something of a ritual.

Beer, quiet, and the silvery snow all around, the flames lashing at my side.

Least my bum leg's not acting up, so I can enjoy it.

Gotta say, I wouldn't mind if Peace had a go at it again.

Being under her healing hands beats the starry darkness and silence.

Thinking her name summons her. The door opens behind me, light spilling across me and then dimming again as it closes, and her soft footsteps take her to the chair on the other side of the pit.

She flops down, bundled up in her big coat, hands in her pockets, and blows out a little cloud of breath before murmuring, "Hey."

"Hey yourself." With a small smile, I set my beer down on the little side table.

"Dinner was nice," she says, quiet but sincere, while she looks up at the sky and the horizon.

"Yep, chef's special," I agree, then add, "Thanks for helping out."

She tilts her head toward me with a little smile. "Just earning my keep, right?"

I chuckle. "You don't have to."

Come on, man, a voice growls in the back of my mind. *It's now or never.*

"I'm sorry, Peace. About before, going off on Holt in front of you." I throw her a heated look.

Her smile fades, her eyes darkening thoughtfully as she cocks her head. She doesn't say anything, just listening while I take a deep breath.

Fuck, I don't want to ruin this quiet, but I feel like I *can't* ruin it with honesty. *We hope.*

That's what she makes me, at least. Honest and real.

"My brother and I, we've got bad blood. Some of it you know about; some of it you don't," I admit. "Still...didn't give me the right to treat you like that."

She's just looking at me, but it's not bad. A second later, her smile comes back, soft and just a little warmer. It's like seeing the sun come up at night.

Ever since my dumb outburst the other night, that brightness was turned down, but now she's ramped it up to eleven.

"Thank you," she says softly, and I duck my head, clearing my throat. "But..."

"But nothing, lady. No use thanking me for apologizing like a decent human being."

"But it wasn't all bad, you going crazy." She leans back in her chair, her face flushing, and it ain't just the fire. "I'd almost think you were jealous."

I shouldn't say it.

I do anyway.

"What if I was?" I counter. "That's Holt's thing—moving in on what's mine—and apparently he's still stuck in high school. I let that shit get in my blood, and next thing you know, I'm practically banging my chest with both fists like *you, Jane. You mine.*"

She bursts out laughing at my silly Tarzan impression, then lifts her eyes to the stars again, her smile only growing. "There's no contest, Blake. You don't have any reason to be jealous."

The humor fades. My eyes fix on her like a hunter's. My blood goes molten.

Then she reaches out her hand, stretching over the warm

glow of the embers in the fire pit, her fingers curled and palm inviting.

I don't even hesitate.

My fingers twine with hers, wrapping up that small soft warmth in my hand.

Her smile only deepens.

So does that heady, possessive burn in my chest.

So does the *ache* below the beltline, the surefire knowledge that one fine day, I *will* mark this woman from the inside out. And when it happens, when we fuck, when we finally speak in flesh and heat and thundering moans, I'm not sure *you mine* will ever be a joke again.

Tracing my fingers over her skin, I try to behave as her hand gets hotter, almost fiery in mine.

Together, we watch the stars.

XIII: ROCK AND ROLL AIN'T EASY (PEACE)

This place shouldn't feel so much like home.

It's hard to remember it isn't.

I haven't really had a home in years.

My home is a burned-out van still going through a ton of body work and internal renovations at Mitch's autobody shop.

I take my home with me like a snail shell wherever I go.

The dream of settling down died a long time ago, after Dad never came home and Mom closed off the way she did.

I made myself believe home was in my heart.

But maybe that's why it's so hard to shake this feeling. Blake's house as home.

He's digging his way deeper into my heart with every touch and snarly-faced glance. And the last two weeks I've spent crashing at his place isn't doing anything to put the brakes on.

I get to see this man half-asleep in the morning with his hair sticking up everywhere and a faded old t-shirt clinging to his chest, his pajama pants threatening to fall off the beastly angles of his hips.

I get to see him taut and ready and rushing to work, slinging into his coveralls at the report of a campfire gone wild in a nearby RV park.

I get to see him tired at the end of the night—covered in grease and soot, shoulders heavy, but half the weight he carries is pride at a job well done.

I get to see him love Andrea.

I get to see him fight with her, too, even if she's clearly trying to be on her best behavior with me around.

Doesn't mean they aren't oil and water.

No, let's be honest, more like gas and flame.

Their fights are combustive, but I try to sit them out.

Except somehow, I always wind up helping, holding somebody's hand until they feel better.

It's only temporary, I tell myself.

I'm not the little woman here, no matter how many times I help around the house with breakfast and dinner and cleaning.

I can't stay forever.

Blake can't be responsible for me when Andrea's his world.

And I can't keep scaring him every time I refuse his offer to chaperone me, and head out to my clients' cabins and houses for work.

I hadn't expected to be as busy as I am in a town this small, honestly.

But there are a lot of seniors here. Arthritis and rheumatism everywhere. Things that flare up in winter in ways some medications just don't help.

It's not all people work, either.

Don't ask me how I spend a day massaging an arthritic cow's knees.

Just don't.

I have the weirdest life sometimes.

But it's a long day out in the boonies beyond the limits of Heart's Edge, and I'm already tired—but I've still got a full night ahead. I drive my little purple people eater rental car as fast as I can to zoom back to Blake's house to shower up and get ready.

By the time I'm finished and dragging on clean, warm clothes, there's a knock at the door.

I don't even have to look outside to recognize Ember's car. Grabbing my guitar case and tumbling down the stairs, I open the door to find her bright-eyed and happy in a white fluffy peacoat and matching gloves and cap.

She doesn't say anything, squealing with a grin.

So do I.

Tonight, it's freaking happening.

We're bouncing and hugging each other before tumbling into my car for the drive to the radio station.

It really does kind of feel like we're in a movie.

Blake invited us in for more than bumper music, to *play* over the airwaves, where we'll get picked up and broadcast not just locally, but as far as Spokane and Coeur d'Alene and Missoula and Seattle.

It's exciting. Terrifying. Enthralling.

I can't *wait*.

But as we buckle into the car, I glance over at Ember, who's empty-handed.

"Hey," I say. "Where's your violin?"

She blinks, looking down at her hands as if she's magically expecting the violin to appear out of nowhere. Her cheeks go bright pink.

"Oh my God," she says. "I was so excited I left it at the clinic!"

I can't help but laugh, too, even as I twist to shove my guitar into the back seat. "No worries. We've got a few minutes, and it's on the way there. We'll stop and pick it up."

She flashes me a grateful smile—then holds on to the oh-shit handles as I back the purple people eater—that's its official name now because snozzberry makes me feel like I'm going to sneeze every time I say it—out of Blake's driveway, doing a little fishtail spin before we hit the road.

Ember lets out a whistle. "You handled that curve like a pro."

"I've gotten used to it." I laugh. "My car's smaller than Blake's, so I can pull off the easy tricks. Maybe my next gig will be a stunt car driver."

That aches, though.

In ways it never has.

I'm so used to packing up and moving on when the work dries up or I just get the itch to be on the road, but...

Somehow, I haven't started feeling that itch here.

I don't think I want to leave.

"Hmm. Don't think there's much work for that kind of driver here, Peace. But if you're ever hard up...we can always use an extra hand at The Menagerie." Ember smiles at me.

"And let me lose my mind around those adorable animals all day?" I half-smile, my throat tight, touched at her offering even though I'm not hard up. "Thanks, but I've got plenty of work coming in. I always find something."

"So you're not staying?" she asks in the gentle way she has that seems to invite people to spill their souls out.

But it's still hard for me to say it out loud.

Hard for me to admit.

"I...I kinda want to." I bite my lip. "I think I want to stay with Blake."

"Oh, Peace!" She lights up with a smile. "How are things going with him?"

"Maybe you tell me?" I whisper, my face flaming. "I mentioned the time he kissed me half to death, and I've been waiting for it to happen again...but I'm starting to worry he sees me like family. As in, *blood* family."

She looks amused. "Nah, I don't think he'd get all roid ragey in his brother's face over you if he saw you like kin."

"He might if he saw me the same way he sees his daughter. You know how he gets with Andrea and Clark. Totally overprotective." I sigh deeply. "I mean, he apologized for that. For getting weird with Holt. And admitted he was jealous. And I told him he had no reason to be, and..."

That's it.

Me, biting my lip like a schoolgirl waiting for the hottest boy ever to *make a big move.*

I groan, thunking my forehead on the steering wheel for a second before straightening up to keep the car on the road.

"He's a tough nut to crack," I mutter. "Every time I think I'm getting under his skin, he just pulls back, gets busy, like he's trying real hard not to make a mistake with me."

"It's sweet," she whispers. "Frustrating as blazes, but sweet that he cares. His first wife died, and he's got a daughter to protect. Even if he's ready to open up, old habits die hard."

"I know," I murmur, watching for her vet clinic's sign. We're getting close. "The thing is, I don't want to push him so hard I break *him*."

Finally, we pull into the parking lot at The Menagerie.

But something isn't right.

There's an old boarded-up ice cream shop next to the clinic, empty, and—

Oh, God.

It's billowing smoke.

Thick plumes jet out of the side window, gathering in the narrow alley between the buildings and arcing toward the sky, flames leaping out of the open windows a second later.

Jets that lash out at the clinic.

And catch on the wood eaves lining the overhanging roof.

Ember lets out a heartbreaking squeal, already scrambling for the door before I can even stop the car. "The animals!"

Oh my God.

Oh my God, there are live animals inside...and the clinic's catching fire.

Heart in my throat, sickness in my belly, I fly out after her, already reaching for my phone.

"Don't rush in!" I cry, though there's no stopping her as she bolts for the front door, ripping her keys out of her pocket.

We need help.

And I know the only man to call.

I'm hitting Blake's contact and I can't breathe for the three rings it takes him to pick up with a lazy, drawling, "Hey, sweetheart."

"Blake?" I gasp, though it comes out almost as more of a whimper. "Help—*help*, you've got to hurry. The Menagerie is on fire."

* * *

THE LAST TIME I watched Blake Silverton put out a fire, I ended up trying to stay out of the way even though I wanted nothing more than to help.

This time, I wind up on the rescue crew.

Because there were over two dozen animals inside the clinic, and Ember couldn't wait.

I couldn't wait, either.

So we formed a relay, ferrying the cages out to my car, and working carefully between us to lift and move a ginormous St. Bernard who was too drugged and injured to walk after he'd been in a car accident. The poor thing whimpered as we eased him along, and I made sure to turn the car heater on as high as it would go before leaving him bedded down on a spare blanket in the passenger seat.

My car is full of grunting, mewing, and squawking in no time.

And my arms are full of wriggling Labrador. There's no more room in my car, and someone's got to hold this chocolate-colored monster while Blake and his crew hose down the clinic and the shop next to it.

At least it wasn't as bad as the fabric place; we called it in just in time. The damage to The Menagerie looks pretty minor.

But they had to break the doors on the vacant ice cream shop to get inside with a fire hose, and the smoke is gone except for a heavy, burning, chemical scent.

Not good.

Not at all.

I don't think fires normally smell like chemicals.

I can't help noticing how grim Blake looks, marshaling Justin and Rich to do a few more runs with their gear to make sure they haven't missed anything.

He looks so troubled, even if he's standing tall and strong in those fireman's coveralls, soot streaked down one angular, chiseled cheek.

I so wish I could go to him.

But it's me, the chocolate lab, and my freezing cheeks. The dog keeps licking me and then leaving it to turn into frost against my skin.

Ember's leaning hard on her husband—Doc.

He showed up even before Blake, rushing inside to save what he could, dirt streaked up and down his normally immaculate button-down. The back of his truck is full of animal carriers and blankets, too.

It took all four of us to get every pet to safety while Justin and Rich started on the flames, but at least we got them all out before they could suffer from the smoke.

Doc sighs, his lips thinning.

"We'll start looking for a new place in the morning, Firefly," he tells Ember.

Her eyes widen, and she lifts her head, looking up at him.

"You mean we're...we're abandoning The Menagerie?" she asks, her voice soft, small, destroyed.

"Not abandoning," Doc growls, his emerald-green eyes flashing behind his glasses. "Making do while it gets fixed."

My heart almost dies.

The man has such a reputation around town for being cold, untouchable, those green eyes flinty and a little unnerving.

But when he looks at Ember, they go so warm. There's so much love in the way he holds her, the way he tucks her hair back, the way his voice softens just for her.

Even when they're sad, they have it all.

A deep, secret part of me aches for someone to look at me that way.

Make that a very *specific* someone.

Doc half-smiles, tired and distracted. "Even if the damage was modest, we can't keep sick animals here for now. There'll be residual smoke and carcinogens, plus the reconstruction noise and sawdust won't help, either. So we'll find somewhere temporary that's safe for them—and us—until we're done rebuilding. It won't take long. Promise."

Her brilliant smile of relief is contagious. I find myself smiling, too, as she lays her head against his arm.

"I'm glad, Gray." She squeezes his arm then, looking up at him in concern. "But are *you* all right? Does this bring back...you know, the memories? The lab fire?"

Doc's face creases, and he bows his head, a flicker of pain crossing his features. He leans in and mutters something I can't hear.

I feel weird.

Like maybe I shouldn't be watching something this intimate.

It's too private. I'm just an outsider here, not privy to all their pains and histories. I'm just standing here awkwardly holding an upset, nervous dog, shut out on the fringes.

I look away, glancing over the rows of pet carriers lining the back of Doc's truck, full of angry cats, dogs, birds, even one very upset-looking pot-bellied pig.

It's the pig's carrier that catches my attention.

Because I think there's a black envelope tucked into the handle of it.

Frowning, I drift closer and take the opportunity to ease my aching arms by setting the lab down in a free space in the back of the truck, right on top of a tarp so the frigid metal won't hurt his paws. While the dog spins around in agitated circles and I try to calm him with scratches behind the ears, I brace my other hand against the edge of the truck bed and peer in for a closer look.

It's an envelope, all right.

"Blake?" I call, looking over my shoulder.

He takes a second to break from his trance, staring up at the building with his mouth set in a grim, forbidding line. Then he looks at me, dark-blue eyes questioning, and I toss my head a little, beckoning him.

He trudges over. "What's up, Peace? You didn't get hurt, did you?"

"Just a little dog spit frostbite," I say with a tired smile, nodding my chin toward the pig's carrier. "That envelope there...that's not normal, is it?"

His face goes dark, almost wary. He leans in to tug it free from under the carrier's handle. It's stuck on surprisingly hard, and he has to yank a few times before it rips loose.

He flicks the flap with his thumb and spills a folded sheet of paper into his palm.

Blue.

Just like the last note he showed me.

Oh, no.

His face goes black with fury as he scans the handwriting I can just make out in dark slashes of ink, though I can't tell what it says.

"Doc!" he barks. "Get your ass over here."

Doc pulls away from Ember with a kiss on her forehead, glancing at us curiously, icing over with his usual stone-cold calm as he steps closer.

His expression barely twitches as he reads the note. But I swear, there's something dark, something deadly in the gleam of his eyes.

"So now it's my turn," he says flatly. "I see."

"I don't understand," I say, stepping closer. "What's happening?"

I'm expecting them to ignore me. This isn't my business.

But Blake turns the note so I can see. When I do, my blood runs colder than the winter wind battering us.

*If only you'd **kept your germs to yourself, Doctor. Heart's Edge wouldn't catch fever.***

Fever.

Fire.

And I know this story, it's the one that made headlines nationwide.

The corrupt company, Galentron, that used Heart's Edge as this secret base to develop lethal weapons, and tried—twice—to cover up their tests with extreme force.

Doc was one of the scientists, I think, before he realized what it was really about and tried to shut it down.

Meanwhile, Leo—Nine—*did* shut it down. But at the cost of so many lives lost in the Paradise Hotel fire drama. His own huge, tattooed body was scarred wild, and he became a wanted man for years.

I feel dizzy.

Until a warm, wet, raspy tongue slides across my cheek.

I groan, pushing at the Labrador's head.

"Stop that," I mutter, which actually gets a smile out of Blake, however tired.

I wonder how much more he can take. All this pressure and stress before he *snaps*.

When the breaking point comes, it's usually explosive, and it can hurt our bodies in ways we never recover from.

Part of me wants to drag Blake home right now. Get him on my table and do everything I can to relieve some of that stress.

But I know I can't divert him from this.

"Stay here, try to keep them warm. Lots more blankets in the fire truck," he tells me.

I can only listen, watching him walk away to disappear inside the ice cream shop.

At least that gives me and Ember something to do.

We grab the extra blankets and start using them to insulate the pet carriers. We know the sickest beasts crowding my car are warm with the heat going, but these poor things shouldn't have to be shivering out here in the wind with just thin plastic walls to protect them. The blankets should help.

And my chocolate-furred friend gets a blanket of his own, wrapped snug around him, bundling him up. He finally calms down a bit, curling up in his spot in the back of the truck, resting his head on his paws. I settle on the tailgate, swinging my legs, scratching behind his ears and watching the few glimpses I can get of Blake through the shop's boarded-up windows.

He emerges awhile later, his expression set in stone. Doc's at his side, the two of them bowed over something held between them, talking in furious whispers.

I'm a little surprised when they beeline toward me.

The thing they're holding...it's some kind of metal contraption.

Looks almost like a cuff, but with a nozzle and some kind of lighter-like mechanism attached, and a little empty metal tank that's been burnt and dented in. It's small enough to fit on someone's arm, maybe.

They stop in front of me, both of them glaring so grimly I wonder if *I* did something wrong.

Then Blake speaks. "Peace, you're absolutely *sure* the person you saw setting fires wasn't Clark Patten?"

I bite my lip.

"Mostly," I say. "The guy wasn't skinny enough, and he was maybe a little taller than Clark? It's hard to tell when Clark slouches so much. Why?"

"Because," Blake grinds out. "This is Clark's gear. The shit he borrows from his Uncle Rog for his little fire shows. I'd like to know why the hell it's here."

* * *

I'M LEFT WITH EMBER, soothing the animals, while Blake, Justin, and Rich do walk-throughs to check for any more incendiaries or buried embers that could rekindle the fire.

Doc's taking photos for assessments already.

He's not the only one.

Justin's got his phone out, his brows set in a fierce line as he snaps shots of different burnt areas of brick and wood.

I'd watched Blake show him the note, and his expression settled into a deep, worried scowl while they whispered to each other.

Something's terribly wrong.

I'm usually a pretty good judge of character. I can't believe I misjudged Clark.

It just doesn't add up.

I don't think Clark would do this.

But considering how highly specialized the pyrotechnic equipment is...

God, I don't know what to think.

Ember leans in next to me, the two of us keeping each other warm at the shoulders. She watches her husband storm around with her easygoing face drawn tight with worry.

"When does it stop?" she asks softly. "When do we finally get to just...live?"

"I wish I knew, honey," I answer. "Wish I had some kind of answer for you."

* * *

IT'S hours before we can finally leave.

There'll be no show at the radio station tonight.

Warren and Haley are next on the scene, because apparently, for now, all the animals are being relocated to Ms. Wilma's place and the central atrium at the Charming Inn. It's not a bad plan, but it's a lot of work getting half of them transferred to Warren's truck for more space—and I give my Labrador buddy one last scratch behind the ears before he disappears.

Doc and Ember are next, hauling the other beasts. They'll swing by to pick up her car before heading home to take solace in each other after taking the other pets off my hands.

Then Justin and Rich and Blake. They get on the fire truck.

I barely catch up with Blake, resting my hand on his arm just as he's getting in.

He looks downright *broken.*

This massive statue of a man that's been struck by a metal fist, and cracks are radiating through his soul. Maybe others can't see them, but me?

I see everything.

And how he's leaning *hard* on his right leg, meaning the left one is acting up.

He stops at my touch, looking down at me with his brows drawn together.

I offer a faint smile.

"Hey," I say. "Drive home with me. Let the guys take the truck back."

He frowns. "Why?"

I glance past him, at Rich and Justin, lowering my voice. "Do you really want to drive on that leg?"

He bristles instantly. I wait for him to shut down, to thrust me away.

Instead, he groans, looking away and closing his eyes.

I hear the driver's door slam. He lifts a hand to signal the guys, then looks down at me.

"Don't know how the fuck I'm gonna fit in that tiny car of yours," he says, and I grin. "But *fine,* Miss Broccoli."

XIV: DEEP TEMPO (BLAKE)

*S*omehow, I fit into that tiny ass huckleberry car of hers.

It's close. Tight. Cramped.

I can't really say it's much better for this bum leg of mine when I'm all tensed up in the passenger seat, my thigh already throbbing. Still, it'd be worse if I had to wrangle that fire truck back to the station and then drive myself home.

It's hard to focus on the pain during the drive home.

Hard to think about anything but the fact that this town's in danger again, and I feel like it's my fault.

Yeah, so the arsonist has gone after Warren, Leo, Doc.

Not me.

Not yet.

But the fact that the scum are using fire?

Maybe it's to hurt Leo and Doc and kick up chaos, sure.

It feels like they're baiting me.

Trying to draw me out, one messy combustion blaze at a time.

It's like in all the little messages to my friends, there's a deeper message:

You're next.

Like hell.

Because if anyone hurts me, that's gonna hurt Andrea.

And it might just hurt Peace, too.

I won't fucking let it happen.

Something stinks *rotten*.

I know where that equipment came from. There's nobody in town who has that shit but Clark and his Uncle Rog.

But Peace said she was sure it wasn't Clark.

So would it be Roger?

What the hell would Roger Patten be doing setting fires like this?

I mean, he's always been a bit of an old weirdo, this drifter type making his life in show biz.

Maybe he's starting to go a little soft in the head, and his lifelong obsession with pyrotechnics is turning dangerous.

Trouble is, I don't even think Rog is in town right now, unless he's laying low. That's the main reason Clark's been taking over the prep for the carnival shows, with Roger off doing stuff in other states for winter, flitting in and out of town.

I still can't stop thinking about my brother.

He's no firebug, not that I've known.

But that's the problem.

We've been estranged for so long. I don't know Holt anymore.

And he's not stupid. He works construction. Even if he's more on the business side now, I've seen him bust his balls before his stint in the Air Force—and he can work some pretty complicated shit.

He'd be able to rig up something easy if he set his mind to it.

Hell, he's been skulking around town, talking to people.

Probably sneaking talks with my daughter whenever he gets a chance. He knows damn well I won't let him back in the house to see her, but I can't watch her every minute.

All she'd have to do is drop hints that I'm trying to beat up her boy over fires he didn't set, and she'd give Holt his scapegoat.

Is that it?

Is Holt setting Clark up?

I wouldn't put it past him.

Still...it doesn't totally jive. I feel like one of the UFO guys who call my show, ranting and raving about the sketchiest rumors.

Like I'm twisting things around to suit wild theories because I don't want to doubt Peace's judgment with Clark. Or Andrea's.

Don't want to doubt my own good sense, either.

Even if I think Clark's a smarmy, proud little asshole...

The kid had an alibi. Langley told me so himself.

And he's not old enough to know who Jenna Ford was other than a name dropped here and there, let alone worship her like some kind of hero we've failed to honor.

None of it makes *sense*.

I'm missing something.

I feel like it's right in front of my face.

I'm still stuck on *what* by the time Peace pulls into the driveway, the empty spot where my Jeep should be. I'll have to go back to where I left it parked at the station in the morning.

I'm almost hoping to see Clark's ratty Pinto there, too, but there's no sign of it. Andrea's window upstairs is dark.

Probably out screwing around in the woods with her friends again.

The only reason I haven't put more of a stop to it is because it'll just make her go overboard.

Girl doesn't even like the taste of moonshine after she spent a night puking it up. She still insists she wasn't drunk that night she came home way back last year, puking her guts out and weaving.

Besides, she's never let teenage shenanigans come between her and school.

I leave her to be smart. If she drinks that crap again, she'll take one or two sips for show, just to fit in with her friends and then pass it on.

"Hey," Peace says gently. "Earth to Blake."

Then her hand is on my thigh—just below the scar.

It should hurt.

Should hurt like hell, but all I get is warmth.

Like it just drifts off her, this gorgeous candlelight of a girl who soaks her heat into me and soothes storms with the lightest touch.

"Blake?" she whispers again.

"Sorry. I zoned out." I jerk away from glaring out the window and look down at her.

"I could tell." She smiles playfully. "I've been waiting for you to get out so I can lock the car for over a minute."

"Uh. Oops." Clearing my throat, I pry myself out of the little purple car, stepping into the snow—and hissing, clutching at the car roof to hold myself up as I try to put my weight on my bum leg, and it says *fuck you, nope*.

Pain like chainsaw teeth ratchets through me, and I growl, closing my eyes. "Fuck."

"Hey—you'll be okay. C'mon."

I feel the car door slam, rocking it, and then she's there, pressed against my side. Her arm winds around my waist as she eases me away from the car, into her warmth.

"It's okay, Blake," she whispers. "I'm here."

"I...fuck. I'm too heavy," I manage to grit out, and she laughs softly.

"I'm stronger than I look. It's okay. Let's just get you inside. It's not far."

My pride wants to rebel, turning into this mangled, helpless thing in front of this beautiful woman.

But there's no room for ego. If I try to be stubborn and stagger my way back, I'm gonna tumble us both into the snow.

So, reluctantly, I lean away from the car, clumsily shoving the door closed, and let my weight lean on her carefully.

She dips a little, but she's right—girl's stronger than she looks.

Then one hobbling, fire-burning step at a time, we make our way up the drive.

It's the porch steps that are the worst. My leg's turned into a brick with every step, and suddenly I can't fucking bend it without feeling like someone's shoving a molten steel rod right through the muscle.

Snarling, I stomp up, then slump against the wall next to the door.

I go stiff as a mummy while her hand slips into my open coat, burrowing down into the pocket of my jeans.

Pain or no pain, I can't really ignore it.

That warmth sliding down my hip, my thigh, way too close to my cock.

Hell, maybe I'm some kind of freak because suddenly it's like the pain just makes my cock throb harder as she twirls her fingers around down there.

Shitfire.

She can't know what she's doing to me.

Not when she looks so focused, so distracted.

And so triumphant, emerging with my keys—then giving me a sheepish look.

"I've been kind of timing leaving and coming home around Andrea," she says, pushing the key to the lock and opening the door. "It feels presumptuous to ask you for a spare."

I'll make you one, I want to say. *You can stay as long as you want. You can be home.*

But the words are locked up behind my teeth.

I don't know if it's the pain that keeps me silent, or just knowing the truth.

She's gonna leave.

Sooner or later, she'll go back to her cabin when I figure out who's setting these damn fires and she's not in danger anymore. Or spring will come, and she'll leave Heart's Edge for good.

She'll leave me.

You don't chain a girl like her down.

That's another bitter crushing pain, keeping me trapped inside my own head, as I drag in behind her and march myself to the couch.

Forget being graceful.

I just flop down on my back, closing my eyes, letting my bum-ass leg stretch out and easing some of the weight on it.

Peace makes a soft sound that's half amusement and half worry. I hear the door shut and the sounds of her stripping off her jacket.

"I'm not getting you up again, am I?"

"Not without at least two Vicodin," I mutter, draping my arm over my eyes. "Sorry. I'm actually keeping off that shit. This leg always gets worse the longer winter drags on. I'm never ready for it. I just need to rest a bit."

"What you need," she says firmly, "is a massage. And if I can't get you off the sofa and on my table, I'll just have to strip you down right here."

Is she serious?

I tense, opening an eye, peering up at her from under my arm. "Damn, woman. Can't say I've ever met a girl *that* eager to get me naked."

"No? So the stories they tell about you are exaggerated?" She flashes a saucy little smile and tosses her hair back, sending it slithering around to lay on the other side of her neck and pour down her shoulder. "They swear you were quite the ladies' man in your younger days."

I snort, closing my eyes again. "I grew out of that shit by my senior year. Think they're confusing me with Holt. He went nuts seeing how many chicks would throw themselves at me, and then kept stealing girls I had just to get under my skin."

There's silence.

When I look, she's just standing there, her hands on her

cocked, curving hips, watching me wryly. I grunt, unable to help cracking a smile.

"I know. I know, it's fucking awful, but I was a horndog teenager, and Holt treated it like a competition. I feel bad for those poor girls, honestly. We were *both* dicks, even if it was him who left 'em in pieces and me who let 'em down easy."

"As long as you've grown up." She settles down on the couch, her weight denting the cushions at my calves, and then those soft hands are pulling on me as she starts working at my bootlaces. "Let's get you ready."

I arch a brow. "You're really gonna strip me on my own couch?"

A wicked grin makes her eyes darken and glitter.

Aw, hell. She's serious.

Peace drags one of my boots off, then catches the toe of my sock and peels me out of it. "I've finally got you at my mercy, Mr. Silver Tongue. And you can't fight back. What red-blooded girl *wouldn't* take advantage of the last standing heartthrob of Heart's Edge in that situation?"

Goddamn.

That might almost be hot in a crazy, bad porno kinda way.

If I wasn't laughing my damn fool head off.

"Heartthrob of Heart's Edge? *Fuck.* Don't tell me that dumb Instagram account Ember's ma runs is still going?"

"Yup! She showed me. It's up to like a million followers. Her mama's pretty crazy for all the hot guys around here."

"Yeah, fuck. Doc told me all about it." Snickering, I pull my good leg back and shove her shoulder lightly with the heel of my bare foot. "Heartthrob, my ass. I ain't nobody's."

She might just be mine, though, with the way my heart skips a beat when she laughs.

"You might not think so," she teases, starting on my other foot with an arched look my way from under her lashes. "But I have it on good authority that every single lady in town pines away into their lattes at The Nest, mourning the fact that you're probably being taken off the market by some out-of-town witch with purple ends."

My whole body prickles.

If she wants to take me off the market...hell, that doesn't sound half bad.

I almost say it.

Almost slip right then and there, but I rein myself in and force a smug smile. "Nobody told them they got the wrong idea, huh?"

She's just staying with me for safety, even if she's getting crazy ideas in her head.

I practically put her under lock and key.

I gotta remember that.

Peace falters a second, glancing at me before fixing her gaze on her hand as she pulls my other boot off. "I don't think it's worth the argument. Most of them will figure out soon enough I'm just a tourist, anyway. So they can stop fretting."

There it is.

That reminder she isn't from here.

This isn't her home.

I'm not her home.

It shouldn't get me so riled up.

I bite my tongue while she drags my other sock off, then shifts her weight up to sit at my side, her hip pressing into my waist.

"Here," she murmurs, pushing my coat open. "Sit up for me a little."

I can't resist her. Not even when these feelings are sinking into my gut like a boulder, and I manage to haul myself up on my hands without jouncing myself too much so she can help me out of my jacket.

Then she's got my shirt, fingers on the buttons, peeling the flannel open.

I can't stop watching her.

She's so close, her mouth red and sweet, a rosebud.

Nah—more like a strawberry.

A thick, luscious, juicy red strawberry you just want to sink your teeth into for a wet bite of tart sweetness.

One taste of her lips was enough to leave me addicted, obsessed, undone.

It's a miracle I'm even looking at her without throwing her on her back and drinking my fill, pain be damned.

She's quiet, her eyes on her hands while she works at the buttons, but now and then there's a glance.

Her, catching me through those long lashes that make the green of her eyes stand out even more.

Her lips part subtly, just enough to see the gleaming tip of her tongue.

And me barely breathing.

This feels too fucking intimate, her hands trawling down my body, parting my shirt. She stands, working me out of it with gentle gestures that make her fingers glide across my body.

When she catches the hem of my undershirt, I nearly lose it.

Her knuckles, her nails, skim over my naked skin as she pushes the cotton up across my abs, my chest. I lift my arms and let her peel it over my head.

Fuck. Don't think I've ever let a woman undress me before.

From anyone else it'd feel diminishing.

Weird.

This helpless, sorry bastard being pampered by this knockout chick.

With Peace, though, it's almost too powerful.

Even just to strip me down for a massage, she's got this certain care for my body. It makes her touch worshipful, like she's handling something important, something that means the moon and the stars to her.

I almost can't stand the silence between us.

The prickling tension.

Or how damn bad I want to put my hands on her body like I own it and just feel her warmth soaking into my fingertips.

She holds my eyes as I flop back against the sofa. Then she settles again, bracing one knee against the cushion, her hands falling to rest on my stomach just above the waist of my jeans.

I can't help sucking in a breath through my teeth, shuddering, her touch so *hot*, my skin so crazy for this mad, sexy woman.

"You okay?" she asks softly. "This might hurt, getting your jeans off."

Real cute. I don't think she guesses the real pain I'm in.

Wanting her so bad I can hardly feel the hissing agony in my thigh. Not when the *need* burning in my gut cuts twice as deep.

So I nod, licking my lips, bracing myself. "Rip the Band-Aid off, darlin'."

"I'll try to be more careful than that." She smiles gently.

So she says.

But she's fucking me up *hardcore* as those nimble fingers flick the button of my jeans open and draw the zipper down.

I try one more time to tell myself this is nothing to her.

It's a job, ain't it? She undresses clients all the time. She's seen human bodies in every state imaginable.

But it's hard to be objective when she's dragging the denim down my hips, and it's pulling my boxer-briefs so tight against me, the fabric rubbing hard, teasing at a reckless hard-on that's pure torture.

Yeah, I'm boned.

Peace can't be blind.

She can't miss what's going on, tugging my jeans around my thighs and leaving me with nothing but my underwear guarding my growing cock, an unmistakable bulge against the cotton.

Her gaze darts downward.

Her cheeks blush that gorgeous shade of sunset, cherries and ocean sky and dawn and every pretty redness in between.

Fuck.

Her lower lip catches between her teeth, and she averts her eyes.

But I think she's breathing a little harder as my jeans come down the rest of the way.

Then the heel of her palm knocks my scar.

Pain explodes over me like a nuclear bomb.

I snarl, rolling forward, clutching at my thigh with a blistering litany of curses. Suddenly, I'm not thinking with my cock anymore.

I'm thinking with every bit of agony in me. Peace makes a distressed sound, tossing my jeans aside.

"Crap," she gasps. "I'm sorry, I—hold on. I'll fix it."

I just squeeze my eyes shut, gritting my teeth, while she darts away from the room.

She's not gone long.

Through the roar in my ears I hear her rattling around upstairs, digging, before she comes clattering back down with the case she uses for her massage oils.

She careens back to the sofa, dropping down next to me. The case hits the coffee table and snaps open. If I wasn't hurting so damn bad, I might almost laugh. She makes me think of an Army medic with a go bag diving in to save a soldier down.

Hell, I feel like a man down right now.

"Let's see..." she whispers.

She rifles through her bottles and comes up with one that has a faint reddish-gold tint to the oil inside. Soon she's got a palmful, rubbing her hands together to warm it with swift friction.

The scent is explosive. Something with a pungent bite like cinnamon, maybe leather. I don't know. But just the scent alone is soothing.

It gets me breathing again, ready for her hands, her heat.

"Ahhh, baby," I growl. It falls out spontaneously. "You're so the shit."

She laughs, giving me a heavenly stroke. I love how fast this stuff numbs me up.

Pure soothing heat drenches me, melts into my flesh, and I groan, shuddering.

The pain relief isn't instant, not by a mile, but it's better than a legion of needles ripping at my flesh.

"What is that stuff?" I ask, focusing on how she kneads my flesh.

"My own custom blend, sort of," she says. Her voice has that steady, soft warmth that she settles into when she's working, like she can heal with the hypnotic rhythm of her words as much as the rhythm of her touch. "Have you ever heard of BPAL?"

I shake my head, leaning back a bit, making myself lie down and letting her work.

I gotta trust her.

Let her do her thing.

And I try to relax as she works her fingers in knowing circles over the scar. Each pulse of pain is a little less terrible, a little less raw.

"Never heard of it," I say.

"Black Phoenix Alchemy Labs." She laughs. "When I was a kid, it was this big thing online. They make these oil-based scents, instead of alcohol-based or water-based colognes. It only takes a dab to last all day, but they're unique because they respond to your body chemistry and mix with your skin pH to make your own scent. Which means what smells really good on one person can smell rank on another."

I snort. "You ask me, most normal cologne smells rank anyway, so this already sounds like an improvement."

"Maybe." Her voice softens and so does her touch.

She switches to using the heel of her palm, kneading my pain like dough to make it more pliant, more malleable. I'm almost starting to enjoy how it hurts as that heady scent drifts over me.

"Keep talkin'," I tell her. "Your voice helps me along."

"Well, it used to be this status thing around the online message boards I'd hang out on. You'd get samplers to try out and talk about all the different scents you could throw together. I was into it because it was this cool thing, but I honestly thought half the people were bullshitting." Her voice hitches up, taking on a snooty accent that makes me grin. "I get heart notes of cardamom, with a secondary hint of jasmine and a delicate underpinning of laurel, lavender, and jock straps."

Can't help myself.

I burst out laughing, the feeling helping to loosen more tension knifing through me. "Jock straps, huh?"

"Yep. I bet not one of them could tell the smell of jock straps from cardamom," she says, laughing wickedly. "I don't know what cardamom smells like."

"Got one up on me, darlin'. I don't even know what cardamom *is*."

"Because you're a dude," she teases, warm and sweet, and it aches to hear that fondness in her voice for *me*. "But they had this one line of scents called Dragon's Hide. It was this leathery smell mixed with something else I couldn't identify. It always made me think of Dad. This leather jacket he always wore, all the time, and I just..."

"You tried to make your own?" I ask softly. "So you'd have a scent that reminded you of him."

She nods and swallows thickly.

I open my eyes and watch her in her glory.

The sweet little smile playing around her lips, the way she touches me with tenderness. This woman might just be an angel come to earth.

"But I made it my way, and it kept me working until I figured out the oil I'm using on you right now. Cinnamon. A little fiery, just like me." She shakes her head with a soft, self-deprecating laugh, and her unbound hair shimmers like the spark she is. "The heat helps, don't you think? It's a good topical remedy for pain. Penetrates deep to loosen up the tension and warm the muscles."

"It's working," I tell her. "How come you never used it before?"

"The smell's pretty strong," she says, flicking an almost nervous glance at me from under her lashes. "I'm always worried people won't like it."

"I do," I answer. "It's deep shit. Intoxicating. Sultry, kinda. Helps me limber up."

Her eyes ignite, even if that pixie smile of hers doesn't change.

"Yeah?" she whispers. "I'm glad."

I am, too.

Not for the reasons she's thinking.

I'm just happy to be up in her world tonight.

Glad that she'd take something tied to an important memory and turn it into something she can use to ease people's pain.

It's like this girl was *born* for that name she carries.

She really is a peace to the world and to me.

And she's everything as I close my eyes and settle into silence and let her go to town.

I don't know when I started trusting her hands this much, but I do, just like that big ol' pissed off lion in the story with a splinter in his paw.

I let go.

Drop my pride, drop my defenses, and let Peace Rabe fix my hell.

Boy, does she ever. Every time her hands glide across my flesh, I feel like she's reaching inside to soften my soul.

I know what she told me, when those bad memories hit during that one session. Massage can stir up old pains. It's only natural that touching those trigger points in the body unlocks things that were buried away.

Thing is, pain's not the only thing that's been branded in me.

I haven't been calm or truly happy for a long time.

But she's coaxing that out, reaching down to where the better stuff's buried. She dredges them up and lets them spread through me in a blissful wash of warmth, rolling through my flesh until I'm a relaxed, lazy mess sprawled on the couch.

No pain.

No hurt.

No heartbreak.

No anger, no tension, no loss.

Just me and this fine ass woman.

Her hands on my skin, my body throbbing, and fuck, I can't stop how that wonderful feeling pools in my gut and pulses in my cock again.

This time, it's slow and riled instead of urgent and tense.

Best of all, she never stops touching me.

Telling me, with every tender press of her fingers, that she's not afraid.

Not repelled by whatever this insane, unspeakable thing is between us.

I don't know how long I lie there, letting her turn me into a mess of contentment.

It seems like forever and too soon at the same time when she slowly eases, stopping with her palms resting lightly over my scar.

"How you feeling?" she asks, her voice pure silk in the darkness behind my eyelids. "Better?"

"Oh, yeah," I breathe, opening my eyes, looking up at her hazily. "Doesn't even hurt now. Feels like hot butter."

"Good."

She looks down at me with her eyes half-lidded, her lips parted, and—

Shit.

There's something there.

Something blazing in the rapid pace of her breaths, the way her tits rise and fall, the thinness of her shirt and bra over nipples that press hard little swells against the fabric.

Peace just holds my eyes for several long moments before her gaze darts away. She pulls her hands back, standing and reaching for a towel from her kit.

"Give me a second," she says, a throaty burr darkening her voice. "I'll get everything cleaned up."

Her tongue slides over her lips, her gaze slipping over me for a drawn out second. Then she turns and walks away just a little too fast, vanishing into the kitchen.

I push myself up on one arm and stare after her.

The sway of her hips, the tightness of her sweet, thick ass in her jeans...

Sweet hell, they're pulling on me like gravity.

Something more, too—this intangible *thing* between us, this connection I can't ignore.

And it's urging me to her.

I don't even realize I'm getting up till I'm up. My body feels light, fluid, like she's taken away every scar and every burden I ever had. She's left me stronger.

Strong enough for her.

When I step into the kitchen, she's washing her hands in the sink.

She glances up as I draw closer, turning to face me, wiping her hands off on a towel. "Blake?"

I can't find the words.

No damn words ever made would matter right now. Words can't express this yawning *hunger.*

It's every kind of wrong and I know it.

She's too young. Too sweet. Too temporary.

I'm too broken.

None of it means dick as her smoky eyes flick over me with lingering heat. That blush comes back, enticing, telling me I'm not the only one who feels this. Begging me to shut the hell up and *do* something about it.

So I do.

As her breaths catch.

As her lips part.

As the temperature flares to a hundred degrees.

And I can't resist that strawberry redness of her lips any longer.

I lean down to claim her with a kiss that shatters both our worlds.

XV: CRANK UP THE BASS (PEACE)

*Y*ou don't know torture until you're undressing the most gorgeous man alive and trying to ignore the thick ridge of his cock pressing up against his boxer-briefs.

I don't know how I kept calm during that massage.

Not when every time I touched him, I was fascinated by the feeling of coarse skin under my palms.

The hard sculpture of his body.

The way his face relaxed in bliss and his muscles went loose until he looked like this portrait of lazy passion, from the liquid flow of corded muscle to the part of his lips.

Blake Silverton could mess me up for life without even putting that Silver Tongue to work at all.

Everything in me wanted him so freaking bad, it's a miracle I didn't straddle his lap and kiss and caress him everywhere, spreading that sweet-cinnamon oil all over his body until we slid together in a slick mess.

But I managed to control myself. Somehow.

Control myself, ease his pain, and walk away.

Only for him to follow me, stalk me like a panther, that tall, honed body hovering over me, still nothing but tawny bare skin and bristling hair and jagged scars and those barely there boxers.

Until now, I never believed a kiss could be indescribable.

But oh, baby, Blake is one *hell* of a teacher.

Ever since our first rough taste of each other, I've wondered what it'd feel like to kiss him without any distractions like work or Andrea in the house or some new crisis.

Nothing I've ever imagined matches up to the truth.

His searing heat, the masculine fullness of his lips, his mouth firm in its claiming, needy pressure and yet so soft in the way his lips mold against mine with a fury.

Oh.

My.

God.

As walled off as he's been, as withdrawn, now, a beast is *out*.

There's no hesitation in his kiss.

Only a dominant, utterly certain *yearning*, a compulsion, a demand.

It's given to me in stroking lips, in taunting dives of tongue-tip to tongue-tip, in the slow curl of his hands against my waist. He strokes slowly down my hips, electrifying me with the texture of his palms, the strength in those fingers, the way he touches me like I'm his new addiction with every graze of skin to the fabric over my flesh.

That demand is undeniable.

You want me.

You really, truly want me, woman.

There's only one answer.

Yes, yes, God, yes!

It's been building between us forever, rising like a crescendo to the thrilling, shivering peak of a song's climax, right before it crashes into a rousing chorus.

And every freaking part of me is *singing* right now.

I rise up on my toes, bury my fingers in his hair, and try like crazy to give it back.

Kissing Blake with everything in me, deep and desperate and hot, trying to show him with every bit of my soul how bad I want him, need him, *crave him.*

This could be my only chance.

He has to understand that whatever he thinks he's hauling around that's too much for me...

It's not.

And nothing's ever too much if we carry it together.

He makes a startled grunt as I nip at his upper lip, teasing it between my teeth.

I smile. He actually recoils for a second, before his hands clench deliciously hard on my hips and he answers with a sharp rake of his teeth against my lower lip. Enough to make my mouth burn with a perfect, searing friction.

Oh, yeah.

I gasp as the feeling rocks right through me, lights me up in little sparks that scorch right down between my thighs.

"You're playing with fire, girl," he growls, lashing his tongue against my lower lip.

I smile against his mouth, feathering my fingers down the back of his neck, tracing the strong muscles of his trapezius, his shoulders, his *back.*

This man is a human truck. He's sinfully broad and sculpted, every muscle as ruggedly hard as a broken cliff face. Every time I've had him on my table, I've wanted to touch so *bad* and couldn't.

I can now.

And I do, smoothing my hands over him, learning his shape by branding him into my palms.

Wherever my hands don't touch, my body makes up for it, pressing in close just to *feel* him from head to toe, to feel how his heat melts into my breasts, my thighs, my belly.

"So burn me," I whisper and capture his mouth again.

He smothers me in another growling kiss.

Maybe I shouldn't be so shameless.

So wanton.

So needy.

But I've never been afraid to chase what I want.

And what I want right now—maybe for life—is *him*.

Especially when he backs me up against the counter, shoves me against it with my spine arching, his body pinning me, making me gloriously aware that he's wearing nothing but those thin cotton boxer-briefs.

And they're doing nothing to hide how much he wants me, too.

His cock presses hard against my stomach.

He's so tall the thickness of it almost slides up between my breasts, over my ribs. I can't help a wicked impulse as I shimmy my body against him, writhing as I twine my tongue with his, wet-slick thrusts of locked mouths mating with the rhythm as I roll myself against his cock and savor his shuddering groan, loving how his entire body tenses under my palms.

"*Peace*," he groans, that ladykiller voice rolling over my name like lust distilled into honey whiskey. "What're you trying to do to me, woman?"

"Not quite sure yet," I breathe against his lips, brushing my mouth against his in little taunts. "But is it working?"

I let my bravery make me bolder still. My fingers dance across his side and then slip down between us, folding over the burning-hot flesh inside the cotton, stroking his length.

"*Fuck.*" He slams his hands against the counter to either side of me, gripping so hard his knuckles go white, his eyes closing, his jaw pinched, breathing like a winded animal.

A gorgeous, glorious, wild creature.

And he's putty in my hands as I stroke him—feeling every throb of his cock against my palm, his underwear so thin. I feel every ridge and vein, just how slick he is with pre-come as I grind my hand against him.

Yes, I'm greedy.

So flipping greedy I devour his face, adoring the way his lips hang slack on panting growls, his expression frozen in bliss.

I've always been good at making people feel good with my hands.

But it's never been as heady as *this*.

I'm pushing my luck, though—I can tell by the tension rippling through his shoulders, the way his fingers dig at the counter, his teeth clenched as he rocks into my hand.

I circle my thumb under his cockhead and give him a tight squeeze just to feel how *hard* he is.

My gut's so tight, so hot, and God...

It's getting me *soaked* just touching him, sweetness running between my thighs, my body clenching up with this fever.

Because I'm doing this to him.

He's this hard for *me*.

I'm the one driving him to the edge.

...and I'm the reason he snaps a second later.

I give him one more squeeze, one more stroke, and he jerks his hips forward roughly, throwing his head back with a feral growl.

"*Enough*," he bites off. "Goddammit, you'll come for me *first*."

Then his hands are on me—lifting me up, gripping my ass, fingers digging in.

Instinctively, I wrap my legs around his waist as he hoists me off my feet.

My head whips back with pleasure as he fits so perfectly between my thighs, the bulk of him spreading me open, leaving me throbbing and empty and exposed. I'm at his every mercy, his cock grinding against my jeans, my panties, so close to fucking me I can't *stand it*.

"Oh God, *Blake*." I bury my face against his throat, licking at his pulse, tasting the sweat of his skin and digging my nails into the back of his neck as I rub against him.

He's got me in heat so easily.

The feel of his cock in my palm, and all this pent-up desire that's been building up is bursting out brighter than the sun, deeper than a riptide, hotter than a wildfire, and sweeping over me in all its sweet insanity.

"Just hold on, you little wildcat," he gasps, biting my shoulders, his teeth ripping my shirt aside to find skin.

I'm gasping as he turns to carry me upstairs, every step punctuated by another rolling thrust of his hips until he's moving us in sinful rhythm. Each stride brings us closer, sharp friction, and I'm trembling, my thighs clenched as I ride those waves of movement, practically riding *him*, arching myself into him and dragging my wet panties to the scrape of his hardness so I can feel him.

I could come just from rubbing on him, my breasts crushed against his chest, my nipples pert, my pussy dripping into the fabric molded against my flesh.

And I'm moaning, panting, practically drugging myself on Blake.

His stubble, his skin, his rock-hard muscle holds nothing back.

A soft cry slips out of me as he kicks his bedroom door open and practically throws me on the bed.

There's a darkness in his deep-blue eyes. Pure inky smoldering depths as he gazes down at me, catching his thumb in the waistband of his boxer-briefs, tugging them down one sculpted hip, baring another hint of that oh-so-kissable, perfect, scarred body.

He looks like he's been put through the wringer and come out of it perfectly honed. Every pain and torment he's ever experienced just makes him hotter.

"Strip," he growls, those bearish eyes raking over me.

I've never been one to give in when a man orders me to do anything.

But when Blake Silverton tells me to strip...

I want nothing more than to obey. To be naked before those eyes already burning through my clothing like he sees every inch of me and wants to devour me whole.

Yet there's still a smidge of defiance left in me.

So I take my sweet time—smiling cattily up at him as I stretch against his sheets, catching the hem of my shirt, peeling it up slowly one inch at a time—and deliberately curving my spine to make my breasts rise against my lacy bra. I pull the shirt over my head, then toss it aside with a little flap of my hair.

And his eyes lock on to me, riveted, following my finger down as I trail it between my breasts, over my ribs, then lower.

Holy hell—*lower*.

His gaze blazes across my belly, making me suck in a gasp, savoring the hypnotic way he watches as I forge a path down to the waist of my jeans. Flick them open. Unzip.

My tongue skims my lips as I catch them at the waist.

And slink my hips from side to side, watching his pupils dilate with every second, as I shimmy them down my thighs to reveal the matching lace panties curving over my hips.

I never get the chance to take the rest off.

Because the second I toss my jeans aside, he growls.

"Fuck it—"

And next thing I know, he's on me like a marauding beast.

His weight pins me down. His naked flesh ignites my body. His hands lace with mine, shoving them to the bed.

His mouth attacks my flesh in taunting bites, all swift kisses tracing my jaw, my throat, the upper curves of my breasts. He catches my bra and bites it away, grazing the tip of my nipple so gently.

Just enough pressure to make me gasp and cry out, tossing my head back before he soothes it with his tongue.

Then Blake's mouth is *everywhere*, igniting me in wildfire sparks, torching my senses as he leaves wild marks all over me.

My arms. My belly. My inner thighs.

But still, no matter how I whine, no matter how I writhe, he won't give up what I want. Not on my terms.

This man plays by his own rules, and he's hellbent on making me *beg.* I don't even have the words because he's driving me out of my mind.

I'm lost.

Caught up in his storm, all the wicked things he does to me, the way he invades my senses.

His smell, aftershave and charcoal and heat, the scratch of his stubble on my skin, the flex of his body, the perfection of his weight.

God.

I can't separate the noise of my gasps from the harshness of his hungry breaths.

I'm just spinning, falling, but then there's a new sound, the rip and crinkle of a condom wrapper.

And that needy ache between my thighs he's been ignoring flares harder, my pussy throbbing as he flicks my panties aside.

His thumb runs down my wetness. One stroke leaves me whining, squirming, flexing and clenching in rippling pulses. He spreads me open and makes me hurt with that hot *emptiness,* every ugly second he's still not in me.

"Blake..." I whisper, grabbing at his hand. "Blake, please."

One glance is all I get. So intense and flaming blue I'm not even sure it belongs to a mere mortal anymore.

Then he grabs his cock, presses the head against me, and bares his teeth.

A thick band of pure, hard heat slides against my wet flesh so sweetly.

"Hang the fuck on to me, sweetheart," he whispers. I've never heard his voice sound more tender, more seductive, more husky. "Gonna take you now."

I grasp at his shoulders, staring up at that gorgeous face. His eyes drill me like he's never seen anyone else, like I'm his whole universe, and maybe his last freaking meal.

I'm just glad I listen and hold on tight as he tears my world apart.

No exaggeration.

I've never felt anything as intimate as the moment when Blake slides deep, bringing our flesh together like heart notes striking in rhythm—and *God*, that rhythm!

He holds nothing back in the music of his hips, crashing into mine almost hard enough to *bruise.*

We're rock and roll and heavy metal. The dirtiest country and the sweetest hip hop. We're the scream of a guitar that's pure sex and the thud of drumming hearts.

You'd better believe he makes me *sing my effing heart out* like never, ever before.

Because the instant I go crashing over into my first O, tensing, my pussy clinging to his shaking thrusts for dear life, there's nothing but our song made flesh.

Just Blake's massive body slamming into mine, the steady *clap* of his balls on my skin, his friction tearing sounds out of me I didn't even know I could make.

And he buries his mouth against mine, stealing my breath, lifting his hips higher to throw his cock into me harder, faster, *deeper.*

My whimpering release just folds me that much tighter to his piston of a body and drives him on.

If I thought he'd lose it and come with me—ha!

That's so not the way this works.

That's so not how this man operates. I realize it a little more in every stroke.

Blake might be off his chain, but he's in scary control. And he's not letting go until he's had his way with me however freaking long he pleases.

So his hips power on, the thrusts coming wilder, his hips jerking and shuddering in sharp staccato, surging us along in rough thrusts that sizzle, rip me apart, stretch me open, fill me more and more until I'm screaming, begging, and still it's not enough.

Never enough.

More, more—I want *more.*

I'll always want more, and with his name on my lips, I wrap my thighs around his hips and pull him into me, lifting my hips to beg for every inch he can give.

And sweet Lord, does he *give*.

He storms my body straight into another frantic, screaming release. I feel it coming, tensing up, my arms and legs desperately tangling with his body, enjoying our sway, and then—

Coming!

My eyelids flutter and white-hot ecstasy erupts from my core, blooming through every bit of me like some insane flower of pure energy. I barely even hear the rising pitch in his growl, even if it's impossible *not* to feel the sudden harsh swell of his cock.

As he slides home, as he finds the darkest, neediest depths of me, as he touches me inside with invasive heat and closeness and sheer, raw, erotic *pleasure...*

I can't detect the difference between his heartbeat and mine.

There's just his body flowing over mine, and I move with him, and every deep stroke bursts something deep inside me as he grabs my wrists, slams me into the bed, and pushes his forehead into mine.

"Don't you fucking stop," he growls. "Gonna go with you, baby."

And he does.

Even through the condom, I feel when his cock roots itself in my depths and explodes in a hot flood that leaves him stiff and twitching. And if I thought my orgasm was done, I was *dead wrong.*

It hits me full force the instant Blake goes off inside me.

He vibrates through me, ignites my bones, makes my body shriek with the pounding, driving, mad push to a crescendo. We share every second of our bliss.

I don't know if I'm singing or screaming.

But I know when we break higher, when his roar drowns me out, when I hit the *zone* where he's already waiting.

Moving in harmony, peaking in perfect time together.

His body with mine.

And my heart with his, even if he doesn't know just how deep these feelings run.

* * *

Wowza.

I don't think I've ever had sex like that in my life.

Sex before Blake was meat and potatoes.

Clumsy college fumblings.

Tantric gurus with bad hair at Burning Man.

Stoner musicians who fell asleep halfway in the middle.

I mean, I've had some good nights, but nothing like...this otherworldly, uncontrolled burn I can't even put into words.

Now there's just my life before sex with Mr. Silver Tongue, and life after.

All that, and then some.

There's nothing like being completely taken and possessed by a man who knows exactly what he's doing, and does it so intently focused on you and *only you.*

I feel wrung out in all the best ways.

Massage is a great release, sure.

But it can't even compare to the hot thrill of an amazing orgasm or six. I let out a soft, sighing sound of pleasure as I nestle myself against Blake's overheated, sweat-slick body, slipping a hand across his chest to toy with the dark bristles of hair.

"You okay?" I murmur, rubbing my cheek to his shoulder. "That didn't hurt your thigh?"

He lets out a chuckle that's half growl, the arm around my shoulders tightening. "Woman, I'd have stopped if something was wrong. You don't need to give the old man his health checks."

"You're not old." I prop my chin on his chest so I can look at him and the lazy, sated expression on his face "I think sometimes you forget that."

"Old enough compared to you," he points out.

I giggle. "Mmm, but I'm an Aquarius. We're all old souls."

Blake lets out another laugh, trailing into a groan. "Don't even know what that means. Please tell me I ain't gonna have to like, look up your birth chart to get to know you better or some shit."

"Nah. I'm not that deep into it." I grin. "And you don't need to know astrology to get that deep into me."

His eyes spark, heating, a rumble vibrating under me and through him. "Truth be told, I wouldn't mind getting deep into you again," he purrs in his velvet, taunting voice.

I shiver, even as I laugh, slapping at his chest.

"Don't be—"

There's a sudden clatter from downstairs.

We both freeze.

And my heart stops.

Oh, crap.

We exchange a single wide-eyed look before we both breathe it.

"Andrea!"

He goes tumbling out of bed first.

"Stay here," he gasps. "I don't know what to tell her, about..." He just waves a hand at me, at the mess of the bed, before diving for his closet. "This."

Biting my lip, I nod, pulling the covers up against me. I feel ice-cold without him, but I cling to the warm spot in the bed while he yanks his clothes back on and then goes bolting out the door, barely closing it behind him.

I close my eyes, pinching the bridge of my nose, too scared to breathe.

I adore Andrea, and I really don't want to hurt her.

I can't even guess what his incoherent-hand-gesture-*this* meant.

Was it just a quick release of pent-up passion and attraction? Or does Blake have feelings and actually wants this to be a *thing*, but maybe...no, too many maybes.

Either way, finding out that I slept with her dad could upset Andrea.

Wanting Blake is complicated. Delicate. Kind of a minefield.

But worth it, I think.

He's worth it, and I don't think he quite sees it.

I frown, though, as voices drift up from downstairs. Blake's, plus another male voice?

One I think I recognize, even if only vaguely.

Holt Silverton.

Blake's brother.

Double crap.

This might not end well for a very different reason.

I should probably mind my own business, but I won't lie.

I'm worried about Blake down there.

And I don't want to see all the work we've done on his leg unraveled when he tenses up again from his brother stressing him out.

So I clamber out of bed and fumble into my clothes, wincing as my panties push up against me. He's left me so sore and well-loved, well-used, that I feel like my legs have almost realigned. *Whoa.*

But I manage to keep quiet as I slip into the hall and head downstairs, hovering on the upstairs railing and listening before I decide if I should make my presence known.

Blake hasn't let Holt through the door, even though there's a fresh flurry of snow coming down outside, Holt visibly shivering on the doorstep.

Blake's made himself a wall.

I guess Holt's still public enemy number one right now. Something he's clearly not happy about.

"Jesus, Blake," he growls. "I don't know what you're mad at me for now. Is it something new, or the same old shit?"

"You tell me," Blake snaps back in that calm, crisp way he has when he's refusing to let his temper get the better of him. Almost the same way he dealt with Clark—asserting his authority but not lashing out when the other person can't take it.

It tells me Blake still cares for his brother, underneath the venom.

Which is why I'm surprised when he says, "I'd run you out of this fucking town if I could."

"But you can't," Holt answers. "It's my home too, and I want to help rebuild it. I want to *stay*. And if I'm going to, we can't keep circling around each other like angry skunks wonderin' who's gonna piss up first."

There's a decided twang to Holt's voice that deepens with every word, a far cry from the smooth, purring voice he'd introduced himself with the other night. *Interesting.*

Blake actually grins. "So you've still got some country boy left in you after all."

"Much as I've tried to beat him out of me," Holt snarls back. "Now you want to let me in to talk or not? My sack's about to freeze off out here."

"Tragic. We don't dare deprive the good ladies of Heart's Edge, do we?" Blake mutters.

But he steps back, letting Holt inside.

Holt stomps snow off his boots, shakes out the collar of his jacket, then rubs a hand through his slick black hair. He glances around, starts to take off his jacket, but Blake shakes his head even as he pushes the door closed behind his brother.

"You ain't staying," he says. "Don't get comfy. Start talking."

Holt just looks at him, rubbing his gloved hands together, then sighs. "Fine. I heard about the arsonist."

Blake's jaw twitches. "Nobody keeps secrets in this town anymore."

"This town is nothing *but* secrets, brother. It's like everyone knows but acts like they don't exist." Blake snorts. "But look, you're hunting him down, right?"

Something about the way Blake looks at Holt, head cocked...it's odd. Wary. "Yeah. Something like that. It's my job."

"Yeah, well, it's not Andrea's. Wait—" Holt holds both hands up sharply before Blake can do more than bristle, baring his teeth. "My point is, you can probably work easier if someone else is keeping an eye on her. And I'd like to get to know my niece. She's seemed pretty pissed at you lately, anyway. Mostly over Ma, but kind of over me. So kill three birds with one stone. Get her out from underfoot, get me out from underfoot, and maybe get her to forgive you with a little space."

"Like hell." Blake curls his upper lip. "You might be talking country, bro, but you're still full of too many goddamn city words. My family's not some fancy contract negotiation."

"No," Holt drawls softly. "But your family is my family too."

Then, suddenly, his gaze snaps to me, and I realize he's known I was there all along.

I swallow hard.

He grins, tawny gold eyes glittering, making him look positively carnivorous. "Looks like your family's gotten bigger, if my eyes aren't deceiving me."

I jerk back, stumbling over words, but Blake tilts his head back, looking up at me upside down before sighing. "You don't have to eavesdrop, Peace."

"Sorry," I say in a tiny voice, unsure if I should laugh or just run.

But I peek back over the railing, then straighten and slip down the stairs, approaching them tentatively. "Hi, Holt."

"Hey, sugar," he says, his grin widening as he jerks a thumb at Blake. "Sorry our last conversation got cut off by this big fucking lunk."

Said *lunk* immediately snares his arm around my waist, making me squeak again as he pulls me in close against his side right there in front of his brother.

It's almost crazed, jealous, overprotective.

My heart turns over, and I stumble against him, resting a hand to his side.

I guess that answers one of many questions about his intentions.

"Go ahead and put your damn eyes back in your head," he growls at his brother.

I feel it vibrating through him into me with a little thrill.

"I'm just being nice to a pretty lady," Holt says, once again raising his hands, his brows arching innocently, but *wow* does he have the devil's own smile.

Not my type—I'm not into the clever guy who can make you believe fallen angels walk the earth—but I can see why women fall all over him.

He sniffs loudly. "I guess you finally decided to do something about it before this girl pined to death. Nice."

I choke on a flustered sound. "I wasn't pining!"

"She was pining," Holt says firmly. "And so were you, big brother."

"The hell I was!" Blake sputters.

But when I look up at him...his face is almost as red as mine feels.

It's impossible not to laugh, burying my face in his side. This is so ridiculous, whatever it's all about.

"Holt, *stop*. You're embarrassing both of us," Blake says.

"I'm just glad I didn't have to nudge you two too hard. Thought I was going to have to play matchmaker, but you took care of it pretty well on your own." Holt chuckles, shrugging and stuffing his hands into the pockets of his leather jacket, looking at Blake rather frankly. "So what do you say? In exchange for that big fat kick in the butt, I get to spend a few days with my niece?"

Blake narrows his eyes, watching his brother mistrustfully. "Only if you tell me why you want to so bad."

Holt's gaze flickers, and he sighs, his smile fading. "It's not obvious? I've got no family left but y'all, Blake. Ma's gone, don't even know my dad's name, and I'm not taking one of those mail-in DNA tests. So maybe I'm sick of being alone. I'm trying to actually have something that matters, instead of a bunch of bimbos and fly-by-night flings."

For several seconds they stare each other down. Holt almost pleading, Blake stone-still and forbidding.

Then he just sighs. "Fuck. Fine. I'll ask her if she *wants* to and make sure she doesn't have any school projects. But if she injures you, breaks anything, or tries to feed you to the boa constrictor, that's on you. And you'd damn well better keep her away from Clark Patten."

Holt's smile transforms in an instant: broad, crooked, *genuine*, and suddenly I can see the faint resemblance between the brothers when Holt drops his smarmy mask. It's totally the lopsided smile more than anything.

"I'll be just like her own good daddy," he says. "Promise. I'll make sure she does her homework and won't feed her junk food or let her stay up too late."

"Hey," Blake says. "You gotta give her some special treatment, or I can't use you to get her to forgive me."

I can't help but laugh, watching them with relief. Crisis averted, thank God.

I'm quiet, but it's a cozy sort of quiet that makes me feel things.

Like I could fit in here.

Like I'm part of this slowly assembling family, too.

Stop reading too much into things, Peace.

They only talk for a little bit longer, then Holt's out the door.

And Blake immediately goes silent, tense, his expression settling into something grim, his resigned smile fading as he stares through the small window inset in the door, watching as Holt disappears down the driveway in his sleek, snow-dusted black car.

I frown, looking up at him, smoothing a hand over his chest. "Blake? What's wrong?"

"I think I'm about to send my daughter into a fox's den," he mutters. "That's the only real way to trap him."

* * *

EVEN AFTER BLAKE EXPLAINS IT, I'm not quite sure I follow.

Even if it makes sense.

Holt comes back into town after years away, and the fires start almost immediately.

Holt knows all of them, the Heroes of Heart's Edge. Their pasts, their hurts, their scars.

He'd have reason to resent them, what with the constant battle scars between brothers left by their mother extending to Blake's childhood friends.

As a boy, he was in love with Warren's sister, Jenna, and would blame Warren for not protecting her when an Army drug lord arranged her murder.

He's got a history of dishonesty, and he's willing to do anything to one-up Blake.

He tried to sleep with Blake's wife.

Not only does he have the technical knowledge from his construction work to be able to set fires with complex equipment, but he has the motive, too. As the newest contractor here, he'd be able to pick up work rebuilding everything he burned down, long after damaged buildings from the big museum fire run out.

I sit across from Blake on the couch, my hands clasped in both of his as he looks at me earnestly.

I shake my head. "But...but why? You really think he hates you so much that he'd do all of that?"

"I think it's more about getting the business," Blake says, staring through the wall. "It's just a bonus the bastard gets to use it to stab me."

"I don't understand. Then why even consider letting Andrea

stay with him?" I frown, squeezing his hands tighter. "Isn't that dangerous?"

"No. So far, none of the fires have hurt anybody. They're too messy, and he left 'em that way intentionally. He wants business and to satisfy his shitty little grudge in the worst way possible, but he ain't a serial killer, darlin'."

"But the clinic, Doc and Ember's place—"

He hangs his head. "That was the worst, coming way too close to hurting them animals. No excuse. Still, it was all small stuff that was simple to douse and easy for folks to get away from. I don't think he'd hurt an actual person on purpose. Especially not a kid. Even if he deserves a whoppin' for fucking up The Menagerie and making those poor critters scared."

He squeezes my hands back, watching me earnestly. "I don't like it, but I need something, dammit. Some proof. Andrea's smart. She can be my eyes and ears. Keep him busy so I know where he is at all times, and if a fire pops up while she's with him...we know for sure it ain't him. But if it is, then she just might find us the evidence we need."

"Unless you've got another girlfriend," comes from the kitchen, "that 'she' you're talking about better not be me."

Uh-oh.

We both look up as Andrea trots through the back door, stomping her feet on the mat and pulling her hoodie back from her wild-colored hair.

Blake and I yank our hands back like an electric shock. She just arches a brow, giving us both a cynical look.

"Really? You two are like third-graders. God, hold hands in front of me, guys. At least you can stop pretending." She rolls her eyes dramatically, shrugging out of her big military jacket as she meanders into the living room with a dry little smile for me. "Just so you know, you can do way better. Buuut I'm not too mad that you didn't. Dad needs somebody."

"Careful." Blake shoots her a deadly look.

I grin, offering my hand to Blake. "Nice to have your seal of approval."

She just wrinkles her nose and sticks her tongue out playfully, while Blake sighs and slips his hand into mine, squeezing it warmly, freely. I flush for the hundredth time at how easily he makes a show of *being* with me in front of others.

We probably need to have some kind of talk soon.

But maybe not right now.

And Blake seems to agree because he says, "Peace and I haven't really had a chance to work out what we're doing yet before we talk to you about it."

Andrea shrugs, flinging herself down into the easy chair and sprawling out with typical teenage ennui. "Do whatever you want. She's gonna dump you for being an asshole sooner or later anyway, so no skin off my ass."

Blake sighs.

"*Language*," he mutters with the air of someone who's said it a million times.

Andrea just rolls her eyes again, leaning forward and snagging the TV remote.

I snort. "Hey. I'm not gonna dump him for being an ass." I eye Blake playfully. "Maybe."

"Haven't run you off yet, have I?" he returns with a warm, lingering look, his blue eyes mellowing.

"*Yet*."

"Ugh," Andrea groans. "Can you stop being gross? And tell me why you were talking about me?"

Blake hesitates, sobering, then says, "Violet, I need your help."

Andrea's eyes widen when she sees it's not a joke. She goes rigid, darting a sidelong look at her dad. "Who are you, and what pod person replaced my dad?"

"I'm serious, Andrea." Blake groans. "It's about your Uncle Holt."

Her eyes narrow. "You mean the uncle I didn't know I had and that you've been a complete dickwad about?"

"Yep, that'd be him."

She sniffs. "I had to turn down a ride home from school yesterday *in the snow* because I knew you'd be ridiculous about it."

"First I'm hearing of it. You should've told me, girl," he growls, his brow furrowing. "See, this is why I don't trust him. He does shit behind my back. And I need you to help me catch him at it."

Andrea's annoyed expression turns puzzled. "At what? What's he doing to crawl up your butt so bad?"

"At figuring out if he's the arsonist who almost burned down the damn Menagerie," Blake says grimly. "And keeping him from setting more fires."

"What!" She bolts forward in her chair, leaning in, staring at him wild-eyed. "No *way*."

"Way," Blake throws back.

Her gaze darts to me. "You...you think he did it, too?"

"Well," I wince, my words stalling.

Oh, boy. I can't take sides. And honestly, I don't know what to think anymore.

Right now, I don't trust my gut with everything so confusing. Not to mention that little wrist apparatus we found at the vet clinic, the same kind I saw Clark practicing with at the carnival grounds...

"I don't know," I say slowly. "I don't know him very well. Your father does."

"Yeah, but my father's a dick who hates everyone in his family," Andrea slurs, her eyes flashing as she turns a glare on Blake. "You're joking, right? You can't actually *believe* it's Uncle Holt? You just don't want me to have *anyone* in my life but you, huh? First Clark, now my uncle?"

Blake's face visibly falls, his brows drooping. "That ain't what it's about, Andrea. Never was. Believe me. Besides, if it's your Uncle Holt doing it, then I've got no reason to stop you from hanging out with Clark, do I?"

"Awesome. So now I have to choose between them?" Her mouth twists up in an upset line. "That's so not fair. It's not fair that both the people you think are doing it are people I want in my life. They're *both* innocent."

Blake's sigh is long, slow, deep, and hurting. "I want to believe that, Little Violet. I really do. But you've got so much faith in your uncle without knowing him like I do." He holds his free hand out to her, pleading. I squeeze his captured hand, offering silent support. "Just shut it and prove me wrong. Can you do that for a couple days? I just...fuck, I need you to *help* me on this, Andrea. He wants you to stay with him, and if you do...you just might be able to end this."

Andrea stares at his hand.

She doesn't take it.

Instead, she turns her nose up, folding her arms over her chest.

"*Arghhh,* fine. I'll help you. So maybe you can stop being paranoid and learn to trust people. Clark didn't do it. Uncle Holt didn't do it." She makes a disgusted sound. "I'll be your little spy, and then *when* you're wrong, you can actually start being nice to your brother. Deal?"

Blake drops his hand, resting it on his knee.

"That's asking a lot," he says flatly.

She shoots him a withering look. "More than asking your teenage daughter to spy on the dude you think is setting fires everywhere?"

"Dammit, you're worse than he is. I just want you to report back if you see anything funny, and if you do, call me ASAP. And call Peace if I'm not answering." Blake drags a palm over his face. "*Fine.* If he's innocent—*if*—then I'll be all smiles for him. Happy?"

"Now I am," she chirps, her mood shifting instantly. "How long?"

"No more than a week," Blake says. "Check-ins every day. I'll drop by as often as I can."

She smiles brightly, bouncing to her feet and prancing over to drop a kiss on Blake's cheek, leaving him looking absolutely befuddled as she singsongs, "Thank you, Daddy. I'll go pack."

He stares after her with wide eyes as she spins toward the stairs, then calls after her, "Don't forget, you're still helping Justin out with prepping his carnival workshop."

"I won't forget!" drifts down the stairs while Blake just sits there.

Looking poleaxed.

Who could blame him?

"That girl's going to be trouble when she grows up," I mutter playfully, and Blake's wide eyes slide to me.

"*When?*" he chokes out.

Suddenly, we're laughing.

And it's good, and right, and while I know we need to talk, not right now.

Not now, when I don't need a fancy name for this thing between us.

I just know that being with him feels good.

At the moment, Blake's music is all I need.

XVI: STAY FOR THE ENCORE
(BLAKE)

*I*t's funny how every time shit goes wrong, we turn the Charming Inn—and specifically Ms. Wilma's kitchen—into our war room.

It's just like when that fucker Nash kidnapped Deanna Bell and left poor Leo hunting for her before her sister, Rissa—now his wife—lost her ever-loving mind.

Only now we're all gathered at the kitchen table—me, Warren, Gray, and Leo—around those three scraps of blue paper with their ominous words.

Nobody's touching their food.

I don't think anybody's got any appetite. We're too busy staring at the scrawled, scratchy handwriting.

*You and your **merry band of assholes aren't as smart as you think, you scarred freak.***

*Jenna was the real hero, **Warren**.*
And you can't even protect her memory.

. . .

If only you'd kept your germs to yourself, Doctor. Heart's Edge wouldn't catch fever.

I'M WARMING my hands against a cup of coffee, the thick omelet Ms. Wilma laid out in front of me left untouched. The others are the same, bracing black coffees like it's the only thing holding us up.

"So we're sure," I say, "that this has nothing to do with those fucks at Galentron?"

"It doesn't have their smell," Leo growls, his tattooed and scarred hands tightening against his coffee mug to the point I'm worried he's gonna crack it. "They leave a real stench. Patterns. We'd see strangers in town posing as tourists, standing out just a little too much. Strange happenings. People spending too much money. Fuchsia Delaney."

Everybody goes still, a nervous hush settling over the room.

Doc actually looks over his shoulder. "Can we *not* say her name this time and invite Count Dracula's mistress in?"

I look up and grin. He's hardly exaggerating. That woman's a black cat.

Bad luck to anyone who crosses her path.

And somehow, she always seems to materialize not long after you mention her, usually bringing trouble in her wake.

But Fuchsia's ghost aside...it's just us in the kitchen, which is always sunny and light-filled even in the dead of winter. Cozy enough to banish the memory of that witchy woman but not enough to remove the dread silence.

"All right." Warren's the man who finally breaks it. "I made a few calls. Nothing to do with the old drug ring, either, or any leftover bad business here in town. I thought maybe someone was coming back for a little revenge after we busted everything up and ruined their cash flow, but they'd have to be pretty dedicated to get this whole vengeful stalker thing down in *this* detail."

"So it's personal, it's local, and we have few options for who it might be," Doc says in his flat, even monotone that says his temper's on the verge of bursting. "Other than a minor who really has no reason to go to such extremes."

"I have one idea," I growl. "And y'all won't like it."

They all wait, just looking at me. I feel like they're already bracing for what I'm about to say.

"Holt. My brother."

War immediately sighs, pressing his face into his hand. "I can't believe that brat's back in town."

"And still a brat. Just bigger and more dangerous," I say. "I'm keeping him busy right now pretending to be the good uncle, and Andrea's snooping for any leads. But he's not stupid. He wants to keep up appearances. Still, right now, he's the one who stands to benefit the most from new construction contracts on the buildings he's burned up."

"He won't be getting my business," Doc snaps. "Not even if he's innocent. You've told me how slipshod he was in high school. I won't have that kind of work on my clinic, a place of rest and healing."

I can't help a smile at that, even if it's tired. "He's...I don't know, man. I don't want to believe my own brother would do that, asshole that he is, but who else has a grudge against all of us who isn't connected to either the drug gang or Galentron?"

"Occam's Razor," Leo grunts. "The simplest, most obvious solution is usually the right one."

"Unless we're overlooking something," Warren adds, cracking his knuckles.

"But what?" I ask.

I'm only answered with blank looks and spread hands.

Leo shakes his head. "The question is, if it's Holt, what do we *do* about it?"

"Flush him out," I say. "He clearly wants to humiliate us, hurt us, get under our skin. This is a game to him. One where he wants recognition, and it's fucking eating him alive that we're the heroes of the town. Sooner or later, he'll do something showy."

"Shit. The thing coming up, the *ceremony*," Warren says. "He'll want to sabotage it, won't he?"

"Exactly," I snarl.

Everybody trades awkward looks over the table.

None of us wanted this damn ceremony at the carnival.

It's not worth it.

Some kind of prideful circus the town council threw together for morale or something. Really, it's just making a big hoopla out of the hell we've been through over the past couple years and acting like we did anything other than try to make sure Heart's Edge survived along with us.

I can't stand it.

The way folks look at us, gab about us. Like they wouldn't do the same if they were under pressure. This town's full of good people.

We ain't special.

We're just the guys who got tossed in the pressure cooker and *had* to come out the other side.

But Holt wouldn't miss a chance to show the town who we "really" are.

The people he still sees.

The big kids who didn't give him enough attention. Because if I know Holt, I know some part of him is still holding old grudges.

Doc cocks his head, watching me keenly over the top of his glasses. "Then the plan is to lure him out at the ceremony?"

"The plan's to keep him away from the ceremony," I correct. "He's gonna try to set some kind of fire, if his pattern holds up. So far it's been juvenile-level prank shit. Easy to pass off as one of the kids. No one really gets hurt. But so many people at the winter carnival...he fucks one thing up, and we've got a lot of casualties."

"So what do we do?" Warren asks.

I grin.

"Easy," I say. "We give him a bigger target."

* * *

It doesn't take us long to come up with a plan.

We're gonna put on a variety show.

Listen. I know it's silly. But people like my radio show, and I know I can bark up a crowd.

And that crowd's gonna be gathering around inside the ice palace they're building.

I can't think of a better place to keep a bunch of people safe from an arsonist than inside a building that's damn-near solid ice bricks.

He can try to pull his shit, but it won't work.

I'll have fire containment on standby, Justin and Rich and the part-timers ready, plus a fire truck or two.

The town council might complain about the aesthetic—but considering they're building a temporary wooden windbreaker wall around the entire carnival grounds so nobody freezes their asses off in the biting winds, they won't even be able to see the trucks.

It'll be fine.

And maybe, just maybe, we'll either catch the bastard red-handed...or just bust up his schemes so he'll turn tail and run right out of town.

Right now, though, I'm out following up another lead. Chasing down loose ends.

Even though my suspicions are fixed on Holt, I gotta cover all my bases.

That's why I'm at the Patten house, eyeing the big white rental truck in the driveway with the Patten Pyrotechnics logo stuck to the side on a big magnet.

Just makes me think back to that dark, glittery truck Peace saw.

Damn.

Why ain't nothing sitting right?

Why does everything keep bouncing between Holt and Clark, but never really falling on either?

At least this means Roger Patten's home.

The poor man looks like a flustered mess when I bang on his door, holding the half-busted pyrotechnic device in my hand from the clinic.

His hair is sticking up everywhere, and he stares at me, then down at the phone in his hand, tapping redial on a listing that says *Clark*.

"Blake Silverton? Thank hell, man, I was gonna call Langley."

"Langley?" I raise an eyebrow.

"Yeah, uh, have you seen my nephew? Is he out with your daughter?"

My lips pinch a thin line.

Ah, shit.

"Haven't seen him. You want me to call Andrea?"

"Please!" Rog says, his throat working in a hard swallow. "Clark hasn't answered his phone in over a day."

Not good.

And I don't want to tell Rog what I'm thinking.

That maybe Clark did it, and he's gone to ground till we lose his scent.

I'm starting to get whiplash from this case. It still doesn't make sense, that whole thing about Jenna Ford when Clark's too young to remember that crap, but maybe he heard enough whispers?

Or maybe nothing about this makes a lick of sense.

I pull my phone out and dial Andrea. I'm half worried she won't answer.

Nobody wants to pick up the phone for their idiot dad—but after a few seconds her voice comes over the line, laughing breathlessly. There's someone else laughing with her, a male voice, but it's not Clark.

"What, Dad?" she asks without a hello, and I wrinkle my nose.

I taught her manners. *I swear I did.*

"Where are you?" I ask. "Is Clark with you?"

"Dammit, Dad, are you really—"

"It ain't that," I cut her off. "Listen, he's not answering his phone, and his uncle's scared sick."

She goes still. Dead silent.

I can just hear her breath turn quick and wild and scared.

"Oh," she says. "I'm...I'm at the carnival grounds helping Justin right now. Clark's not here. He was supposed to come help, but I thought he just ditched me and was busy with his uncle."

Fuck.

"What's wrong?" Justin asks in the background. "Drea, you look pale."

She pulls the phone away enough for her voice to mute a bit, though I can still make out, "It's Dad. Clark's missing, he thinks."

There's a fumbling sound on the other end of the line, then Justin's voice comes over. "Chief? It's Justin."

"Hey," I say with a flush of relief. At least I know my daughter's somewhere safe; Holt must've dropped her off. "You seen Clark Patten around?"

"Not hide nor hair," he says. "But I'll keep an eye out. Ask around. Somebody had to have seen him recently. Half the town's been in and out of here getting the last stuff set up."

"That'd be appreciated." I pause. "Say, if you run into him, keep him busy, Justin. Don't let him out of your sight."

"Chief?" Justin sounds puzzled.

"Trust me, I got a funny feeling," I say. "That's all."

We exchange a few more terse comments, then I hang up and look down into Rog's watery, worried eyes.

"We've got fire crew out at the carnival grounds," I say. "They're keeping an eye out and asking around about Clark. Wherever he is, they'll figure it out."

"Oh, thanks! Finally some good news," Rog says, clutching his phone to his chest, closing his eyes. "I'll go have a drive around and see, too."

"Good man. I'll keep my eyes peeled. But you should let the sheriff know, too, just in case. Missing minor and such. He can put the word out to his deputies."

I pause, though, fingering the device in my jacket pocket. "One more thing...I don't wanna add to your woes, but I came by to show you something." I hesitate a moment longer, then pull the device from my pocket—and I know by the click of recognition in his eyes even before I ask.

"Is this yours?"

* * *

IT'S HIS.

And that's another nail in Clark's coffin.

Except Rog says it's been messed up by someone who doesn't know how to use it.

He says it's a little magic trick, not meant to hold more than an ounce or two of fuel. Magicians use them all the time for dramatic bursts of flame.

He said someone who knew how to use it wouldn't have dented up the little fuel can like it is. They're fragile and have to be opened just right. Whatever the person who used it did, it also fucked up the firing mechanism, so it only gave off a weak flame.

Somebody clueless tried to rig it to go off by itself once he left the building.

But since he didn't know what he was doing, he just broke it, and sabotaged his own arson attempt.

That's a pattern pointing at unfamiliarity with pyrotechnics, and once again steering away from Clark.

So if Clark's missing, and he ain't the arsonist...

Where'd he go?

That question's still weighing on me like ten tons of bricks by the time I make it home.

The burden lifts a little as I step inside, and I'm greeted by the sound of singing.

Peace.

She's practicing that song from The Nest.

The one about a desperado who's got a heart of gold inside gunmetal plating, that tired man looking for a reason for his heart to still beat.

Can't help but smile. It still feels like she's singing that song for me.

Like she's singing it to guide me home.

And I can't resist following the sound upstairs, where she's curled up in my bedroom like she belongs there.

I *want* her to belong there.

Hell, she's gorgeous.

Just simple and natural, swimming in one of my oversized t-shirts and a pair of pajama shorts, her legs bare and lush with the guitar in her lap pressing down on her thighs.

They give in to the soft pillows of flesh around it, her bare feet tucked up under her knees.

Her hair falls and sways around her face as she bends over the neck of the guitar and strums away, her lashes lowered in quiet focus, strawberry lips moving in low, lyrical thrums that turn simple words into pure soul.

It's like she *knows*.

Just how bad she's messing me up, screwing me for life and for any other woman.

My eyes fuse on her sweet face, wait for her gaze, and I smile like a total fool when it comes.

Fresh need erupts out of me like a howl, this fierceness ripping through me, making my blood pulse in time to her music.

And before I know I'm moving, I'm striding toward the bed,

reaching for the guitar, pulling it out of her fingers and setting it aside where it won't get busted.

Goddamn if I can resist when I'm alone with her sweetness.

Her eyes widen, a gasp catching in her throat.

"Blake?" she asks. "What's—"

No. Don't talk, darlin'.

That's what I'm telling her by stealing her mouth, robbing her voice, begging her to sing to me with her lips instead. I'll pull the moans out of her if I have to.

There's something about her voice.

Whether she's murmuring sweet things to me, teasing, laughing, sighing, or crying out in pleasure.

No matter what she does, it's always *music* to me.

And I need to make her sing her pretty heart out right the hell now.

I don't think I've ever touched a woman like I touch Peace today —shoving my fingers under her clothes, playing over her body in animal touches, exploring every inch of her with just my fingertips.

Her tits fall into my hands. I knead her rough. Loving her for being fragile, but loving her even more for being something I can *break.*

She arches for me, giving up these lush whines as I flop her back against the bed, stripping her one garment at a time.

Taking my time.

Taking her in.

Taking my woman.

Making this last when it's one thing I can hold on to, with everything else being so fucked.

She's a flower in the wind. One fine day she might blow away.

So I let my lust memorize her.

With every bleeding look that follows the curve of pale shoulders, the swell of her body, the hourglass taper of her thighs.

With every touch of my fingers.

With the way I savor every frantic sound she makes, how responsive she is when I grab at her hair and pull just right, taking her lips like I'm starving.

I pluck every string she's got, making her quiver.

And oh, hell, does she *sing* for me.

Her voice rises in moans almost lyrical. They slur perfect notes even when she's crying out for me as I taste her.

"Blake!" she whimpers, pushing her pussy against my thigh.

"Not yet," I growl, giving her hair a fierce tug that makes her eyes flash. "Hold still."

And she listens while I run the full gamut of Peace and then some.

Her honey lips, the dark inviting depths of her mouth, her wildflower tongue.

Then her snowy throat, sucking at her pulse, *trying* to leave marks.

I know I've lost my shit.

I *know*.

But I'm feeling territorial, and it doesn't help one bit when my nostrils flare, smelling how bad she wants me. Her scent comes thick on the air, something luscious and sweet like cream and cake.

My mouth sails onward to the dip between her tits, already filming with sweat as her temperature roars, glistening in a sheen against pale flesh.

The pink, tempting tips of her nipples, delicate and pale as candy, roll against my tongue in perfect hard swells. I can't help but toy with her again and again, drunk on the way she jerks, tenses, shudders, ripples flowing down her in waves.

My cock beats like a jackhammer, so hard it could bust up cement.

I'll tell you one thing.

A man doesn't know intoxicating till he feels a woman respond to him like this.

Like all I have to do is kiss her—pressing my lips to her belly just below her navel where that little gem shines—to make her desire overflow.

Hell, she can't contain her voice, her writhing, the mad, sexy way she fists at my hair.

"Blake!" she whines my name again.

I love how open she is.

So free, so easy, so hungry.

Her hips show me exactly what she wants when she spreads her thighs and lets me *see* her—every delicate pink fold, every wet curl of flesh, the way her pussy moves like she's already craving me for dear life.

It ain't even a tease.

As if I could deny her invitation.

As if I could resist her feast laid out in front of me, begging to be ravished with the psycho hunger burning me down.

And goddamn, *do I feast.*

She smells so fucking good I can't stop myself.

My tongue goes to work, skimming up her thighs, dipping between her folds. I lick hard and wild over every inch of her like a starved beast, tracing delicately along the outer flutters of pink to gather that first tart wetness on my tongue, then searching deeper, craving more.

She's better than any booze ever invented.

Pure addiction, drawing me in, driving my tongue to coax her wet heat even as I drink every bit of her with a desperation that scalds my blood.

Fuck.

I'll remember this for life, the way her thighs clench against my shoulders.

The way her belly tightens and ripples.

The way she screams *Blake!* like she's in agony, her fingers clawed in my shoulders, both pushing and dragging me closer still.

Finally, I let her clit have it. Suck it between my teeth, hold it, lash it with one fiery lick after the next. The devil himself couldn't eat pussy any hotter than I devour her just now.

And she responds. Oh, mama, her body spikes up in a tight arch, and I growl, pinning her down.

I'm not done, woman.

And I delve my tongue inside her, thrusting again and again and again.

Telling me she wants me.

Telling me she's *ready*.

Telling me that she's so mine I won't let her leave this town.

Gonna do whatever the fuck it takes to keep her here.

Especially when her body goes rigid, twitching, electric, and comes for me so sweet I think I'm hooked on her for life.

Peace goes off like a wildcat, hissing her pleasure, every last bit of her rolling. My tongue never stops, fucking her through it, totally obsessed with owning her as she comes, now and forever.

My cock is on fucking fire by the time she lets up.

This hell between my legs might be worse than my bum leg—good thing I'm looking at the cure.

I flow up her body, capturing her mouth, tasting her lips, giving her back the taste of herself. She takes it with a shrill moan that just makes my cock jerk even harder.

Damn, I love a girl who isn't afraid of herself. Who can lose herself in sex and passion without restraint.

There's something both deliriously filthy and angel pure about the way I delve my tongue in her mouth, priming her till she's begging again in little whimpers.

Who am I to deny a lady?

Nudging my knee against hers, spreading her, I curl my hand against her hip, pulling her up as I kiss her deeper, softer, slower, longer.

I hold her spellbound in that kiss as I slide in. My eyes waver shut. I let those silky depths slide over me, pull me into the heavy, sweet fullness of her flesh.

She drives me out of my mind.

The way she moves against me, the way we fit together.

I almost can't fucking stand the idea of ever pulling out when it's so hot inside her, so *right*, and the pleasure we make is deeper and headier than anything I've ever known.

But my body's pure greed.

I want all of her.

And I don't have a prayer of stopping this rhythm any more than I could stop the ocean tide. Not when she's already rising up, pulling me into her, looking at me with her eyes so dazed and so hot, with that sweet pleading expression on her face, this thing almost like pain, as if she can't endure the intensity.

I know, darlin'.

I know.

Can't stand it myself, but I don't want it to end, crashing my body into hers.

I bring our strokes together till somehow I'm not sure who's pushing or pulling anymore, only that we're bound and twined and frantic and breathless, trading kisses and sighs and whispers of each other's names. I can't stop saying hers, over and over again.

And I can't get enough of hearing *Blake* on her lips, or how she holds on like she's never wanted for anything else.

The world could shatter and burn around me, right now, but I wouldn't know anything but her.

I'm in too damn deep.

Her rolling tide pulls at my desire, turning it into something more than the hot-burning lust threatening to burst right out of my veins. It goes molten, something that's stitched into my skin and bones.

Pure instinct has me moving harder, faster, trying to get deeper inside her, even though I'm filling every bit of her. I try to bury myself where she'll never forget me, where I'll never be without her. I make her unforgettably *mine* in every stroke, claiming her body, mind, and soul.

Never. Leave. Me.

That's what I'm saying as I make her writhe, make her twist, make her clutch with her thighs shuddering and tight. She won't be long.

Her eyes flutter open, sunny jade-green staring up at me, her strawberry lips parted in an O, waiting for me to say the magic words.

"Come for me, darlin'. Come like you mean it," I growl. "Gonna go hard, gonna go with you."

There.

Her face tenses. Every last bit of her convulses, her hips insane, tits thrusting up against me and her face so slack, so gorgeous, so completely *lost* as she falls apart.

I'm roaring when my cock explodes, sending lightning up my spine, reckless in my release.

I never had a chance today.

Not when I'm this riled.

She takes me with her, that tight flux gripping against my cock, destroying my self-control.

Don't leave me.

In every thrust, in every pulse of black magic between us, every seething breath as pleasure cuts through me like a flaming sword, I hear the same word.

Stay, darlin' lady.

Stay, stay, stay, stay...

* * *

It's almost zero degrees outside, but it's got to be running at least a hundred in my bed.

I'm a sweaty mess, and I don't give a damn.

Not when I'm tangled up with Peace, content and lazy with her stretched half on top of me. Her fingers lace in mine and her mystic-flame hair spills over my shoulder.

"So," she teases softly, her voice husky in the way that makes me burn. It's how she sounds when she's been singing for ages.

And how she sounds when I've been making her hit high notes for other reasons.

"That happened," she continues, a smile playing at her lips. "Again."

"Sure did." I chuckle, trailing my fingers up her back just to feel her shiver against me. "And I wouldn't mind it happening again and again, either."

"Mmm...I guess that means we should have the talk."

I blink. "Broccoli, you realize no man has ever wanted to have *the talk?*"

"You're not every man." With a sunny smile, she kisses my shoulder. "And I don't think you're scared to talk to me about your real feelings. Or about what this means."

Shit, she's right.

Still, it makes me pause.

I know this girl's practically been after me ever since she laid eyes on me, if I'm being honest about the way she was looking at me that night I found her standing on the side of the road next to a burning van.

But I don't know if she gets what wanting me means.

I turn that over for a minute, picking my words carefully before I say, "I can't do casual."

Might as well be blunt and get it out there. She's watching me intently.

"Not with Andrea to think about, I mean. After the way she lost her ma, I can't afford to have someone in her life who's just gonna leave her. So when I say I like you, that I feel things when I'm with you...I ain't saying that easy, Peace. Not saying it light. It's serious shit. If we're gonna do something, I'm gonna treat it that way. Serious." I look down into those rich, warm green eyes that watch me without judgment, without even a flicker of hurt. "But I know you don't do permanent. I know you don't *stay.* And I don't wanna tie you down. Especially at your age. No twenty-five-year-old wants to jump in with a family and a kid already waiting."

Her eyes sparkle.

There's a long, breathless silence. Like waiting for a verdict.

Then she smiles.

"Blake Silverton, you might just be the dumbest man I've ever met," she says firmly.

Huh?

She pushes herself up, breasts plush against my chest, and kisses me like mad.

It's a fierce kiss full of half-breaths of muffled laughter, her mouth curling on mine, and despite myself I can't help but laugh against her lips as I lift a hand to weave my fingers through her hair.

When I nip her upper lip, though, starving for her taste, she pulls back, smirking down at me, and I grin.

"So you wanna tell me why I'm dumb, why you're laughing at me, and what I did to earn *that*?"

"Easy. Did you ever *ask* me if I do or don't do permanent?" she asks softly. "Or did you just assume because you're scared I'm going to leave?"

I want to tell her that's not fair.

Dammit, though, she's right.

She's right, and it's almost frustrating, how easily she sees through me.

"I didn't ask," I admit. "I should've. Sorry."

She settles against me again, folding her arms on my chest and watching me thoughtfully. The way her eyes glow, rich and deep makes me feel like I'm the only man she's ever looked at in the world.

"Maybe I wander," she murmurs. "Maybe I take flight. But it's because I'm looking for a home that's not my poor van. It's not that I can't stand staying in one place. It's just that I haven't found *the* place I want to stay just yet. That doesn't mean I *won't* stay, once I find it."

Am I it? I wonder. *Are* we *it?*

Because there ain't no denying.

I'm a package deal.

Love me, love my daughter, pain in the nub she might be.

I smile faintly, coiling Peace's hair around my fingers. "So what about Andrea?"

"I adore Andrea." She smiles shyly. "As much as I adore her father. I think she likes me, too." Then she laughs, biting at her lower lip playfully. "Not sure about her dad, though. He gives me a lot of mixed signals. Especially when he's hurting and grouchy."

"*Hey*," I grumble. "Pretty sure what we just did wasn't a mixed frigging signal."

"Okay." She rolls her eyes playfully, wiggling her body against me, and fuck if my cock isn't already springing to life at the feel of her. "So are we coming through loud and clear and reading each other, then?"

"Yeah," I growl thickly, tightening my fingers in her hair, drawing her toward me. "I'm addicted to Broccoli now. And I want you to be addicted to me. So get your cute ass down here and kiss me, lady, and I'll show you *exactly* what kind of signals I'm giving off."

XVII: OUT OF TUNE (PEACE)

If I wasn't on birth control and Blake wasn't stocked up on condoms, I'd be in major trouble.

Because as often as we fall into bed together, I'd be giving him a second kid after an entire week of this.

A week of passion.

A week of pleasure.

A week of emotion bordering on pain, whenever I wrap myself around him and beg him to take me, beg to come deeper, beg him to never stop touching me with his hands, his mouth, his silver voice that's like a physical caress every time he grinds out my name.

Peace, Peace, Peace, he growls.

God, I'm flushed just thinking about it.

And I need to keep my eyes—and my wits—on the road.

Life goes on, even with great sex and the sweet insanity of falling in love.

Honestly, I don't know how we find time for so *much* sex when we're both so busy.

Blake's working quintuple duty.

Looking for arsonist clues, working with Sheriff Langley to put an intensive search out for Clark Patten, helping prep for the carnival and run safety checks, doing his job as fire chief with people and home inspections, and still sneaking in a radio show or two in between breathless nights with me.

I don't know how he does it and still has the energy to sweep me into his arms.

I'm just exhausted, running around keeping up with my clients.

Everyone wants a spa day, I guess, before the big carnival officially opens. They're keeping me busy with massage and aromatherapy sessions.

Not that I mind. It's good money, it lets me feel useful, and—

Okay.

This is silly, but it makes me feel like a contributing member of Blake's household, instead of a freeloader. Papa Bear let me buy groceries the other day, and it made me weirdly happy.

Like this could be everyday life, if I—if *we*—gave it a chance.

We could have this comfy, lovely home where we might both be busy people, but we always find our way back to the same warm place every night.

Am I just dreaming while wide awake?

Hoping for more than I can have?

I don't know how to be a mother. A stepmother. Andrea's honestly too old to need one; she'll be eighteen in two years. I don't think I offer much, really, jumping right into the terrible teens.

But I can be her friend. Hardly a bad thing to be.

Maybe it's because Andrea's on my mind that the girl I see as I drive past the carnival grounds looks just like her.

I glimpse her through a gap in the temporary wooden fence they're erecting around the carnival grounds, several workers pounding tall, thin planks into the earth to form a safe windbreaker.

I don't blame them. The nights have been getting colder, the days greyer, the Montana wind sharper with winter's biggest roar.

I don't think anyone could enjoy the carnival with frostbite.

Blake says we're maybe a week or two off from a big one—a blizzard that buries everyone in place, and when people just hunker down and stay warm.

Roads get snowed in, sometimes covered by landslides.

I look up from the road just now, though, watching in my mirror as the girl leans against a familiar tall figure—Justin. He's holding up his phone again, snapping quick selfies, before laughing and clapping her on the shoulder, watching her as she trudges off.

She heads through the open gate, pausing outside and looking briefly left to right before bowing her head into the wind and pushing forward, thumbs hooked in her backpack straps and shoulders hunched. The sharp gusts blast her bright purple rainbow-tinted hair away from her face, making her wince, turning her head away from the blast.

Wait.

What the hell.

That *is* Andrea.

And isn't she supposed to be with Holt, instead of out here walking alone in the freezing cold?

I slow my car, then pitch a U-turn and go cruising back.

When I stop next to her, she doesn't notice at first, until I lean over and put the window down. At the whirring sound, she lifts her head, squinting suspiciously.

Her face clears, and a bright smile of relief breaks across her face.

"Hey," I say. "Looking for a ride?"

* * *

However I expected to end this day, it wasn't with a tearful teenage girl in the passenger seat.

We're parked at the diner.

She insisted she doesn't want to go home, she doesn't want to go to Holt's. She just needs some space from stupid men with their dumb opinions and dumber egos.

And that's when she bursts out crying, and it all comes spilling out.

Clark isn't missing.

He ran away.

"Because Dad's such an asshole," she says.

Because he blamed Clark for the fires and Clark knows it, and he just wants to lay low until everything blows over and they find the real person doing this.

Andrea was sneaking out from Holt's to see him, to bring him food, to make sure he was warm and safe wherever he's been hiding.

But they had a fight this morning.

She'd tried to actually defend her dad.

To tell Clark that if he just talked to Blake, if he came home, her dad would listen and believe him, and that right now Blake was out trying to find Clark not because he thought he was guilty, but because his Uncle Rog is worried sick about him.

But that wasn't what they'd really fought about in the end.

My heart nearly tumbles out of my chest when she looks up at me with her eyes gleaming bright and wet, tears streaming down her face, her expression so pink and miserable.

"He knows," she says, gulping the words. "He...he knows who did it. And he won't fucking tell me because he says I might get hurt."

I can't breathe.

How?

"I don't understand." I grip her hands, squeezing them warmly, silently begging her with the touch to focus on me when this is *critical*. "How does he know? How did he find out? Is it a friend of his?"

"That thing Dad had," she mumbles, sniffing and lowering her eyes. "The wrist flamethrower or whatever...Clark's the one who gave it to the guy. He made him do it. He made Clark be quiet, and he said...he said if Clark tells anyone, he'll kill them, then kill his Uncle Rog, then kill *him*."

Then she bursts out sobbing again, and I gather her close, murmuring softly, offering her the only comfort I can.

God.

I feel like crying myself.

Clark's innocent.

But I can't possibly believe Blake's own brother would kill someone, either.

There's something deeper going on here than a family feud turned ugly.

And I don't know what to do to help.

Or if I even can.

* * *

Andrea cries on me for almost half an hour, but at first I can't coax her back home.

So I talk her into having a late lunch and something hot to warm her up. We're already at the diner so no use in wasting the opportunity.

After two cups of hot cocoa and a breakfast platter piled high with pancakes—which, frankly, is the best lunch—she reluctantly agrees to go back with me and talk to Blake.

It's the only way to protect Clark.

Get him where the arsonist won't find him.

And once Clark's under adult supervision, once he's *protected*, once he's cleared his head, then maybe he'll give up a name and put an end to this madness.

"I don't think it's Uncle Holt," Andrea says woefully. "I know Dad thinks that, but...I never saw one thing out of place when I stayed with him. And I told Clark I'm staying with Uncle Holt, he would've freaked if that's who made the threat." Her lower lip thrusts out. "Ugh, I don't understand. Why won't he tell me? He says he cares, but if he did, why doesn't he trust me?"

"He cares about you," I assure her, reaching across the table to squeeze her hand. "He does. Or else he wouldn't be holding back to protect you. His heart's in the right place, even if he's going about it wrong."

I pull my hand back as the waitress returns with my credit card and the receipt. I quickly sign off on the bill.

"C'mon," I say. "Let's go home. Mr. Hissyfit's been missing you."

* * *

I WAS WRONG.

Mr. Hissyfit isn't lonely.

He's *pissed off.*

And I don't blame him, when Andrea and I pull up outside the door and see it.

Someone's broken in.

I realize something's off the second I park. The front door is open, swinging loosely on its hinges, and the lock's busted out, splintered wood in jagged little spears against the frame.

A sick, nervous feeling curdles my stomach.

"Stay here," I murmur. "Stay in the car, keep the engine running. Doors locked."

Andrea just gives me a wide-eyed, frightened look and nods.

I creep out of the car, moving stealthily up the steps, skipping around the one porch board I know creaks every time and edging over the threshold.

Only to nearly jump out of my skin at the loud smacking sound inside the house. It takes me a slow motion second to peer into the living room.

Mr. Hissyfit darts his head hard at the glass of his heated enclosure, banging against it with a little *bonk*, his teeth bared, a loud hiss erupting over the room.

"Peace?" Andrea's voice echoes behind me from the open window, panicked and sharp. "What's wrong?"

"Nothing," I croak, barely getting the word out, pressing my hand over my chest and my racing heart, then calling over my shoulder, "Nothing, honey. Stay in the car while I finish looking around."

Not that I even know where to start.

Jesus. It looks like the entire house was trashed.

The sofa and easy chairs are turned over, the glass coffee table in shards, the shelves are tipped, books scattered everywhere. The cushions have even been cut open, stuffing erupting out in big white puffs, the rug slashed into ribbons, the coat rack cracked in half and stabbed like a wooden spear into the underside of the overturned sofa. The huge HD TV is broken in half, like someone body-slammed it over their knee.

Holy crap.

Someone clearly had rage issues, and they took them out here.

The only thing that hasn't been touched is Mr. Hissyfit's aquarium.

Good thing, too.

As cold as it is in here, I think whoever did this has been gone for a bit.

Long enough for the heat to leak out through the open door, leaving the entire house absolutely freezing.

But Mr. Hissyfit's safe inside his heated enclosure, protected from the cold that might have killed him.

And maybe, just maybe, the snake is what scared the intruder off.

At least, I *hope* he's gone.

So I back out slowly and run for the car, diving into the driver's seat and shivering with more than just the cold.

Andrea stares at me, her lashes trembling. "Peace? What happened?"

"Someone broke into the house," I say, already digging my phone out, tapping Blake's number. "But I don't think they took anything."

"Mr. Hissyfit?" she whispers with a worried look.

"Safe. Warm inside his tank and just...agitated," I tell her.

She starts to open the car door, her breaths sucking in, but I catch her arm, shaking my head firmly as I lift the phone to my ear.

Blake's line rings. Again and again and again.

He doesn't pick up.

Crud.

I start to dial again, only to stop as I hear the roar of an engine.

Something finally goes right. Blake's Jeep comes tearing into the driveway.

I go tumbling out of my car just as he screeches to a halt, nearly spinning the Jeep and sending up a spray of snow.

He leaps out, his face set and tight, flushed with fury, but it's the worried darkness in his eyes that gives away his real concern.

"Peace?" he strides toward me. "Where's Andrea? Have you seen her? Holt called, and—"

"Dad?" Andrea says behind me, emerging from my car. "I'm right here."

Then they're crashing into each other.

Blake hugging his daughter tight, Andrea clinging to him hard, letting out a soft little whimper that he echoes in a deep, reassuring growl. Dad buries his face in his daughter's hair.

"He said you were missing," he chokes out. "Fuck, Andrea, I freaked out."

"I'm fine," she mumbles but clings to him even tighter. "I didn't tell him I was going to the carnival, but I...Dad, I gotta tell you something..."

Blake pulls back enough to look down at her, gripping her shoulders. "Anything, Little Violet. What's up?"

She bites her lip, looking up at him worriedly. "Clark's hiding. He's afraid you think he did it when he knows who really did," she says hesitantly. "But he won't tell me who. I don't know. And now someone broke into the house."

"*What?*" It comes out of his mouth like a gunshot.

Blake stiffens, parting his lips—only to stop and go stone-still, lifting his head, staring at the house, his eyes blue fire as he finally notices the door.

He detaches from Andrea, and then it's my turn. His huge, fierce arms lift me right off the ground, and I'm suspended in the air for a couple seconds before he lets me down again.

"Did they hurt you?" he growls, his eyes flashing to mine.

It's so sweet but almost scary. The edge in his voice is a death warrant for anyone who'd ever *dare.*

"I...no. They were gone before we got here, I think. I've already been inside," I say. "The living room's trashed. I didn't check anything else because I think they're gone, but not a hundred percent sure."

"We're about to find out, sweetheart," he says darkly, then nudges Andrea toward me. "Stay here. Both of you. Keep 9-1-1 handy. And if I tell you to run, get in your car and drive. Don't look back."

I can't stand watching him go in there by himself.

And I know if something happens, I won't leave him.

Andrea and I huddle together, clutching each other's hands, watching the door.

I strain, listening for any sound, any hint of a fight, but all I catch is a bit of furniture scraping and moving—then a flicker of motion in the upstairs windows. Blake's tall, dark shape moves past the curtains. All seems well.

But I still don't breathe easy until he's back outside.

"No one home except one mad snake," he says grimly. That tired stoop bows his broad shoulders, his eyes blue shadows. "It's only the living room. Bastards didn't touch anything else. Didn't seem like they were looking at anything in particular, just wanted to piss out some rage. Maybe send a message."

He stops, though, squinting down the front steps and toward the snow along the side of the porch.

Several heavy footsteps leave prints in the packed snow surrounding the house.

And I'm pretty sure they aren't mine, his, or Andrea's.

Blake slowly descends the steps and moves to the edge of the walk, then crouches down, peering at the closest tracks.

"And send a message he did," he mutters tightly. "Shit. I recognize these prints. They're standard safety issue for work crews...including hired construction contractors."

* * *

SOMEHOW, we've come full circle.

With Blake's house a mess and the door refusing to totally shut, we can't stay there.

So after a call to Sheriff Langley, we end up packing everyone up and heading back to my cabin at the Charming Inn.

Sure, the arsonist tried to set it on fire after I'd already left, but it's somewhere warm and safe where we can all be together.

In a town this small, the arsonist could get to us anywhere.

We're with each other.

That's all that matters.

That's what's going to keep us safe.

Not the location of the four walls we have around us.

Still, it's somber as we load our things into my car and Blake's. No one talks—except Mr. Hissyfit, who's entirely vocal about how unhappy he is with having his aquarium moved, and as riled as he is, Andrea can't even soothe him without risking getting hurt.

So we settle in with a very angry snake and a very upset teenage girl.

And Andrea doesn't even argue about being sent to bed early.

Leaving just me and Blake.

He settles on the sofa in the living room, while I turn the

thermostat up to warm a cabin that's been left idle and freezing for over a week. Not even the insulation on the windows stops the cold from creeping in. I'd piled Andrea with blankets before sending her to bed.

By morning we should all be nice and toasty, but these first few hours are going to be chilly.

Blake doesn't even seem to feel it. He props his elbows on his knees and presses his mouth against his clasped knuckles, staring blankly at the coffee table.

I've never seen his face like this.

This terrible mask. Not quite anger.

It makes me think of grief, deep and painful.

And it makes me hurt for him so much.

Once I've got the warm air circulating, I settle down next to him and lean against his side, offering my support without intruding.

And he leans back against me, letting me in.

I curl my hand on his arm, resting my head to his shoulder. "It's not looking good, is it?"

"I don't want to believe it," he says, deep and gritty and pained. "My own goddamn brother. But with all the evidence, who else could it be?"

I don't have an answer.

I wish I did.

I can only press snug in his arms and hold him as close as I possibly can.

* * *

I can't stand seeing him like this as we settle into bed.

Maybe that's why I'm almost expecting it when he moves on me, hard and swift, his thick, hard weight suddenly on top of me. His fingers push through my hair.

"How?" he growls out his question.

"Come again?" I'm totally lost, even if there's no mistaking what he wants. His hips move against mine, pushing his bulge between my legs.

"How the hell you stay so beautiful in the middle of all this ugliness, darlin'?" His eyes shine so bright, two blue gems set deep in his tortured face, almost like a wolf's.

I answer him the only way I can. With a kiss so long and hot and intense it's all twirling tongue.

If I made some mistakes today through this mess, it might be my best mistakes ever.

Because soon he's throwing off the covers, tearing at my clothes, then shedding his own like a second skin. He winds my hair around his fingers, then guides my face to the huge, pulsing, angry hard-on throbbing between his legs.

"Take me away, baby. Make me forget," he orders.

I only let myself blush in stunned silence for a split second before I obey.

I'll never comprehend what makes men so hot when they're tense and pissed off. But tonight, Blake freaking Silverton just might burn me down.

He lets out a sharp, muffled groan as my mouth sinks down on his length. He's so big, so full, so *wired* I can barely fit him in my mouth. My fingers wrap around his base, pumping, going to town on his steaming skin.

I play him like an instrument, loving how he plays me back so effortlessly. He grabs my other hand, pushes it down, and gives me a feral look.

"Play with your clit. Only thing better than getting sucked off by that sweet mouth is hearing you, seeing you, while you do it."

"But—" I ease off him for a second, staring into his eyes.

"Play, woman. You heard me."

Holy hell.

I don't even think I have any words.

So I do what he wants, trying to keep my focus tight on his magnificent cock. Heat flares against my hand, hot and wet and thick. It isn't long at all before we're losing control together.

Blake starts thrusting in my mouth, his hips moving in angry strokes, keeping my concentration with his fingers in my hair, guiding my head down. I find the sweet spot just under the head of his cock and *push,* murmuring a helpless moan.

My fingers move faster, circling, technically *this close* to bringing me off. Only, that's not quite right.

Because it's Blake who ignites my body, my blood, every time he pulls his lip with his teeth.

Every time he picks up his speed.

Every time he growls, cursing, trying to stay quiet for Andrea's sake.

If my mouth wasn't full of him, I'd totally be in trouble, too.

He never peels his eyes off me. They just stick to my body, so intimate and intense, stripping me barer than stark naked, watching my nipples swell and my pace quicken.

I try like the devil to bring him off first, but it's too intense with his gaze, his taste, his soft grunts and echoing *fucks* like thunder in my ears.

I'm—

Coming!

Oh, do I ever.

And it's somewhere in the middle of my first twisting, shaking tremor that Blake goes off, his cock swelling in my mouth, pulling my lips down on his shaft. It only takes a second before I'm overflowing with him, his heat pouring all over me, more than I could ever hope to swallow.

My body hitches again and again, even as I try to keep my lips pulsing up and down his cock.

Muscles I didn't even know I had are freaking trembling when it's over, and there's nothing but the sound of our heavy breathing in the night.

Except, *over* isn't even the half of it.

Blake barely rests for five minutes while I take a breather in his arms. Then his rough, calloused hand circles my ass. And those caresses turn into greedy handfuls while the warm, loving look in his eye goes pure caveman.

Maybe our little talk about birth control the other day was an invitation to forget the condoms. Or maybe he's just that into it—and so am I.

If he was a savage before, he's an absolute beast-man now, pushing into me raw, his forehead on mine as he spreads my legs and claims my wet heat.

There's no holding back.

Everything we've done tonight was just a warm-up for a therapy far deeper than anything I could ever do with words or my hands.

He grabs my wrists and pins me down, a sharpness I adore, a contrast with the sweetness of his kiss and the scratch of his beard on my bare, trembling skin.

Our mouths try to match what's happening *lower*, Blake pistoning into me, each stroke gliding me a little higher. It's pure friction. Delicious agony.

The angry, pent-up desperado—my gunslinger—throwing himself into me with a passion and a heat that takes me places I never dared imagine.

"Blake!"

I can't stop gasping out his name.

He can't stop his heat, his furious strokes, the sweeping slash of his tongue as we crash together like two cymbals. It's reckless and wild, a frantic race to the end.

There's nothing on earth like the way he growls out my name, drilling deeper, when he goes off the edge.

Of course, I'm a goner, too.

His hips pound so, so deep.

The friction of his pubic bone melts me from the inside out.

And next thing I know, every inch of him swells, his whole body tenses, and he's shoving fiery words through his teeth.

"Fuck, Peace!"

I think it's hearing my name on his lips in so much rapture

that does me in. My body seizes. There's barely a second to tangle my limbs around him as his final strokes lift me completely off the bed, before slamming us both into the mattress again.

We dive right into the electric heat of our release together. So intense I feel like I've been ripped right out of my body.

But Blake Silverton stays imprinted on every sweet convulsion and breathless sigh.

XVIII: CAMERA BLUES (BLAKE)

It takes me a long time to fall asleep.

Partly because it's so damn cold in that little cabin, though the small space makes it easier to warm up fast, especially with Peace tucked against me, sharing our body heat underneath the blankets.

Partly because I can't stop thinking about Holt.

About that bootprint.

See, the town council can't afford a workers' comp lawsuit for construction injuries, or any other kind of injuries on the job for town contracting work.

So they issue their own safety equipment when they hire people.

Cops, firemen…construction workers.

And Holt went clomping around the house in those boots, ripping my home to shreds while I panicked over my kid running away.

Bastard scum. I bet he called just so I'd go running home to see what he did.

It's a growing certainty in my mind, and I hate it.

Hate that it ruins any chance that the last scraps of my tattered kin might be able to hold together.

Guess it's just me and Andrea, after all.

Me, Andrea, and Peace.

That last thought finally lets me find refuge in sleep, deep into the night.

I'm not expecting to be woken up by the sound of my phone ringing.

And I'm sure as hell not expecting it to be Sheriff Wentworth Langley.

"Blake?" Langley says. He sounds tired—but he always sounds tired lately, and I think that man needs a damn Xanax. "You're gonna want to come in. We picked up Holt and...it ain't looking good."

Shit!

I bolt upright, making Peace squirm sleepily, burrowing harder against me.

"Give me twenty minutes," I bite off. "I'll be there."

* * *

I won't let Peace come with me to the police station, not even when she looks at me with her big green eyes so wide and soft with worry.

She's dealt with enough of my ugliness.

I won't let Holt make it worse.

When I get to the station, he's pacing in the drunk tank—and favoring a bloody hand that's been slashed up like he, oh, fucking kicked my door in, punched my windows out, smashed my TV.

And he's still wearing his construction coveralls, rolled down around his waist over a dirty, blood-smeared shirt.

He's still wearing *those* boots.

The moment he sees me, he flings himself at the bars, ignoring Langley's wince as they rattle. He grasps at the iron, staring at me desperately.

"You never called, asshole!" he accuses. "Andrea. Is she okay?"

For a second, I blink, dumbfounded.

I have to hand it to him.

That's one hell of an act.

He's good.

Too good.

I stare at him coldly. "Stop it. You weren't worried about Andrea. You just wanted to show off what you'd done."

"Done?" Holt recoils, staring at me. "I haven't done a damned thing, and why the hell did you send Langley after me?"

I work my jaw, staring at his bloodied hand. "How'd that happen?"

Tell me the truth, goddammit.

Tell me the truth, and tell me you aren't a total loss.

Holt pulls his bloody, scabbed hand back from the bars, staring down at it. "I was helping out with the reconstruction. One of the old cinder blocks we were tearing out came loose, fell on me," he said. "I dodged, but it ripped down my hand pretty bad."

"How convenient," I growl, fighting to control the black, ugly rage rising inside me. "Considering I've got your fucking footprints all around my house after you broke in and ripped my living room to shit."

He stares at me like I've grown a second head. "Wha—what are you talking about, Blake? Broke into your house? Why?"

"You tell me. Why the fuck did you break into my house?"

"I *didn't!*" he roars, his voice deepening to a frustrated snarl. "What the hell's wrong with you?"

"What the fuck is wrong with *you?*"

I lose it.

I'm slamming myself against the bars, and so fucking help me if not for those rods of iron between us I'd be wringing his chickenshit neck.

"Were you looking for the evidence? Sorry, bub, I already turned it over. And once they find your prints on it—"

"Prints on *what?*" he demands, only to go still, staring at me, eyes widening, his tanned face going pale beneath his dark five o'clock shadow. "The hell...what the hell? You think it was me. You think it's been me all this time, with the fires."

"Tell me it hasn't been," I snap. "You're the only man with motive. And you showed up in town right when it started. Real big goddamn *coinkydink* if it ain't you."

"I told you. I want to help rebuild this town," he throws back, lips peeling away from clenched teeth.

"But only after you burn it down first, right?" I retort, taking a step back. "You almost fooled me, Holt. Almost made me think maybe you'd changed. But I never trusted you before, and I'm not about to now."

I turn and walk away then.

I can't stand to look at him.

Can't stand to think that the man who'd endanger Heart's Edge is my own blood.

And I ignore him, even as he calls after me, "You idiot, be careful! It's not me—it's not me, Blake! He's still out there...and he's going to really hurt someone."

You already hurt someone, I think bitterly as the door to the station slams shut and I step out into the harsh, unforgiving February wind. *You hurt me and obliterated any chance at all for a relationship with any of us.*

* * *

I ALMOST WISH we could cancel this stupid variety show.

There's no real reason for it anymore.

We've got our perp and evidence to back it up.

Everything points to Holt, even if I don't want it to.

Now, I just gotta coax Clark into coming out of the woodwork to confess Holt's the one who took his equipment, and that'll cinch it. I'm sure Andrea's wrong about Clark thinking it ain't him. The boy just didn't want to tell her and rip his girlfriend's heart out.

Too bad we're on the hook with the Heart's Edge council.

We told them we'd stand up here and entertain them like the big damn heroes they want us to be and let them ask their questions.

So that's what we're doing. A town hall question and answer of sorts.

It's surprisingly warm inside the ice palace. No small feat, really, considering it was put together by a bunch of townies with basic engineering and art.

It kind of looks like the Ice Palace in *Frozen*, complete with spiraling ice stairs leading up to the stage. Thank fuck they're textured so we don't go slipping down like fools as me, Warren, Doc, and Leo stand up here with our mics and big fake superhero smiles.

Mario's here with us, recording everything and transmitting it to the station. They're doing a live broadcast for the folks in the surrounding counties.

Nothing's happening except people asking me lewd questions and teasing everyone else about being henpecked and settled down with kids.

Figures. The folks in this town would much rather talk romance than rehash drug kingpins and evil corporations trying to biohazard us to death.

The men are too quiet. Most of the teasing comes from their own wives and kids in the audience, making the entire town laugh with warm affection.

I mean, it's not bad.

I don't much like being the town darlings, but these people make no secret of the fact that they care about us the same way we care about them.

Still, I can't shake being uneasy.

Doesn't help with Holt behind bars.

This ugly sixth sense prickles on the back of my neck.

I can't help repeatedly peeking backstage, where Peace is quietly warming up on her guitar, and Andrea and Justin have their heads together, working out how to do the safety presentation without Clark's help.

Peace catches my eye from behind the curtain, lifting her head and smiling.

You're doing great, she mouths. I shrug, turning my gaze back to the crowd.

It's calm. Peaceful. Happy.

And I don't trust it one bit.

I hate that I still feel this irrational doubt.

Like some small part of me wonders if Holt's telling the truth.

But if our man isn't him, then *who?*

Gritting my teeth, I tell myself to knock it off and get through this.

Because it means something to Peace, to Andrea, to Justin.

Because it means everything to this beat-up little town, and this town means something special to me.

After an hour of making an ass of myself, I finally escape with the others, exiting the stage so the ice crew can re-texture the melted areas to give traction for the next act.

It was supposed to be Clark, but of course he's nowhere to be found.

I don't want to interrupt Peace's music practice before she plays for the crowd later, so I reconvene with the boys behind the ice palace.

Leo says it before anybody. "You feel it too, don't you?"

I grunt. "Something ain't right, yeah. Everything's pointing to Holt." I glance at Langley and one of his guys, making the rounds along the big wooden windbreaker fence. "I mean, I don't like that they left him alone, but hell. He's locked up. He's not a prison breaker like you or Fuchsia, Leo. So we shouldn't have to worry."

"Snow's coming in. I can smell it," Warren says. "There's something in the air."

"I'll do the rounds," Leo says. "See if anything looks suspicious."

I nod. "The rest of us should take up positions, inside and out. The goal is to keep as many people covered as possible so if anything happens, we can coordinate an evacuation."

All three of them nod tightly.

We split up then, breaking off in different directions. We've all known each other so long and been through so many baptisms by fire we don't even need to ask questions to coordinate.

We know each other's strengths, the way we all think.

And we work together like a well-oiled machine.

As I'm heading back inside the ice palace, though, Andrea comes tumbling outside, searching left and right only to land on me. Her eyes are too wide, her messy, half-shaved hair spiked up from running her fingers through it.

"Dad?" she asks. "I can't find Justin anywhere. We're supposed to go on in forty-five minutes, and I...I can't do this by myself!"

Shit, here we go. Another problem.

Another fire to put out, and I can't ignore my daughter when she's actually *into* this, and I don't want to disappoint her.

"Give me a second," I say, fishing out my phone. "I'll give him a call. If we can't dig him up in time, I'll do the demonstration with you. No worries."

"...*fiiine.*" She wrinkles her nose at me but slumps against the carved, spiraling archway that acts as the entrance to the ice palace, folding her arms over her chest.

Not really a surprise reaction.

I just flash her a smile, waiting for Justin to pick up.

He doesn't.

The call goes to voicemail, and again when I try a second time.

On the second call, I leave a quick message. "Yo, Justin, you're up soon, and Andrea's looking all over the place for you. Let me know where you're at."

When I hang up, she lets out an exaggerated sigh. "Of course he bailed on me. Of course. Everyone always does."

Fuck.

That one cuts deep.

Yeah, I guess everyone's been disappointing her lately. Her mom checked out for good. Uncle Holt's a fire-setting prick. Her boyfriend's hiding out somewhere. Her old man's just the kind of dick dads *have* to be.

And now Justin, her cool new older friend, ditched out on her.

I already know I'm gonna go to stupid lengths to find that guy, just to make her happy.

"Head backstage with Peace," I say, offering her a smile. "Just wait. I'll hunt him down."

"Okay, fine," I get again.

She gives me a skeptical look, but after a moment turns and flounces inside.

I catch Leo's eye across the carnival grounds, through the steadily growing crowds of people moving through booths selling funnel cakes, fried things that probably shouldn't be fried, hot drinks, trinkets, all the little touristy things people like to take home with them even though they ain't good for much. I see a lot of out-of-towners, folks I don't recognize who came just for the carnival. Makes it harder to spot anyone acting fishy, but I trust the guys to have things under control.

So I signal Leo that I'm ducking out, then let myself blend into the crowd.

I check the entire grounds up and down for Justin, every nook and cranny, every storage shed, every backstage area—even looking under the stage. It doesn't make sense, they were together less than an hour ago. Did he forget something at home?

I do some more checking.

Nothing.

And after a few more calls go unanswered, I've had it.

I'm about to go and drag Justin out of his apartment if I have to, if it'll make my little girl happy.

Dammit.

I trusted him with this, trying to make him feel like he was part of the team. Part of my *family*.

Look, I know he's got heavy shit he's dealing with, but I need him not to duck out on me like this right now.

So, reluctantly, I stop for a holler at Warren, letting him know I'll be back and to call me if anything goes down. Then I climb in my Jeep and head back into town.

The apartment complex isn't far. Heart's Edge is so small we've only got a few of these multi-unit buildings since most people buy or build their own homes.

Justin's truck isn't in the parking lot when I pull up, but I go up to check just in case.

And find his door open.

Unlatched, just barely pulled closed a crack, like he left in a hurry.

I frown. After finding my own home ransacked, I've got a bad feeling.

But before I can push the door open, my phone vibrates in my pocket. I snatch it out, not even checking the name on the caller ID, and answer.

"Justin?"

"Nah, Blake," Sheriff Langley says. I can hear the music and noise of the carnival in the background, chatter and people moving about. "It's me. Listen, I got bad news."

My chest goes heavy, and my breath goes thick with dread. "What's that?"

"I left the new junior deputy watching the station, and uh, well..." He clears his throat. "Apparently, Holt stole his keys right off his belt and managed to get loose."

I close my eyes.

Fuck.

I don't need this right now.

"Watch for him at the carnival," I growl. "Be ready to evacuate people, but don't cause a panic just yet. I'll be right there. If you need help, get the guys."

Langley makes a nervous sound of agreement. I already know when push comes to shove, he probably won't be much help.

He picked the wrong town to bumble into.

I'm already forgetting Justin, turning away, but my elbow bumps the door as I do and sends it swinging open.

And I go cold, frozen in place, as I see the interior.

Gone is that sterile lifelessness that made me think Justin's existence, his home, must be so empty, so lonely all the time.

All the photo albums have been yanked down from the shelves.

They're scattered everywhere, their pages open and slashed in ominous red ink.

What the hell?

I almost don't want to look.

I have to.

Because suddenly what I've been overlooking is right here in front of me.

I drift inside, crouching down to look at the first photo album on the floor.

The pictures in it are old.

But I know them, because I know the *people* in them.

Warren. Jenna.

Me.

Back then, we were a trio, after Leo went underground and before Doc moved to Heart's Edge. We're young, fresh out of boot camp, hanging on each other and laughing at Brody's.

The picture's shaky. Taken by someone real inexperienced.

But me and Warren are slashed out in red, while Jenna's face is circled in a curly red heart.

My jaw drops.

It's the same weird shit in every other picture.

Dozens—no, fucking *hundreds*, some just seconds apart, capturing our lives. Us working. Us laughing. Us coming home from deployment to see our families and friends. I see myself and Warren and Jenna over and over again, but more and more it's Jenna. Jenna. *Jenna*.

Shots of her tossing her hair back, shots of her dirty with grease because she wasn't afraid of manual labor, shots of her leaning on her brother and laughing until her eyes scrunch up.

Then shots of that folded American flag on a coffin.

Shots of her grave.

And then no more of her as I move from album to album...but there's me again. This time, it's a photo from an old local paper, taken by some reporter.

Right outside the Paradise Hotel, or at least what's left of it.

And Justin's mother leaning on me as I haul her away from the smoking rubble.

I don't even remember that.

That night was such a fucking haze. My gut's in knots as I realize that in the rush of doing what needed to be done, I must've been the guy to notice the woman collapsed in the ruins was still alive, wheezing, her body blackened with soot.

I don't get it.

Don't understand why he'd save all this crap. Why he'd be taking pictures of us all these years without us knowing.

There's something very wrong here, I'm realizing.

Something wrong inside Justin's head.

More and more, I'm flipping through page after page, barely breathing.

Watching as the photos get better in quality but more obsessed, more strange. More of me and Warren on our lonely fishing trips, and visits to Jenna's grave captured in black and white.

Then Doc, too, as he opened up The Menagerie, practically

chronicling his integration into Heart's Edge. Even a few secret shots of Leo back when he was Nine by night, concealed in the shadows, watching over the town from a distance, just a silhouette with an edge of moonlight glinting off his mask and hood.

Justin's been everywhere.

Watching our lives.

Obsessing over us.

And *hating* us, because too many of these photos are scratched, slashed with ink.

Enough of them show an unstable rage.

Blame, in jagged scratches of red pen strokes that rip right through the paper.

Snarling, I sift through more, coming up on recent stuff.

Then I hit on a trend that terrifies the ever-loving fuck out of me.

I start seeing photos of Andrea.

My *daughter*, and goddamn if every goose pimple on my body doesn't stand up. I recognize her gangly pre-teen lope, her crooked gap-toothed smile. More and more photos that seem to track her growth by the *month*, hearts circled around her face...until it's not her face at all.

The photos are altered in this strange, fucked up collage.

My daughter's punky clothing and knobby knees, but pasted over her face, it's Jenna Ford's.

Hundreds of cutouts of Jenna's face, meticulously trimmed down and pasted over my daughter's until Jenna lives again in these sick doctored photos.

They paint a clear picture.

One that makes me want to vomit.

Justin was obsessed with Jenna, even though he'd have been so young when she was alive she probably never noticed him as an awkward teenager.

Obsessed with all of us.

They call us saviors, heroes, but we didn't save the woman he idolized.

Or his mother.

And now he's transferred his warped obsession to my daughter.

Fuck isn't strong enough a word.

I can't decide if I'm more pissed off or freaked. If he's willing to punish us by fire, if he can play the victim so easy that even *I* was fooled into taking him under my wing...

I don't even want to think what he'd do to feed his obsession with Andrea.

I just know I've got to protect her.

And I've got no fucking time to lose.

XIX: BROKEN PITCH (PEACE)

I don't think I've ever seen Andrea looking so despondent.

I'm trying to practice backstage, but it's hard when she's dragging around looking like the apocalypse just hit.

I feel for her.

Truly.

Justin's vanished, and she can't do the safety presentation on her own. She needs someone official backing it up from the town fire crew.

"Hey," I say, trying to catch her attention. "It'll be all right. Blake will totally find him in time."

"Yeah, sure." She rolls her eyes, sighing heavily as she flops down on one of the benches backstage. "I should just give up now."

"No way," I say softly. "Listen, honey, if it comes right down to it, and he doesn't make it back in time, I'll wiggle into Blake's coveralls and do it up there with you."

"You don't know it." She smiles wryly. "But thanks for offering."

"Plan B. Dead serious. I've been around enough showy fireworks and circuses to know how to give a spiel. Nobody'll ever know." I wink at her.

She stares right through me, letting out a deflated laugh.

There's a tired maturity in Andrea's smile that hurts to see.

She shouldn't have to deal with this crap. She shouldn't be so used to disappointment that she learns to accept it.

And when she stands, coming over to squeeze my shoulder, I decide I won't let her.

Catching her hand, I grip it tight for a moment, before she pulls away.

"I'm gonna go find a bathroom, okay?" she says. "Yell if he ever shows up."

"Will do," I say, watching her straggle off before I bow over my guitar again.

She's not the only one with jitters today. Playing at The Nest was a sliver of this crowd.

I try to shake off my nerves, losing myself in practice chords. That song about my gold-hearted desperado still rolls real easy off my tongue.

It's now or never.

It seems especially fitting right now, when the whole town is honoring Blake and his friends. I guess they'll all see the heroes of Heart's Edge in the song, though I'm really just singing it for one very special man.

My man.

I'm so lost in the melody and lyrics I don't realize how much time blurs by until one of the stagehands ducks in the back. "Uh, Peace? Hey, it's almost time for that fire safety thing? Where are they?"

Oh.

I lift my head, looking around.

No sign of Andrea. No Justin. No Blake.

It's just me back here, all by my lonesome with my guitar.

I flash the stagehand a distracted smile. "Let me see if I can find them."

My heart throbs sadly. I bet Andrea just moped off somewhere to give up.

Poor girl.

Maybe Blake and I can take her out for a special dinner tomorrow to make up for the disappointment.

I'm still thinking of things I can do to help her feel better as I head off toward the row of temporary bathrooms backstage that aren't much better than port-a-potties, just cleaner.

But I don't start worrying until my foot catches something.

I look down and recognize the ragged patchwork colors of Andrea's neon-stitched messenger bag. There's a scrap of blue notepaper poking out of it I can't help but recognize.

"No!" I whisper, my hands already starting to shake.

My vision flashes, a sudden hot rush of panic, vertigo, adrenaline.

And as I bend down, slow with dread, to pluck the paper out, I see the familiar, scratchy handwriting.

The same handwriting on the notes left by the monster.

*Hey, **babe, let's make up. Meet me out beyond the fence. I'll be waiting. You were right. Love you. -Clark***

Clark didn't write this.

No flipping way did Clark Patten write a single word.

The tone is too adult, the script too obvious, and why would Clark say *love you* when they aren't even technically *dating?*

My heart pounds so hard it's making me sick.

There's a time to meet scribbled below his signature.

Fifteen minutes ago, and Andrea's *still not back.*

I feel like I've just swallowed razors.

Quickly, I look up, darting my gaze around. I'm in a narrow corridor leading out beyond the backstage staging area and around to the dressing areas, the bathrooms, other little enclosed bits of the ice palace that were thrown together for construction and maintenance.

I'm alone.

No Andrea.

No anyone.

I need to find Blake, before the worst happens.

His daughter needs him.

I need him.

And maybe this whole town needs him. Again.

Because whoever wrote this note...I think they want to hurt way more people than just Andrea.

Choking back the sickly panic in my throat, I spin on my heel, darting to the exit.

That's how I slam right into something solid and warm.

I stumble backward, reeling, my vision crossed for a second.

Then my eyes refocus, and I'm staring up into a masked face. A pair of murky hazel eyes I recognize now with a horrible familiar chill.

A single dark, Grecian curl escapes the mask, drifting across his eyes.

And I don't even get a chance to scream the horror rising up from my darkest depths before he's on me, his hand clapped over my mouth.

A foul, acrid smell washes over me.

Everything goes cloudy, dark, distant, and I'm gone.

* * *

I WAKE TO A POUNDING HEADACHE, brutal nausea, and the deepest cold I've ever felt in my life.

It's like I've been sleeping on a slab of liquid nitrogen.

As my vision clears, the clarity coming back in the darkness, I realize I'm close to the truth.

I don't quite recognize where I am.

Only that it's dark and closed off with billowing cloth walls.

There are chunks of ice everywhere. Stacked and tumbled in towering crumbles, slabs the size and weight of two or three men, many of them dirty or broken in half.

It's the leftovers from building the ice palace. The mistakes, the unclean bits, the oddly shaped bricks.

And I'm lying on top of one of them, numbly aware of the freezing cold so deep it practically burns my skin. *Oh, God.*

Frostbite city, here I come.

But I'm less worried about that than the fact that I can't feel my left leg, and I think my cheek might be fused to the ice.

I can't lift my head.

There's something around my ankle, too, cold and heavy.

But if I roll my eyes, I can just make out the source of soft whimpers rising in my peripheral vision, paired with this strange, disturbingly *happy* masculine humming. A man's voice.

And Andrea.

She's in worse shape than me.

She's been stripped out of her coat, down to a sleeveless shirt and thin leggings under her skirt.

And she's sobbing in sheer misery as the tall, lean demon in black stands over her, painting her lips red, ignoring how she writhes against the handcuffs. They've been stabbed like icepicks into the ice block, keeping her bound in a crucifix position, arms spread, ankles together.

And her poor bare skin touches the frigid slab, already looking red and irritated.

Oh, God.

Oh my *God*, it's Justin.

It's *been* Justin all along...and I don't think he even remembers I'm here.

He's so utterly fixated on Andrea's face, watching her with a sort of scary, obsessed adoration.

"Almost there," he says, stroking his long finger down her cheek. Andrea flinches away, turning her head to one side. "You look so much better now. Except for that shitty clown hair, but we'll fix it up. We'll make you right again, Jenna."

"I'm not Jenna!" Andrea half screams, half rasps, her teeth chattering, her voice weak.

I get a sick sense it's hardly the first time she's said it.

"You will be." Justin's expression goes colder than the ice, his voice flat, his eyes a total black void.

"Justin!" I snap, just wanting to get his attention.

Anything to distract him from this shitshow. This senseless nightmare.

Anything to keep him from hurting her more.

"That's Andrea. It's not Jenna. Let her go. Let us *both* go."

"You don't tell me what to do. You're not even his wife!" He whips toward me, his upper lip curled in a sneer. Even with that twisted, hateful expression, he's still so empty it's unnerving, his voice toneless. "Did you honestly *think* I'd let you take them from me? Take Chief from me? Take *her* from me?" His eyes glow eerily as he steps closer to me. "They're *family*. My father and...and Jenna. You can't have them."

That's when my heart stops and the gravity of what we're dealing with sinks in.

Fear hits like a tsunami wave, making me numb, yet hyperaware. I can't look away from this psychopath—from those chilling eyes, that blank stare.

"You can't have them if you hurt Andrea," I whisper. "She'll die of frostbite like this. And Blake will never forgive you. He'll never be your dad if you hurt her."

I swallow hard.

Jesus, I hope I'm doing this right. It's not like there's a guidebook or anything for talking down someone who's gone dangerously off the deep end.

I can't even begin to understand what Justin's going through.

What's happened to warp him *this freaking much.*

But I remember overhearing it when they were washing dishes, that day we all had dinner.

How he's always seen Blake like a father.

And Jenna Ford, Blake told me about her, how she died thanks to another man gone crazy with greed.

Whatever happened to twist Justin's need for a surrogate to the point where he thinks Andrea is Jenna and Blake is somehow his father...

I have to stop it.

I've got to snap him back to reality before it's too late.

But I flinch as he slams the heel of his palm into the ice next to my head, and nearly scream as my cheek pulls against the ice. It rips free from the thin skim frozen against my skin, leaving half my face on fire.

Breathing hard, I stop panicking, struggling not to burst out crying, fighting not to black out.

I don't think I'm bleeding, just a little frost burned, but *God* does it smart in the nastiest way.

And Justin seems to enjoy it.

His mouth forms a vicious jack-o-lantern grin as he leans over me.

"I know your ways," he whispers. "Siren-seductress-*Medusa*, destroyer of men. I won't listen to your lies, witch. But if you really want to save them, you'll do what I say."

I lick my parched lips.

Andrea's sob eats into me, but I can't look away from Justin.

"What? What do you want me to do?" I ask, forcing the words.

"I," he hisses, catching a handful of my hair and making me cry out, "want you to make them take me *seriously*."

He jerks my head, neck whiplashing, and suddenly I can feel heat again as the sharp spikes of agony rush through me. He shakes me roughly a few more times, then stops, leaning closer, leering at me with his eyes too wide and his teeth bared.

I've never seen anything scarier in my life.

No movie monster compares with the insane terror of a man pushed over the edge.

"Everyone calls them heroes," he hisses. "*Everyone!* When they bring nothing but pain and misery to this town. The real heroes die so they get all the praise. Jenna. My *mother*. They might as well have killed them themselves. And everyone always sees them—*them!* They're so strong, they're so brave, they've suffered so much...what about *my* suffering? What about *my* strength? What about what I've lived through? What I've suffered? What I've lost?" His voice cracks like a very dangerous, very lost little boy.

I don't even know if I want to cry for myself...or cry for him.

I have to try again to talk to him. To *reach* him through the terrible pain he must be in that turns his world into this black-and-white projection of every wrong he's ever suffered, amplified a thousandfold.

If I can ease my clients' pain, I can stop this.

Can't I?

Even if I'm shaking down to my core, in so much pain I could pass out, I keep my voice low, soothing. I try to channel Blake from his advice line, the voice that made me fall in love.

"I'll listen, Justin," I say. "I see you. I see how much you're hurting. You deserve recognition for everything you've lost. And if you want...I'll write a song about you. I'll tell the truth about everything you've fought through. Just please, let Andrea go. I'll sing for you until everyone hears it."

For several long seconds, he stares.

Justin's grimace widens, his jaw shaking—and he flings me back against the ice slab, letting go of my hair.

"Bullshit. You sing only lies," he whispers in a slow and eerie tone. "But I'll tell my own truth. I just want you to give me a nice little soundtrack for dramatic effect. Something to get their attention." He cranes his head like a doll, watching me with those unblinking, empty eyes. "And you'll do it, or I'll leave my Jenna right where she is, and they'll have to cut her in half to peel her frozen body off the ice."

"Don't!" I plead, while Andrea's whimpers peak even higher,

wordless and terrified. "I'll do it. I'll sing for you. Are you going to do a presentation?"

"Oh, no, little peacemaker."

I recoil as he reaches for me, curls his knuckles, strokes his fingers down my temple, my cheek—and reignites the hot pain where he touches my frost burned skin.

"I'm going to burn everybody in Heart's Edge alive. Right down to ashes," he purrs with a deep, hideous pleasure darkening his voice. "And then they'll know *exactly* how it felt when my mother died, charred and choking on her own charcoal-blackened lungs. And he'll be right in the middle of it. My father and all his little friends...and so will you."

It takes everything I have not to shake. I don't understand his logic, his reasoning.

Much later, I realize there isn't any.

He taps his fingertips almost playfully to my nose. "Sorry for this. You're not from this fucked up little town. But you chose your side, Peace, and you looked at me *just like them*. Like I was nothing. Like I was just this hollowed out puppy. It's time for me and Jenna to leave this place behind. In our *dust*, where you all belong."

Crap.

Crap, crap, crap, and also *crap*.

"What are you going to do? I don't understand," I whisper.

I'm not expecting him to tell me. Not really.

I'm just trying to stall him for a little while longer.

Especially when I see movement.

We're in some kind of tent, I realize, and there's a frosted plastic window stitched into the fabric. Over Justin's shoulder, I catch a glimpse of someone.

Clark.

He's looking inside, his face white with fear.

Oh, thank *God*.

Someone who knows we're here.

Someone who can help.

But I'm dragged back to Justin as he lets out a short, barking laugh. "Wouldn't you like to know?" he mocks, folding his arms over his chest, looking down at me with contempt. "You just do your job. Give Chief a little more incentive to come running for you. The fool loves you more than he loves his own son and daughter. That's why I have to take her away. That's why I have to take you away from them, too."

"That's not true," I whisper. "You have no clue how much Blake loves Andrea. He'd die for her."

"Maybe he will," Justin snarls, giving me the most dead-eyed look yet.

I shake my head sharply, but past Justin, I'm watching Clark, hoping not to give him away. But he's got to *do* something besides stand there.

"You're wrong. You'll never *get Blake*," I spit back at Justin. "You hear me? You'll never *GET BLAKE*."

Please, I plead silently.

Please let Clark understand. Let him find Blake before it's too late.

Justin has no intention of letting anyone get out of here alive.

He swings around, hefting a thick tank with a strap on it and a nozzle, and it takes me a second to figure it out.

It's a flamethrower.

"Don't worry," he says, his nasty, cunning smile returning, making him look like a nightmare scarecrow come to life. "One way or another, I'm going to get *everyone*. Then Heart's Edge will know how it feels to really burn."

XX: PERCUSSION SHOCK (BLAKE)

Too many damn people.

That's all I can think right now as I bolt out of my Jeep and through the gate, back on the carnival grounds.

There are too many people, hundreds, and fuck if calling ahead didn't do a single thing to help.

I'd warned them.

Leo, Warren, Doc, even Langley.

I told them, while I barreled my way down the road toward the grounds at top speed, breaking every fucking speed limit in the county while I barked into my phone.

Justin's crazy.

He's obsessed.

He's the *arsonist*.

And he's out for revenge against the people he thinks failed to save his ma, Constance, and failed to save the girl he was obsessed with...

...and now that dumb kid is about to ruin his life.

It doesn't matter who's to blame right now.

We can talk guilt, unfortunate circumstances, and how somebody always gets hurt when evil companies like Galentron cause tragic hotel fires.

Later.

After I see my daughter and my woman alive in one piece. The fact that Andrea's not picking up her phone and neither is Peace has me scared shitless.

Crazy or not, I have to fucking stop Justin from inflicting his pain on anyone else.

A *whole* lot more people, because apparently the townspeople aren't listening when Warren and the others try to get them to *leave*.

Most folks don't even hear the announcement.

They're too caught up in their chatter and funnel cakes to cast more than odd glances at the crazy men waving their arms around everywhere and shouting.

I shove my way through the dazed, milling crowd, toward Leo, who's closest, standing on the fence around a pen with thickly furred woolly sheep dressed up in cute costumes for kids to play with.

"Hey!" I bark, reaching up to snap my fingers for his attention. "Andrea! Where's Andrea?"

Leo stops shouting and looks down at me, then growls and vaults off the fence in front of me. "No goddamn clue, man. I've turned this place inside out, and I can't find her or Peace."

I swear under my breath, pacing roughly left and right.

Fuck.

I need a plan.

Shame all my training and emergency response skills go right out the window when it's my daughter and the woman I love possibly in danger.

I make myself stop, take a deep breath, press my fingers to my temples, and calm down. Just like the way Peace would. I can almost hear her soothing voice washing over me.

Wait.

That ain't my imagination.

I hear Peace. Her voice echoes over the intercom system mounted to the power poles spaced around the area.

She's singing.

This slow, intense, oddly distorted version of "Ring of Fire" I'm not sure what old Johnny would ever make of.

And it sounds like she's never wanted to sing anything less in her life. The pain and fear in her voice make every word tremble. It's ugly and unmistakably different from those soaring sweet notes from the heart I love so much.

Leo lifts his head, staring up at one of the mounted speakers. "What the hell is that?"

"Trouble," I mutter. Just like that, people start clustering toward the middle of the carnival grounds, milling around and staring, whispering among themselves in curious tones. "And we'd better put an end to it now."

That's when I realize I'm hearing Peace's voice *twice*.

Once over the intercom.

And echoing from the center of the carnival grounds.

Where people are streaming toward her, gasping out. Some seemingly delighted by what they're seeing like it's some kind of show, others crying out in concern.

I shove my way through the crowd, using my size to my advantage to part the sea of people.

Until I reach the front.

I stop, staring in horror.

Peace stands on the tall wooden stage that's been erected for the silent auction later tonight.

She's perched on a stool and surrounded by a literal *ring of fire.*

Some kind of accelerant must've been sprayed down on the wood and ignited. Now, it leaps up around her, and she's trapped on all sides, no more than two feet of space in any direction from the stool where she huddles, strumming her guitar.

And singing her heart out.

I don't understand.

I don't get what's happening.

Why she's singing her heart out, when past the flickering

flames I can just barely make out her face, the sweat beading on her brow, mixing with tears.

That's why her voice is so thick.

She's sobbing.

And my heart hits my throat like a bullet.

Especially when I see the side of her face, red like someone struck her.

Someone *hurt* her.

Someone hurt *my girl.*

"Peace!" I roar, reaching out, charging toward the steps.

Her head snaps up, her eyes widening, fear transfixing her face as her tear-bright gaze locks on me. "Blake, *don't!*" she cries, the song breaking.

Too late.

I just don't realize it till my foot comes down on the bottom step.

And I feel something *snap* under the sole of my boot.

Some kind of trigger, I realize—freezing far too late, sudden flashback, the feeling of a shell exploding too close on a hot, Afghan day.

But it's not the earth around me that explodes.

It's the snow around the temporary windbreaker fence built around the carnival grounds.

Plumes of snow rocket up in sharp blasts, followed by gouts of flame, jetting up in red-gold tongues from concealed devices beneath.

Holy fuck.

Those fence planks are just dry wood, not very dense, and—

And it's like throwing a match into a stack of newspaper, they're so flammable.

They go up instantly, illuminating like fireworks, flame racing up along the planks and spearing toward the sky in a roaring rush, wood crackling, a ring of flames completely encircling the carnival grounds in hellish light. Heat that melts back the snow so furiously the wetness doesn't even have a chance to dampen the sparks.

The barrier that was supposed to protect the townspeople from the cold traps them in an orange-flickering cage of fire.

Dimly, I'm aware of screaming. Shouting.

People begin their stampede, shoving, pushing, rushing for the exits—only to break back with frightened cries as leaping walls of fire make them recoil, the heat beating them back. One man tries to rush it anyway, then stumbles, throwing himself down in the snow and rolling frantically, beating out the flames on his jacket while people grasp at his smoking frame and drag him back.

Shit.

I'm the fire chief.

I'm supposed to be taking control here.

Instead, I'm frozen, staring, the only point of stillness in the chaotic crowd.

This is my fault.

Because I was blind.

Because I let my biases rule me.

Because I was too goddamn naïve and trusted the wrong people, mistrusted the people I should've put some kind of faith in, let my own issues get in the way of keeping people safe, protecting the people I love.

And I still don't know where the hell Andrea even is.

My hands form rigid fists at my sides. I hold in a scream. I'm just frozen.

Freaked that I might lose her, and lose Peace.

And suddenly my leg is all rigid pain, and I'm down on my knees, dropping as everything inside me locks up and pulls that tension in a paralyzing knot.

Hissing, I hit the ground hard, losing sight of Peace as I strike the frozen earth, clutching at my thigh.

No, dammit. *Not now.*

I can't.

Fucking mind over matter, and it's my mind making my matter act up.

All because I had a slow-motion half-second eternity of doubt, of fear, and I'm pounding at my thigh, but it ain't doing a thing but driving that pain deeper like a nail in a coffin.

"Blake!" someone cries, only it's not Peace.

Someone comes slamming into me, hard enough to nearly bowl me over, dropping to his knees in front of me and staring at me with total desperation.

Clark Patten.

He's wild-eyed, scared, shaking me.

"Get up!" he gasps, begging me, pleading me. "You have to get up. You have to come. She needs you."

I don't even know what *she* he means, and it doesn't matter.

All that matters is I can't let my fucking body destroy me like this.

Or anyone else.

I grit my teeth, pushing past the pain, grappling at Clark's arm, forcing myself up. It feels like I'm ripping my leg out of its socket, but I don't have the luxury to care. He holds close to me, letting me steady myself on him, and I give him a tight nod as I brace my feet and start for the stage.

Peace.

I've got to get her free.

And then I've got to get this crowd under control and to safety.

Then I've got to get through the flames myself, to the fire truck outside.

Remember my duty.

Remember my calling.

And take it one step at a time, until everyone's out of danger.

But Clark thrusts himself in front of me, staring up, shaking his head as he braces his hands against my chest to stop me.

"Let me help," he says, already shrugging out of his jacket—

fire-retardant material, I realize, just black like the rest of his clothes, a hazard of his job.

For a second, I can't help but feel a spark of admiration in him, and I get it—why my daughter likes him. He's mustering up all his bravery even when I can tell he's piss scared.

"Andrea?" I growl. "Where is she?"

Then he says the words that make my gut ice over, that beat back the heat of the roaring flames to leave me completely cold.

"He's got her," Clark whispers. "Justin's got her. He was calling her *Jenna*, and he...he was hurting her. I couldn't get inside. I couldn't get to her without him seeing me. He's armed, Blake."

I've never felt such pure murderous rage like what I'm feeling now.

Never felt such sheer certainty that I could kill someone with my bare hands without even half a second's thought.

My anger is a wall of ice.

And strong enough that I swear to fuck, I'll break Justin Bast into pieces against it.

Without hesitation.

"Where?" I bite off coolly, and Clark points over the rioting, shoving, out-of-control crowd, toward the far end of the carnival grounds.

"Inside a tent," he whispers, then lifts his chin, tossing his head to me urgently. "*Hurry*. I'll help save your girl, Mr. Silverton. Just promise me you'll save mine."

He doesn't have to ask.

I trust him to beat down that little ring of fire and let me get her free of the flames.

And no one has to tell me to save my daughter.

For a moment, over his head, I catch Peace's eye through the flames, slowly tightening around her. I know now that she's bait.

Justin knew, though.

He knew I'd react to seeing Peace threatened, and charge right at the stage.

He used my own feelings against me.

He's *been* using my own feelings against me—to lead me astray, to cloud my judgment.

No more.

I see clearly now.

And I see so clearly the faith in her big green eyes. She gives me a small nod, her lips trembling but her jaw firm, her shoulders square.

Then I slap him on the shoulder, and it's go time.

The boy knows what to do. He's charging in ahead of me, positioning himself near a natural sliver of a break in the fire. He crouches, letting the flames pour against his stretched out jacket, just long enough for me to fly right past.

I dive for Peace, rip her off that chair, up into my arms.

The hard part? There's no time to even steal a kiss.

Not while the fire keeps lashing like deadly whips all around us.

Not while a fucking madman I thought was my friend has Andrea.

Fire resistant or not, the boy's jacket isn't made to last forever. We barely make it past him again, Peace clutched tight in my arms, folded around me.

I leap off the stairs holding her and we hit the snow, topple over, and roll.

I only realize after the fact the snow hisses out a small part of my jacket that caught the flames.

It's a miracle I can even stand, sparing just a second to give her a fierce look and a furious hand-squeeze. "Stay here, darlin'. You're safe. Be right back."

Then I turn away, striding in the direction where Clark's pointing, forging through the crowd. I slip my fingers between my teeth, letting out a piercing whistle before thrusting my hand in the air.

It's like summoning hunting hawks. Warren, Leo, and Doc appear almost out of nowhere, sweaty and dirty and rushed,

Warren's jacket singed from where he's been beating at the flames. Rich materializes next, breathless and streaked with soot.

"You know what to do," I say. "Calm everybody down. Keep 'em away from the flames. Slow and orderly, before anyone hurts anyone else. Tend to the injured. Tell everyone to get low, under the smoke. Look for a weak spot in the wall, and get them out of here. As soon as you can get to the truck, fire it up."

"On it," Warren snaps, while the others already peel away, jogging out, raising their voices in loud shouts. "What are you gonna do?"

My answer gets cut off by a sudden spout of flame erupting from between two booths. My head whips around.

Justin steps out, a fucking flamethrower strapped to his back, the nozzle clutched in both hands.

He jacks it and sends flame spraying out in front of him in an arc that burns through the snow to catch the dry grass underneath, igniting it like some kind of crazed smile painted in flames against the ground.

Almost as disturbing a smile as the one on his lips. The flames light up his eyes and he plants his feet, staring me down.

I stop in my tracks, locking my gaze on him, wishing it could kill. My fingers clench slowly into fists as that anger inside me erupts into a sense of purpose.

"You go on," I whisper to Warren, never taking my eyes off Justin. "I'm gonna save my daughter."

XXI: DRUMROLL (PEACE)

Of all the weird things I've seen today, one of the weirdest *has* to be Clark Patten wrapping his jacket over his upraised arms and face.

Then charging through the wall of flames around me, parting them in a burst of sparks, giving Blake just enough room to save my almost frying bacon.

I can't stop crying.

Because I'm so *angry*.

So angry Justin used me as bait.

And I had to play along, or he would've hurt Andrea even worse.

I'll never forget Blake folding me in his big, strong arms and taking a leap of faith through the fire. The way the heat washed over us reminded me of surfing back on Oahu.

There's this moment where you lean into the curl of a wave, and there's this glass wall of crystal-blue water that you can see right through, skimming right along your shoulder. It's so fragile and yet so powerful, and you're aware, in that moment, how quickly it can crash over you and drag you under.

That's what diving into fire feels like.

Only it's hot and flickering and so terrifying I never would've been able to do it without Blake Silverton.

Please, I think desperately. *Please let him get to her in time.*

I try insanely hard not to think about his last look, how bright his blue eyes burned, how he squeezed my hand with a grip that could've made Hercules jealous.

Back on the ground, Clark wraps his jacket around me.

"Come on," he says, his voice only cracking a little. "I...I promised Mr. Silverton. You're gonna be okay. My jacket's fireproof."

I stare up at him. He's just a kid, but his smile is brave and fierce and toothy. "Clark, what about—"

"Don't worry about me," he says. "Fire's my game. You just hold the jacket tight, move fast, and if any of those flames from the fence start coming toward you, dive for the snow. *Go.*"

For a moment, I'm just frozen, my eyes locked on the huge, flaming fence that makes any hope of escape impossible. Blake's friends are in the thick of the crowd now, trying to calm them, barking orders.

It isn't easy for even these men with their booming voices to make themselves heard in the disorderly roar. Warren and his friends shout louder, marshaling people away from the flaming walls. But there's more shadows now, fire from another direction, closer.

Oh no.

I crane my head, turning toward the space where Clark is still staring with dread.

I can see the tent where I'd been bound up with Andrea.

I can see Blake's broad back.

And I can see Justin, standing between Blake and the tent, blocking him with a fountain of fire he keeps spraying from that flamethrower along the ground.

There's no way Blake gets past Justin in time.

That's the point.

That's what Justin really wants to do, isn't it?

Force Blake to suffer, knowing he's just feet away from his daughter, and he'll die before he gets to her.

Like hell.

I won't let that happen.

Slowly, I catch Clark's eye.

He nods, decisive, and I know—we're on the same page.

Without another word, ducking low, we take off running.

The booths lining the carnival space are our shield as we circle around, trying to avoid Justin's line of sight. He seems totally focused on Blake right now.

I can't make out what they're saying to each other, Blake's voice just a growling steady rumble, Justin shrill and crazed and leering, but they're facing each other like gunslingers at high noon. The chaos and the crowds and flames don't even divert them one bit.

I can barely breathe in the choking smoke, so I pull my shirt up over my mouth and run faster.

With Clark on my heels, we dive behind a tent several feet from Justin, breathing hard, watching him warily as we crouch down.

"Do you think he's seen us?" I whisper, and Clark shakes his head.

"Nah. He's a fucking loon."

I hope he's right.

But for a moment, past Justin's tensed back, his jerking shoulders, and the flames...

Blake's eyes flicker.

He seems focused entirely on Justin, but I know he's looking at me.

And I nod slightly, offering him a tiny smile, mouthing, *I've got this.*

I've got *her.*

I'll save her, Blake.

Just trust me.

Please.

He turns into even more of a statue for a split second. Then there's an almost imperceptible nod. His gaze flips back to Justin.

And he takes a deliberate, aggressive step forward.

Justin shouts, firing off another burst of flame, his voice cracking, manic.

Blake's buying us time. Distracting the madman.

We can't waste this opportunity.

"*Go!*" I hiss, shoving at Clark and tumbling along after him, scrambling for the tent.

After what feels like forever, we duck inside.

Andrea is still bound up on the ice slab, moaning in pain, whimpering so quietly it nearly kills me to see her when it's like she's too weak to even work up full, deep sobs.

That creeping redness against her bare skin scares me.

Clark lets out a hoarse, raw sound, sheer anguish, and rushes over, capturing her face in his hands. "Andrea? Andrea, oh my God, I'm sorry I didn't get here faster..."

Her head lifts, her eyes opening. She stares at him muzzily through her tears.

"C-Clark?" she whimpers, and Clark smiles, his eyes brimming with tears, his lips quivering.

"Yeah, baby girl. Yeah, it's me. Gonna get you out of here."

He grasps at the cuffs drilled into the slab, pulling, but they're ground in deep, the ice solid.

Ugh, can one freaking thing go right?

I let out a despairing sound, searching for an ice pick, a drill, some kind of power tools, *anything*—

A blowtorch!

I dive for it, grabbing and thrusting it at Clark.

"Here," I say, holding his eyes steadily. "You know fire, right? So do what you do best. *Quick.*"

He gives me a nervous look, so utterly terrified it can only be born from the fact that I think this boy really loves Andrea.

He doesn't hesitate, though, snatching the blowtorch out of

my hand and firing it up, that fear in his eyes turning to grim determination.

I glance nervously out the frosted plastic window of the tent, keeping watch while he goes to work—but what I see makes my heart stop.

Plumes of blinding hot flame. Justin spraying wildly, shouting, his face red, veins bulging in his temples.

I can't see Blake anywhere.

And everything in me wants to find him, but I know I'd be in the way.

Andrea needs me more right now.

And suddenly I get what it means to love *this* much.

I don't know when Andrea crept so close to my heart.

Maybe the same time her father did.

But Clark is fast—so quick and focused, handling the torch with the deftness of an artist with his brush, working his way through the ice sealing the cuffs without ever coming close to Andrea's delicate skin.

Then she's sagging, and I'm there, catching her, grabbing Clark's coat and wrapping her up in it.

I don't see her clothes anywhere, but I shrug out of my own coat and wrap it around her waist, trying to bundle her up. Clark and I lift her weight so I've got her torso and he's got her legs, and she doesn't have to touch bare, raw skin to the frigid ground.

She's still conscious, just barely, letting out a sniffle as she rolls her head against my shoulder, one hand coming up to cling to me, gripping at my sweater with shaking, desperate fingers.

She can still move them.

Thank God.

If her extremities aren't damaged beyond repair, then there's hope for the rest of her, too.

My hope turns into a cracking, aching sensation as she whimpers, burying her face against me.

"Peace," she gasps, sobbing weakly, her tears just barely soaking through to wet my skin.

"It's okay, Andrea," I soothe, peering through the tent flap, watching, making sure we won't get caught. "It's okay. I've got you."

"Wh-where's...where's Dad?" she sputters out. "I have to t-tell him..."

"He knows about Justin, honey." I squeeze her tighter. "It's okay."

"No!" she gasps out, her fingers tightening against me before she goes limp again. "I...I h-have to tell him...I'm sorry."

Her tears are downright infectious. I tear my blurry gaze from scanning the flames outside, looking down at her, my nostrils prickling.

"He knows, love. I promise you, he knows."

Clark bites his lip as another arc of flame rockets into the night, lighting up the tent fabric from outside in hellish silhouettes.

We both flinch.

He tightens his hold on Andrea's legs. "What's going on out there?"

"I don't know," I say, peering outside again. "But I think we need to make a run for it."

It's sheer bedlam now.

Fire everywhere, an unruly mob of scared people in the distance, and I can hardly see through the thick black plumes of smoke, the burning stalls.

Everything catches fire, from the banners stretched between the stalls to the string lights. The bulbs *pop* with shattering squeals, sending more sparks flying. Louder *pops* hint at bigger lights breaking, flares of electrical current jumping, catching on display signs and flyers like wild lightning.

Oh my God.

It smells like every nightmare ever, charred and dark and hellish.

I can't see Blake *or* Justin.

But in the center of the fairgrounds, I can just make out the shapes of people huddled like damned souls crouching away from the flames of hell, and barely make out familiar voices—Warren, Sheriff Langley among them—begging people to calm down even while screams and sobs of despair rise.

They're walled in.

Nowhere safe, the flames are closing in.

Nowhere safe for us, either.

Then the tent catches fire with a sudden *whoosh!*

The scouring winter wind—no longer blocked by the burning wall—washes over the sea of flame and sends a wave of it lapping at us.

Cruuud.

Fear spikes through me, but we have to move. Clumsily, with Andrea heavy between us, Clark and I go stumbling out, skittering away, tripping over fallen debris and around flames burning in powerful clusters with hardly a free space to step.

"Come on," I gasp, running toward the crowd, practically swinging Andrea between us. "We have to get somewhere safe."

"*Where?*" Clark cries. "How do we get out here?"

I don't have an answer.

Not until I stop, staring at the one thing that isn't burning. The ice palace is almost gorgeous in the reflected light of the flames, the entire thing lit up in kaleidoscopes of red, blue, gold, purple, and infinite orange.

"We don't get out," I breathe. "We get *in*." I tighten my grip on Andrea, hefting her. "Shift her onto my back. Come on."

Awkwardly, Clark helps me maneuver Andrea so she's riding piggyback, her weight bending me over, but I don't *care*. Adrenaline sends me charging forward, raising my voice, using those pipes I've trained to project over the years to shout over the sounds of crackling flame and panicked people.

"Sheriff Langley!" I cry. "Leo! Doc! Warren! Get them inside the ice palace! Everyone move; it'll be safer in there."

A few heads turn toward me, confused mumbles. I jog closer before Warren cuts through the crowd, his hard eyes drilling into me. He just stares at me, then at Andrea, and he nods sharply, raising his arms, bellowing.

"She's right—the ice will shield us! Get the hell inside, people!" His voice is ten times louder than mine, a lion's roar that carries, and people slowly start moving, following his commands. "Stay low! If you have children, make sure you cover their mouths. Cover your own mouth—breathe through your hand, your jacket, your shirt, whatever it takes. Just avoid the smoke inhalation."

For a moment, I just watch him, Doc, and Leo, the way they work together. I can see the gap where Blake should be. And I can see why they're all called heroes.

They're the town's knights who step up when everyone else is afraid.

But there's a glint of approval in Warren's eye as he turns back to me, looking me over before giving Andrea a worried look.

"You too," he says. "Get inside. Blake, he'll murder me if I let anything happen to either of you."

I bite my lip, adjusting Andrea's weight. "But Blake—"

"Needs you to look after yourself," he growls gently like he knows exactly what I'm thinking. "Now go."

Then his hand is on my shoulder, steering me forward, his other hand grasping Clark's arm and drawing him gently behind as he guides us through the throng, finding a clear path through the flames. He ushers us to the only safety we can find when the entire world is falling down around us and we're trapped inside a ring of fire.

But before I disappear under the gleaming arch of ice, I can't help but look back, searching the flames.

Nothing.

And I send a prayer up, aching and terrified, to anything that might be listening.

My dad, the universe, the stars, God...even Andrea's mom, if she's looking down and watching over the daughter I cradle so close right now as I find a safe spot near the stage and huddle on a bench with the teenager in my lap.

Please.

Please don't let Blake be gone.

XXII: IT AIN'T OVER (BLAKE)

Minutes Earlier

When I get out of this, I'm gonna tell her.

I'm gonna tell Peace I love her if it's the last damn thing I do.

I knew I could count on her to keep my baby girl safe.

I'd hated having to leave her in Clark's hands, even though I knew she'd be fine. That's the thing with Peace. She doesn't need me holding her hand every step of the way. She's scrappy and smart and takes care of herself, which makes it so much more amazing that she *wants* me.

Hell, maybe I'm the one who needs her.

Yeah.

Fuck yeah, I do.

But I had to put her out of my mind as I stepped closer to Justin, listening to the sounds of the crackling flame, the whipping wind, the walls slowly burning closer to the ground.

Not good.

Low flame plus high wind with no windbreak?

Bad, bad cocktail. It could send this fire blanketing across the landscape, consuming the carnival grounds first, and then the entire town, and anyone left in it.

If there's anyone out there.

I hope there fucking is, and they're on their way to help us out of this shit.

Because with the fire truck outside that wall of flame, I can't do anything but try to find an opening to get people out of here.

And try to stop Mr. Pyro Man from making things worse.

He lets out a harsh, ugly laugh and sprays another burst of flame, holding the flamethrower up and deliberately torching one of the small banners flapping in the breeze.

I take a step closer, spreading my hands, trying to look nonthreatening.

"Hey," I say, keeping my voice low, soothing. "C'mon. You don't want to do that, man. Just stop already with the flamethrower stuff before you hurt Andrea."

I can't fucking call her Jenna, however much it might appeal to his madness.

Justin stiffens, whipping the nozzle around and pointing it at me.

I halt in my tracks immediately.

It's got a medium range, no more than ten feet or so, looks like. Small fuel canister on the back. If he wants to keep on being a threat, he's gotta keep to short bursts so he doesn't use it all up too fast.

But that means I gotta hang back.

And hope I can talk my way through this shitshow.

"*You* hurt Andrea," he hisses, baring his teeth.

I pinch my jaw, still trying to comprehend who I'm seeing. Gone is the enthusiastic, wide-eyed puppy of a young man who sometimes gave in to the sorrow always hanging on his shoulders.

He's been replaced by a maniac with a vicious smile and hard, hateful eyes that bore into me.

"Justin—"

"Shut up! You hurt her, just like you hurt everybody. This whole stupid town calls you heroes, when you're the reason everyone gets hurt. If you weren't here with your friends, *none* of this shit would've happened. Jenna would still be alive without Warren. No one would've tried to kill us again and again and again without Doc and Nine. My...my *mother* would still be alive." His face crumples, and then he spits on the ground, disdainful. "You're no hero, Chief. You're just a fucking curse, and *everyone* will know it tonight. They'll know it's your fault this whole town died because you can't save it now!"

"It won't be," I say softly. "But it is my fault your mother died, Justin. I didn't get to her soon enough that night, as hard as I tried. Doesn't mean you need to pass that pain to anybody else. Only me. Just let me get Andrea out of here, and you can do your worst. Right the fuck here." I reach up, giving my chest a thump.

"Nooo! You aren't taking Jenna from me again!" he howls.

The flamethrower barks, burping another jet of flame that scalds the air. It catches on the support arm of a nearby stall, biting the wood with hungry hot teeth.

Fuck.

I feel for Justin.

I do, even after all this.

I had no idea he'd been so psycho obsessed with Jenna as a boy, but it makes sense now. After his ma up and left him by dying...Jenna Ford would've seemed like some untouchable goddess, enlisted in the Army, this strong soldier who'd go away on deployment but come back every time after walking through hell, returning unscathed.

Until she didn't.

And I guess those reserves of grief inside Justin cracked.

Building his hatred over time as he kept looking for someone to blame. It must've fucking eaten him up to see Warren and me and the others getting all the credit for recent events when he hated Warren for surviving Jenna...

...and hated me for not being good enough, fast enough, to get his ma out of the Paradise Hotel in time.

Maybe he's right to.

I'm only human.

Only one man.

And there just wasn't enough time, enough resources, to get through all that chaos when no one knew what was going on, who was alive inside, who was dead. Nobody knew about the lab incinerating itself in the mountain nearby, causing the fire.

Maybe nobody could've saved Constance Bast that night.

That don't mean he's wrong for needing someone to hate.

Or for hating me.

But even if I hurt for him, even if I get why he's gone off the deep end with a festering wound that never healed, I won't let this crazy SOB do this.

I'll kill him if I have to, or let him kill me if it puts a stop to this shit.

And I take another step closer, careful, wary.

"Andrea isn't Jenna, man. You know that," I say. I can't get him too excited, but I gotta snap him out of this fantasy. "You can't bring Jenna Ford back. None of us can. You're just taking my little girl away from me. Is that what you want? To make me hurt the way I made you?"

"*Yes!*" Justin roars. "You deserve it! You deserve pain, and yet you still get *everything!* You get to have Andrea. You get to have Peace. You get to be Mr. Fucking Radio Man, fixing everybody's problems when you aren't talking about your stupid conspiracy shit and—"

"And a dead wife," I growl. "A dead ma. A brother I can't stand and don't know how to talk to even though he's trying his damnedest to get through to me."

He stops, staring, a wild tear sliding down his cherry-red cheek.

"I know what it's like to hurt, Justin. I know what it's like to miss 'em. And you wanna be mad at someone for taking them away. But really, no matter what things were like when they were alive, whether they were good or bad people...you're really mad at them for leaving you before you can set things right."

It's raw, how painfully true that is.

How long it's taken me to figure it out.

Yeah, things were bad with me and Abby.

With me and Ma.

But I keep feeling the same thing.

Like they checked out before I had a chance to make things better.

Like they just left me with these scars while they got to run away, and maybe it doesn't make sense, maybe it's selfish, but we're human. We get to be selfish when we're hurting.

Fuck, I'm mad.

I'm furious at life, but as soon as I realized it, I didn't go postal with a goddamn flamethrower.

I let it go.

And this calm rushes in to take its place.

A calm that tells me I can do this.

Somehow, I can talk Justin down. If I can just get through to him.

As I start to open my mouth again, that's when I see her.

Peace.

She's with Clark, creeping along the edges of the carnival grounds, using the flames and the stalls to mask their movements, ducking behind some of the tents set up all around. This is a hellscape, a mess of jumping sparks, just waiting for the right one to catch the wind and turn this into one of those forest fires it takes an entire statewide effort to stop.

But I know, the moment I see her, we're gonna get through this. She stops, peering around from behind a tent, catching my eye.

I can't be too obvious looking at her.

Can't tip Justin off that she's there.

But she mouths *I've got this.*

And I know Andrea's gonna be fine.

Because she's got Peace's love to hold her through.

And so do I.

I just gotta keep Justin distracted and trust Peace to do her thing.

Even if it means letting him hurt me.

And I deliberately move within his reach, within range of the flamethrower, even as I keep my hands up.

He jerks the nozzle of the flamethrower up, taking aim at yours truly, his eyes narrowing. "Don't you fucking think I won't."

"I know you will," I say, locking my gaze on him as I drop my hands, bracing myself, ready to move. My thigh burns hotter than any flames around me, but I can't fucking care right now.

Peace is moving, darting toward the tent Clark pointed to, disappearing inside.

I inch closer to Justin, making sure his attention stays riveted on me.

"If you hate me that much," I say, "come and get me."

He lets out a wild, savage scream like a war cry.

Then charges dead at me, his hand clenching the flamethrower's trigger.

Fire erupts like dragon's breath in front of me, lashing out in burning tongues.

I throw myself to one side, hitting the ground hard on my shoulder and rolling, the flames licking over me so close I feel the hairs on my beard singe.

Shitfire!

Literally.

I'm gonna have to move faster if I want to stay alive.

Breathing hard, I spring up to brace my weight on my good knee, tensed and ready. He swings the flamethrower in a guttering arc, sending fresh bursts everywhere and catching on more banners, signs—dammit, *everything*.

I hope like fuck somebody got on their cellphone and called Missoula.

'Cause right now, we're trapped in an oven of our own making, and Justin keeps turning up the heat.

He lunges at me, whipping the flamethrower back and forth like he's trying to cross swords, only I got no damn sword to fight back.

So I throw myself left, right, and for a second my bum leg actually fucking saves me when he jets that thing right at my face. My thigh goes out under me, dropping me to the ground flat on my back.

Good timing.

That last burst would've seared my face off.

He moves to lord over me, grinning wide, pointing the flamethrower at the center of my chest. "You're too slow. Too pathetic. I don't know what anyone sees in you. What I tried to see, once..."

"Me neither," I say. "Guess folks stick around 'cause I'm one stubborn son of a bitch."

He barely gets a second for his eyes to narrow.

I shove my good foot right at his leg, hitting him hard in the knee.

He goes down with a howl, fingers clenched on the flamethrower, sending hellfire right at my chest. The burn hits me hard even as I roll away, scorching through my jacket and shirt. I hiss through my teeth, smacking my hands against the fabric to put out the embers, but I got no time for pain.

All I got are endorphins.

Desperation.

And the hopeful sight of Clark and Peace ducking and weaving through the flames, with Andrea bundled between them.

I'd scream with relief.

If only Justin wasn't up again and charging right at me, stabbing that stupid flamethrower like a spear.

I dive to the side, making it look like a deliberate stumble, leading him around. Leading him away, keeping his back to Andrea as I constantly duck and weave just out of his reach, pulling him in my wake like I'm fishing, and I've got him on the hook.

Please, I think. *Get my baby girl out safe.*

Please get yourself out safe, darlin'.

Forget about me and just run.

Wish I could follow my own advice.

Justin backs me up like he's feinting with a bull, swishing the flamethrower back and forth in arcs of bright orange, making trails on the air. Everything's falling down around us, his wild spray catching booths, tent poles, tent cloth, light fixtures...

It's all just glowing orange, black, the colors of destruction.

Even if we survive this, there'll be nothing left of this field but embers and ash.

Maybe nothing left of me but dust. I hit a wall of flame at my back, all around me, the heat blistering, pushing me forward like a forcefield.

Pushing me back toward Justin.

He's got me cornered now.

And he knows it, too, stopping with a grin and that fucking thing held ready.

He can't have much fuel left after this rampage.

I hoped he'd spent it all, but I guess I'm just not that lucky.

Slowly, I hold my hands up, breathing hard, sweat licking over me and soot sticking to me.

"Okay," I gasp. "Okay. You got me."

"You're damn right I do. Finally. Points for making me work for it, I guess."

He steps closer, pressing the nozzle right against my chest, the metal ring burning-hot, searing at my already burning skin and making me wince.

Too damn bad.

I won't flinch, won't back down.

If I jump him right as he lights me up, I can take him down with me. I'll hold my whole flaming body to his, burn him up with me, trigger that fuel line to blow him to kingdom come.

For Peace. For Andrea. For Heart's Edge, I'm ready.

The Reaper doesn't scare me. Neither does this crazy little shit.

His leer turns cold, a dark and ugly grimace—but there's a familiar sadness there, too. Sorrow, loss, and I think it's sinking in already that killing me won't end his pain.

Won't bring anybody back.

But that ain't gonna stop him.

I brace myself for a world of hurt as he whispers, "You can tell Jenna and my mom hello when you get there—if you're worthy of anything but hell."

This is it.

My legs tense, ready to jump as soon as he lights me up like a candle. I watch him like a hawk.

His finger tightens on the trigger.

And a massive, roaring crash explodes behind him.

My face jerks up as a fire truck comes roaring through the blaze, smashing through the last of the burning walls and bursting out of the riot of flames, bearing down on Justin like a freight train.

It's my brother behind the wheel.

Holt's eyes set and grim, his grip on the steering wheel strong as he comes plowing at us without a second's hesitation.

We lock eyes for barely a breath, and in that moment, I want to scream like I've lost my shit.

I trust my brother.

And I throw myself out of the way, while Justin turns with a wide-eyed scream.

He doesn't have a chance.

I go tumbling into a snowbank and almost roll right into another flaming booth.

There's a horrible *thwack!*

Justin disappears under the fire truck's wheels, crumpling up like a doll with no sound but the crush of bone and the crinkle of collapsing metal and wet spurts of fuel.

Then nothing as the fire truck goes completely still.

Holt kicks the door open, leaning out, breathing hard, then flashes me a grin that can't mask his tension and the sense of horror in his whiskey eyes, dancing in the firelight.

"Sorry I'm late," he gasps out. "Got locked up."

"You just gotta make a joke now?" I groan.

He jumps down from the driver's seat and lopes over to give me a hand, hauling me up with a strength I don't have.

I start to collapse the second I manage to stand—but he loops an arm around my waist, and I drape mine over his shoulders. He helps me as we limp toward the fire truck.

Plus, the battered, broken body protruding from behind one wheel.

He's still alive. *Fuck.*

Justin's eyes are glazed and blank but open, flicking back and forth, his lips parted as blood trickles out. His body is a twisted mess, limbs contorted in ways no human body should ever be.

I think he's looking right at me till I hear his words.

"I see her..." he whispers, his voice guttural, as broken as he is. "Mom, hey...Mom, it's *me...*"

I ain't gonna cry.

I ain't.

But fuck if that don't stab me right in the guts.

He's so young, so screwed up, and if things hadn't gone so goddamn wrong...

I push Holt away, my strength coming back, taking a halting step toward him.

"It didn't have to be like this," I choke out. "Fuck, I saw you like *family.* Why'd you have to go and..."

The words just die in my throat. Questions can't fix this shit.

Justin's eyes clear and focus on me.

And he smiles, this pained and awful and accepting grin.

"H-hey, Chief," he grinds out. "...y-you...you were a good dad. I'm sorry...when I get mad, I just...can't think straight. But it's okay, now. I can think again and I'm sorry, I'm *sorry*, it hurts, Mom, it *hurts*..."

He trails off in a broken, hushed sob.

I've seen that look, heard that anguish before, that trembling, crumpling expression.

It's loneliness.

The fear that death's coming, and dammit...no matter what this poor misguided idiot did to me, I won't let him spend his last seconds alone.

"Help me," I mutter to Holt.

He gets me down, both of us on one knee.

I reach for Justin's bloody hand, his shaking fingers, and clasp his weak grip in mine.

"It's okay, kiddo," I grind out, my throat so thick I can barely talk. "It's fucking okay now. You can let go."

He blinks at me slowly, blankly. My eyes blur, right when his go clear.

His fingers go limp.

And then slip free, falling to the ground with a heavy *thud* as his head lolls to one side.

I know.

I shouldn't feel shit for someone who hurt me and mine so bad.

But I meant what I said about him, and I can't help but think.

That could've been me or Holt in another life.

There's a heavy, somber silence before I reach out and brush my fingers over Justin's eyes, closing them so he looks more at peace.

"Let's get him out from under there," I say. "And then let's go clear a path."

XXIII: TILL THE FAT LADY SINGS (PEACE)

When I was a kid, there was this film I loved called *Meet the Robinsons*.

It was this cute CGI thing, with a boy getting whisked off to the future with a time traveler to recover some stolen device. I can't remember the entire plot, but I remember one scene really well.

The bad guy sends a T-Rex after the kid heroes.

But the T-Rex chases them into a corner and can't get to them because every time it charges in, its massive head hits the wall while its tiny arms can't reach, wobbling and flailing and always falling short of the boys.

It's the best line in the film, the T-Rex talking in this weird Charlie Brown teacher voice to his furious master.

I have a big head and little arms. I'm just not sure how well this plan was thought through.

That T-Rex?

That's me right now.

I had the brilliant idea to buy everyone a few precious minutes and shelter them inside the ice palace.

Too bad that brilliant idea doesn't hold up very well under the simple truth that ice *melts*.

So.

I've got a headache and arms full of unconscious girl, and the walls are wet and running and growing thinner as the flames work their way through. People cower back, screaming, whimpering, hopeless, trapped on all sides like fireflies inside a jar.

And I'm just not sure how well my plan was thought through.

Clark edges in closer, staring at the leaping flames through the translucent walls. "Peace...I think we gotta make a break for it."

"I don't think that's a good idea." I catch Leo's eye across the room.

He's got his wife and kid with him—ugh, I hadn't even realized they were here, but he's using his massive bulk like a wall, keeping people inside. I tilt my head his way, but he shakes his in return.

"If we run, everyone runs," I tell Clark. "And people are going to get hurt in the chaos. We can't have a stampede. There are *kids* here."

"So what are we supposed to do?" he begs. "Burn to death? Shit, I don't know..."

"There's still time," I whisper, and hold Andrea closer, trying not to sense the change in the air.

It's getting warmer.

It was frigid before, but the fire's licking deeper against the ice. It's warming up fast inside the enclosed space, the air heating as the flames eat through the ice shell, closer to us.

One of the walls is thinner than the others, just a paper-fine shell of ice keeping the fire out, and people start backing up. They're crowding each other, retreating as the flames leap higher, catching on something with a deafening roar.

Some kind of fuel tank, something, I don't know what. But suddenly there's a flash, and I hear the ice cracking, and everyone's screaming, shoving, and I can't move or I'll hurt Andrea, but I don't know what to do—

Until a loud hiss echoes over the clamor.

I clutch Andrea to me, squeezing one eye open.

I'm just staring as a huge spray of water comes arcing out of nowhere, splashing against the walls and splattering down, dripping down to smother the flames outside.

Not all of the red outside is fire. I see it now.

Some of it's a fire *truck*.

Holy hell.

I tumble to my feet, barely keeping my grip on Andrea, staring at the two wavering figures outside. Blurry or not, there's no mistaking them.

Holt Silverton.

And *Blake!*

The two of them stand strong, fighting to wrestle the massive high-powered fire hose hooked to the truck. They're spraying the walls down and smothering the flames under jets of water that freeze as soon as they touch the palace.

Others cry out in relief, and Clark lets out an awkward laugh, realizing the same thing I do.

We're going to be okay thanks to one jaw-droppingly beautiful hero man.

"Holy crap," he says, sinking down next to me, leaning against Andrea. "I *knew* he'd come through."

I'm the only one silent.

Crying.

Tears of hot, uncontrollable joy.

Yeah, I knew he'd come through, too.

While the face I want to kiss forever ducks through the half-melted archway, looping his arm over his head to beckon to everyone, I burst out sobbing with the gorgeous, wonderful feeling of relief in my heart.

"Everybody get moving!" Blake calls, that voice as wonderful, as soothing, and as strong as it was the night he picked me up on the side of the road. "Train's moving this way, people, and we're all goin' home."

* * *

It's hours before the fire's fully out.

Even longer before the chaos starts to fade.

Blake and Holt couldn't put the flames out on their own.

Not with just one truck and its reserve tank.

But they cleared a critical path.

They cleared an opening that let people escape the ice palace and spill across the highway to take refuge in the fields on the other side by the school, many retrieving their cars from along the road, forming tight rings like pioneers used to circle their covered wagons for shelter, huddling for warmth.

By the time everyone was out and accounted for, the backup someone called in came wailing down the road—more fire trucks and ambulances with *Missoula* stamped on the side.

The whole time, I never let Andrea go.

And the whole time, I don't take my eyes off Blake, who still hasn't found us in the commotion.

Not even as Andrea and I are bundled into the back of an ambulance. They check me for burns, look her over, and give us the verdict.

Stable.

Oh God, she's going to be *fine*.

"She's got a little frostbite, no doubt," the EMT says, checking Andrea's pulse. "Hurts like hell, but it's only surface level. No deep tissue damage. We just need to keep her warm and hydrated, and she'll heal up just fine."

I'm grinning through my tears, squeezing Andrea's hand so tight.

"Can you wait?" I ask thickly, struggling to find words that aren't sobs. "Before you take her to the hospital. I just...I need to find her dad. Her dad needs to be with her."

The EMT nods. "I'll be here getting her settled and checking her vitals, but move it."

With a grateful sound, I go tumbling out of the back of the ambulance.

The entire field looks like a refugee camp at this point, people getting medical treatment, hot liquids poured into them, salves for burns, bandages. People give witness statements to the cops, firefighters checking over the smoldering ruins.

I find Blake talking to a group of firefighters, standing in the way that says he's trying to be stubborn, be strong, but he's carefully keeping his weight off *that* leg. The last glow of dying fires glints off his hair, turning it to bearish rusty brown and ash.

I can't even describe the *feeling* that bursts through me when I see him like this.

Standing so firm, even dirty and burned and covered in soot and sweat.

That stubborn pride's everything I love about him.

It's like I'm on fire now.

And I know this is one flame that'll never go out.

I start forward hesitantly, then stop.

"Blake," I call softly, my voice small.

He stills like I just shouted his name from the rooftops.

Slowly, he turns, this warmth, this light, breaking over his face—before he's loping toward me, his bad leg dragging, but he doesn't let it stop him as he catches me, lifting me off my feet, letting out a ragged sound as he buries his face in my hair.

"*Peace*," he gasps. "Thank God, *Broccoli*."

I never thought I'd be so happy to near that stupid name.

"Blake," I manage raggedly, burying my face in his shoulder, clutching on for dear life. "I was so scared for you, when Justin..."

"Shhh. Quiet," he soothes, his hands strong and firm and warm against my back. "It's all right now. He can't hurt nobody anymore." Then he pulls back, looking down at me, those intense blue eyes flickering with trepidation. "Andrea?"

"She'll be just fine," I promise, unable to help grinning even though I'm crying so bad I'm practically *melting*, but I've never been this happy, this relieved before. "Justin had her against the ice for a while. She's got frostbite, but no permanent damage. The EMTs got her, and she's gonna be fine."

His eyes light up before softening as he leans into me hard, curling his hand against the back of my neck, pressing his brow to mine. "Fuck, Peace, you saved my baby girl."

"How could I not?" I whisper. "Don't you know how much she means to me? How much you *both* do?"

He stares at me intently, so much raw, rough emotion burning in his eyes.

"Tell me," he growls, his clutch on me turning hard, possessive. "Tell me what we mean."

"I love you!" It falls out without hesitation, without even the slightest hint of fear, because I need to be honest about this bright flame inside me. I need him to *know* when we all came so close to losing each other. "I love you like everything I've ever needed, and I love her because she's everything sweet and bright and free. I *love* you, Blake, even if you don't love me."

That's the fear of it, right there.

That even after everything we've been through, everything we've been to each other...

What if he just doesn't feel this so deeply, so hotly, so truly?

My heart twists with apprehension, like even my pulse is holding its breath.

Then Blake smiles his lopsided grin, the most heartbreakingly handsome smile ever.

"How the hell could I not love you, darlin'?" he rumbles, and all the love in the world makes that sinful voice of his musical. "You're the peace I've always wanted."

I choke out a laugh.

Ohhh, that pun, it's terrible and wonderful all at once, but I barely get a chance to part my lips before he's just *there*.

Kissing me, dragging me against him.

Stealing my mouth, taking my soul, tearing me up inside with how amazing it feels to be with this man.

To finally—finally!—be *his*.

And to give myself over to him in wholehearted surrender.

I part my lips and let him take my mouth in delicious, languid strokes and twining thrusts of tongue for all the world, the sky, and the townspeople scattered around us to see.

I don't care who knows.

I flipping love Blake Silverton.

He's my desperado.

My gunslinger with a heart of gold.

And no matter what soft and melancholy songs I sing for him, it's a done deal.

I'll never let him be lonely again.

* * *

Months Later

Spring in Heart's Edge.

When I first came rolling into town in January, I never thought I'd stay long enough to see spring fully erase the snow and leave flowers. They're coming up in pink and blue fields, clouds of vibrant color bursting across the hills.

Absolutely gorgeous is an understatement.

Worth staying for is more like it.

But not nearly as much as the man by my side, his fingers twined snug in mine as we walk the paths through the hills, moving quietly beneath new leaves that turn the sunlight green-gold and sweet.

Blake and I walk like this often now.

It's part of my therapy, putting a little more heft on his leg with the slope of the hills.

It's also just become part of us.

Part of our routine, after we see Andrea out the door and

before we go our separate ways for work, only to come together again in the evening.

I can't shake how Andrea seemed troubled this morning. Heading off to school with a frown pulling her lips down. She'd barely talked to me when normally we chatter our heads off through breakfast, whether or not she actually deigns to acknowledge her father's existence.

Sigh.

Probably boy trouble.

Even after everything, she and Clark are still dancing around in this are-we-or-aren't-we way that only teenagers do.

I'm not her mother. I can't force her to talk to me.

But I am her friend, and I know she'll talk when she's ready.

When she needs me.

"Something on your mind?" Blake rumbles, his thumb stroking over my knuckles.

I look up with a smile, taking in the brilliant blue depths of his eyes.

"Yeah. I just think Andrea's bickering with Clark again. I worry about her."

Blake grimaces. "I'll *stop* worrying when she finally gets sick of him. He's still a punk, even if he did me a solid."

I laugh. "You'd think any boy who likes your daughter is a punk."

"Because he *is*."

"Oh, stop!" Laughing, I lean on him, resting my head to the delicious tone of his upper arm. "You'll get used to it someday. He'll grow on you."

"Never," he vows, but those eyes gleam with mischief and amusement. "Honestly, that's better than what I thought you might be worrying over."

I cock my head, my brows knitting. "What else would I be worried about?"

He hesitates, gaze darkening, that hint of a smile fading.

"California," he grunts finally.

Ah. Right.

That envelope's been sitting on the table in the foyer for a week now, waiting like a royal decree.

Waiting for me to make a phone call, a choice, a decision.

Because there's an artist in California who wants to sign the rights to my song away and make it part of her catalog.

A really, *really* famous artist.

A really obnoxious, infamous pop artist who took a shine to my music and my story when it made some news along the West Coast. Apparently, she went through her own fair share of big bad danger before the men of Enguard Security came to her rescue.

But there's a catch. There *always* is.

She wants me to leave.

She wants me to come be part of her entourage and help write songs just for her.

Everything I've always wanted.

That song I wrote with all my heart, for Blake and Blake alone...

But I've still given it to so many hearts on the airwaves, so they can feel what I do.

I guess he doesn't know.

I already made the phone call this morning, while he was in the shower.

I tilt my head back, looking up at him with a faint smile. We make our way out of the trees, toward the inn waiting in the distance with that long, curving cliff dropping down over the valley.

"California's lovely in summer," I say. "Have you ever been?"

"No." Blake looks dismayed, wrinkling his nose. "Never been much for the big city life. That's more Holt's thing."

"No? So you wouldn't want to visit?"

His expression looks strained. "You saying you're heading out there?"

"Next week," I say—then relent as his face falls like a kicked puppy. I can't do this to him, and I laugh, stopping and squeezing his hand and leaning into him. "For a weekend, I mean. Just to handle some contract stuff. Then I'm coming right back."

Blake breathes in sharply, his cragged brows lifting, those intense eyes locked on me with something like hope. "You're not leaving Heart's Edge?"

"Why would I?" I drape my body against him, wrapping my arms around his neck. "Everything I want is right here. I don't need to live in California to write music, Blake. I make the best music when I'm here. At *home*. With you."

Even after two months of lovely sweetness, domesticity, our time together a mix of comfortable silences, laughter, and devastatingly hot passion...

It still makes my heart beat hard to be so forward, so true with my feelings.

Yet Blake has proven time and time again that I can trust him.

I can let him have every last piece of my heart.

He smiles, slow and hot and pleased, settling his hands on my hips. "Then I guess it's a damn good thing we're right where we are," he growls.

I don't understand.

Suddenly, he pulls back, takes my hand, and leads me to the edge of the cliff.

"You remember the legend? About lovers making wishes here?" he asks. We stop together, looking out across brilliant blue skies and flowers stretched below, as far as the eye can see. All around us, too, waving around our calves in delicate pink and blue dots. "About the cliff."

"I do," I say, flushing, looking up at him, his profile so strong, so handsome against the brightness of the sun. "You want to make a wish, Blake?"

"Sure do, darlin'."

He pulls his hand free from mine then, and sinks down on

one knee, digging in his pocket. I don't know why I'm surprised—but my pulse still kicks up hot and fierce anyway. A current rushes through me with a wonderful thrill as he pops a little velvet box open.

Inside, there's a pretty silver band, set with a stone as violet as the tips dyed in my hair.

"What I wish, more than anything," he says gruffly, his voice thick with emotion, "is that you'll say yes, Peace. Give me forever."

I laugh—I can't stop myself. My voice needs to do something with the joy overflowing inside of me.

How can I say anything but yes? He's the part of my song, the muse to my melody, everything I've been searching for all my life.

I fling myself against him, gasping out my *"Yes"* as I kiss him with my all.

I lose myself in it—the warmth of his mouth, the scratch of his beard, and I'm lost in so many sensations, taking in the world around me and feeling connected to *everything*. The scent of wildflowers, the taste of this man, the brightness and warmth of the sun, the heat of his hands on my waist, my back, then buried in my hair and pulling me in deep until I can't feel anything but *him*.

His tongue traces my lips jealously, leaving me gasping. His teeth graze, a reminder how sensitive he can leave me with the smallest movements.

I'm gasping, breathless, by the time he lets go, clinging to him to stay upright as we lean hard into each other.

"So this is us," he whispers, pushing his forehead to mine.

His cadence, his breath, his strength wrapped so tight draws me deeper into our own little universe.

I smile, rubbing my nose to his.

"This is us," I answer as he slips that ring on my finger, lacing our hands together. I squeeze his fingers, then glance out over the cliff. "Shall we?"

"Hell yeah."

Together, we gather up handfuls of flowers, weaving them together in alternating links of pink and blue, making them into wreaths, laughing as he tickles a soft flower head under my nose.

Then we throw them over the edge, sending them sailing, watching the wind catch them and make them float down gently, slowly.

It's too peaceful, too hopeful, too perfect. Until Blake tosses something else.

A little string of firecrackers snaps and crackles, making bright bursts of light as it follows the flowers down. He looks at me and winks.

I let out a startled laugh, tugging at his hand. "Idiot. That's a fire hazard, you know."

"Wrong." With a rumble, he drags me in close against the hardness and heat of his body, his eyes sparking bright as fireworks. "*You're* the only fire hazard here today, darlin'."

"That doesn't even make sense."

"It would if you knew how hot you get me," he says, leaning into me, all the desire in the world darkening his eyes as the distance between us grows smaller and smaller, hotter and hotter.

Okay, so maybe it does make sense.

"Show me," I whisper, folding my fingers against the back of his neck, my body already growing warm with my need for him —a passion that will never end. "Show me again and again, Blake, for as long as we both live."

* * *

Weeks Later

LEAVE it to me to sing at my own freaking wedding.

It's not quite planned. It's not quite what anyone intended, but my wedding, well...

It turned into as much beautiful chaos as the rest of my life.

And I love every hot messy minute of it.

The sound system to play the wedding march malfunctioned and caught fire. Blake singed his tuxedo putting it out. The doves that were supposed to be released over the cliff got out of their cage and burst free in a squawking flock over the sky.

One of them tried to nest in my mother's hair.

And she actually laughed. I hadn't seen her smile even once since she'd flown in from Oahu.

Holt tried to hit on Ember, not realizing she wasn't just my bridesmaid, but Doc's wife, and nearly got pushed over the cliff for his troubles. Good thing Blake insisted on having two best men in Holt and Warren.

Leo's son Zach coerced Andrea into carrying him on her shoulders, and they charged around playing horsey while everyone was trying to find their seats.

Everything was a *mess*.

But it was ours.

I've never been happier.

And I don't think the priest has ever seen anyone laugh through most of their wedding vows like Blake and I did.

It's hard not to.

We met by total accident in disaster, and it's like uncertainty and mishaps follow us around everywhere.

All the more reason to be certain of each other.

And there's not a moment's doubt in our eyes, our voices, when the time comes.

We lace our fingers and say "*I do*."

It should be our moment, something sacred and private.

But somehow, we belong to the entire town, too. I swear I can feel Heart's Edge nodding its approval with the mountains, the trees, the gorgeous flowers tilting our way as all the guests break into laughter and applause.

Soon, we're whisked away to dance with everyone but each other, then thrust back together for that one special slow dance. I cling to my new husband—*husband,* how crazy is that?—breathlessly for dear life. Blake just smiles so easy, like he was born for this, and maybe he was.

Because we're each other's refuge in the whirlwind.

Yesterday, today, and forever.

Before long, we get pulled apart again after dancing a few rounds.

There's a whirlwind of people. Everybody from Felicity to Ember to Warren and Haley's little niece, Tara, who's visiting this summer. Someone pulls on Blake's arm. He looks up and grins.

"Best damn wedding shindig I've ever seen, brother," Holt Silverton says, his whiskey colored eyes flashing. "Here's one more gift for the road."

Uh-oh.

For a second, Blake's face goes blank. I wonder if they're about to get into their usual scrap over their mom's inheritance. Then Holt holds up a big bubbly bottle of very expensive-looking champagne.

"Only if I'm raising a toast to you, bro. Without you and the cavalry, no way would I be standing here a married man, grinning like a fool." He takes the bottle and slaps Holt's shoulder.

Thank God. Relief steams out of my lungs, and I smile, feeling this giddy serenity coming over everything.

"We gonna be seeing you again after the honeymoon, or are you jetting off to Chicago or New York?"

Holt gives back a near-identical lopsided grin that makes me laugh.

"Actually, I've been doing some thinking. With the building contracts I've got lined up, you know...I might just settle into Heart's Edge for a little while. Just traded up my little rambler Airbnb rental for nicer digs at the Charming Inn till I can find something more permanent."

Blake nods, smiles again, and starts to tug me forward by the hand again before stopping. He looks back over his shoulder. "It's good to have you back," he tells Holt.

"Good to be back, Blake."

Just like that, we fade into the crowd, pressing hands with friends and acquaintances and maybe even a few low-key journalists. All the drama going down here the last couple years is close to putting this little town on the map.

Then someone says they heard that catchy song on the radio, and they beg me to sing it, and suddenly I'm standing under my own wedding bower with a mic thrust in my hand. Half singing, half laughing, I give the people what they want while they dance together and talk and throw wild humor back and forth.

The meaning hits me just as deeply. It's a struggle not to cry every time I catch Blake's eyes at my side, staring gently, while I sing about a gold-hearted desperado I just freaking married.

It's more of a party than a wedding, honestly.

I'm okay with that.

I'm happy with the rest of my life starting like a celebration.

But it's maybe just a *little* much when we get piled into the back of the fire truck.

Then driven through town at the head of a parade of cars, the siren going at its lowest volume and the fire truck trailing cans, ribbons, and big bunches of flowers behind us. People appear from the stores and houses along main street to wave and whoop and yell our names.

Blake looks so embarrassed, and it's adorable.

I lean my shoulder to his, snug in my empress-waisted white wedding dress with its scalloped bodice and trailing train that makes me feel like a princess.

"Get used to the attention," I whisper. "You may not want to be everyone's hero, but you are."

"I'm no hero," he growls, his face flushing as he looks down at me, but he grudgingly waves to the crowd. "I'm just your husband."

Husband.

God, I love it.

I lean up to kiss his cheek, curling my arm in his.

"You're my husband now, Blake," I say, and squeeze his arm, lacing our fingers together, our wedding rings touching, simple gold bands warmed by body heat and endless love. "But you've always been my hero...and you always will be."

EXTENDED EPILOGUE: KEEP IT BURNING (BLAKE)

Years Later

I'M GETTING real damned tired of being called a hero.

But after this many years, well...

I guess I ain't gonna get people to stop.

At least it's given me the chance to do one of the most amazing things I've ever done in my life.

This year, there's an Olympic torch relay going across country, all the way to Canada.

That cross-country race that keeps the same flame lit from town to town, border to border.

And with the flame coming through little old Heart's Edge, the town council had a meeting six months ago, deciding who they want to represent our little town.

Guess who?

Yep. I'm the man they picked to carry it, from one side of town to the other, before the next relay runner picks it up and shuttles it onward.

Just a few years ago, I wouldn't have been able to do it.

I could handle short bursts of speed, sure, but my bum leg?

Nah.

There was too much pain bound up in it.

Bound up in me.

Now, I've learned how to let the hell go of so many things.

My pain. My hatred. My resentment. My guilt. My sorrow.

My pride, the shit that made me too stubborn to go back to physical therapy in the first place.

Don't get me wrong, my wife's hands are magic. They do wonders on my leg whenever I need a little relaxation.

But pair that with physical therapy, and I've never felt stronger.

Close to completely pain-free.

Hell, I feel like an animal bucking at its leash as I stand at the starting line painted across the highway, bouncing on the balls of my feet, keeping myself warmed up and limber.

The whole town's lined up along the side of the road, making a wall of people, from my friends to my neighbors to the familiar folks I've known my whole life.

My brother's even there, watching me with a small smile.

Holt looks so much more settled now, so much happier with a good woman by his side. Took him a nice jaunt through hell to get there, but that's a story for another time.

I know the feeling.

But that calm inside me ignites into a bright flare of eager enthusiasm. I hear the sound of sneakers on pavement, coming up behind me—paired with an engine.

I glance over my shoulder.

The runner approaches trailed by the pacer car, his expression strained, face dripping sweat, but he's got that torch held high and proud with his chin raised.

And it's with just as much pride and a burning grin that he comes tumbling up next to me, strides almost windmilling to a halt as he slaps that torch into my hand.

My turn now.

I go shooting forward, taking off from the block like I'm running a race.

Hell, maybe I am.

Outrunning the man I used to be.

Using the body that belongs to the man I've become, and pushing on toward the man I'll still become.

With the help of an amazing, beautiful, sunshiny woman at my side, anything's possible. Peace showed me I can be more than I ever thought I was.

It's like my wife's calling me onward as I go flying down the street, holding the torch high. Cries of joy and approval trail after me in a wave, everyone clapping, calling out my name, cheering, lifting me up on their warmth and excitement.

Maybe I don't ever want to call myself their hero.

But when they give me so much of their approval, their support, their encouragement, I relent.

I can't deny them anything.

I'm running for this weird little town just as much as I'm running for me.

And I'm running toward the siren head of crimson and purple hair waiting at the finish line, Peace's eyes flashing so brilliant green in the bright sun, glowing like emeralds.

Andrea's right next to her.

It's strange to look at my little girl and see a young woman now—a real stylish one, turning her punk look into her own brand. She's already planning her own fashion line when she's only been in design school for a year.

Girl's got big dreams.

And I know she's got the gumption and the smarts to reach every one of them.

Right now, she's reaching out for me, grinning with that familiar lopsided expression. As I breeze past, I slap her a high five before catching my wife's hand in a squeeze.

"Run, Dad!" Andrea calls, while Peace just laughs.

"Look at you go, Speedy!"

I snort, but I don't slow.

Speedy? No.

Goddamn, though, it feels *good* to not be chewed up by pain.

Though I think I could handle any agony just as long as I've got family by my side.

My sprint's not long. Heart's Edge ain't a big place, and there's another relay runner waiting at the end of Main, ready to take the next leg with the pacer car to the next town. And as I break free from the crowd, slap that torch into his hand, feeling the heat from the burning flame...

It's like someone lets the town off its leash.

The second the next runner sprints on down the highway, they're swarming me like bees.

Lifting me up.

And my lovely wife is right there, reaching with both hands, until I draw her up with me. Together, the crowd carries us on their shoulders, jostling us through town as we laugh and cling tight to each other.

I get this funny damn feeling.

Something I can only describe as wonder.

It fills me as deep as this love that seems to have no end as I look down at Peace, holding her tight. They finally lower us to the street, surrounding us with laughter, with warmth.

We're just quiet, though.

We've only got eyes for each other as I kiss her palm and whisper, "How did we get here?"

"Simple," she says, laying her head on my chest, the place where she's always belonged and always will. "We were made to fly, Blake, and we just flew together."

* * *

It's a long day.

The town makes a showy celebration out of the whole thing, bordering on a festival. Andrea comes home with us for dinner.

I try not to notice whose ugly-ass truck shows up to pick her up and spirit her away afterward, leaving me and Peace alone. Clark has traded up from his ratty Pinto over the years, and it doesn't look like I'll get rid of his ass anytime soon.

More like planning a wedding, whether I like it or not.

Together, we sprawl on the couch. Peace draped on top of me like a lazy cat; me melted and tired and sore, sighing as I settle on my back and let my eyes drift closed.

"Worn out, old man?" she teases softly.

I chuckle, smoothing my hand down her back till I get a generous handful of that full, gorgeous ass, pulling her into me.

"Not too tired for you." I grin. "I could do another race in bed, if you asked me."

"Oh, I don't ever want you to race." She pushes herself up, straddling me, settling those lush thighs around my hips and bracing her hands against my stomach. "I want you to take your sweet time. Forget the bed." Her eyes are dark, her voice husky. "Show me what you can do right here, Blake."

I don't need to be told twice.

Not when I'm as hungry for her as I was the very first time.

The past few years have only made her more gorgeous as she blossomed into who she was always meant to be—this vibrant woman full of music, and rather than growing bored from knowing every inch of her...it only makes it that much more fascinating to rediscover her with caressing palms, to taste her with hungry lips.

The familiar ain't routine.

Even when I know everything that makes her shiver and shudder and beg for me, it just amps up the anticipation.

I fucking crave her reactions, the song in her voice, the melody of her pleasure so badly.

They say music soothes the savage beast.

Well, she's the living song who soothed me—and made me into who I was always meant to be.

If I can show her that with my touch, you'd better believe

I will.

So I sneak my hands under her clothes, caress her skin, then slip up to cup her breasts. It makes her arch, moving her hips against me, rocking slow and deep in this sultry rhythm that only makes me crave the real thing that much more.

I know exactly how she looks when she hits her peak, when she finds that perfect release, when she comes herself rigid and sweet just for me.

And I know exactly how to tease her to that point till she loses her sexy mind.

Her thighs tighten against my hips.

Her body jerks in short, sharp pleasure shocks.

I flick her nipples with my thumbs, then tease them in circles, stroking, guiding the cups of her bra down.

There's something almost twice as dirty about teasing her by touch alone, everything hidden beneath her shirt. My hands move blindly till I'm so much more sensitive to the creamy texture of her skin, the weight of her breasts, the heat of her skin.

Fuck, she's beautiful.

And fuck again, she's *mine*.

I don't even know what I did to get so lucky that this angel thinks I'm worthy of her love.

What she saw even when I couldn't.

But I'll damn sure give her everything I can to repay her.

From every bit of pleasure I can wring from her body to the sugary love pouring out of my heart.

I can't even hope to contain it. The feeling just spills out of me with a groan.

"Peace," I snarl, pushing myself up to steal her gasping, ripe, red mouth for my own.

Goddamn, the way she kisses me.

Like she's a slave to this pleasure, like she can't think of anything else but our mouths locked and our tongues sliding together, our bodies pressed tight. She digs her knees into the sofa and gyrates her hips over me till suddenly I'm not the one in control anymore.

Not when she knows me as well as I know her—and she turns me into a panting, mindless animal for her, my cock rising hot against my track pants, thrusting up toward that warm softness her fucking jeans are keeping me from.

I need it.

I need *her.*

With a rough, wild sound in the back of my throat, I lift her off me long enough to rip her jeans away, tearing her panties aside, baring those thick curving hips that do *wild* things to my self-control.

She's built like an instrument of pleasure, lust, heart-deep emotion captured in trembling flesh.

And when she comes down against me, already dripping, wet for my probing, stroking fingers, I marvel again at the truth.

This wild, gorgeous woman wants me just as bad as I want her.

As much as I'll *always* want her.

Five days or five years from now, or fifty or five hundred.

She's my forever.

She's the reason I fly, every frigging day—even when life wants to punch me down.

And she flies with me now as I drag my pants down, bare my cock, and press it against her hot, slick pussy.

Pure thunder rips at the back of my throat. My eyes roll back as she sinks down on me, meeting me halfway. Always halfway, always right there with me.

One mind, one heart, completely in tune.

I can't imagine life without her.

I can't imagine pleasure deeper than this.

I can't imagine love that could ever be truer.

It's like a favorite song I can queue up on repeat. Every time those perfect notes and gorgeous lyrics strike my heart pure and true with the same amazing feelings.

We're pulsing drumbeats, together. Especially when we fuck so good.

My hand goes to her throat, adding this rough, animal edge she likes.

"Come on, woman. Let's go," I growl.

"Blake!" she whines my name, singing so sweet it just might be tied with that old desperado tune she still sings for me.

I take her hard and long, sweeping long strokes into her body, my free hand tangled in her hair. When she goes off the first time on my dick, my mouth attacks hers. I steal the whimpers from her lungs.

No matter how long we're married, I'm still *greedy.*

And she knows "one and done" ain't my style. My cock goes to work, faster and harder, the instant her twitching pussy eases up.

I fuck her through one release straight into the next, storming a little deeper into her body, into her soul.

Ever since Andrea moved out, she sings louder on nights like these. We make *a lot* of noise. And I'm adding to her shrill melody with my bass, my sandpaper drumroll, my earthy growl as my balls catch fire.

"Fuck, sweetheart, can't hold back! Come on." I give her a playful, desperate smack on the ass, the last little trigger she needs to go.

My whole body blows up in white-hot fire, starting at my balls and the ripping up my dick, straight to my brain. I'm bathed in this sticky-sweet insanity of her velvet heat pulling everything out of me.

This woman steals fucking *ropes* of Blake Silverton.

And that's how it is for the next few minutes of sweet, panting fuckery.

Our own familiar tempo, the perfect peaks of sound and rhythm, breath and whispers, pleasure and pain, push and pull as she rides me to hell and back and I give it *all.*

It takes me a minute to shake myself out of the coma when

she tumbles into my arms. Then she looks up shyly, this nervous glint in her eyes. "Think we did it?"

"Darlin', I think I could've knocked you up from ten feet away coming that hard. But even if we didn't...don't mind trying another hundred times."

She gives me a playful whack.

I chuckle.

We fall back together.

We decided to try for our first kid the other week, agreeing to get to work as soon as the relay was over. And if there's one thing I've learned about my wife over the years, she ain't a patient woman when it comes to the stuff that matters.

No big, though.

I sweep her flaming-red hair back and stare into her eyes, already feeling myself getting hard again.

She's the soundtrack of my life.

The tune to my soul.

There's never, ever been a more perfect song.

* * *

Peace came into my life like a wildfire—who knew broccoli could burn?

Bad jokes aside, she's the only blaze I've ever been truly proud of conquering.

If I was this screwed up, wounded thing before—damaged goods every way you cut it—then she made me something infinitely better.

She made me whole.

She patched my family quilt.

She made me believe in love actually existing off the airwaves.

And every day I get to spend alive with this pixie spark, when she gets to burn me down again with her kiss, her voice, her everything, I know I'm the luckiest desperado who ever lived.

ABOUT NICOLE SNOW

Nicole Snow is a *Wall Street Journal* and *USA Today* bestselling author. She found her love of writing by hashing out love scenes on lunch breaks and plotting her great escape from boardrooms. Her work roared onto the indie romance scene in 2014 with her Grizzlies MC series.

Since then Snow aims for the very best in growly, heart-of-gold alpha heroes, unbelievable suspense, and swoon storms aplenty.

Already hooked on her stuff? Visit nicolesnowbooks.com to sign up for her newsletter and connect on social media.

Got a question or comment on her work? Reach her anytime at nicole@nicolesnowbooks.com

Thanks for reading. And please remember to leave an honest review! Nothing helps an author more.

MORE BOOKS BY NICOLE

Heroes of Heart's Edge Books

No Perfect Hero
No Good Doctor
No Broken Beast
No Damaged Goods

Marriage Mistake Standalone Books

Accidental Hero
Accidental Protector
Accidental Romeo
Accidental Knight
Accidental Rebel
Accidental Shield

Stand Alone Novels

Cinderella Undone
Man Enough
Surprise Daddy
Prince With Benefits
Marry Me Again
Love Scars
Recklessly His
Stepbrother UnSEALed
Stepbrother Charming

Enguard Protectors Books

Still Not Over You
Still Not Into You
Still Not Yours
Still Not Love

Baby Fever Books

Baby Fever Bride
Baby Fever Promise
Baby Fever Secrets

Only Pretend Books

Fiance on Paper
One Night Bride

Grizzlies MC Books

Outlaw's Kiss
Outlaw's Obsession
Outlaw's Bride
Outlaw's Vow

Deadly Pistols MC Books

Never Love an Outlaw
Never Kiss an Outlaw
Never Have an Outlaw's Baby
Never Wed an Outlaw

Prairie Devils MC Books

Outlaw Kind of Love
Nomad Kind of Love

Savage Kind of Love
Wicked Kind of Love
Bitter Kind of Love